THE ONES THEY TOOK

BY

SARAH K. WEST

A TINY FOX PRESS BOOK

Library of Congress Control Number: 2023938608
ISBN: 978-1-946501-54-7

Tiny Fox Press and the book fox logo are all registered trademarks of Tiny Fox Press LLC

Tiny Fox Press LLC
Parish, FL

For Anthony,
who made me fall in love with LA
and inspires me more than he realizes

And for Seymour the dog,
who diligently kept my lap warm
the whole time I was writing this

CHAPTER ONE

Los Angeles was burning again.

Cora Somerville was no stranger to dry-weather warnings or ash riding the Santa Ana winds from the valleys. But that's where fires typically began and ended: places many Angelenos knew only as freeway signs, rarely worth braving traffic to get to.

These fires, the ones glowing against the night-darkened sky two neighborhoods over, weren't lit by power lines or vehicle sparks or errant cigarettes. They were lit by an uprush of human fury, by people demanding answers and not trusting the ones they were given.

Low-hanging marine layer mixed with smoke to blind the streets beyond the 405 off-ramp. Cora eased off the gas and turned up the radio, half hoping it could chase away those old pieces of her lurking in the haze.

She nudged her old station wagon, Lucy, into a spot against the curb, grimacing when it kissed the bumper of the sedan behind her. Lucy wouldn't mind another dent, but Cora bet the Audi owner might.

Wonderful. The neighbors would be thrilled she was back.

Watching for movement on the edge of the fog, she killed the engine and grabbed her duffel bag from the passenger seat. The whine of a distant siren drifted on the breeze, rustling through the skinny fan palms dotting the roadside like crooked toothpicks.

Santa Monica had become a hodgepodge of aging beach shacks squeezed between boxy, modern fortresses that, year after year, replaced more homes like the Mission-style bungalow in front of her—a house her aunt Mindy had bought from an artist in the eighties and hadn't changed a brick of. Probably never would.

As Cora crossed the threshold of an agave-flanked porch, the arched living room window filled with light. Warding spells, at least, were easily masked from hunter patrols, and Mindy's would have warned her of Cora's approach.

The heavy scrape of one deadbolt, another, set Cora's teeth on edge, and Mindy filled the open-door frame. Her graying curls were wild as ever. "There she is." Mindy grabbed Cora's face and crushed a kiss onto her freckled cheek, brushing Cora's copper-brown hair out of the way. "Were you able to grab something to eat?"

"Um, no. It's fine, though. Sorry it took so—"

"Don't be silly. Come inside." Mindy ushered her into the house with a tight-lipped smile, shoved the deadbolts back into place. More hallway sconces flickered to life as they passed. "Curfew only started at ten, but it might start earlier tomorrow. You know how things get." Mindy's voice still held some of the Georgia parish where she'd grown up, but all the years in California had given her back her r's.

Nature had been kind to her, and aside from some softness in her jaw, she wore sixty years with grace. Her house reflected that same youth: funky woven baskets, loud pillows, her own eccentric multimedia artwork. Nothing matched, and the result was usually cheerful. But tonight Cora's palms were still red from her stranglehold on the steering wheel, adrenaline only just now ceding ground to weariness—the brightness chafed, the artwork sneered, and it all seemed frantic, disconnected.

Somewhere, a tea kettle shrieked.

"I couldn't sleep." Mindy gestured helplessly toward the kitchen. "I figured you'd need something after the drive, anyway."

Always a fuss to be made, over someone, somewhere. "That's...you didn't have to..."

"Don't be silly."

As Mindy dashed away to silence the kettle, Cora followed, sinking onto a barstool and dropping her bag by her feet. She hadn't eaten since noon and should have been hungry. She wasn't, but she sipped the tea and ate the bagel Mindy toasted for her anyway. "Thanks."

"Everything went smoothly, then?" Mindy sat next to her at the bar, stirring honey into her own mug.

6

"We avoided the worst of it. Downtown is quiet for now. But I don't know why she couldn't have just stayed with Ezra and Quinn. Or us."

They'd argued this before, and Mindy's expression betrayed her unraveling patience. "There's an order to these things, sweetie. A system. We chose every safe house for a reason—"

"I know that, but you didn't have to leave Nell there." Cora pinched the bridge of her nose, where a headache threatened. "You didn't have to see how scared she was and promise her it would be okay and then just pass her off to another stranger like a hot potato. She's only sixteen, for fuck's sake." The drive from San Diego to Downtown LA had been tense, and Nell, her charge, had barely spoken. The girl was going to need a lot of therapy when she finally got to Whitefall.

It was just one of many concealed cities witch refugees could flee to if they'd been exposed, or suspected they'd been. The cross-coven Runner network that Cora served stretched from coast to coast, but she'd only dealt with their local chapter, ferrying witches between safe houses until Whitefall could accommodate them.

"Nell will be just fine with Poppy. She couldn't be in better hands." Mindy sipped her tea and sighed. "It doesn't get easier. It never does. Especially with the orphans."

"Quinn said her parents had only been taken." Cora's friend Quinn, another Whitefall Runner, had given them the lead in the first place. Nell wasn't originally part of Cora's plan to move back to LA, but her guardian, her grandmother, was losing a battle with dementia. When Cora mentioned she was moving, Quinn asked if she could take Nell up with her, unsure how much longer she'd be safe there.

Mindy gave her a pointed look, and Cora knew. She should know better than anyone. She'd been as good as orphaned, herself.

Because there was no coming back from wherever the hunters took you to. And she didn't blame Mindy for not saying it aloud, not wanting to put words to her own nightmares. But it didn't matter because whatever tenuous grasp Mindy had on her self-control shattered. She pressed her fingers to her lips to stop them from quivering, and three weeks' pent-up grief bubbled over.

Cora gripped Mindy's shoulder. It was bonier than she remembered. "I'm here now. I'm not going anywhere, okay?"

"I just...I just stood there while they took Oscar, I couldn't..." She dissolved into tiny, hiccupping sobs. "I watched them from the front window, dragging him from his house. Right through the new flower beds he'd just planted. We picked them out together. Santa Barbara daisies."

"What could you have done?" Anything else would have condemned herself to the fate Cora's own mother and twin brother, and so many other witches like them, had suffered. "What do we tell people, all the time? Not to be a hero. And why's that?"

"Oh, come on. Anything, something. That's what I could have done."

"Would you say that to Nell? To me?"

"Of course I wouldn't."

"Then give yourself that same fucking kindness."

"Why should I, if you won't?"

Cora drew up short. The irony of the whole exchange wasn't lost on her, but it was easier to say the words to Mindy than to herself. "Oh, no you don't. This isn't about me."

"You know how hard it is to watch someone you love destroy themselves because of something that isn't their fault?" Mindy sniffled, crumpling her tissue into a fist.

They hadn't talked about Cora's sobriety in months, and she outright refused to give it any more of the air in this room. Cora got a grip on herself. "You're hurting, Min. You're angry. I know what that dredges up. Push me away to make a point if you want, but this is going to be bad enough without you making it harder on yourself."

Mindy's forehead fell into her hands and she sniffled, raking her fingers through her hair. "I know. Fuck me, don't I just know." She looked Cora in the eyes again. "Oscar...his son-in-law wasn't his biggest fan, but he said, 'Oh, Min, he's harmless. He's all bark.'"

"His *son-in-law?*"

"Oscar's ex-wife wasn't a witch, and their daughter didn't inherit. So they decided not to tell her about him. Easier, you know. And the man she married always had this...look about him when Oscar came around. Now I'd bet my life he just wanted Oscar out of the way so he could have the house." Mindy burst into tears again. Oscar had asked her to move in with him not weeks ago.

Cora rubbed her back, letting her cry out everything she'd held in for the last three weeks. Mindy shouldn't have been alone here so long, but Cora had loose ends of her own to manage. Quitting her nursing job, packing what would fit in Lucy, shoving what wouldn't in storage, breaking her lease.

She'd visited, sure, since she'd moved down to San Diego, but the demands of trauma nursing kept her free time in a vise. So coming back felt a lot like those earlier days, the aimless ones they'd spent together down in their grief. Cora didn't know how Mindy had done it, juggle the loss of her sister-in-law and nephew with the sudden responsibility of raising a teenage girl, all the while pulling doubles in the ICU and performing miracles on unwitting patients.

Now this pillar of once-indomitable woman was crumbling again, and Cora tried not to show how much it shook her.

She took the easy way out and changed the subject. "Think they'll declare martial law?"

Mindy laughed bitterly. "The governor won't go that far. Besides, I'm sure it's all some morbid measure of success to the hunters—anytime emotions are high, magic follows. People keep exposing themselves. Around we go."

The riots were somewhat recent—the hunters weren't.

The earliest years of the witch hunts were quiet. People just vanished. Pleas to the police for help were met with rug-sweeping, accusation dodging, gaslighting. Governments don't abandon their humanity overnight, after all. Theirs was a war of attrition, fought in the dark.

Until some FBI whistle-blower was killed for revealing a conspiracy to the public: witches, sometimes entire families of them, were being injected with magic-inhibiting sedatives and locked away in prison camps. Witches had known as much since the kidnappings began, but it was news to everyone else.

The riots began soon after, ebbing and surging as new information leaked. And now that people were afraid, aware, looking for trouble, sharing videos, you couldn't just covertly wipe the memories of those who witnessed magic—you had the entirety of the internet to deal with. Not even the Council's team of master technomancers could cover up that mess.

"Are these all because of that necromancer?" Cora asked. A medical examiner on the east side was caught reanimating bodies, and his coworker posted the video on social media.

"People like that just can't get out of their own way. And then you have others who are so careful, but they still..." Mindy's voice caught in her throat again, and she just shook her head. "I'm just relieved you're here in one piece. I've made up the pullout in the den for you—go get some rest. You're dead on your feet."

Cora couldn't argue with that. She dragged herself into the den, and as fatigue bore down, she sank with it.

The specter of last night's fog burned off in the early rays of dawn. Across the street, a fresh For Sale sign stabbed Oscar's dew-slicked yard. His son-in-law hadn't wasted any time.

Janice Ford Realty, the sign read. A tan, blonde woman with too much lip and cheek filler smiled at Cora, promising a two-bedroom, two-and-a-half-bath floor plan with a pool.

Bitch.

Cora walked down the curb to her clunker and grabbed the surfboard in it, the only thing she owned of actual value. It had been an early graduation gift to herself, bought with the little money she had after haggling for Lucy.

The last few years she'd kept her head down in the ER as a trauma nurse, scraping together the courage to come back to LA for good. But she'd poured too much of herself—and her magic, when it was safe to—into her work, preferring to heal others instead of face her own problems. And it didn't matter how many hours she put in—discontent and loneliness still found dark places to breed off the clock. So she spent more and more time with a board and a wetsuit...among other things.

Things she couldn't think too much about these days, or she'd fan that little ember of need she'd worked so hard to douse.

The rambling stone pathway led her through the garden to the back of the house, into the sun-room. Its terracotta flooring and bright Talavera tilework had always fit Mindy's undying sense of optimism, her strength of spirit. She'd come through hardship with more grace and tenacity than anyone had the right to.

This house had anchored both of them through the most difficult chapters of their lives.

Propping her board against the smooth stucco wall, Cora was immediately drawn to a scattering of photographs sitting on a wrought-iron side table. There was her third-grade photo with both front teeth missing—her brother Sebastian's photo was parked next to hers, except his adult teeth had already grown in, too big for his mouth. He was wild-eyed, wild-haired. He'd hack those red locks off with kitchen scissors the following year, to their mother's horror.

Beside those sat a younger photo of her mother, just shy of thirty, near Cora's age. Soft auburn waves feathered around her face in the defining style of the decade. She crossed her legs on a horrible floral sofa, mid-laugh, head on Mindy's shoulder. She, like Cora, had been terribly vain about her hair.

And oh, the freckles. Cora's and Sebastian's weren't the cute sprinkle across the nose that their mother had—they were the kind grade-school bullies made careers out of. Clusters of speckles like a thousand tiny coffee-stain droplets, dancing across shoulders and elbows and knees with very little symmetry and rhyme or reason, only darker the more time they spent in the sun. Which was a lot.

It had taken years for Cora to accept them. Maybe one day she'd love them, but she wasn't there yet. She was still resentful that she'd had to give up on most makeup beyond mascara.

So her hair was the thing she'd poured her energy and money into. Even when she'd been at rock bottom, even on the days when getting out of bed was an effort, she'd always taken care of those elbow-length waves. It was her pride and joy. Her basic-as-hell wardrobe, all jeans and t-shirts and beat-up sneakers, was just a blank canvas for it. That suited her just fine.

She moved down the row, and the third frame held a picture she'd never seen. A young Cora and Sebastian cheesed with wide, ice-cream-cake smiles next to a balloon shaped like an eleven. Sebastian wore some frosting on his head, and he'd stuffed more down the front of Cora's striped sailor bathing suit. The backyard they stood in tugged uncomfortably at her memory.

Cora jumped when Mindy lay a palm on her back. "Morning, hon. Didn't mean to startle you." She peered over Cora's shoulder. "That was Teddy Ryland's eleventh birthday, do you remember? I found it in an old album when I was cleaning out the attic last summer."

"It's not you. I'm a little jumpy after...I'm having those dreams again." Cora looked closely. "Ryland, huh? There's a name I haven't heard in years."

Theodore Ryland, their old neighbor, had always hated Mindy's little nickname for him. To the twins, he'd just been Ryland. Their mothers' close friendship meant the kids had more or less grown up together, but they lost touch after... well, Cora didn't want to invite those memories back in, either. These pictures had stirred up enough emotions for one morning, thank you very much.

"What dreams? About Sebastian?"

Cora nodded, and because it was there, sipped the coffee Mindy handed her.

Mindy sank into the chair next to her, and up close, it was obvious sleep evaded her too. "I get them about Oscar. Mostly we're gardening together." She white-knuckled her mug. "You don't have to talk about Sebastian if you don't want to."

Cora searched for words. It felt important to acknowledge him, at least. They hadn't yet. "Being back here is...claustrophobic, I guess? Like a knot of nostalgia in my chest that keeps pulling tighter. You ever go somewhere and want to leave as badly as you want to stay?" Helplessness sat in her throat—a thick, tangible reminder of everything she hadn't been able to do, the impossibility of hoping she'd ever see the people in those photos again.

She'd tried to find them, once before. Tailed one of those big, black vans the hunters took people away in. She'd just swapped out her learner's permit for a shiny new license and stole Mindy's car, only to crash it into a fire hydrant—something they'd both be thankful for when their heels finally cooled.

Cora had never heard Mindy beg before then. *Goddess help me if you leave me alone in this world,* she'd cried into Cora's hair. *I likely won't survive it.*

"It helps me to think about how many millions of miles Earth has moved from the point in the universe where a memory was made. Gives some places less power over me." Mindy lifted her coffee to her mouth with trembling hands. "Will you go see Quinn this morning?"

"That was the plan."

Quinn would want an update on Nell, and Cora was anxious to see how badly the Westside had deteriorated in the months since she'd last visited, so it seemed as good a time as any to rip off that band-aid.

But before Cora got in her car to head down to Venice, she paused by Oscar's garden across the street, smeared dirt on Janice Ford's too-white teeth.

A small rebellion. A safe one.

CHAPTER TWO

Traffic was kinder than usual, and whether it had anything to do with the unease in the air or the tail end of rush hour, or a mix of both, Cora was grateful for it as Lucy puttered into a spot along the curb outside a boarded-up surf shop.

Graffiti splashed across the plywood and the sidewalk in front of the door. Papered over that, as well as across five other storefronts down the row, posters as tall as Cora displayed the official Arcane Assault Hotline.

ADVISORY FROM THE BUREAU OF ARCANE COMPLIANCE ENFORCEMENT
IF YOU SUSPECT YOU OR A FAMILY MEMBER HAS BEEN A VICTIM OF ARCANE HARASSMENT OR ASSAULT, CALL IMMEDIATELY

What does arcane assault look and feel like? There are many kinds of magic, some more visible than others. For a list of known types, visit magichurts.gov.
Ask yourself the following questions:
1. Am I, or someone I love, behaving in an inconsistent or suspicious manner?
2. Have I experienced hallucinations, confusion, loss of time or loss of memory?
3. Does my body physically do the things I intend it to do?
4. Do unusual or unnatural things tend to happen around me?

5. *Do my pets tend to react to things that aren't there?*

6. *Have I dealt with the sudden onset of unexplained health problems?*

If you answered "yes" to more than one of the above, you might be a victim of arcane assault. Call our toll-free hotline for round-the-clock support. If you suspect your life is imminently in danger, call 911 instead.

Goddess, it was such useless, fearmongering bullshit.

The shop beneath the posters used to be a local favorite called Last Glass, owned by a witch she'd only known as Georgie. Now it was just a reminder of someone else they'd hauled away and a mouthpiece for more of their fucking propaganda. Tempting as it was to rip these down, she couldn't take the risk—too many eyes here.

Hugging herself, Cora continued down the block toward Bungalow, the hotel where Quinn worked. People milled about the pier, fishing and skateboarding. Just one slate-gray and black uniform further down the boardwalk, arcanometer in hand, but not all hunters were visible, anyway.

Hunters were, officially, the only organized faction with true government funding, some with innate magic sensitivity and some without. Those without carried a machine to mark magical activity in the general area, picking up readings like a Geiger counter. Scarier than the sanctioned hunters, though, were civilians who lashed out on suspicion alone and reveled in the grim theatrics of a good old-fashioned mob.

Fear, that great mind-narrower, didn't care how progressive society claimed to be. All it needed to do was cast a long shadow. Imaginations would do the rest.

Cora wandered further, passing low-slung shops and offbeat eateries along slender roads better suited as alleyways. Venice had, out of spite and pure cultural inertia, mostly survived the development trying to squeeze the color from it. Bungalow was a salient example of that stubbornness, a little slice of old-school Venice. Weather-beaten brick and peeling stucco lay beneath vivid murals Cora knew were painted over twice a year by local artists.

Ezra, Quinn's boss, owned this place, and took pride in being one of the holdouts.

A cool blast of air met her at the lobby entrance, where the twisting metal tendrils of a welded sculpture reached down in an otherworldly greeting. All was quiet aside from the murmuring of the receptionist, the clink of plates from employees clearing breakfast. She tensed. A familiar tingle at the base of her skull suggested another witch was nearby.

A lounge nestled between the entryway and the espresso bar, arranged with cozy leather wingback chairs. From the other side of the counter, a leggy barista with a wild crop of pink hair stared at Cora—Quinn would have sensed her the instant she entered, too.

She floated through the lounge, already untying her apron and flinging it behind the register. Quinn smelled like a library—leather and parchment and spice, a favorite from her collection of unusual perfumes. "Took you long enough. I'm fucking dying of boredom."

"Oh, *hi*, great to see you, too, and I'm fine, thanks for asking, how's—"

"Not here. Come on." She grabbed Cora's hand and pulled her outside.

Strolling down the pier arm in arm, they made a mismatched pair—Quinn's tall, slender dancers' features beside Cora's petite-but-dense, muscular build from long hours spent surfing. "You remember how we used to bike over here, insisting we wouldn't pay nine bucks to park for a four-dollar cup of coffee?" Quinn had a faraway look in her eyes.

"Where the hell were you getting those four-dollar cups of coffee? Six, minimum."

Few people were out fishing this morning, but the two still found a bench where the wind would carry their voices away from curious ears.

"She's okay," Cora said, and Quinn looked sharply at her. They both knew she was referring to Nell. "Missing home, and a little shaken up by the transition. I know we're not supposed to tell them anything about Whitefall, but damn it, it was hard. She looked so lost. I wanted to give her more to be excited about."

"Ezra's upset she can't stay," Quinn said, referring to her boss. "But with all the construction...There's just people in and out of his place, constantly. He picked a shit time to remodel."

"They're...what, first cousins? Second? Are they close?"

"First. It runs on his mom's side of the family. Nell's grandmother, who you met? She's Ezra's adopted aunt, who ran off and eloped with that Italian guy, remember? So her son, Emilio, and his wife...hunters took them last year. No warning, no nothing—just poof, bye."

Nell's parents, then.

Quinn shrugged. "Not close, though, Ezra and Nell. I don't think. He doesn't see the Italian side of the family much. But family's family."

As they watched gulls circle overhead, Cora's mind wandered to Georgie. "When did Last Glass close?"

Quinn scrunched her nose in thought. "Two months ago, ish? Poor Georgie. Someone said the place boarded up the day before, though. I'm sure he knew."

"I hope he got out."

"Me too."

"Why haven't you?"

Quinn played with her necklace, a nervous habit. "Jules and my parents are here. I'm still acting, can't really do that anywhere else. I'm not desperate enough to try for Whitefall yet. Things are worse in the Midwest, forget the South...and besides, I'm making decent money."

"I'm glad Jules is okay," Cora said.

"Well," Quinn said bitterly, "none of us are okay, are we? But we're together. That's more than most—" she fell silent, remembering Sebastian. Her voice was softer when she spoke again. "How's Mindy holding up?"

Cora stared at her once-white sneakers. "The guy...he was a neighbor of hers. They'd been dating two, three years. Gardening, renovating. She was weeks away from renting her place out and moving in with him."

"So, not great then."

"Yeah. Not great."

Quinn's hands fisted in her lap. "Fuck, they can't *do* that."

They. The ubiquitous, proverbial they. Every car in Cora's rearview taking one too many of the same turns she did. Every set of eyes lingering just a bit too long as she walked past. "Yeah?" Cora asked flatly. "You want to be the one to tell them?"

Silence fell again. A mouse scurried along the weather-beaten wood, casting a wary glance at a seagull perched on the guardrail, too close for comfort. Cora picked up a pebble by her foot and absently tossed it at the gull, which backed away and reconsidered its snack.

Something seemed off about the way that mouse moved...

The air shimmered, and Cora inhaled sharply. It wasn't a mouse at all. It had become a shapeless thing, cloudlike, not quite solid or liquid but somewhere in-between. A rainbow of colors shifted within, approximating a set of bright dots for eyes. No larger than her closed fist, it darted behind a wooden post and stayed there.

If she'd blinked, she might have missed it.

Quinn saw her stiffen. "What?"

16

"You didn't see that sprite?" Cora did blink this time and left the bench to peek around the post. Nothing there.

"Aw damn it, I always miss them! Jules can practically catch them blindfolded."

"It's the time of year for it," Cora murmured. Cora and Sebastian once set an elaborate trap in the backyard, watching from the treehouse with binoculars for an entire week. Southern California was a nexus point for several magical ley lines. Sprites were tiny enough to slip through the veil keeping the mortal realm separate from the spirits' realm. Their curiosity often got the better of them, and they liked to mimic mundane things they saw around. Small animals, insects, and inanimate objects, mostly.

They never did catch one, but she had fond memories of those nights they spent camped under the stars, keeping watch while the other slept.

Cora's burning eyes caught her off guard. Back here, that memory was so visceral. She shoved it aside and sat down again, switching gears. "How's acting going?"

Quinn brightened a little. "I just did a thing for oat milk! I'm on a bus shelter in Silver Lake, too. I'm hoping it'll open some doors. There's an audition coming up for a medical drama, the love interest of the broody cardiologist." She winked at Cora. "Maybe you can help me rehearse."

"Sure, if you want." Cora raised a brow, waiting. Quinn looked like she wanted to say something else. "Out with it."

"Speaking of...medical stuff."

"Mhmm."

"I know you said you didn't want to jump right back into the ER."

Ah. Cora knew where this was going. She'd mentioned she wasn't eager to work full-time again, at least not right out of the gate. The first order of business? Deciding how permanent this move was. Couldn't hurt to be around more for Mindy, either.

"Have you thought any more about that position at Ezra's surf shop? I know retail isn't the most glamorous thing in the world, but..."

"Compared to the hours I'm used to? Might as well be a vacation." Cora finger-combed her hair, picked at a split end while she considered. "It's funny. I had this daydream, a few years back, when things were...really bad. Burnout, you know. I imagined quitting on the spot and opening a surf shop of my own, right down the block from my favorite break."

She'd build a shower in the back so she could roll up after an early morning, go straight from the beach to work. Maybe she'd give lessons.

Maybe even learn how to build boards herself. She'd serve coffee and tea and bake chocolate croissants the way her mother had taught her.

It had never been more than a brief fantasy. She'd never enjoy any of it knowing that Sebastian and her mom wouldn't ever get to see it.

Of course, that implied there'd be something to see, which was laughable in itself. Back then, most of her disposable income went to drugs. Lots of her non-disposable income, too. The way she'd decimated her credit, no sane bank would ever approve her for a small business loan.

"A change of pace might not be so bad," she finally said. "Enough to help Min with some bills, since she's refusing to charge me rent."

"I already talked to Ezra. It's yours, if you want it. He knows what you've done for Nell."

Beneath the weight of Quinn's gratitude, Cora looked down, away. She'd only chauffeured a teenager for three hours. But she squeezed Quinn's hand. "Thanks. I appreciate it."

"It's called Boardroom. It's close to Georgie's place. Just...be careful. It can get dicey at night. Venice has changed..."

"Darn." Cora snapped a finger. "I was all set to hang a sign in the window saying, 'Howdy neighbors! Now offering palm readings and crystal healing seminars!'"

Quinn rolled her eyes. "I'm off tomorrow night—I'll take you to his taqueria, and you guys can talk shop."

"Thanks. I mean it." Cora felt the knot she'd been carrying in her chest loosen just a little. "What's your deal, anyway? You and him."

"He's my boss, Cor." But red bloomed across Quinn's neck and ears.

Cora raised an eyebrow. "He wasn't always." They'd met through the Runners, and he'd offered Quinn a job at the hotel so she could keep an eye on the refugees coming through there. A self-proclaimed 'starving actress' cliché, she'd had experience as both bartender and barista—so it was a no-brainer.

"Your point?"

"What's *your* point?"

"*My* point is that you're blushing."

Quinn rolled her eyes. "It's a crush. Crushes fizzle."

"Sure. Handsome, self-made real estate mogul, risking his life for the greater good. That'll dry anyone right up."

"Fire season in Topanga dry," Quinn agreed emphatically. "Death Valley dry. It's a shitty idea, anyway."

18

Cora knew why. Nobody had bigger targets on their backs than the Runners. Giving the hunters anything or anyone else to use against you was just asking for trouble. Being tortured for information was a very real occupational hazard most of them were prepared to endure—trained to, even—but watching someone you love being tortured? Not so much.

"Anyway," Quinn said, standing, "I should probably get back. I'll make sure to update Ezra."

Cora stood with her, winking as they headed back across the planks toward Bungalow. "I just bet you will."

"Don't make me push you off this pier. I'll do it."

"I know."

———— ✺ ————

Ember, Ezra's unassuming taqueria, squatted between a barber shop and a Latin American grocery just off the main drag of Venice Boulevard. Garage doors gaped between the bar and the patio, and a dusty canopy of string lights tried for cozy—an effort underscored by the heady bouquet of weed, grilling meat, and charred elotes.

A crop of pink hair drew Cora's eye from across the room. The black man to Quinn's left draped a tattooed forearm over the back of her chair, holding himself with that telltale assuredness of the indifferently wealthy.

Spotting Cora, Quinn waved her over to their high-top, then pressed a sweating pint glass into Cora's hand and gestured to the man beside her. "Ezra, Cora. Cora, Ezra."

Ezra's locs brushed his broad, muscled shoulders. Cora guessed he was edging forty, with the tiny threads of grey along his temples, and a bright, slightly crooked smile reached his whiskey-colored eyes. Cora would've bet good money Quinn made his cable-knit sweater. Interesting.

When Quinn noticed Cora frowning at the glass, she added, "Ginger ale, hon."

Cora blinked. Of course Quinn remembered. And if Quinn remembered, she'd given Ezra the heads up, too.

Well, this was awkward. She wished being eighteen months sober wasn't the first thing Ezra learned about her, even if it wasn't about the alcohol, specifically—but it sure opened doors better left locked. Doors to things that had quieted the guilt, depression, and anger long enough to be able to live in her own head.

Cora coughed. "It's good to meet you."

19

To Ezra's credit, he'd pretended not to notice, even when the gratitude for that made her cheeks redden, too. Holding out his hand, he saved her the trouble of finding a segue. "Nice to finally put a face to the name. Heard a lot about you and from a long way back, too."

His grip was warm and firm, his voice steady, and Cora immediately felt less adrift. "How far back, exactly?"

"Orange County far." Quinn gave her a meaningful look. He knew about Cora's family.

"You don't meet many lifers," Ezra said, not missing the exchange that had just occurred. "Seems like everyone's from somewhere."

"Which are you?" Quinn had mentioned he was involved in the community. He acted like a local, but she wasn't sure just how deep his roots ran here.

Ezra shrugged. "Been here long enough to claim it. Spent a chunk of my childhood in OC too, before I bounced around the South Side a little and wound up here in Venice. Came up on some of the best waves you can find." He sipped his beer, taking the measure of her, and pushed some chips and guac her way. "Quinn says you know your way around a board, yourself."

Relaxing a bit more, she said, "My brother and I split weekends between San Onofre and El Porto as kids."

His brow climbed upward. "San-O I can see, but El Porto? That's a hike from OC."

"My mom's favorite brunch spot was near there. We'd make a day of it. Nothing beats the break at San-O, but mom was doing the driving, so..."

"Fair enough. You ever compete?"

Cora snorted. Back at the OC house, she'd been perfectly content with her shelf of various youth sports league participation trophies. Unlike Sebastian, there wasn't a competitive bone in her body. "It's...not for me. I just like being out there, even on the days I suck."

His crows' feet crinkled. It had been the right thing to say. "Howsabout you swing by tomorrow, get a feel for the place?"

"Sure." With another swell of gratitude, she added, "Thanks again for the opportunity."

He waved a hand. "You're doing me the favor. I'm just racking them up, aren't I? After what you did for Nell, anyway. I won't forget it."

As he excused himself to take a call, Quinn leaned across the table. "What do you think?"

Cora sipped her ginger ale and glanced at her, sidelong. "Well, he didn't try to recruit me for his multi-level marketing racket. So that puts him a step above—what was her name? Lily? Lulu? The last one you dated."

"Lexi." Quinn grimaced. "That breakup sucked. We were the same shoe size...and she had so many amazing ones..."

With what she hoped looked like a sympathetic nod, Cora thought about the beat-up sneakers she hadn't bothered to change out of before coming here. She shifted a little in her seat. "Does he know...about..."

Quinn blinked. "Oh, Goddess no. I'd never tell him that. I just gave him a heads up about the drinking, since his first idea was meeting at a brewpub."

That was a relief, at least. Because Cora hadn't even heard about Ezra from Quinn, not at first—that had come from Mindy, and the Runners, when he'd purchased a small B&B in San Diego. They'd sent her to help place wards before it could officially be used as safe house.

Wards weren't her wheelhouse, but most witches had learned to cast basic ones out of necessity. Leyweaving was what they called it—drawing raw power up through the ley lines in the earth and turning it into something you hadn't inherited an affinity for.

Cora's healing magic came from her father and Mindy's side, her terramancy from her mother's side, but most wards relied on neuromancy or abjuration. Simple wards warned you when unwelcome visitors were near or could mask the presence of magic. More involved ones could compel someone to turn back without them realizing why. None, though, were easy to do when you were high as a kite on Bliss.

Which Cora had been that day Mindy called. Head spinning, stomach roiling, the job took her hours. Halfway through, she'd begged Mindy to send someone else. Anyone else.

But Mindy had known what it would take to break Cora out of her spiral of self-destruction. She'd told her about the family arriving the next day, the horrors they'd been though, even the cats they'd had to leave behind.

That was her first job for the Runners, and her last hit of Bliss.

She found a witch chapter of Narcotics Anonymous, *A New Thread*. Later that week she'd pour out all the liquor in her cabinet, the dregs from the jars of powders and tinctures she'd been saving for a rainy day, and begin clawing her way back to something resembling a functional human being's life.

21

Some days she was still clawing her way there, but at least she was never back at the very bottom of the well, squinting at the pinprick of light above her, wondering what it would take to haul herself out.

It was progress, at least.

"I was with him when Nell's parents happened, you know," Quinn said, lowering her voice more. "His cousins."

"You were?"

Quinn glanced back toward the street, where Ezra still paced with a phone to his ear. "So I'm working late at the hotel one night, and he comes in all distraught. He sits at the bar and orders drink after drink, not saying a word, until he's the only one left, and I cut him off. He gets mad at me, says I can't cut him off in his own bar. I say like hell I can, and close up so I can drive him home.

"He doesn't want to go anywhere, though, so I ask the front desk for the key to the suite he works out of, and we go up. I practically carry this guy, Cora, he's so out-of-his-mind plastered. I get him to chug some water and take off his shoes, make sure he's lying on his side when he gets into bed. I start to leave, but he asks me if I'll stay with him."

"And did you?" Cora asked.

"Well, of-fucking-course I did, he was my hot boss, but beyond that, I was worried about him. I grab a blanket and get all set to sleep on the couch—oh, god, don't look so surprised, I can control myself—and I could see he was a little disappointed, like maybe he'd been hoping I'd lie down with him, but he passed out and that was that. We haven't talked about it since."

"At all?"

"Like it never happened. And hell if I'm going to be the first to bring it up. It's been a year, anyway. Don't want to make it weird."

Cora snorted. "You can never have an uncomplicated crush, can you?"

"You know me. Simple's a snooze fest."

"Well, nothing brings people together like shared trauma."

Quinn ran a hand through her hair, and her words took on a bitter edge. "Lots of that going around, so I'm sure you two will be the best of friends soon enough."

And as they both downed the last of their drinks, neither knew just how quickly Quinn would be proved right.

CHAPTER THREE

Theo's phone buzzed once, twice, three times on his nightstand before he fumbled around and answered it. His voice was thick with sleep. "Yep."

"Ryland, you've got an Alpha-12 near Little Tokyo. Apartment complex. Santana's ETA is twenty minutes." He recognized the dispatcher's voice as Sid's. The smile in it was no doubt the schadenfreude of knowing Theo had forgotten he was on-call this morning.

Eyes still closed, Theo said, "Riot protocol was extended?" Occasionally real arcane activity was behind an Alpha-12, but usually it just meant someone had a bone to pick with a neighbor or had hit a blunt too hard. Ricky Santana would have taken this call himself, but all the riot protocol meant Tactical Arcane Compliance Specialists were being sent out in pairs.

"Until 0900," Sid said cheerfully.

Glancing at his watch, Theo cursed under his breath. It was 8:47. "Who called it in?" And why couldn't they have waited ten fucking minutes?

"A Lieutenant Miller, LASD."

"Alright. En route. ETA twenty minutes." Theo ended the call and sat up, kneading a kink in his shoulder with a thumb. Lately, he'd felt every one of his thirty years and most of them in his neck. Gone were the days of getting tapped out and bouncing back the next morning.

He splashed water on his face, his beard, and brushed aside a curl of dark hair to examine the progress of his cauliflower ear in the bathroom mirror. The swelling along the outer shell had shrunk, and it was hardening again. Last night, a brown belt had gotten the drop on him at the gym. Next time they wouldn't.

Through the receding fog of sleep, he dressed and ambled into the kitchen, cool concrete beneath his bare feet. The espresso machine whirred and chirped as he set it to brew, and while he waited, he dumped an old glass of water over the creeping vine under the window. A pothos of some sort, the home store clerk had said. The kind you can't kill without trying to, which was just his speed. He'd done too much killing already.

Fingers of sunlight poked through sheer curtains, stretching across the polished concrete floor. It was as bachelor a pad as any, nestled in the Arts District between the spires of downtown and the tent metropolis of Skid Row. Things changed swiftly from street corner to street corner, and while the Arts District was undergoing its own renaissance, it was a still world apart down there. A world apart and a scant two blocks away.

With his duty weapon tucked into his waistband, he locked the fifth-floor walkup. He carried an FNX 45, which was pretty heavy-handed for a concealed carry sidearm—but when against a witch, you'd be grateful for the extra firepower.

Then there was the other thing.

Normally, a short-range tranq projector pistol was unwieldy as hell. But ACE, the Bureau of Arcane Compliance Enforcement, didn't mess around. As soon as they'd developed the magic-inhibiting sedative Crash, they requested a proposal from every gun manufacturer who wanted a piece of that sweet taxpayer money.

Zev Tech won the bidding war, and what they gave ACE was something sleek, ultracompact and quiet—with the density of a dying sun. So TAC Specialists carried theirs in a specialized shoulder holster, like the one Theo wore now over his gray and black uniform.

As for the name, well...after a dart took out a telekinetic who'd been levitating a car over a squad fresh out of the Academy, the name Crash had stuck. Their deaths were a cautionary tale to ACE recruits who got trigger happy with the serum.

It was damn strong, and for a reason.

Little Tokyo wasn't far from Theo's place, so he opted to walk instead of taking his motorcycle. He loved the city on foot, the grit and grime of it. Artists' studios had flourished here since the seventies when it was only a wedge of industry straddling railroad yards and the LA River. Now, galleries and co-ops filled unassuming warehouses. High-concept cafes raised vegetables and chickens in alleyways, and the old guard gave up on their skyrocketing rent.

But the perfume of sewage and stale urine grounded all of it, no matter what else changed. And if anyone asked him, he'd say LA's heart beat here, on the grills of roadside taco trucks or under the rainbow umbrellas of sidewalk fruit vendors—not on Hollywood sound stages or the freewheeling crescent of Westside beach towns.

He waved through the propped-open door of his favorite coffee shop, owned by an old woman named Mrs. Moradian who always pinched his cheek and handed him a free pastry if she thought he was looking thin. He reminded her of her son, she'd said, who'd moved away a few years before. Theo helped her put plywood up before the violence rolled through last night, and she seemed a little shaken, but determined to stay cheerful in the face of it.

While many of the riots began as well-meaning protests, different groups always joined the fray to say their piece and things escalated from there. It brought the crazies out in droves—conspiracy theorists, religious extremists, violent personalities looking for an outlet.

But plenty thought it was all a hoax, denying video evidence because it might be doctored; more still saw it as needlessly politicized; others only cared about their day-to-day, like the cadre of pro sports players who tried to use the "unfair magical advantage" to justify their own doping.

There was no consensus on how to untangle the mess, but one thing most people seemed to agree on was that they were afraid—afraid of what they didn't understand and couldn't quantify, couldn't see enough of to protect themselves from. ACE Special Response Teams had operated in secret long before the leaks, but the fear and unrest made it necessary to come out of the shadows and show civilians something was being done about it. In the beginning, the riots had been worse.

Much, much worse.

When he neared Little Tokyo, the LAFD and LASD were out in force. Yellow tape cordoned off the soot-darkened bones of his favorite sushi place, but tempers here had cooled for now. Shattered glass reflected the early morning light, and a trampled rainbow of paper strips cluttered the streets.

Bending down, he examined one. These had been torn from The Wishing Tree, an old ficus outside one of the plaza's art galleries. The smooth, gray trunk was usually layered with handwritten notes from locals and tourists alike. Once, the paper wishes had been part of the yearly Tanabata festival, but in recent years, they had become a more permanent symbol of hope in the neighborhood.

The strip beneath his boot was in Portuguese. A few feet away, another read, *A wish to find Auntie Lauren, or that she's healthy and safe wherever she is.*

He wondered if Auntie Lauren had been a witch. If he'd been the one to make her disappear.

Standing, he tried to shake whatever feeling clutched at his chest and nodded at an officer directing the lingering trickle of traffic. The beat cops knew him well since this was one of his districts, but a uniform he didn't recognize approached from his left. A lieutenant, actually, from the bars on his collar.

"Special Agent Ryland?"

Dipping his chin in the lieutenant's direction, Theo said, "Morning, L.T."

"Miller," he said by way of introduction. They shook hands. "Hell of a night."

"You're telling me. What do you have?"

"Electrical interference up in that apartment complex—" he gestured to the end of the block, "—there."

Theo followed his eye line, squinting against the morning sun. "Explains these traffic lights here. But an outage after a riot isn't unheard of."

"It's not a true outage. Other intersections are fine. We noticed a pattern to the surges, and like, a hum, or a musicality to it. Hard to explain. But I guess you'll do your woo-woo thing and figure that out for yourself."

Once the police delegated any arcane activity calls to ACE, they were shut out, and they weren't exactly thrilled about it. But this man was a lieutenant, and Theo still had respect for the bars, so he swallowed his retort.

Miller stayed on Theo's heels as he moved down the block toward the offending high-rise.

Once within range, the hair on the back of his neck stiffened. The echo of the energy was stronger in his peripheral vision, threads surrounding the building taking on a bluish hue and thrumming in the odd rhythm Miller described. His fingers and toes tingled like they'd fallen asleep and were just regaining feeling.

Well, fuck. An electromancer generating that much interference was one he'd need backup for.

He pulled out his phone, dialing Dispatch. "It's Ryland. Bump my Alpha-12 to an Alpha-9."

"Confirming Alpha-9. We'll send transporters to your location. "

"Be advised I'm awaiting Santana's arrival before moving in."

"10-4."

Theo dismissed Miller while he waited, all the while shifting his weight from his heels to his toes and back again. When Ricky finally arrived, he still hadn't shaken off the pins and needles.

Two rookies trailed behind him, and Theo recognized them as Jamie Harris and Terrell Thompson, recruits six months or so out of the Academy. They were bright-eyed, young, keen to prove themselves. But their probation would wring out the enthusiasm and hang them up to dry.

Still, he couldn't begrudge them their excitement. Field training was always a step above riding a desk.

Ricky craned his neck toward the looming apartment block. Though lanky and built like a boxer, his interests ran more to hockey. Wide, mischievous brown eyes sat under heavy, expressive brows and a hairline that Theo had never seen look less than razor-sharp. Ricky's hair was the second great love of his life; the first was his mother, and he was adamant he'd never marry unless the woman could cook sancocho the way she did.

Predictably, Ricky had yet to settle down.

The compass-like arcanometer he held could measure magic, though it wasn't as accurate or effective as Theo's talent, which formed a more complete picture of the magic being used. Theo could tell what kind it was, where it was coming from, and the passions driving it. But sensitives like Theo were a rarity and couldn't be everywhere at once, so they made do.

"A 6.2," Ricky murmured, watching the tiny gauge click back and forth. When his observation was met with silence, he coughed. "Which I'm certain one of you is *writing down*, yes? For the mountain of paperwork you'll need to do later?"

Thompson and Harris looked at each other, suddenly fumbling for their field notebooks and pens. Ricky rolled his eyes. "The first to tell me which bracket that falls into doesn't have to do the writeup."

"A 6.2 is classified as a Moderate Arcane Disturbance, sir!" Harris blurted, and Thompson tried not to look delighted as Ricky closed his eyes and prayed for patience.

"Thompson," Ricky said sweetly, turning toward him, "Please inform Harris why this is incorrect."

Thompson sounded smug. "Moderate Arcane Disturbance is 3.0-5.9, sir. A 6.2 would be classified as Significant."

"It is, but—" Ricky pointed a finger as Thompson's grin widened, "You still have to do the writeup, because you were a little shit about being right."

Harris snickered when Thompson's face fell, and Ricky turned back to Theo. "Fletcher really undersold being an FTO. You should try it."

Theo had been there, done that, and would never touch field training again. Not to mention he wasn't exactly a social butterfly. The friends he made were usually by accident or forced proximity. Ricky had started as a mix of both. "They must be desperate if they're trusting you to teach anyone."

Ricky snorted. "That's what I said! These assholes don't stand a chance. Alright, tell me what we've got here."

"Electromancer," Theo said, and briefed him in on what Miller had said. "Fourth, fifth floor, maybe. Feels young, or at least...not fully realized. Hard to tell from here. Let's go on up."

At the flash of their badges, a stout, grizzled man in the lobby waved them through. He introduced himself as the onsite manager. "Thought you looked a little kitted-out to be electricians. These surges have been happening since the riots came through. Elevator's on the fritz, so I'd avoid it."

Theo nodded and led the team up the stairs. The pulses intensified with each floor they climbed, a bizarre hum ebbing and flowing with the flickering lights above.

Taking point with his .45 drawn, Theo eased open the stairwell door and moved through the long hallway. It was a clean enough building, if not dated. Peeling baseboards skirted spartan white walls, escorting the team's muffled footfalls over threadbare green carpeting. He halted in front of apartment 506.

28

He felt the shape of the magical ward before he saw it, thrumming along to the cadence of the dancing overhead lights. It was young energy, definitely, green and unrefined. Unskilled witches often lashed out with strength they couldn't understand or control, and it made them all the more dangerous.

If he touched the scarred blue door, he'd probably fry—but his boots had rubber soles. He signaled Ricky to go in high so he could go in low, then turned away and poured his strength into a hard mule kick.

A little give. He tried again, and this time door splintered off its hinges with a bang that echoed through the narrow corridor. From the corner of Theo's eye, Harris waved a curious resident back into their condo.

Unwilling to test the strength of the magical ward, he and Ricky pointed their tranq guns through the doorway and peered into the tiny studio.

God damn it.

A teenage girl scrambled off a blue sofa with a panicked yelp. She couldn't have been older than fifteen or sixteen. Energy crackled through the air and her long black hair fluttered about her head in a static halo, like she'd just brushed against a balloon. "Stay back," she spat angrily, her magic flaring brighter.

His heart skipped, chest tightening the way it always did when kids were involved, and he lowered his tranq gun a tick. He hated this the most. Who he had to be, right here.

He was the thing marking the before and after. They might not remember his face in their nightmares, but they'd remember the fear. He relived his own fear constantly, and maybe that was his penance.

The TAC Specialists who took him had come much the same way, found him crying and angry. He'd begged his parents for help. They'd thought they were helping, by giving him over to people who could teach him to control himself.

He'd never actually said he forgave them, not in so many words. After a time, the anger just became part of him. Drove him forward like steam in a turbine. And now the most he could do for these kids was keep them from getting hurt.

He didn't have time to give it more thought as her magic rose, hovering on a knife's edge – he felt it all along his arms as she put the couch between them, glancing backward at the window. She was going to open it and jump, he realized with a stab of dread. "Don't come any closer," she said, her voice wavering. "I know who you are."

"Then you know if you attack us, you're in worse trouble," he said, deciding to level with her. Her brown eyes were shrewd—she wouldn't stand for being patronized.

"I can't do anything about it," she snapped, though her tone didn't disguise the fear in her eyes. "I don't know how to make it stop. I usually can, but—" she shook her head, as if wondering why she was even telling him. "You guys don't even care, do you? About what they do out there." She jerked her chin down at the wrecked shops below them. "I bet they could burn this whole street down and you wouldn't care."

Ah. The riots, it seemed, set her off. He ignored her question and shot back one of his own. "Where are your parents?"

She shook her head and hugged herself. "You'd know better than me."

The girl seemed to make a decision, then, and he felt the magic just before she snapped it toward him. She was fast, but he was faster, and his Crash dart sailed through the veil of electricity and into her arm.

Eyes wide, she hissed and then slumped against the wall. All at once her hair obeyed the laws of gravity again, and the flickering lights steadied. Theo probed the sole of his shoe through the entrance and, verifying the wards no longer held, rushed in with Ricky on his heels.

The girl fought to keep her drooping eyelids open as Theo crouched next to her but lost the battle. "Jesus." Harris peeked through the doorway, eyes wide. "Just a freakin' kid. About her parents—what do you think she meant?"

"Probably that we have 'em already," Ricky said, looking around the condo warily. "Or killed 'em. Wonder who's paying for this place, then."

Theo glanced around the condo too, deciding it didn't look lived-in— no pictures on the walls, no knickknacks on the shelves. The shoddy furniture was mismatched, probably thrifted. "It looks like..."

"A safe house." Ricky finished Theo's thought.

Theo stood, carefully hoisting the girl's limp body over his shoulder. She smelled sweet and floral. Probably a perfume sample from the open Vogue on the breakfast bar. His stomach churned again and forced his mouth to move. "Do a sweep and make sure there aren't any other surprises waiting for us," he told Harris and Thompson. "Look for a phone. She's a teenager—there's no way she doesn't have one." And if she didn't...that

30

meant someone was looking out for her. Someone who knew what the hell they were doing.

Ricky holstered his tranq gun and turned back toward his rookies. "After that, you're on lookout duty. Fix the door and watch the place. I want pictures and names of everyone who comes in and out of this building. If there aren't cameras here, see if any next door or across the street are aimed this way. Whoever left her was planning on coming back."

Theo would return and question the neighbors later, himself. He wasn't about to do it with an unconscious kid slung over his shoulder.

As they started back downstairs, Ricky said, "Fletcher's gonna want to hear about this. Fits the pattern."

Theo nodded. An untold number of witch smugglers operated up and down the coast, and most of Theo's leads had fizzled or outright disappeared. They were careful not to draw attention to themselves while they were being moved, but this kid was so frightened she couldn't control her magic. "Stupid of them, leaving her alone."

Downstairs, the onsite manager stared as they crossed the lobby. He made the sign of the cross in the air and hissed, "*Bruja.*"

An armored, blacked-out SUV idled by the curb outside. Two transporters in dark uniforms beelined for Theo, relieving him of his charge, then stowed her in the backseat.

When they handed him the clipboard to sign off on her intake paperwork Theo fished out the IDs he'd found in her wallet. One of them was a well-made fake that he might not have caught if he hadn't seen the learner's permit behind it, which bore a slightly younger photo. It read *Tesauro, Daniela Savina,* and listed an address in Chula Vista.

But the silver necklace she wore just said *Nell.*

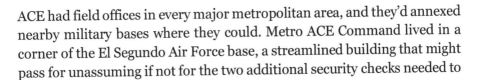

ACE had field offices in every major metropolitan area, and they'd annexed nearby military bases where they could. Metro ACE Command lived in a corner of the El Segundo Air Force base, a streamlined building that might pass for unassuming if not for the two additional security checks needed to enter it.

Theo grabbed a sheaf of papers from the printer in his office, a stack of folders from his desk, then made his way up to the third floor. He nodded at the receptionist, a middle-aged brunette with a down-turned mouth and a sculptural helmet of hair. She waved him through. Fletcher's office door was ajar, and Theo poked his head in.

Thomas Fletcher was the Metro ACE Commander for LA County, a three-tour Air Force vet. That much was clear in everything from his gait to his posture to his haircut. Quiet, soft-spoken danger coiled in his gaze, unsettling most, but making him ideal for the role he'd inherited. On paper, he and all the other Metro Commanders reported to the Regional ACE Director in Sacramento, who answered to the brass in D.C.

Under Fletcher, Theo led his own Special Response Team, as did every TAC Specialist who was also a natural sensitive. But when an investigation bled beyond their jurisdiction, they had to loop in Command.

"Ryland." He gestured for Theo to sit. "I read your prelim report."

Theo slid a file across Fletcher's desk. "Been digging since then. The girl matches the description of Daniela Tesauro, missing daughter of two witches we picked up last year in Chula Vista."

Fletcher pulled the file toward him and thumbed through it. "What do we know about them? They must've had contact with someone who could help her, maybe sent her away if they caught a whiff of us."

Theo tossed two more dossiers on the table. "Emilio and Sonya Tesauro, serving time at The Beach. My hunch is someone brought Nell to LA, planned on smuggling her further north."

"Nell?"

"A nickname she goes by."

"A big ring was just shut down near Seattle," Fletcher murmured as he read.

"When?"

"Happened this morning. We rounded up nearly thirty of them, and we're hoping for a few to turn, but you know how that goes. We lost one potential already."

He did know. Covens had measures in place to keep their members from talking, and sometimes it wasn't pretty. "I went back through Vanguard to see who might've been around to take care of her after her parents were arrested. A year's a long time for even a sixteen-year-old to be on her own. No other family in the database, but this guy popped for me." Another folder slapped onto the growing stack. "Ezra Foster."

Opening it, Fletcher glanced at the picture of a fit black man in a windbreaker. The man leaned against the front of a bank while he spoke into a headset, his locs pulled back in a ponytail. "Why'd he pop?"

"Big-shot who owns a lot of real estate on the Westside. I pulled property tax records. Two hotels, three dive bars, a club, a surf shop—they're all in the file. INN|LA has a sister property in San Diego, also."

"You think he's using the hotels as safe houses." It wasn't a question.

"Guess who used to own that condo."

"Son of a bitch." Fletcher paused. "*Used* to own?"

"Sold it a year ago. Some woman in Chicago rents it out now. Allegedly."

Sifting through the rest of the papers, Fletcher rubbed the stubble creeping along his chin. "Squeaky clean, this one. Not even a speeding ticket."

"And here's what makes me pretty certain he's our guy," Theo said. "He's big in the community. Look at the charity fundraiser he did two years ago." He tapped a photo in a newspaper article he'd printed. "That's Emilio Tesauro with him. They're cousins. Mother was adopted, from what I could gather."

Fletcher whistled. "This is good work, Ryland."

"Don't cheer just yet. This guy? He has his fingers in half a dozen political pies. He's made some inroads with the police commissioner, he reinvests a lot in small businesses on the South Side, and his father graduated UCLA with Governor Folsom, same class, same frat. I hear he'd been cut off as a twentysomething, but patched things up with his dad, and I'd hate to assume they couldn't raise hell for us if Foster wanted them to. Folks would listen."

"There's always a fuckin' catch." Sighing, Fletcher took off his glasses, cleaned them, and looked down at the dossier again. "If we get anything solid on him, I'll handle the PR song and dance. But right now, you worry about making sure this shit stays quiet. Keep Santana on it if you want, maybe his two rookies for the grunt work, but no more than that."

"Understood, sir. Not a peep."

CHAPTER FOUR

The immersion blender in Mindy's hand groaned and sputtered to a stop, spraying her shirt with flecks of green.

Cora grimaced. "Want me to..."

"No." Mindy inspected the stuck blade and banged it on the edge of the sink. "I'd trade the efficiency of this fancy thing for the catharsis of a—" the blender roared to life again, she had to yell over it, "—mortar and pestle right about now."

Cora eyed the mixture. It was a murky, questionable green-brown, but if it would give her dreamless sleep, she'd deal with it. Nightmares about her family's arrest had dogged her for the last two nights. Coming back here had triggered them again.

And she couldn't keep them at bay, herself...at least not the way she used to.

Over the years, she'd never dreamed of the old house in Orange County; just the backyard, the streets, looking in from the outside. She should have been able to go back.

She almost had, weeks after her escape, but they'd be watching the place, waiting to stick it to the fourteen-year-old girl who'd eluded them, outsmarted them. Then they'd have seized it and sold everything in it. Her bed with the flowered quilt; the stuffed animals beneath it that she couldn't bring herself to give up; the vanity mirror Sebastian once drew penises on with the very first lipstick her mom let her buy. It was bright coral, clashed horribly with her complexion, but damn it, it was hers. Until it wasn't.

Mindy mumbled an incantation over the mixture, added a scoop of powder from a tin, and Cora snapped out of the memory. "What's that?"

"Oh, nothing."

"Min."

"Okay, it's fiber. Just a little. You have such a troubled aura, dear, and regularity goes a long way toward—"

Cora rolled her eyes.

"—easing the burden on the soul. You eat so poorly."

"I eat like a normal human being." She took a calculated bite of a cheese doodle.

Mindy sighed. "You won't even taste it." She stuck the pitcher in the fridge. "That should last you a week or so—just a quarter cup each night, before bed." A knock at the door interrupted Cora's less-than-enthused thanks.

As Mindy moved through the foyer and opened the arched slab of wood, Cora noticed Quinn's long gel nails were violently pink today, and a fresh piercing hooked her right eyebrow. Quinn rushed forward, planting a kiss on each of Mindy's cheeks. "Ms. Mindy Somerville, as I live and breathe. Are you aging backwards? Just look at you! Please tell me you made those earrings."

Mindy beamed, tugging at the mismatched clay shapes dangling from her ears. "Oh, these old things? They have a sister set...I could be convinced to part with them..."

"Say no more! I'll bring you my mom's lemon bars next time I come around."

Cora and Quinn made their way into the den. At this time of morning, natural light flooded the converted office space, illuminating the colorful spines of books on floor-to-ceiling shelves. Anchoring the other wall was a careworn leather couch, with just enough room for a wooden writing desk and the robust string-of-hearts vine wandering down its hutch.

Quinn dug in her purse for some folded pieces of paper and waved them at Cora. "You get to play Dr. Blackheart."

"Let me guess: he's surly, sexy, with a terrible bedside manner and dark, mysterious past. But he saves lives, so we're able to forgive him for being an asshole, and it'll take someone like..." Cora snatched one of the papers from Quinn. "Nurse Haven? Ugh. Someone like Nurse Haven to break through that tough exterior."

Quinn frowned. "I didn't tell you about this already, did I?"

"Oh, Goddess. Okay, let's get this over with." Cora cleared her throat and plopped on the couch. Quinn stood in the middle of the room and did a few vocal exercises before Cora began to read.

"Int...Hospital Cafeteria, Day—"

"You don't have to read that part. Just start from where I come to sit at your table."

"Right. Okay." Cora skipped ahead, doing her best impression of a sexy male voice.

                    DR. BLACKHEART
        "You've got some nerve coming over here, after what
        you pulled in the OR."

Quinn summoned a little gust of wind to blow her hair backward, and Cora snickered. The perks of being part aeromancer.

                    NURSE HAVEN
        "I did what needed to be done, Victor. You'd know
        something about that, wouldn't you?"
                    DR. BLACKHEART
              (shutting her down)
        "You know nothing about me."
                    NURSE HAVEN
              (coy)
        "Would you like me to?"

Quinn shrieked and chucked the script across the room. "Motherfucker!"

Cora frowned, flipped the page over. "I don't see—"

"Look! Look, right there!"

A small brown and gray intruder scrambled up the trailing leaves of the plant on top of the desk. Nose peeking out of the foliage, the mouse blinked at them.

They blinked back.

Cora crouched to bring the tabletop to eye level. "I think it's staring at me." She crawled closer, trying not to startle it—its little nose twitched, sniffing the air. Just as quickly as it had appeared, it was gone.

What the hell?

Something cold slithered along the back of Cora's neck and she squealed, swatting wildly with the handful of papers. "Get it off! Get it off!"

"Wait, Cora, stop! Stop!" Quinn yanked the script from Cora's hand and grabbed her shoulders, turning her around. "You'll scare it away!"

Cora opened her mouth to explain that was exactly the goal, but she looked where Quinn had pointed her. On one of the bookshelves, behind a vase, sat a small, glowing blob of light and color. It didn't appear to realize the vase was transparent, and therefore ineffective as far as hiding spots go.

She released a measured breath to control the adrenaline crashing through her and lowered her voice to a whisper. "I think...I think it's the same sprite from the pier. Maybe. That one took a mouse form too."

Mindy had poked her head in the room when she heard Quinn's scream, and now they both turned to her, as if she had any idea why a sprite would want to follow them home.

"Oh, wow!" Mindy breathed. The sprite peeked out from behind the vase, then lost its nerve and hid again. "I know what'll coax it out. Hold on."

Mindy dashed away and returned moments later, fishing through a small sewing box. She held up a quarter-sized piece of mother-of-pearl for Cora, probably broken off an old button. "Go ahead. You do it."

Cora took it, gingerly turning it over in her palm. Sprites were partial to shiny things, and she let the mother-of-pearl catch the light from the window. The sprite tentatively peeked around the vase again.

She stepped closer, breath held, placing the broken button on the other end of the shelf. "Go on," she said softly. "It's for you."

The sprite's tiny glowing eyes shifted from her, to the button, back to her.

"I'm sorry for hitting you," she said, taking another step closer. "I didn't mean to. You startled me."

The sprite flowed across the shelf like spilled liquid, snapping up the button and holding it close. It didn't quite have arms or hands, but it seemed to be able to form bloblike appendages at will. It turned its eyes to her again and she felt something...almost a smile, or a purr, but not any she could see or hear. It was more of an imprint in her mind. A thank-you.

And then it folded the button into its body, some kind of otherworldly pocket to hold all its treasures in.

It leapt from the shelf to her outstretched hand, pooling there, warm and cold, solid and ephemeral, like weightless putty. She wasn't sure what to do with it, so she reached out a finger to stroke it. Shuddering in a way that registered as satisfied, it flowed up her arm to hover above her shoulder.

Turning back to Quinn and Mindy, Cora took care not to make any sudden movements. "Um. What should I...what's the etiquette here?"

Mindy shrugged. "Why not ask its name?"

Of course. As a sentient arcane spirit, it probably had one. The warm-cold sensation crept under Cora's hair and over to her other shoulder as the sprite looked Quinn up and down.

"It's Pip," Cora said, not sure where the knowledge had come from, or her confidence in its absolute truth. "His name is Pip."

Pip flowed down Cora's arm and dove between the couch cushions. Then, bubbling up from beneath a pillow on the other side, he lofted a quarter high above his—head? body?—and held it out for Cora.

She thanked Pip and pocketed it, not fully understanding the exchange that had just taken place, but knowing it was important, somehow.

———⁂———

It would take time to adjust to the suddenness of Pip's comings and goings. Sometimes he preferred to be a mouse, and he had already sent Mindy shrieking up onto the kitchen chair. Other times he enjoyed living on the countertop as a mug or the TV remote or a spatula. Expecting to pick up a solid object that instead shifted and pooled through your fingers like molasses was...unsettling. She'd begun prodding things first before handling them but was grateful for the extra company—whatever form it decided to take.

Pip's presence offset nostalgia's grip on her, too. So much of the Westside nagged at Cora's memory, snippets of past lives lodging between her heart and her throat. She considered what Mindy had said—about the millions of miles of cosmos separating these places from the things that happened in them years ago—and it just made her lonelier.

But Ezra's store, Boardroom, was somewhere she'd never been. Stepping into it that first afternoon was a strange kind of refuge. Here was a place no ghosts could claim, not yet. It smelled of fresh wood, the rubber of brand-new wetsuits, the pages of new books. Its displays were bright and uncluttered. It was cozy, unpretentious, and she loved it immediately.

Pip did, too. As a ballpoint pen, his vantage point from behind her ear offered a good view of general goings-on without the risk of being picked up by an unwary customer. That was the last thing Cora needed.

She'd worked retail before, so learning the register was just muscle memory. Ezra let her geek out over the custom boards and showed her how to work the juicer in the break room. It surprised her how much time he spent there.

"I like the simplicity of it," he'd confessed. "I get tired of investors and revenue reports and sitting in boardrooms—"

Cora's eyes lit up. "And so the name was born."

"Just a little joke with myself."

She fell into an easy rhythm in the days following, enjoying the guardrails of the new routine, but the honeymoon didn't last.

At the end of her first week, Ezra dropped off the map to deal with a family emergency, leaving Marlo, the manager, to finish Cora's training. She'd nudged Quinn, asking if she knew what had happened, but only got cryptic non-answers.

That wouldn't have been so strange on its own—it wasn't her business, really—but on that same Saturday, Mindy cried more often than usual, speaking in hushed tones on the phone late into the night. She wouldn't have given that a second thought either—not after Oscar—but Mindy made two crucial mistakes. She dodged Cora's questions, and she lied.

Mindy was too honest to be anything but a clumsy liar, too open about her emotions to convince Cora that "fine" covered all the nuances of her heart. An empath like Mindy was never simply "fine." She was either ambivalent, or content, or apathetic, or bemused, or unperturbed, or preoccupied, or underwhelmed. "Fine" was a four-alarm fire.

And so a thick, amorphous unease charged the air overhead as the week wore on; Cora could almost smell the ozone before a storm, like the sky might open up at any moment.

One slow afternoon while she was taking inventory of a new shipment of wetsuits, it did.

A muffled ooof drew her attention toward the board rack at the front of the store. She set down her scanner and headed towards the window display, half-expecting the neighbor kid to be playing hide and seek in it again.

Instead, a tall, broad-shouldered man with a riot of sable curls tipped a longboard back into place. He paused, hands outstretched, waiting for it to fall again.

"Did you miss the sign?" she asked, hand on her hip.

He turned, locked eyes with her. His were nearly black, sparkling with a familiarity that made her shoulder blades itch. By his shallow crow's feet, she'd put him at thirty, or a bit past it. A short-cropped beard a shade lighter than his hair hugged the strong line of his jaw. His plaid button-down, jeans, and boots might have been expensive once, but he'd gotten his money's worth out of them and then some.

Even with features more brutal than handsome, all her hormones sat up and took notice. Tanned skin was marred by a thick scar dividing his playful left brow in two. A cauliflower ear outed him as a fighter, and his nose had been broken before. Maybe more than once.

The room instantly became smaller.

"This sign?" he asked. She got the impression every word was a deliberate choice, not a single one wasted.

She looked at the sign he gestured at: PLEASE ASK FOR ASSISTANCE. All too aware of the muscles filling out his shirt, she swallowed. "Um, yes. That one."

He raised the other eyebrow. His eyes flitted toward the ten-foot board, then across the otherwise empty store. "From who? You?"

Her ears grew hot. She might be short, but she knew her way around a board, and her quads and shoulders showed it. She summoned her most diplomatic tone. "You'd be surprised what people will sue over."

He smiled—*smiled!*—at her and wandered over to a display of coffee table books, thumbed through the glossy photos with disinterest. "I prefer Bolloré's first book."

And Pip really, really didn't like him. That much she could sense. But she knew this man from somewhere. She knew she knew him. Where did she...

He ran a finger along the spine of a different one, pulled it out, tested the weight of it, slid it back. "The others feel too polished. I think he's forgotten what it's like to find sand in your—"

"Can I help you with something or not?" Curiosity simmered under the annoyance.

He casually unfolded a shirt on the pile she'd folded half an hour before. "I've got it. Thanks."

Cora would've happily left him alone and finished inventory. But as she headed back to womenswear, his words punched her in the gut.

"A friend gave it to me a long time ago. Bolloré's *Salt*."

Throat constricting, she turned. A wave of memory crashed through her, wild and furious, before settling uncomfortably in her chest. She aged him down in her mind: lose the scar, the beard, the hard line of jaw. Skinnier, lankier. Keep the chin dimple, the riot of hair—though it was longer back then, a curly stub of ponytail.

She'd been the one to give him the book, on his birthday. She'd been so nervous, she remembered because he was two years older, two years cooler. The most adult thing she could think to give him was a book. A massive one, full of surf photography. Something a sophisticated guy might put on a coffee table.

She wondered if he still had it.

"Theo Ryland." The sound had come from her own mouth, jarring her back to the present. Her chest was tight, her body hot and cold all at once. He grinned at the recognition in her voice, and she couldn't stop the tears, couldn't stop herself from leaping toward him, and suddenly she was in the air, legs around his waist, and he was spinning her, laughing.

She buried her face in his neck and breathed him in, and the scent was so new and strange but still wholly Ryland, and Goddess he was strong and so much taller and—

She remembered the last time she'd seen him, and the day after, and when he set her down she shook her head in disbelief. Her shock and joy had fizzled fast, leaving room for everything else to rush in. She took a step back, and another, and when he frowned, she finally found her nerve. "You...asshole."

41

He blinked, as if shaking off the whiplash from her reaction, then stuffed his hands back into his pockets. "Right. I guess I deserve that."

"You couldn't call? Text? What happened to you?" Bracing herself on a nearby shelf, she tried to gather her emotions, her thoughts, into something coherent. "Did you think you could just...stroll in here? Like you hadn't just vanished one day and never spoken to us again?"

He had the sense to look bothered. "It was...complicated. It wasn't my choice."

"What. Happened. To. You?" she repeated. Giving him any chance, any at all, to explain to his closest childhood friend why he'd nearly kissed her one evening behind the bougainvillea and disappeared, along with his parents, days after.

"Have you really never been kissed before?" he'd asked with all the nonchalance of a sixteen-year-old who'd probably only been kissed once or twice and didn't want her to know it. "I could show you what it's like, for the hell of it." He'd coughed, looked around, scratched the back of his head. "Wouldn't have to mean anything."

"I can see why all the girls chase you," she'd said with a dramatic eye roll. "Weirdo. Come on, my mom's making lasagna." And she'd left him in the little patch of garden before her blush climbed high enough for him to notice in the dark.

Okay, so maybe that wasn't nearly a kiss. But it didn't change the way it hurt when she'd walked by his house a few days later, seen the For Sale sign and the movers, followed the cardboard path through the open door, looking for him. Realizing.

She'd been fourteen. And when you're fourteen, those things seem a lot like the end of the world, because your world takes up all of about two square miles. But seeing Ryland in front of her, with looks and swagger and charm he didn't deserve to have, stirred up a couple of feelings she thought she'd buried.

"I wish I could tell you," he said. "I didn't plan on running into you—"

"Of course not. Why would you, especially now? Better to stay gone."

He held up his hands. "I didn't mean it like that."

Cora blinked. The balls on this guy. Her mother couldn't make him go back to his own house for dinner most nights.

"I was heading down the boardwalk and I saw you closing the shop," he said. "I wasn't sure it was you at first. I thought..."

"You followed me?"

"Just long enough to be sure."

"Why are you here?" she asked.

"I had to see for myself that you were okay."

She focused on re-folding shirts until she had the courage to look him in the eye. "I'm fucking peachy. In fact, I've been doing fine without your sage advice for—how many years has it been? You weren't the only person to disappear, Ryland. You were just the first."

The bell over the door tinkled. A middle-aged woman entered, teenage son in tow. Grateful for the distraction, Cora turned her back to Ryland and forced her lips into a smile. "Welcome!"

The kid rolled his eyes at her, so she must have laid it on thick. The mother didn't seem to notice. "Hi. My son starts surf lessons soon, and he needs a board."

"No problem." Cora eyed the kid, who gazed with longing at a $1,300 custom job. "We'll want to start him on a foamie. We have a few Wavestorms over here..."

While she showed them the different colors available, Ryland's eyes burned holes into her back. By the time she'd finished, he was gone.

It was probably for the best.

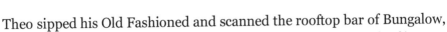

Theo sipped his Old Fashioned and scanned the rooftop bar of Bungalow, taking in the sprawling view of the marina and everything north of it.

Tiny lights flickered in neighborhoods that climbed the base of the Santa Monica mountains and reached towards Malibu, making the stuttering gleam of the Ferris wheel seem garish by comparison. The coastline beyond faded into a swath of liquid night, and while the bar was hardly the wildest place to be in LA, he wished for that distant promise of quiet.

When Ricky had suggested they check the place out, Theo wasn't about to turn down an excuse to drink—and work was a damn good one. Especially after the day he'd had. After the look Cora had given him. *You weren't the only person to disappear, Ryland. You were just the first.*

The bartender was young, pink-haired with an eyebrow piercing. Except to refill his drink, she steered clear of him, and he tipped her well for it. Meanwhile, Ricky had abandoned the arcanometer in his pocket along with any pretense of work, more concerned about chatting up a blonde in the hotel uniform, probably fresh off her shift.

The other customers fit a solid demographic: attractive, trendy try-hards.

Did Cora come here? It wasn't far from the Boardroom, and Ezra probably gave her a discount. Or maybe she preferred dives. Maybe she was more of a homebody.

Honestly, what the hell did he know about her, anyway? And did he want to learn, or was he just drawn to what she represented—the only uncomplicated chapter in his life, a sliver of childhood normalcy he could never reach through time to get back?

The way she ran to him, at first...it cast everything else about that moment in sharp relief. Knowing what it felt like to hold her after so damn long just made what came after sting more.

But what else did he expect from her when he stepped into the Boardroom? Relief? Gratitude? An admission she'd missed him? Any of that was laughable, and it didn't matter now. He'd been selfish to think she wouldn't be hurt, surprised by the seed of guilt that planted, foolish to think he could just drink it away.

Hell, he shouldn't have left things like that. She deserved a goodbye to make up for the one she hadn't gotten years ago.

But he knew why he'd done it.

It was the part of him that didn't want her to see who he'd become if he stuck around long enough to show her.

Maybe it was because—no, not maybe, it *was* because he'd worn the edges off his sobriety that seeking her out seemed like a good idea. Better, at least, than brooding about her a few blocks away.

If he left now, he might be able to catch her before she closed up.

Cora locked the front door of Boardroom and began to tidy up. Saturdays were the longest, and kept her here the latest, so she was looking forward to crashing. It filled her with a sunny little buzz, though, to talk about surfing all day with people who loved it as much as she did.

That buzz muted when uniformed hunter patrols prowled past the window, arcanometers in hand, but Pip hadn't set anything off. Sprites drew their magic from the ley lines differently than witches did. Still, he had the good sense to stay hidden.

After breaking down empty cardboard boxes from the morning shipment, she dragged them to the recycling one block over, a wary eye sweeping the alleyway. During the day, Venice was chock-full of tourists, artists, skateboarders, sidewalk drummers, folks walking dogs as they roller bladed in banana hammocks. But at night the energy changed, like a spell losing its grip, returning the streets to their pre-Abbot Kinney ambiance.

That particular bastion of gentrification flourished just a few blocks away: a refuge for all things designer and people who defined themselves by owning them. But even it hadn't gone untouched by magic paranoia.

She'd seen the evidence of it that afternoon as a clean-cut man lofted a sign on the street corner, bellowing at passersby. A small crowd of supporters had gathered on the sidewalk. Cora had kept her head down and crossed the street, but he pointed, jowls jiggling.

"YOU can't walk away from the corruption gripping our neighborhoods, infecting our schools, festering in our government! This can't continue unchecked! How can we defend ourselves from the unseen, the unknown?"

As she hefted the cardboard into the recycler, his words echoed in her head, stirred her up a little. She slammed the lid shut. *Fuck* that guy.

What right did he have, did any of them have, to claim ownership of those things?

Witches had lived in these communities for years and contributed to them like anyone else, done charity work, owned businesses. They weren't this amorphous, unknown entity. They were friends, and neighbors, and teachers, and nurses like her aunt who saved the lives of people who might otherwise try to turn them in. They had just as much a right to exist as the idiot with the sign on the corner.

Stewing in that, she turned back toward Boardroom. A heavy, shuffling footstep snapped her out of it.

She spun around and looked up, and up, meeting the wide-eyed stare of an unkempt man with a bulbous nose. Even with a few steps between them, he stank of booze. She patted her pocket and realized her mace was safely tucked away in her purse, which sat uselessly on the counter inside.

"Can...I help you?" she asked, backing up as he moved forward.

"Maybe you can," the man said, sing-song. He took a swig from a flask with his free hand. "Maybe you can't. Depends what you got."

"Um, not much." She fought to keep her voice level, circling to his right. "I don't get paid 'til Friday. Come back then?" If she could just get around that truck parked between her and the main road...

"What's that? Gimme that." He gestured at the tiny gold and opal pendant she wore.

She hesitated a hair too long and he rounded on her, shoving her against the dumpster with meaty hands. She choked out a noise of surprise, gasping for the air he'd knocked out of her lungs.

Suddenly a blob of light slammed into his face, forcing him backward and muffling the scream that followed. He clawed at it, but now it had stretched across his eyes and hair, holding fast. He blindly stumbled into the hood of a parked car, then fell backwards onto the asphalt.

Cora stood, dumbfounded, as the man scrambled along on hands and knees. Pip flowed upward and pulled his length of unruly hair towards the alley's mouth, not strong enough to drag him there, but certainly annoying enough to encourage the man's movement in the general direction of it.

When Pip released him, he pitched forward on unsteady feet and disappeared around the corner, sputtering. His sharp gasps for air and erratic footsteps faded as he put distance between them, and only when it was silent did she remember to breathe again.

Pip bounced back into her hands, self-satisfied with an edge of concern. "Goddamn it, you," Cora managed. She waffled between gratitude and horror, eventually landing somewhere in the middle.

Sprites without frequent exposure to humans struggled to grasp the nuance of worldly concerns. Pip couldn't know why helping her might have been bad. He only knew she was in danger and didn't want her to be. "You need to be more careful. It's not safe for you to..."

Pip stiffened in her palm, his cloudlike form solidifying as he twisted his eyes to the left. Cora felt the warning, an urgent tug on her mind, and instinctively dropped beside the nearest parked car. As she rolled under it, clutching Pip to her chest, footfalls drew near—quiet, measured.

They stopped.

"Hide, now," she breathed, and Pip disappeared with a faint *pop*.

46

She could only see a pair of boots, unmoving, beside the trunk of the car she lay beneath. Cora didn't dare breathe. Seconds passed like hours. A crumpled In-N-Out bag sat two inches from her face, suffocating her with the stale smell of grease.

By the way they stepped forward again, stalking, she ruled out a concerned bystander. Her heartbeat filled her throat, her ears, and she was certain they could hear it thundering as they walked around the side of the car, then—mercifully—away, towards the other dumpster.

Cora inched sideways on her elbows, scraping her forearms along the pavement until she was out from underneath. With the parked car now between them, she rose to a crouch and weighed her options.

Peeking over the hood, she could see the outline of a man, his back still turned. She could crawl under the next car and wait him out, but she'd never have as good a chance to run for it as she did now.

Only a split second to decide. She said a silent prayer and bolted.

"HEY!"

Cora shouldn't have looked back. She almost didn't, but...

That voice.

She'd kick herself, in the coming days and weeks, for giving in to the urge, for slowing down just enough to—

A weight slammed into her from behind, strong arms grabbing her, and she cried out. The pavement shot upward, and she felt the skin rip from her palms as she tried to break her fall. A crunch—her bones? Something she landed on?—then pain, singing from the heel of her hand to her elbow.

She gasped for air and writhed beneath the weight—no, the man—who'd pinned her to the ground. He'd shifted her onto her back, and she stared up at him now, those familiar dark eyes meeting hers with equal shock.

It was Ryland.

"*You*," he said, blinking down at her in surprise.

Vision swimming, Cora groaned and tried to sit up. The weight on her chest eased as he rocked back on his heels, looking at her left arm. "I'm sorry, I..." He cursed and yanked something sharp out of her shoulder.

Stars still dancing in the corners of her eyes, she tried to understand what he was holding. It looked like a dart, or maybe a syringe. "What...what have you..?"

47

But even through the haze of pain, she knew. She fought the hard lump in her throat where her vocal cords should've been. One half of her brain still warred with the other, trying to make sense of the man in front of her. "You're...one of them. They made you one of them."

A muscle in his jaw twitched, like he was biting back the urge to deny it.

One ragged breath followed another, faster and shallower, as her limbs became leaden. A wave of exhaustion swept through her undulating panic, forcing it down. She tasted metal, then bile.

"Cora—" Ryland moved closer, and she flinched away.

"No. No, no. Don't you dare touch me. Don't you..." The world lurched under her. Nausea roiled within her. There were two of him, then one, then two again. "How could you?"

"Cora," he tried again, but she cut him off a second time.

"We trusted you." Her cheeks were wet now. "We trusted you, and we brought you into our home, and we..."

She felt strong hands cradle her head as she slumped backward, fighting whatever had been in that syringe. Pulling away again now seemed an impossible feat of strength. Instead she searched his dark eyes for any sort of regret, an apology, anything.

But they were impassive, even as she reached up to his face, tracing the line of the beard she'd never get used to. The world fell away and there was only his face, hot stab of his betrayal; nothing else felt real or important.

She tearfully whispered, "Where were you when they came for us? When they took them away?"

That stung, she could tell, and he opened his mouth to speak...but she was dragged under before he could try.

CHAPTER FIVE

Theo stared at the sleeping woman handcuffed to the exposed pipe in his living room. She was everything and nothing like he remembered.

The top-heavy curve of her mouth, the generous dusting of freckles, the long lashes under thick eyebrows she'd always complained about. As a girl, her hair had always been cropped short, a wild mess of shoulder-length waves, but she'd let it grow to her elbows, threaded with bronze from the sun.

She hadn't gotten any taller since he'd left, but she'd clearly refused to settle for tiny and meek. It showed in the powerful cut of her arms and shoulders, in the tanned sweep of quads that had seen many a squat rack, in the solid core he'd felt as he carried her upstairs. Curves softened her shape, but beneath them, she was a force to be reckoned with, and hell if that didn't look good on her.

Jesus, what was wrong with him? Shaking it off, he looked away. He couldn't think.

He should have taken her straight to Fletcher. It's what Ricky would have done if he hadn't been preoccupied on the roof of Bungalow.

That she worked for Ezra Foster sure complicated things, but he set it aside for now. He had more than enough to unpack already.

"That's right," he could practically hear her say. *"You might have bought yourself some time, but you can't delay this fight forever."*

He'd resigned himself to that. An explanation was years overdue. But until he'd seen her the other day, followed her to Boardroom, he thought he'd never have to give it to her. He figured he could steer clear of the beach cities, stick to the east side. Let her be someone else's problem.

He was relieved when Cora finally stirred. Just shy of noon and he already needed to get out of his own head.

Her eyes fluttered open. Groaning, she sat up, using the pipe for leverage when she realized one hand was bound. She tried to make sense of her surroundings, then noticed him sitting at the kitchen table.

Yanking at the cuffs, her eyes darted to the front door, the patio door, the windows, looking for a way out. He could see her fighting panic. "What is this? Where the hell are we?"

"My apartment." He leaned forward with a sigh, rubbed a hand over his face. "We need to talk."

She must have begun remembering the night before, because her glare seared right through the haze of the Crash. "Not going to drag me off to wherever you stash the rest of us?" Her voice quavered, and he wasn't sure if it was anger, fear, or a mix of both.

He stood and wandered to the kitchen window, focusing on the steadying familiarity of those skyscrapers. They rose on the shoulders of one another, stabbing through the blanket of smog.

Truth was...he didn't have an answer yet.

Clanging the cuffs against the pipe, she drew his attention back to her. "Hello? Is this really how you want to do this? Like I'm some kind of animal?"

Theo steeled himself. "I've had hours to think on this, Cora, and the truth is, I don't know you." He leaned backward against the counter. "I don't know what you're capable of. I know who you were, but we were just kids."

"My mother treated you like her own. Doesn't that mean anything to you? Didn't *we* mean anything to you?" Grief and frustration glistened in her eyes.

The memory of their old street, receding in the rearview mirror of his parents' van, was a gut punch even now. But he didn't let it show. "I didn't have a choice."

"Of course you did."

"It's not—"

"I think maybe you like feeling powerful."

"I don't—"

"Was it jealousy? Was it about control? Didn't have magic, so the next best thing was to hurt people who did?"

"I didn't have a *choice!*" he snarled, icy, and she shrank away from him. "They drafted me, Cora. They came to my house and took me away."

"Drafted?" The word was incredulous, and the next four barely a whisper. "A sixteen-year-old?"

"They put my parents up in an apartment near the base where I was going to be trained, and my dad stayed behind only long enough to make arrangements for the house." Rage simmered in his chest. "You knew I was a sensitive. But before I met you, before I was old enough to know what it meant, I was scared shitless by the things I was feeling. I didn't know what was happening or how to tune it out, and my parents heard of a doctor in Pasadena who might be able to help me."

Her anger softened. "I...remember. I remember you telling me about the doctor." Her gaze became unfocused, drifting into the middle distance. She'd gone back to that place, and he met her there.

They were skipping rocks in the small pond behind Theo's house, sheltering in the long shadows cast by the pampas grass and dipping their feet in the shallow water. He'd moved in just a few weeks earlier.

"Watch this!" Nine-year-old Theo leapt up and drew his arm back, then chucked the smooth stone with all his might. The angle was wrong, he knew it immediately, but it bounced. And bounced. And kept bouncing, all the way to the other side and into the grass.

His hairs stood on end, that chill crept up his spine, and he jerked his head toward Cora, then back at the lake. "*What* did you just do?"

Alarmed by his tone, her bottom lip began to quiver. "You wanted it to go all the way across. I helped."

Tears would bring his mom running, so he softened a bit and knelt beside her. "How...how did you help?"

Cora sniffled and wiped her nose on her sleeve but calmed down. "I just...I asked it to keep bouncing. The dirt and the rocks and the plants, they listen to me sometimes. I can also make hurting go away."

"They listen to you?"

She shrugged. "They listen to Sebastian more, but they're very nice. Are you angry?"

"No, I'm not angry."

"You sounded angry."

"I didn't mean it."

"Oh, okay." She played with the little pink bow at the end of her braid, shying away from his inquisitive stare.

"Could you do it again?"

"Why?"

Theo took her tiny hand in his, turned it over and examined her palm. She let him. "Because I get a funny feeling when it happens."

"What kind of funny?

He let her hand go, pulled his knees to his chest. "Like I'm really cold, and my hair gets prickly. You're seven, so you're too small to ride rollercoasters, but I rode one at Disneyland, and your stomach gets kind of weird when you go down a hill. Like that."

"My mom says sometimes people are sensitive. Are you sensitive?"

"Dr. Goldman says maybe. He's an important doctor. My mom told me. She says he understands a lot of things that normal doctors don't." He watched her grab a fistful of dirt and squeal in delight when she found a ladybug.

"Oh, no." The ladybug crawled up Cora's finger, one wing jutting out at an odd angle. It twitched, trying to fly. She smiled and the faintest thread of gold pushed the wing back into place. "You're all better now."

"He sold me out later," Theo said, yanking them both back to the present. "Convinced my parents to sign me up for a program that was supposed to help kids like me. But it was a front. ACE used whatever resources they had to find potential sensitives. I was in one of the first groups of kids forced into the program. They preferred kids sixteen and younger...it was easier."

Barely a breath past childhood. Old enough to have a taste of the freedom he'd lose, young and impressionable enough for his training to change who he thought he was. "They still take adults, of course. They test everyone who joins up now."

Cora stretched one leg, rubbing her calf against the other as if trying to fight pins and needles from sitting too long. "I'm sorry. I didn't know."

She was chewing on another thought, so he waited. "But I'm allowed to be sorry and disgusted at the same time. I'm sorry," she repeated, "your childhood was taken from you. It's a bummer, and nobody deserves it. But you're free. They're not responsible for what you're doing now, the decisions you've made since. They drafted you, so what?"

"Now, wait a second—"

"So what, Ryland? Here you are. What are you going to do about it? Do you have an ounce of empathy for the families you tear apart? Half the people you lock up are just trying to avoid a war or protect the people they love. Don't stand there and tell me you believe what they brainwashed you to believe."

He'd anticipated her anger, understood it, but his patience was unraveling fast. He paced in front of her. "You have no idea what I've seen. Horrific things—"

Cora's wide eyes flashed. "Don't sell yourself short. Nonwitches are capable of horrific things, too. Have you forgotten about school shootings, genocide, sex trafficking, organ harvesting—"

"I've seen a family burned alive in their home because their pyromancer son couldn't control himself," he interrupted her back, taking three quick strides to crouch in front of her. His voice was low, icy. "I've seen a man peel his own skin off because a neuromancer hexed him into thinking spiders lived beneath it, and I've watched a telekinetic collapse an entire office building because he was mad about being fired. People are just people, Cora. Sometimes they're shitty, and sometimes they're selfish, and sometimes they're none of those things but they make mistakes, or have a bad day, and when they have magic to boot...there's no telling what they're capable of. They might not know what they're capable of until it's too late."

He was near enough to feel her breath on his face, to count each individual eyelash around her defiant hazel eyes. "People *are* just people," she repeated softly, lifting her chin, "and I have the same right as you do to be here. As anyone has to be here."

That look, those words, hollowed out the righteous anger inside him. He knew she saw it, too. When he spoke again, his voice was hoarse. "I can't just stand by and watch it happen, Cor. I can't."

A shadow passed over her face at the old nickname. "You already are."

He needed air. Before he could lose his nerve, Theo stood and grabbed his jacket off the back of the kitchen chair, then slammed the front door behind him.

———————⌘———————

Cora had slipped in and out of sleep a few times since Ryland left, her system still reeling from the sedative he'd given her the night before. It was dusk now, and she wished she could reach a light switch.

The headlights of passing cars danced across the vents and shafts of the exposed ceiling. If she hadn't been a prisoner in the apartment, she would have admired his taste in decor. Minimal and masculine, it was all hard edges and soft leather. Everything had its place. Every surface gleamed.

How long before he returned?

Her limbs were still heavy with warmth, head throbbing in time with her pounding heart, a cadence of desperation growing louder the more conscious she became. She strained against the lethargy, trying to reach what remained of her magic. The drug was still doing its job.

She shouldn't have riled him up, but plugging that dam of indignation was difficult once it burst open. Years' worth of pent-up emotion wanted out.

Mad as she was...she knew what witches could do. She didn't doubt he'd seen what he described. And anyone kidnapped as a teen and told who to be would have trouble letting go of it. Especially if those prejudices were fed for a decade after.

Could he let it go? Let *her* go? He hadn't turned her in yet. In fact, it seemed like he was going out of his way to keep her alive.

Something soft brushed Cora's ear, chasing her from that haze of thought. She recoiled at first, then her chest flooded with warmth as a tiny ball of light and color bounced around the Theo's living room. It knocked into a standing lamp, which wobbled, but didn't fully tip over.

"Pip?"

Pip ricocheted off the couch and darted across the polished concrete floor to sit at her feet. He was almost vibrating with worry, and she had to fight to keep the imprint of his emotions from sending her own into overdrive.

Suddenly, an idea struck her. Might be a long shot, but... "Hey, do you think you could turn into a key for this thing?" Cora rattled the handcuff against the pipe.

Pip sat up taller in a kind of salute, then leapt down to her lap, leaning forward to inspect the handcuffs. His little eyes narrowed, but with a soft *pop* he became an exact copy of her car keys, then Mindy's, then the tiny key to the backyard shed.

She shook her head. "No, but it's okay. Thanks for trying." She'd suspected he could only mimic things it had taken the time to study, and Ryland kept this key close at hand. But maybe once he was asleep...

The scrape of the deadbolt on the front door startled Pip so badly, he transformed into one of Mindy's gaudiest cocktail rings and clattered to the floor, rolling just out of reach. Shit.

Cora stretched out a leg, trying to nudge it closer with her shoe, kicking it under the credenza in panic when the door swung open.

Sorry, Pip.

Ryland shouldered through and piled takeout boxes on the kitchen table. "Mao's," he offered, tossing a large manila envelope on the counter, almost angrily.

She raised an eyebrow. "This your way of apologizing?" She'd meant for it to sound sharper, but she was starving. And she did have a weakness for Mao's, damn him.

"I didn't know what you liked, so I got a bit of everything." Ryland approached her and reached into his pocket. She shrank away from him, but he sighed and held up a small key instead. "Are you hungry or what?"

Well, when he put it that way.

He crouched next to her, and she was unsettled by his nearness all over again. She caught a hint of his aftershave as he unlocked the cuffs and let them fall away.

"Aren't you nervous I'll try something?" She rubbed her sore wrist and pointedly ignored his extended hand, getting to her feet. It was nice to finally regain some of the feeling in her fingers.

He led her to the table and patted the gun in his waistband. "I'm armed. You're not. I'm twice your size. And your magic's gone. The Crash we use in the field—that's part sedative, part Recantanyl, which keeps your magic locked down long after the sedative's worn off."

He must have decided to turn her in, then. There's no chance he'd be revealing that otherwise. It explained the tension in his shoulders, the set of his jaw.

Adrenaline kicked, but she pushed back. She couldn't let him see it yet and fought to keep her voice casual. "I've always wondered what Crash really was." She grabbed the nearest container and looked inside. Orange chicken. "We have lots of wild theories."

The adrenaline kept coming. *Oh, fuck. Not here.* Her chest kept tightening, her breath uneven. She couldn't have a panic attack right here. She focused intensely on the chicken, trying to ground herself in the moment, counting the pieces. *One. Two. Three.*

"The blood of captured witches," Cora said, trying to sound nonchalant, walking herself back from that precipice, "or reptile venom, or just straight-up heroin are a few I've heard."

"You make Recantanyl sound disappointingly clinical." He frowned. "Where did *you* go? Were you in LA all this time?"

Why? Had he looked for her? *Four. Five. Six.*

And did she wish he had?

"What does it matter?" she asked.

"I don't know. Hard to imagine we could avoid running into each other."

"It's a big city." *Seven. Eight. Nine.* She sipped her water. "But no. I got a job in San Diego." She didn't offer up any details, nor did she think he expected her to. *Ten. One. Two.*

"What brought you back?" She pushed a piece of broccoli around her plate with a chopstick while she decided how honest to be. He knew Mindy, had cared about her once. But she sure as hell didn't owe him any explanations now. "That's none of your concern."

He raised an eyebrow but said nothing. They continued eating in silence.

When she couldn't bear the quiet anymore—maybe five, ten minutes later—she asked, "What would you have done if they hadn't taken you?"

He stopped mid-chew. She'd hit a nerve. Then he fired back so quickly it gave her whiplash. "How'd you end up working in Ezra Foster's surf shop?"

Something twisted in her stomach. That was not the face of someone purely indulging curiosity. She started counting broccoli florets. *One. Two. Three.* "How do *you* know Ezra?"

Taking a long swig of Sapporo, he let that question hang between them. Cora kept a wary eye on him as he slid his chair out and stood, wandered over to the counter, and picked up the envelope. *Four. Five. Six.* His fingers slipped along the opening. He paused. Considered.

"What's in there?"

Ryland pulled out a few photographs, shuffling them, deciding whether to show her. Her heart stuttered. A reel of the last few weeks flipped through her mind—what had he seen? What did he know?

He turned, his eyes steely as he approached her again, and slapped the stack down on the table. She looked.

And then she thought her dinner might come back up.

56

The first security photo was a bit grainy, but it was her—at least, to her own eyes. Anyone else looking at it might just see a woman in a flannel shirt with a baseball cap over long, dark hair. She was carrying a duffel bag into the lobby of an apartment complex. A teenage girl wearing a backpack trailed behind her, rubbing the sleep from her eyes.

Nell.

It took every ounce of self-control to keep the horror from playing openly across her face. If they had these photos, they had Poppy. They had Nell. And if they had Nell, and they'd made the connection to Ezra, the Runners were compromised. If the Runners were compromised...

"What is this?" Cora asked, feigning ignorance even as sweat collected on her palms. "What am I supposed to be looking at?"

Ryland's heavy brows knit together. "Quit playing games, Cora."

"No games," she said, swallowing back the bile in her throat and lifting her hands as if surrendering. "You asked about Ezra. I don't see how—"

"This isn't you, then?" Thoroughly unconvinced, Ryland sat again, leaning forward on his elbows. His stare was a visceral thing, and she wanted to pry it off of her. "Escorting Nell Tesauro, Ezra Foster's cousin, into a condo he used to own?"

Fuck. Fuck fuck fuck fuckity fucking fuck.

"I don't know Ezra's family," she shrugged, not directly answering him.

"How long have you worked for him?"

"Not long."

"Why there?"

She didn't have to fake the incredulous laugh. "I burned out. Hard. I needed everything to just be...not life-or-death for a little while." She sucked in a breath, trying to find the calm, praying he didn't hear the catch in her voice. Aiming for deadpan, she said, "I'm sure you can understand that, of all people."

Ryland's scarred eyebrow twitched. He tapped the photo. "You must really think I'm stupid."

Cora plastered a casual smile across her face. "The truth doesn't care what you think. You say that's me, fine. Doesn't change where I'm going to wind up."

It did change, though, whether they decided to torture her for information. And the less worried she seemed about it, the less certain he might be. She didn't need to win him over completely—she just needed him to doubt.

To overthink it. To maybe buy her a little bit of time.

Because she had to find a way out of here, and she had to warn the Runners. She had to warn Ezra.

A crash, and she jumped. Ryland had swept an arm across the table, knocking his glass to the floor and shattering it. He scrubbed a hand over his face, down his beard, suddenly looking lost. "Goddamn it, Cor. God fucking *damn it*. It changes everything."

She felt Pip edging his way closer, mustering up some courage. He was much more afraid of Ryland than he'd been of the drunk. She prayed he'd stay hidden. "I...don't understand."

He fisted a hand and relaxed it. Then he pointed at the photo. "This is logged evidence. My partner got this from the security cameras the night after..."

His nostrils flared. Oh. *Oh.*

He *hadn't* been about to turn her in.

He was mad because now, he wasn't the only one who knew about her. Who might be looking for her. "Your partner," she repeated. "Does he know I'm here?"

"No."

She was right. Cora swallowed hard as she processed it all. She'd been so ready to put up a fight that her adrenaline had nowhere to go. Her next words shook with it. "Why not?"

Ryland leaned back in his chair, folding his arms, assessing. A long silence. Then: "I've been asking myself the same thing all day."

The look on his face dragged her back to the alley behind Ezra's shop, where she lay crumpled on the asphalt. The realization of *who* she was— the split-second decision he'd made to remove the needle—almost a reflex, overriding the logic of *what* she was. She could see it in him now, again. The war being waged there. The vein bulging in his temple.

The doubt. *Feed the doubt. Make him face it.*

The wall clock was ticking loudly, so loudly. She'd only just noticed. She finally said, "Do remember my mother's secret garden?"

Confusion darted through his eyes. He inclined his head slightly. "I remember it."

Her mother's garden lived in another realm of possibility entirely. That had been Cora's only explanation for how incredible it was. So much love and care poured into it, day after day, all for nobody but herself, and her kids. Flowers too fickle to grow anywhere, trees that always bore fruit, vines interlocking with intricate patterns and forming benches to sit and read upon. Hidden away in a pocket of magic along the side of the backyard, where none of the neighbors could see.

Cora had shown Ryland, once. Just once.

He saw her expression and said, "You got in a lot of trouble for that, didn't you?"

A small grin ghosted across her lips. "Sure did."

"Do you think you'll go back?"

She hadn't been prepared for the question. It settled in her chest like a lead weight. "I...I don't know. The new owners..." And then she realized what he'd said, what it implied. Her eyes widened. "You mean...?"

Ryland's face might as well been carved from granite, for all she was able to read him. He got up again, walking to the pantry and pausing in front of it, hand on the door. She waited.

Finally, he opened it and grabbed a broom. "You should go." Still facing away from her, he said, "But I can't promise others won't come after you."

She rose slowly, unsure of what else to say. "I..."

You should go. That's what he'd said, right? She'd heard him correctly? She could leave. He was releasing her.

Her legs, suddenly free to walk her right on out of there, felt leaden. Something kept her there for just a second longer, waiting for him to turn around, so she could look him in the eyes again. And when he did turn, there was nothing warm in them, nothing but steely resolve, a decision with consequences that neither could reach forward in time to see.

"*Get out*," he barked again, and she stepped back this time. "Before I change my mind."

Cora swallowed and knocked the chair over as she scrambled backwards, riding a fresh kick of adrenaline. As she fumbled at the front door, Pip darted between her feet, and she scooped up the little ball of light between her hands more roughly than she'd meant to.

Theo's eyes widened when he noticed the sprite, but she was through the door before he could say anything else.

Go. *Go!*

A cool rush of night air, and then she was in the hallway, down the staircase, down the block, feet pounding the pavement, breath rattling inside her chest. There were people out and about, music pumping from bars and restaurants, sirens, crickets, car horns.

Faster!

Color and sound swirled together and receded as she flew past, until all she heard was the blood rushing in her ears, the gasps for breath that came shallower and harder.

She didn't know how far she'd run—blocks, miles—when the panic attack finally bowled her over. She was on an arcing bridge somewhere over the concrete basin that held the trickle of LA river, skyscrapers looming at her back, train tracks dipping under the road in front. Few cars were crossing at this time of night, as if allowing her the space she needed to unravel.

Her footfalls slowed and then stopped as she doubled over on the sidewalk, one hand gripping the cold steel railing, the other on her knee. Her chest heaved. Tears came, sharp pinpricks at first, then all at once. There was nobody else around to see them.

The train tracks were quiet. A line of empty cars sat on one of them, rust-darkened and still, sleeping off the day's work. She focused on them as she righted herself, following the arrow they made toward the next bridge to leap over the concrete channel.

Pip slid out of her pocket and crept up her arm to rest on her shoulder. The tiny, soft, warm-cool weight steadied her breathing, then her heartbeat. The sprite's glow was dimmer than she'd seen it before, but she chalked it up to stress. "It's okay. I'm okay," she said, not fully believing it herself.

He'd let her walk out of there. She repeated it a few times, waiting for it to sink in.

She wasn't going to be taken away. Not like Sebastian had been. Not like Nell had been.

Nell. Cora's chest caved in as the girl's face filled her mind. That safe house was new. That they'd discovered it so quickly...had Cora been sloppy, been followed? Had she led the hunters straight to Poppy's doorstep? What had she missed?

She was there, again, in her backyard, in the hammock, her mother's voice pressing into her mind and begging her to run. The grief, the darkness, the loneliness in those days first days without them...it swelled up within her again, filling her lungs and throat, sapping the strength from her knees. She leaned into the steel ledge for support and gazed down into the anemic rivulet below.

No matter how many people she was able to help the Runners save, no matter how many times she got the message that someone else had crossed successfully into Whitefall, it would never mean her family was safe. It would never mean they were free. It just meant someone else would have what they didn't.

Maybe it was selfish of her to let that steal her happiness, but she couldn't help it.

This was the devil she knew: this endless cycle of needing to be useful because anything less was a betrayal, while every victory felt hollower than the last. That's why she had to keep moving, keep busy, deflecting the lows with the promise of something feeling different next time she tried. And the *guilt* of it—that she couldn't find fulfillment in helping, only a short reprieve—ate at her, too.

Why wasn't it enough? Why couldn't she *make it* be enough?

Relying on that to numb the pain was almost worse than drugs and booze because there was supposed to be forward momentum in sobriety. The feeling of building something: a life, a way of coping, a way of healing.

Not...whatever this was. Stumbling forward in the dark. Hating the world, hating yourself more.

She wiped her face on her sleeve and shivered, only now noticing how chilly it had become. She needed to find a corner store, or someone who'd let her borrow a phone. Hers had been left back at Boardroom, along with her purse. As she pushed off from the ledge and straightened, continuing across the bridge, Pip sought the warmth beneath her hair and settled across the nape of her neck.

Theo was right—he didn't know her. She didn't know him. Not anymore. But he'd still done it, let her go.

And gone so far as to warn her what the hunters already knew. Why? Why risk it at all?

It didn't matter, she supposed, since she'd probably never see him again. She shoved all thoughts of him down, down to a dark corner in the back of her mind. She couldn't afford to let any of it derail her. There was too much at stake.

What mattered now was getting word to Mindy...and navigating the inevitable chaos her news would bring, after.

CHAPTER SIX

That night, Cora drifted in and out of...something. She couldn't really call it sleep. Every creak of the house settling, every flash of headlights across the ceiling jolted her back out of that twilit limbo.

She must have dozed off at some point, though, because she awoke to voices drifting in from the kitchen—Quinn's and Ezra's. At Cora's insistence last night, Mindy had called them as early as she dared. The sun was barely up.

Wrestling her hair into a long braid and shrugging on a sweatshirt, Cora weighed her approach. She didn't have it in her to stifle the rising fury. Not on four hours of shuteye, anyway.

As she burst from the den, heads swiveled toward her.

Mindy hadn't slept either. That much was obvious in her unkempt gray curls and colorless cheeks. Quinn and Ezra sat beside her at the kitchen table, exchanging a look that evidently spoke volumes in whatever silent language they'd developed. And in the fourth chair sat the owner of the unfamiliar lilt she'd overheard.

To call the woman petite was an understatement—she couldn't have been over ninety pounds soaking wet, feet barely brushing the floor, though she held herself with the dignity of someone six feet tall. Silver darted through her short black hair, and large, round glasses magnified her green eyes to comical proportions. Costume jewelry dripped off her wrists, clinking softly against the table as she set down her mug of tea.

Alta Ghislaine, one of the three LA coven elders.

Returning to LA meant Cora had become Ghislaine's responsibility. It also meant she had to make a show of kissing the ring, no matter what kind of mood she was in. She cleared her throat, awkwardly halting mid-rampage in the kitchen doorway. "Um. Hi. Good to see you again."

Ghislaine's brows nudged ever higher, into her blunt-cut bangs. "Likewise." It was nearly a question.

Casting around for some way to parry that dubious stare, Cora added, "Look, I'm sorry to catch you in the crossfire, but I have a bone to pick with these three."

Finishing a sip of tea, Ghislaine made a noise of affirmation and waved her jeweled fingers in a 'carry on' gesture. "By all means."

Which Cora did, icily. "Who," she said, locking eyes with each of the remaining three at the table, "was planning on telling me Nell had been taken?"

Quinn opened her mouth, but Mindy got herself together first. "How do you know about that?

"That isn't an answer." Cora moved on to Ezra, but he shook his head. "Hell no. Not my circus."

Quinn was next, and Cora knew she'd cave. With pleading eyes, she said, "Mindy didn't want to worry you—"

"Worry me?" Cora might have laughed if she hadn't been so angry. "I could have been out there helping you look; I could have *done* something!"

"It wouldn't have mattered," Ezra said, the brokenness and smallness of those words deflating her, just a little. His stubble-sprinkled face was haggard, clothes wrinkled as if they'd been slept in.

"Well, I know that *now*." Cora threw up her hands. "But before I saw the photos, before Ryland told me—"

"Ryland?" Quinn looked blankly at Mindy, who gestured back at Cora with her mug.

"The hunter," Mindy clarified. "Who, as it turns out," she added dryly, turning to Ghislaine, "is actually an old friend of the family." She took a bite of toast from the plate in front of her. "Teddy, I used to call him."

"Imagine that," Ghislaine said slowly, quirking a brow. She had the faint whisper of a French accent. It was unnerving how someone her size could still make Cora feel an inch tall.

"Darling," Mindy said to Cora, "We knew Poppy and Nell hadn't gone to ground, otherwise they'd have sent word. And we couldn't locate Nell through scrying, so Crash seemed the likely culprit. Now the safe house is being watched. We've got eyes on their people. They wouldn't sit on that place unless they'd found something they thought we'd come back for."

"We had two witches on scrying shifts," Quinn cut in, "and two more on the ground with us, people who knew the area, the hunter haunts. We figured it'd be better to let you—"

"Sit around on my ass while you guys ran all over town?" Cora finished for her. "Who's 'we' here?"

"It was my call," Mindy said, her mouth set in a stubborn line. "If you're gonna be angry at anyone, let it be me. You were finally starting to settle in...I wanted to give you some time, that's all." *And I was afraid of what it would do to you,* she didn't say. "It was handled, and I wanted to give you a few good days in this house before it all went to shit. So sue me!"

Cora silently begged for patience. Her breath might as well have been visible, for all the ice in her words. "Don't. Sideline me. Again."

Because I can't stand your pity. Because the only way I'm going to be able to live with myself is if I fix this.

She knew she wasn't being fair to Mindy, who was remarkably calm for everything she'd been through in past twenty-four hours. Especially so soon after Oscar. But Cora couldn't dig herself out from under the bitterness long enough to care.

After a tense moment, Ghislaine folded her hands in front of her and gave the table a saccharine smile. "Lovely. Now that that's settled, shall we discuss what Cora's learned from her little...detour?"

A mug of coffee lay untouched before the empty seat, and Cora eyed it. It was almost certainly a bribe. An effective one. She sat.

They waited for her to take a sip. She immediately felt a little more human and finally spoke. "Ryland kept me in his apartment. Somewhere downtown, in the Arts District."

"And who was this 'Ryland' to your family?" asked Ghislaine.

A loaded question, and the alta knew it. It took Cora a second to dredge up the words for an answer. "A neighbor. Or, he was. Sebastian and I used to surf with him, and our moms were college friends. He disappeared one day, and I hadn't heard from him until the day he came by the shop."

Quinn stiffened, and the hurt on her face was plain. "You didn't say anything."

"I didn't have much time to." Cora felt the caffeine beginning to work its magic. "What happened after I...left?"

Ezra sat back in his chair; eyes cast toward his plate. "Marlo called me up. She'd forgotten something at the shop, and when she went back to get it the back door was unlocked, the lights were still on, and you were nowhere to be found. But your bag was still there, so we figured out pretty quick that something was wrong. And when scrying for your location didn't work, well..."

Ghislaine reached for the sugar spoon with knobby, ringed fingers. "Why did he take you now, but not when he first saw you?"

The spoon suddenly burst into a ball of light and color. Mindy and Cora had gotten used to Pip's abruptness, but Ezra jerked backwards with a yelp. Ghislaine didn't so much as flinch. "Oh, you're a sneaky little thing, aren't you?"

Pip stood a little taller as Cora explained how he'd saved her from the man in the alley, and then puddled when she got to the part about drawing Ryland to them. "He didn't know it was me there, not at first," she said, scooping Pip into her palm and making sure he knew he was forgiven. "But he'd already given me the Crash, so he brought me back with him."

"And then let you go?" Ghislaine asked.

"Not only that," Cora said, suddenly finding her coffee cup very interesting, "he left to get those security photos. He didn't just have them on hand—he came back with them."

Everyone let that sink in.

"And these photos," Ghislaine prodded, "they did not show your face?"

Cora shook her head. "Just Nell's. I had a Dodgers cap on."

"But he knew it was you."

"I'm not sure he would have. Not without seeing me in the shop and connecting me to Ezra." Cora jerked her chin at the man in question. "What happened, exactly? Did they get ahold of Poppy, too? What the hell was she even doing?"

"It was not her fault." Ghislaine's voice bore an edge, a warning to rein in the attitude, which Cora obliged. Here was a woman who put up with very little. Who had clawed her way into the role of coven alta, not charmed her way there. "And no, they did not catch her. She is shaken, but...fine, considering."

Ezra glanced warily at Ghislaine, who dipped her chin, as if granting him permission to speak. "She was gone maybe two hours, tops, running errands. By the time she got back, the rioters made it impossible to get through. She was arrested in the sweep. The cops released most of them by morning, but Nell was long gone by then." He swallowed. "Poppy recognized one of the hunters watching the building and didn't go back."

"They're still sitting on it?" Cora asked.

He nodded. "Far as we know."

"And Bungalow? Any sign there?"

"Hard to say, right on the boardwalk." A shrug. "It's way too busy to get a read. But safer to assume any place of mine has eyes on it now. Especially the hotels."

Cora's stomach knotted. They had to move the witches in them—all of them. Anything associated with Ezra was compromised. No telling how much time they had. And the look on Ghislaine's face, on Ezra's face, said they were thinking the same. "How many people?"

"Two at Bungalow, a pregnant couple. Three more at INN|LA, all adults, and a family of four at a duplex in WeHo." Ezra scratched his chin, thoughtful. "I should take the duplex, but I'll need my other car. The Mustang's not big enough."

Cora stood, sliding her chair back. Quinn nodded at Ghislaine, standing too. "If we take Bungalow, you guys can manage the others?"

"I will make a few calls," Ghislaine was already scrolling through her phone. "Your home is not far from here, yes?" she asked Ezra. "We will stop there on our way."

"Not you." Mindy jabbed a finger at Cora. "You still need rest. And you don't have your magic back yet."

Mindy had healed the sharp pain in Cora's ribs from her fall, but this morning her quads screamed from her mad sprint across Downtown, and her system was still coming down from the Crash—not to mention the lack of sleep weighing heavy on her eyelids. Adrenaline could keep her going, though. Adrenaline and...something stronger than the coffee in front of her.

"So? Not like any of us can risk using it." Cora blew past her aunt, crossing the kitchen to rummage through the pantry for the potion she knew Mindy used on the night shift.

"Cora. Be reasonable." Mindy glared at her, then Ghislaine, silently demanding the Alta say something.

Annoyance simmered hot, then hotter as Cora found what she was looking for and poured a shot. "I think it's reasonable to agree to disagree and get on with it." She gulped it down and made a face as it singed her throat and nostrils. Her fingers and toes tingled with warmth, and the weight on her eyelids eased.

Mindy's chair scraped the floor and she moved to follow Cora, who had already left the kitchen to shove her feet into sneakers. "That won't last you long, I ran out of arrowroot—"

"Then we'd better be fast," Cora snapped over her shoulder, not bothering to look back at Mindy as she breezed through the front door with Quinn, desperately fighting the urge to say something she'd regret.

Ezra matched their stride as they crossed the driveway, handing Quinn a room key. "Take the Master. They're in 607. And..." He slowed, sucking in a breath as he pulled out the car keys. "Be nice to the Mustang, okay?"

Quinn's eyes sparkled as she took the keys from him, a thing which appeared to cause Ezra physical pain. "No insulting the Mustang. Got it."

"I mean it!" he said, turning toward where Ghislaine had parked, a few houses down. "If I see just one scratch—"

"Priorities, Ez!" Quinn called back and unlocked the car. Her grin faltered, though, when she looked at Cora and slid inside. "Come on. Let's see how fast this thing can go."

Not very fast, as it turned out, because the 405 South was doing its twice daily transformation from highway to parking lot. It left them both thrumming with anxiety, which Quinn poured entirely into giving Cora the fourth degree.

They stared down the row of taillights. "So, Ryland, Teddy, whatever," Quinn said far too casually. "A hunter—one you *know*—"

"Knew," Cora corrected, "before I met you—"

"—just shows up at Boardroom one day, why? To see you? Or was he, what, shopping?"

A pause. "He followed me, actually—"

Wrong thing to say. The chill in Quinn's voice melted into outrage. "Followed—? Okay, and you didn't even mention—Fuck!" Slamming on the brakes, Quinn flipped the bird at the sedan that had just cut her off and stuck her head out the window. "Welcome to my lane, lady!"

Cora swallowed back her nausea, gripping the handle above the passenger's side door. "I was going to, but he took me that same night, and we didn't have a chance to talk before..."

"And then he kidnaps you," Quinn continued, as if not hearing her, "and lets you go." She gestured with an impatient open palm, waiting for an answer to fall into it.

The car lurched again. Cora closed her eyes as Quinn pulled angrily into the next lane, which was moving a bit faster. Behind them, someone leaned on their horn.

Cora felt a pang of sympathy for Ezra, remembering the look on his face as he'd handed over the keys.

"He was as good as family," Cora finally said. "And we were young, but...I *never* felt like I had to hide who I was around him. I never saw any of what I saw in him last night. I never imagined..."

Something like humiliation clutched in her chest, a bitter kind of vulnerability. She plowed through it, explaining how he'd just disappeared—drafted, unbeknownst to her—and the argument they'd had in Boardroom, the look on his face when he'd realized she was the one he'd tackled in the alleyway.

Her feelings congealed with that memory. He'd have been fine if she was just another witch. He'd have carried on with his night. And she'd have been gone.

She hadn't deserved that mercy any more than Nell had, and yet, here she was.

Quinn's fury made sense all at once, that Cora had been spared and Nell hadn't, that some cosmic stroke of luck found her a way back from somewhere witches never came back from. And that in the space of just a few days, Quinn had watched Ezra go through the cycle of panic and helpless frustration, only to be dragged through it herself.

"I...Goddess, I hate him." Cora fisted her hands in front of her, released them. "I hate him," she said again, tears welling but refusing to fall. It was cathartic to say aloud, to finally put her finger on what it was. "*I hate him.* That he could just...stand there, in all of his stupid self-righteousness, and make me feel so damn small. That any of them could, but especially him."

Because she had trusted him with so much of herself, the way kids do, before they're old enough to know better. She wanted to take it back.

Quinn's brows knit together, but her gaze didn't stray from the road. "You don't know who he is. You know who he *was*. And guess what? You don't owe him any understanding, either, of how he went from shitty to shittier."

Cora knuckled an angry tear away. "I can't help but want to believe the person I knew is still in there. I have to believe it."

"You don't owe him that," Quinn repeated, a little louder.

"I owe *me* that," Cora snapped, her composure slipping. "He's..." Her throat constricted. "He's all that's left, from..." She couldn't finish.

He's all that's left from before.

Quinn fell silent, glaring at the stupid stick-family window decal on the van in front of them. Her jaw worked like she wanted to respond but thought better of it.

Cora's next words were bargaining, as much with herself as with Quinn. "Why else wouldn't he just turn me in? Why else would he have shown me the photos, unless he still...cared, even just a little?" She sank lower in her seat. He could have just let her escape. But he let her escape with information. He let her escape with hope.

Quinn's sigh suggested she didn't know whether to comfort Cora or wring her neck. "Maybe he's a fucking idiot. Or maybe he's laying a false trail. Maybe he sent us scattering, right now, to lead him straight to Ezra's safe houses, and we're walking into a trap. How the hell should we know?"

That hadn't occurred to her. "You don't think—?"

"Doesn't matter what I think," Quinn said with resignation, "because we're five minutes out, and we can't just *not* move these people, knowing what we know."

She was right. Cora's heart sank into her feet, and her stomach leapt into her throat.

None of it was due to Quinn's driving.

Cora flattened the skirt of her borrowed maid's uniform. The fit was off— whoever wore this before her wasn't as bottom-heavy—but it would have to do. She and Quinn nudged open the door of room 607 and wheeled the laundry cart inside.

The decor was all clean lines and smooth, light wood, with large potted plants and deliberate bursts of sage green from the odd wall accent or vase. Only a small kitchenette and single king bed, but Cora had looked at Bungalow's prices. Ezra was still losing a lot of money on this room.

Not that it was why he'd put the McDaniels here, instead of someplace bigger. Because the apartment she'd brought Nell to was guarded by that same air of unassuming restraint—*nothing to see here, carry on.* Comping a friend's room for a while wouldn't raise eyebrows, but comping an ocean-view suite might get the staff talking amongst themselves, wondering who was so important.

John and Fatima McDaniel sat in the breakfast nook by the kitchenette, and Cora was struck by how young they were. Neither could have been over twenty-five. The man's heavy, strawberry-blonde eyebrows and angular cheekbones offset the woman's soft, dark features and delicate chin. Silky black hair spilled down her shoulders to brush a very pregnant belly. The hand not draped over it instead wound through her husband's fingers.

John stood, a question in his eyes, and didn't let go.

"John, Fatima." Quinn nodded at them both. "This is Cora."

Cora edged around the laundry cart and shook hands with them both, noting the clamminess of John's palms.

"Ezra called," he said, buzzing with tension. "We're all packed, but...he didn't say where we're headed."

"We can't tell you yet," Cora apologized. It was the Runners' policy, just in case something happened, which she'd never admit to their faces. "We're not going far, though. About forty minutes."

With some effort, Fatima got to her feet, waving John's offered hand away. "I'm pregnant, you know, not bloody crippled." Her accent was English, and her deep brown eyes lasered on Cora. "What's so urgent? How worried should we be?"

"Everything's fine," Quinn reassured them, sitting on the edge of the desk. "We're shuffling a few folks out of an abundance of caution, but it's probably nothing."

"An abundance of caution," Fatima repeated, deadpan. "Well, that's me convinced, then." She looked pointedly at the laundry cart, then at Cora's outfit. "What happened to the illusionist who brought us in?"

"We...can't wait for him, unfortunately," Cora said, "So we'll have to work with what we've got."

Sensing John's mounting anxiety, Quinn offered what little information she could. "The car's waiting in the loading bay." She jerked her chin toward to the pair of suitcases by the dresser. "I'll grab those and meet you downstairs. We outsource laundry to a contractor, but today's not a pickup day, so nobody will be down there but us."

"Should we...check out?" It was a helpless question, from a man at a loss for how to be useful. Fatima looked like she was swallowing a laugh for the sake of his ego.

Ah, love.

"Don't worry about that, I'll take care of it." Quinn got up and began stripping the bed linens.

Cora gestured to Fatima. "Come on, let's get you in first. John, can you help hold this steady—thanks, and—there we go."

Fatima lowered herself in, tucking her legs beneath her, and John followed. She shifted her weight to make room for him, wincing, but didn't complain.

Cora grabbed the duvet Quinn handed over, draping it over the couple.

"Alright." Cora exchanged a look with Quinn. "Here goes."

Cora had to dig her heels into the carpet to force the cart forward now that it carried multiple times its intended weight. Quinn followed them out with the bags, banking a right down the hall as the cart went left, and then they were alone.

The hallway seemed to lengthen as they rolled towards the maintenance elevator, and every muffled voice, every door shutting urged Cora's heart to beat faster. Up ahead, a bellhop walked purposefully in their direction, and she held her breath.

As he approached, he noted her struggle with a raised eyebrow. Closer...closer...and then he was past them, continuing on.

The elevator meandered up to them, doors whispering open at a snail's pace. Everything was taking too long, everything. Precious seconds dragged as they descended, the display blinking at each floor.

5...4...3...2...1...L...P1...

They lurched to a stop at P2. Cora exhaled and eased the cart down the ramp into the loading bay, gritting her teeth as she kept its weight from propelling them all downwards like a runaway train.

Quinn waited by the Mustang, having already stuffed the bags in the trunk. She helped John and Fatima into the back while Cora ditched the cart, then they both slipped into the front seats; Quinn pulled away from the curb before Cora could heave a sigh of relief.

For ten minutes, nobody spoke. Every red light made them sitting ducks. Every patch of congestion, every flower-seller and unhoused person pacing the medians kept them on edge.

And then, Cora noticed it. She twisted, squinting past the two cars at their backs. "Quinn."

"Yeah."

"White Camaro. Behind the Chevy. Do you see it?"

Quinn checked her mirror. "I see it."

"Take a left here and see what they do."

Nudging them into the next lane over, Quinn's hands tightened on the wheel. They inched forward, waiting for a break in traffic, and watched the Camaro shove its way into the turning lane behind them.

Cora's heart stuttered in her chest. They'd been made. She whipped out her phone to call Mindy, but Quinn had...other ideas.

"Oh, hell no. Fuck this," Quinn said, gripping the wheel harder. "*Fuck this*. You guys better hold on."

And then all hell broke loose.

Quinn slammed the gas and blew through the intersection as the light turned yellow. Engine roaring, the Camaro arced around the cars slowing down in front of it. Horns blared as it careened through the now-red light, swerving to kiss the side of a box truck before advancing in the rearview.

Fatima was repeating something under her breath—a prayer, maybe, as they all lurched back against the leather seats.

The Camaro gained as Quinn dodged a sedan trying to parallel park on the street. They blew through a stop sign, narrowly missed a crossing pedestrian, banked a hard left.

"Where did you learn to drive like this?" Cora was shrill, clinging to the handles above the passenger side window.

"Ez takes me to the Porsche track sometimes!" Quinn shouted over the scream of skidding tires.

Goddess, they were all going to die.

Sailing back onto a main artery, they wove in and out of slower traffic with hard jerks of the wheel. The Camaro dogged behind them, but the *woop woop* of a cop car brought their attention to the front.

The police cruiser passing them skidded to a halt, then made a one-eighty and dug into the asphalt to catch up with the Camaro. There'd be more before long. But the Camaro didn't seem at all worried about the black-and-white behind it, single-minded in its pursuit of their precious cargo.

"Hang on!" Quinn floored it through another stoplight and cars screeched to a halt around him, piling up and filling the air with the stink of scorched rubber. Banking again, she stole down a narrow alley while the Camaro swerved past, unable to make the turn in time. As they clipped a dumpster, Ezra's mirror snapped off and Quinn visibly cringed.

"I think I'm going to be sick," Fatima said as the car shuddered on the rough pavement. Cora, fighting nausea herself, didn't dare open her mouth to agree.

They broke out of the alleyway and watched the cruiser shoot down a parallel road after the Camaro. Quinn plowed through the next cross-street and the Camaro veered in their direction, sliding as it tried to find traction behind them. How much longer before more cops swarmed?

As if Quinn heard her, magic began to curl around them. Shit, shit, shit. What was she about to—?

The threads of magic rippled, contorted. "Quinn, don't!" Cora said in a panic, but it was too late. The magic snapped backward, a sharp lance of air spearing towards the Camaro. She felt Quinn lean on it, pressing harder and harder, her face flushing red with exertion.

The Camaro's front tire erupted with a pop like a gunshot.

The driver slammed their brakes, fishtailing from one side of the road to the other and catching the front of the police cruiser. Together both vehicles tumbled forward in a mess of twisted metal, coming to rest on a grassy median that retreated rapidly in Cora's mirror.

As Quinn folded into southbound highway traffic from the nearest 405 on-ramp, nobody breathed except Fatima, who made good on her earlier promise to vomit.

CHAPTER SEVEN

Lying face-up on the jujitsu mat, Theo blinked the sweat from his eyes. The world came into focus, slowly, then all at once.

Someone was talking to him. His legs were off the ground, elevated, and he realized Ricky was holding them. Shaking them, actually. "Rise and shine, fucker!"

Theo jolted upright and Ricky released his legs, laughing. Adrenaline surged through him, almost euphoric, as the blood rushed back to his head. He spat his mouth guard into his palm. "Fuck this. I'm done." Whenever Ricky choked him out, he never heard the end of it.

"My boy Icarus over here, too stubborn to tap!" Ricky held out a hand to help him off the mat. "What's got you so worked up?"

Theo ignored the question, wiping his forehead on the sleeve of his gi and getting to his feet.

He hadn't slept at all. Just kept replaying that moment he'd shown Cora those photos, her shock plain as day beneath the flimsy veil of nonchalance. All the confirmation he'd needed.

She was in over her head, and she had no idea how bad. If she did, she wouldn't have hesitated when he'd told her to leave, like she was waiting for something else—waiting for a real goodbye. One he couldn't bring himself to give her, even with a second chance to.

But it was better to forget. Because he'd set her free on his own conscience, and he wasn't ready to square with that yet.

So he'd gotten up early to roll with Ricky, who often spent mornings in the gym on base before their shift began. While Theo preferred evenings so he could sweat the day out of him, he'd needed to clear his head, and this was—usually—as good of a way as any.

They walked together towards the locker room, and Ricky opened the door with a flourish. "Step into my office. Take a load off. And don't bullshit a bullshitter."

A damn good nose for the truth, that one. He'd only poke around more if Theo shut him out, so he decided to give him a little, leave out the details. "Fine." Theo found his bag, unzipped it, and pulled out a towel. "There's this woman."

"Ah!" Ricky pounded a fist on the nearest locker and called over his shoulder. "Vega, you owe me twenty bucks."

Dorian Vega, a brown belt who had joined them, yelled a hearty "Fuck you!" from the other side of the locker room. Ricky winked and gestured at Theo to continue.

Sighing, Theo shrugged off his gi and folded it. "I knew her when we were kids. We were close. Our families, too." Just inviting the memory made him weary. He wandered over to an empty shower and ran the water, slumping beneath it, palms flat on the slick tile wall. Ricky shut the door of the stall next to him. "They took me for the Academy, and we lost touch."

Ricky's shower sputtered on. "And you ran into her again."

"I did."

"You sure it was her? Did you say anything?"

A pause. "I was sure, but no," Theo lied, closing his eyes as he scrubbed his face with soap. "She didn't recognize me, and I let it go."

"Ouch." Ricky let the shower fill the silence for a minute or two. Then: "You two hook up or something?"

Theo spat out the water he'd been collecting in his mouth. "What?"

"You heard me."

He abruptly shut the tap off. They hadn't, but whatever was between them didn't just boil down to that.

He hadn't been willing to ask himself how he felt all those years ago, and he sure wasn't ready to go there now. Cora had liked him—eventually he'd gotten his head far enough out of his ass to notice. Even when his friends were preoccupied with saving for cars, crushing on older girls, throwing parties, he'd been sneaking out to smoke weed on her roof.

No matter where her mother hid her stash, Cora always found it. He'd almost forgotten about the nights they'd spent together up there, trading stories about teachers they hated, revealing plans for the future, wondering what college might be like.

Sometimes Sebastian would join them. Sometimes a light would turn on in a window downstairs, and he'd panic and scramble down the trellis so quickly he'd misstep and fall, but she'd enchant the flowering vines to catch him and set him down gently.

He passed the towel roughly over his hair as if trying to scrub away the memory. "It wasn't like that." Not an answer to Ricky's question, or his own. Wrapping the towel around his hips, he headed back over to his bag to fish for his clothes.

"That's a shame. Shoulda met me sooner. I'd have helped you work up the nerve. Vega's sister can vouch for me."

Vega, parading around without a scrap of clothing, dumped the icy contents of his water bottle into Ricky's steaming shower stall. Ricky howled a string of curses.

"What did you bet on, earlier?" Theo asked, jerking his chin at Vega.

Vega sauntered away from the shower, still snickering. "Me? I bet him you were pissed 'cause your fancy espresso machine shit the bed."

Theo considered, then shrugged. "Solid guess, though."

———◦∞◦———

"Which CI is this again?" Theo asked.

Ricky was driving them past a sloping mosaic of densely packed houses on the East Side, heading further away from sleek wooden slat fencing and into corridors flanked by rusted chain-link. Florid sweeps of lawn withered to sparse patches of green and brown, while LED signs screamed about pink slip loans, bail bonds, and cash for gold.

"Nobody you've met," Ricky said. "I need you to promise you'll be cool, though."

Theo sat up a little straighter, interest piqued. "And by that, you mean?"

"It's not exactly...kosher, this place we're headed."

They pulled up to a crumbling stucco building sandwiched between a convenience store and a laundromat. Ricky parked, killed the engine, and turned to Theo. "To get in here, you gotta be escorted by someone who can vouch for you. I'm putting my ass on the line by bringing you, so if you screw this up, you're screwing us both."

Theo felt it, then. The hairs on his arms stood at attention. Faint traces of magic hovered around them, sharp pinpricks in his fingers and toes. Wards, he realized. The shape of dread, slithering across his skin, oily and dark. Deterrents to force second thoughts about approaching.

His hand instinctively found his .45.

Ricky jabbed a finger at him. "See, that's the kind of shit I mean. You can't do that. If you're gonna do that, you need to let me go in alone."

"Where the hell are we?" Theo kept his hand on the gun, not sure he wanted the answer.

"This here's a kind of...open secret, I guess, among some of the guys. But it's not *just* ours, so you can't waltz in there packing or with that cop look on your face, you know? It ruins the vibe."

"The vibe," Theo repeated dryly.

Ricky opened the door and stepped out, already shedding his Crash holster and his duty weapon. "You gotta trust me on this, or just stay here. I'm serious."

Theo released a controlled breath, doing his best to ignore the way his eye twitched, the way every muscle in his body screamed at him to *turn around, go, get out of here, just walk away.* He sure as hell wasn't about to let Ricky go in there without backup, guns or no. "Fine," he said through gritted teeth, and rounded the sedan to lock his gear in the trunk with Ricky's.

His fingers brushed the outline of the knife in his jacket, then dropped to his side—that was where he drew the line.

Theo let Ricky lead. They approached the metal grate covering the door and found it unlocked, and every step rang fresh alarm bells in his head, told him to GO, TURN BACK, WALK AWAY, louder and louder still. But as the entrance spat them into an empty, high-ceilinged photography studio, the ominous feeling dulled. He released another breath, flexing his fingers, the pins and needles easing.

Before them, a dirty white cyc covered one wall, and some peeling gaffer's tape followed long lines of old power cables that led nowhere. Beyond the archway of an empty truss, a dark, dingy corridor bent and narrowed. Their footsteps echoed on the concrete, and while most things in here bore a thick layer of dust, Theo noticed none had settled along the path they were walking.

This studio probably hadn't been used for years, and was picked clean of anything valuable, but shouted its message with gusto: *Nothing to see here, folks. Carry on.*

They followed the corridor to a stairwell and then down, where the faint pulse of music bled through the peeling paint on the walls, beckoning them toward a heavy steel door on their left.

Ricky paused at the handle. "Remember what I said," he murmured, then knocked twice, paused, three more times quickly, and two more about five seconds apart. Magic shifted around them, and he heaved the door open.

A tsunami of enchantments nearly knocked Theo off his feet.

From his vantage point, this place looked like the lovechild of a threesome between a speakeasy, a weed dispensary, and a strip club. Completely windowless, it was dark enough for the high warehouse ceiling to completely fade away behind thousands of tiny floating spheres of light, which winked above their heads like aimless fireflies. Velvet sofas divided the main room into lounge areas, one facing a crowded bar, the other angled toward the counter of what looked like an apothecary. Tendrils of cigarette smoke mingled with the miasma of incense, herbs, and liquor. It made the atmosphere a physical thing to maneuver through, to be choked by.

Music thrummed in his ears, his bones. He'd never felt anything like it and had to summon all of his TACS training to keep his poker face intact.

His eyes followed a skinny, beautiful man directing a glass of glowing amber liquid through the air and into the waiting hands of a sly older woman sitting next to him; another woman with full-body tattoos led her conquest through the crush of people toward a series of private rooms to the rear. A bodybuilder with a half-buttoned shirt pulled a cigar from his lips and blew smoke rings that curled into the shapes of dragons and flew away. One of them darted in front of Theo's face, and he swatted at it.

A dais rose in the center of it all, where a pale woman with ethereal white hair sang at an inhuman pitch. A chill raced down his spine as he realized she wasn't singing with just her voice but with several. An iridescent dress split over the sweep of her hip, more liquid than fabric, but for all its glittering translucence, she might as well have not been wearing anything at all.

He tore his eyes away, snapping out of it.

Most of this was a relatively tame display of magic, but it made sense as he observed the clientèle. There were definitely other TACS here, other government types in expensive suits (and various states of undress), but civilians, too. Just enough weirdness to engage their imaginations, but nothing dramatic enough to make them nervous. A playground for hypocrites.

Ricky led Theo toward the two male witches manning the apothecary counter. One bent over a mortar and pestle while the other used a razor to separate lines of a fine blue powder on a scale, then emptied the rest into a small velvet pouch.

Above the shelves of uplit booze bottles and unlabeled glass decanters hung a neon sign that read *Malleus Maleficarum*.

Theo would have laughed if he hadn't been so dumbstruck—it was Latin and translated to Hammer of the Witch. The theological text it was named for sustained witch hunts well into the eighteenth century. Somebody here certainly had a morbid sense of humor.

"You said you need a sponsor to come here," he remembered, trying to ignore the tingling all over his body. He glanced at Ricky, eyes narrowing. "Who vouched for you?"

Ricky coughed and looked away, chewing on whether or not to answer. "You have to promise you won't bring it up to him. Ever."

"Who?" Theo said through gritted teeth.

"Fletcher." He jerked a thumb at a platform where a green-painted woman danced in black leather. "Comes to see Elphaba over there."

Theo's lips pressed in a hard line. He'd suspected there were places like this, even TACS like these—greedy, or morally bankrupt, or just jaded enough by their jobs to justify the morale boost—but he hadn't imagined he'd learn their names. He hadn't imagined he'd be friends with one, let alone take orders from one.

Who had vouched for Fletcher, then? Someone higher up the chain of command? One of the brass?

"How long?" was all Theo asked, because it was all he could manage. How long had Ricky kept this from him? How long had Fletcher been coming here? How long before all of this backfired spectacularly, got them court-martialed, got them killed?

Ricky shook his head. "I'm gonna need you to hop off this fuckin' high horse you rode in on, okay?"

His initial shock, denial, was melting steadily into anger. "Of course. Why don't I just ask one of these ladies to take the stick out of my ass?"

Ricky rolled his eyes. "Dios mío. Maybe you should. Because I'll tell you what: each of these people was arrested for something and given a choice. *They* chose this for themselves. They get a safe place to go all hocus pocus, and we get a little...you know." He eyed a cocktail waitress walking past. "They like it—ask any of 'em. They get to sleep in their own beds, in their own houses. They can still see their families. We watch them, of course. But if they get tired of it? They can leave whenever they want."

"To go to the prisons, you mean." Theo looked around again, caught an undertone of desperation. He also noticed movement in the shadows that he'd been too dumbstruck to see before, dark silhouettes with steel glinting at their hips. More TACS.

This kind of exploitation...emotional blackmail...

Ricky followed Theo's line of sight. "We can't carry, so they do. It was one of the owner's rules."

The owner? Who the hell might own a place like this?

"Come on." Ricky jerked his head at the apothecary. "Let's go. That's our guy."

The thin, tanned man behind the counter winked at Ricky as they approached, eyes glowing golden. "What can I help you with, sugar?" A sculpted undercut of blonde hair was marbled with pale blue, and his skin shimmered like he'd rolled in fine glitter. "Name your poison. I'm feeling creative today." He spoke from the back of his throat, subtly cutting his w's into v's and his g's into k's.

"Actually," Ricky said, leaning an elbow on the bar and lowering his voice a tick, "we're looking for something else."

Harry's brow quirked. "Hate to disappoint, but I'm not on the menu."

"Is there a place we can talk?" Ricky's voice lowered even more. "Is *she* around today?"

Harry's gaze snapped back to Ricky. "I told you; I'm done with that."

"You really think you're in a position to make that call?"

From the corner of Theo's eye, he noticed the man behind the other end of the counter grow still, then disappear into the throng of guests.

Harry tapped his manicured fingernails on the sleek surface of the bar, making a show of thinking hard. "Yes, actually, I am. Swing that tiny dick around all you like, my friend. See where it gets you."

"Ezra Foster," Ricky said, not taking the bait. "What have you heard?"

Harry's reaction was almost imperceptible—he was *good*. Theo supposed he had to be, working in a place like this. Living this life. "That name supposed to mean something?"

80

"You tell me."

"Mr. Santana." A musical voice curled around them from behind, and Theo swiveled. "And you...you're new."

The black woman who'd spoken was mere inches from him, and he stepped back from her piercing brown eyes. A long, black tumble of tight curls was threaded sparsely with gray, and the shallow lines framing her full mouth suggested some of her youth was behind her. She radiated power and grace in a very expensive, ivory silk suit. There was something truly terrifying about her that he couldn't place.

Her handshake was firm and strong. "Helena. Pleasure." The moment their skin made contact, his mind became blissfully blank—he didn't doubt it was magic at work, but found himself unable to care.

She stared past Theo, not yet letting go of his hand, and cast Ricky a look of disapproval. "What did I tell you about interrogating my employees? Is that one *tiny* rule so hard for you to understand?"

Her hand slipped out of Theo's, and he had the distinct impression his brain had just been sifted through. Ricky flushed, a rare thing. "Theo," he said, doing his best to sound contrite. "Helena owns Malleus."

Theo knew that must be important, knew he should have questions, but his thoughts were murky, then gone—formless and irrelevant, whatever they'd been.

"Join me for a moment, won't you, darling?" She winked at Theo and turned, leading him to an empty booth in the corner of the room. He sat, wanting to address her somehow, but she saved him the trouble of remembering how his mouth worked.

"I've heard much about you already, Specialist Ryland." She drew out his title as if dismantling it in her mouth, syllable by syllable.

The fog lifted from his mind and words came again. "Don't do that," he warned her, suppressing a shiver. The only explanation for how she knew his name was neuromancy, but he couldn't separate those threads of magic from the others writhing in the air around him. It was such a chaos of enchantment that he was, essentially, blind to it.

Her laugh slid around his shoulders, a serpentine thing. "I find it helpful to begin a conversation without the preoccupations one tends to carry through the door with them."

"Whatever you're offering, I'm not interested." Maybe bluntness would end this before she tried anything else.

81

"Who said I was offering anything?" she said sharply, leaning back. "I only wished to talk, but I did not want your friend to see my curiosity ended there."

He was too grateful to take that for an insult. "Why?"

"Because if you think what he has shown you today would make him more receptive to learning what you did last night, you are mistaken. He already knows more than he should."

Theo kept his voice mild, his mind blank, despite the jolt of surprise that shot through him with her admission. If she was reading him with neuromancy, he'd at least make her work for it. "Does he, now?"

"I hear things, as I said. And what I've heard is something I cannot make sense of. Would you care to help me?"

"I'm not in the helping kind of mood."

Her eyebrow lifted. "Well, then. I will make a guess, and you will tell me how close I have come to the truth."

Moving closer to him, she traced slow circles on the back of his hand with her forefinger. For all it disturbed him, he couldn't pull away. She was toying with him, making sure he understood who held the power here. "You wonder why you feel guilt for showing mercy. And you wonder why good people like Cora must suffer while some of you allow yourselves to bend the rules when it suits. Because all around you, people you trusted to help banish corruption are instead reveling in it."

How had she known about Cora? Did they belong to the same coven? The questions swirling in his mind dissolved again, forgotten, though not because he'd made the effort to.

She continued, softer this time. He had to lean forward to hear her over the music. "If you are searching for clarity, only she can give it to you."

Helena released him from her thrall again and Theo quickly twisted his palm upward, clamping his fingers around her wrist. She inhaled sharply as he tightened his grip enough to bruise. His voice was measured, belying the fury building within him as he said, "This conversation is over."

His hold slackened and he stood to leave, but she laughed, rubbing her wrist absently. "It does not matter who you run from as long as your own mind holds you hostage."

The music roared back into to his ears, the cloud of smoke and incense invaded his nose and mouth, and with his mind now firmly his own, his goal was singular: *get out, get out, get out.*

He shoved past Ricky, whose voice followed him toward the door and sounded again, somewhere behind him, in the stairwell as he ascended. "Hey—hey! Wait a second—"

His shoes echoed over concrete again, then scraped across asphalt.

Perched on the sidewalk curb, sun beating down on his back, Theo found his bearings again. The only thing more disconcerting than having his brain picked over by a neuromancer was that she was right. He'd have to face Cora if he wanted clarity.

If.

"Theo. What the hell?" Ricky came up behind him, knelt beside him.

"You blindsided me in there." Theo stared at passing cars because Ricky's face was looking pretty punchable right about now. "On top of that, your CI is a real piece of work."

"Yeah, but he knows something," Ricky grumbled, taking a seat next to him. "You saw it."

Not only had Theo seen it, he'd been grateful for the dead end. He still wasn't sure how to move forward with the investigation, knowing it would lead them back to Cora, but was more than happy to punt that decision down the road. His magic sense had been so thoroughly overloaded, the deterrent wards felt like a pleasant tickle as he sat beside the car.

Ricky's phone signaled, and he pulled it, checking the screen. "It's Dispatch."

Theo scrubbed a hand over his beard. "Put them on speaker, I guess."

"Santana here," Ricky answered. "You got Ryland, too. What's up?"

"Report to UCLA Medical Center, Santa Monica Emergency Room," the dispatcher said. "Thompson, Terrell has been killed in action. Harris, Jamie is in the ICU. You've been cleared to see him once he's out of surgery. Sending over the address for next of kin."

Ricky went very still. Theo could've sworn he'd stopped breathing. "Sorry, what's that?"

"A vehicle collision with a beat cop near Mar Vista. They might have been tailing a suspect from Bungalow, but we'll know more when Harris wakes up."

Ricky had gone pale, so Theo spoke. "Might have been? They didn't check in when they began pursuit?"

"No." The dispatcher sounded annoyed. "Nobody had eyes on it until the cop radioed for backup. And even then, he only described the car *he* was tailing."

Harris and Thompson had made a rookie mistake. A bad one. Ricky's hands begin to shake. "We're on our way."

Ricky stuffed the phone in his jacket, walked over to the car, and yanked open the driver's door. "Get the fuck in. Holy shit, holy shit, holy shit." He fumbled the keys, dropped them once before jamming them into the ignition. "The kid is...he's dead. I can't believe the kid is dead."

"Let me drive, Ricky." Theo, though somewhat numb, would at least be able to get the car to the hospital in one piece. He hauled Ricky out from behind the wheel.

"I just had dinner at Thompson's on Sunday." Ricky's hands shook as he walked around the car and buckled into the passenger seat. "His wife made chimichurri. She's...god, she's three months pregnant."

Formless dread gathered in Theo's stomach as he slammed the gas.

"She's so young, man. They were high school sweethearts...How do I tell her?" Ricky's voice broke. He looked over at Theo, palms open on his lap like he was waiting for an answer to fall into them. "How the fuck do I tell her?"

CHAPTER EIGHT

Two weeks after the car crash, Cora still wasn't speaking to Quinn.

A dozen kinds of anger twisted inside her, but the brightest, hottest thread of it was how they'd had a thirty-six-weeks-pregnant woman in their care, and Quinn had decided to zip around LA playing *Fast and Furious*. She'd put all their lives at risk—and didn't even seem sorry for it.

In fact, she'd had the nerve to double down on those choices in front of Ghislaine and the other altas, who'd insisted she explain herself. Cora had heard about that dressing-down through Mindy's coven gossip grapevine.

After that, retaliation was a real fear. From the crash's brief mention on the local news, they knew about one casualty, another in critical condition, not counting the cop who'd survived with minor injuries.

That meant Quinn had killed a hunter. In broad daylight. Even if no one could prove it wasn't an accident.

And while Theo had promised he wouldn't come after her, she was anxious to know the dead hunter's name.

"I'd had Mindy's number half-dialed," Cora grumbled to Fatima one afternoon. She sat between the woman's open legs on the bed, hands pressing on her abdomen. "They might have been able to send—sorry, I'm almost done, just another second." Fatima winced as Cora felt around for the shape of the baby's head. "Yup, there he is. Ready to get out of there, I think."

"Don't beat yourself up, love. What mattered was making it here in one piece." Fatima's smile was tight, gaze locked on the ceiling.

"What *also* matters," Cora said, reaching between Fatima's legs to check her cervix, "is making sure a covert fucking hand-off doesn't end up on the evening news." Sighing, she gestured at Fatima to sit up. "I'm sorry. You have enough on your mind without having to listen to me rehash this."

Fatima's smile finally did reach her eyes as she pulled her skirt back down. "You're under a lot of pressure. I understand."

Cora found it in her to smile back. "The good news is everything looks fine. Baby's heartbeat is strong. You're about three centimeters dilated, and forty percent effaced, so we're moving along."

"Oh. I haven't felt anything." Fatima looked at her belly. "Not anything different, I mean. He's still a little night owl, and nowadays I mostly sleep sitting up." She kneaded a knot in her neck absently.

"Your body does a lot without you knowing." Cora stood up and peeled off her latex gloves. "Which is pretty awesome, considering the amount of work you have left to do. Here, let me take care of that."

She placed a hand on Fatima's shoulder and moved her curtain of hair out of the way. Then she narrowed her focus to the current of magic deep beneath the ground—the nearest branch of ley lines.

Through the earth below them, magical highways crisscrossed from one natural site of arcane energy to the next. Cora drew those threads of magic inward, tuning them as she went, imbuing them with the power to heal and then spooling them out again.

What civilians didn't know was that witches couldn't *create* magic—they only inherited the ability to draw it in and tell it what to be. Although some witches could only tune magic to the power of one parent; others could do both, and still other kinds of magic skipped generations altogether. Lots of money had been made over the years by diviners who calculated the chances of passing certain affinities along.

And while anyone could learn how to leyweave, it was incredibly difficult to do more than small cantrips. True Leyweavers were mostly coven altas.

Cora's golden threads of healing wove into Fatima's muscle fibers, releasing the knot. With something between a sigh and a gasp, she said, "Oh. Oh wow. The pain is..." She rolled her neck, then her shoulder. "You angel, you. John's been trying to get that out for days."

Such a simple thing, that relief, but Cora was thrilled she could give it to her. "How are your feet lately? Swelling much?"

"I can barely get shoes on these days," Fatima said, somewhat sheepishly. "And not just because I haven't seen my feet since the second trimester. You don't think you could...?"

Cora grinned. "Use me while you've got me." Kneeling, she took off Fatima's socks and prodded the puffy flesh at her ankles. "You know what my mom told me, once? She said the day after she gave birth to me and—" she paused, swallowing, "my brother, she got up in the middle of the night to use the bathroom, and peed longer than she'd ever peed in her life. Lost ten pounds that night, no joke."

"How is that possible?"

"Bodies are weird." Cora urged the pooling fluid to circulate again. "Luckily, this doesn't look like edema, but even still...keep your feet up as often as possible, and low sodium foods for now. The only permanent solution is to give birth, though."

"Great." Fatima's voice was edged with sarcasm. "How much longer do you think it'll be?"

Cora shrugged. "Hard to say, since he's your first. Usually that means they'll take their sweet time. But I'll be back in a couple of days and let you know how you're progressing."

She couldn't fault Fatima for wanting out of this place. As safe houses went, it was one of the nicer ones, with the original wood flooring and a charming garden that the runaways passing through enjoyed tending, but it wasn't home for her. It never would be.

And her son would have to start his life here, somewhere strange, with the threat of hunters bearing down.

"If you feel any contractions, time them out for me, okay?" Cora followed Fatima back out into the living room. The smell of onions and garlic filled the air, and John was bent over a sizzling pan. "Call me if they're intense and regular, anywhere from three to five minutes apart. And you—" Cora waved at John and smiled. "Your wife needs more foot rubs. Doc's orders."

"Thank you so much, for everything." Watching Cora descend the garden path, Fatima hesitated in the doorway. "And—sorry, I hate to give unsolicited advice," she said as Cora turned, "but it's a hard habit for a teacher to break."

"Don't listen to that nonsense. She loves it," John yelled from inside.

Cora raised a brow.

Fatima ignored him and gently said, "You might consider trying to mend things...you know, with Quinn. It seems like you could really use someone to talk to."

The heat of embarrassment crept up Cora's cheeks. She spun around so Fatima couldn't see it. Was she really so transparent?

"Thanks," Cora said over her shoulder, continuing towards her car and wishing the ground would swallow her. "I'll think about it."

———— ⌘ ————

It seems like you could really use someone to talk to.

As she drove back from Redondo, Pip nestled into her shoulder, sensing her unease. She stroked the little sprite absently. "Am I that pathetic? Do you think she's right?"

Pip, of course, couldn't answer, though she could feel him pressing into her mind, trying to ease the hollow ache it found there.

She was used to loneliness, and even enjoyed it sometimes, but lately it was bone-deep. The more time she spent with people, the further away from them she felt. And it wasn't about Quinn, not entirely.

It was this Sebastian-shaped phantom limb she dragged behind her everywhere, that constant reminder of a connection she'd never feel with anyone else.

She'd moved forward and created a life for herself sans Sebastian, sure—but those bricks had been laid without mortar, and she had no right to any of it. It could just as easily have been her, that day. Why hadn't it been?

When she missed him like this, there was still one place she could find him.

Veering off the highway a few exits early, she snagged a metered spot in the narrow lot by Manhattan Pier. Fall had begun to bite, so most of the daytime beachgoers had set off for the evening, but a handful of surfers remained. As she wriggled into her wetsuit, a solitary runner huffed past along the boardwalk.

She yanked her hair from its band and trudged across the still-warm sand, board in tow. The Pacific, in contrast, was numbingly cold, and would only get colder in the weeks following.

Low-hanging sunshine ignited the ocean—ripples of orange and pink caught the light and shimmered as the waves curled and crashed. The rhythm of it calmed her as the board lurched and dipped through the ocean. She ducked beneath an oncoming swell she was too far in to ride, gasping when she resurfaced, blinking the freezing water from her eyes.

Once clear of the next wave, she stopped paddling and sat back on the board, relishing the solitude, watching the horizon. Sebastian never liked this part—the sitting-still. He'd never been patient, not in any sport he tried. She imagined him behind her, whooping as he leapt to his feet and carved his way down the shoulder of the first rideable wave he saw, unwilling to wait out the best ones.

But he could surf anything, even the closeouts, so it didn't matter. He'd taken to it so quickly, more naturally than she had, and it was mesmerizing to watch. Their Sunday mornings together had been sacred— while the neighbors were at church they joked about their own kind of baptism.

She stayed out until the sun sank below the water, hemorrhaging darker shades of orange and purple. As she finally rode in towards the shore, something deep in her chest broke along with that last wave. She stumbled forward until her legs buckled, sinking to her knees in the shallows.

There she sobbed, maybe for Sebastian or her mother or herself or all of it. Their presence was so visceral here. She saw her mother under the umbrella in her striped one-piece, flipping through a steamy paperback— Seb, dumping his board face-up so the wax melted while he ran to the food shack for a hot dog. And rewind a few years, there was Ryland.

No. No, no, no. Stop.

She splashed water on her face and got to her feet, hefted her board across the sand and toward the shower. She wouldn't let him intrude here. Especially not here.

Except as she rinsed the salt from her hair and peeled down the top half of her wetsuit...there he was.

He'd dressed for a run, ditching his leather jacket for a thermal shirt and a black windbreaker with reflective stripes. She ran her hands over her face, blinked the water from her eyes.

Nope, still there.

"I don't want to do this with you," she began, grabbing her things and breezing past him toward her car.

"You're upset."

That only made her madder. He had no right to sound like he gave a shit, to knit his brows together that way, to make her feel an inch tall. "Just sand in my eye."

Ignoring her, he casually kept pace, one long-legged step for every two of hers. "Why were you crying?"

She popped Lucy's trunk, leaned her board against it and began peeling off the rest of her wetsuit. The weight of his gaze was a visceral thing as it skimmed down her body, taking her in. Even in her swimsuit, she might as well have been naked.

"Cora."

He shouldn't be allowed to say her name like that. Part tease, part scold, part honest-to-god concern, all gravel and thunder. Straightening up, she put her hands on her hips. "You want to talk? Okay." She glanced around the near-empty lot. "Talk. You have ten seconds."

He stepped towards the car like she was an animal he didn't want to frighten.

"And you can say it from right there," she said.

He took another step forward, testing her. "For someone so determined to avoid me, you're doing a lousy job of it."

She lowered the towel and stared. "What? You're the one following me."

"I jog here all the time," he said easily. "The only new variable is you."

"Great. Then let me leave, and you can get on with it."

"Is that what you want?"

"Yes."

He folded his arms. "Liar. You just tugged your earlobe."

Her mouth fell open. "No, no, no. You don't get to pretend like you know me now. You don't get to stand there and bring up the one random thing you remember about me like you know anything about who I am now."

"Interesting." Amusement sparked behind his eyes. "You sure seemed to think you knew a lot about me, back at my apartment."

"My mistake." Fighting for calm, she shoved the towel and board into the car. Goddess, he was a jerk. "Guess you'll actually turn me in this time?"

"I didn't report it."

She froze. She'd been right. He hadn't sent the other hunters after her—so who had chased them from Bungalow? "Why not?"

"That's what I've been trying to figure out." He leaned against the parking meter, cucumber-cool, like they were discussing the weather. "Should be easy, right? Follow orders, move on."

Something snapped inside her and her face grew hot. Maybe if he'd had even a little anger or confusion in him, if he'd given her something other than that insufferable poker-face, this rage wouldn't have felt so bright and sharp, and she wouldn't have let it win.

"Well, go ahead then!" She got in his face, poking his chest, now close enough to pick out the amber threading through his deep brown irises. "I sure don't deserve any special treatment. You've made it clear we're not friends. Why are you still here?"

"Because we *were!*" he roared back.

At the regret in those three words, Cora blinked. She didn't know what to say.

He kept going. "And because even though so much else has changed, *you*—the core of you—it hasn't. I keep remembering things I haven't thought about in years, that I buried because I wouldn't have survived in that place if I didn't."

He looked like he was standing on the edge of a precipice, muscles poised to leap. Like he desperately wanted to shake sense into her. He didn't close the distance, though.

After an eternity of staring at him, she found her voice. "If you think there's any chance of salvaging this friendship, you're absolutely out of your mind."

"There are worse places to be."

Cora backed away. Every muscle in her body protested. His nearness made it impossible for her to think. "I have to go." She stuffed her feet into shoes and yanked open the driver's side door.

As the car sputtered on, he walked through her headlights to the sidewalk, but didn't look back.

Tires squealing, she shot through the parking lot towards the main road, and only once he'd retreated in her rearview mirror did she realize her hands were trembling on the wheel.

———— ⌁ ————

"No."

A metal screen filled the doorway between the blonde man and Cora, who stood on the second-story front patio of his apartment. He held a little dachshund mix under one arm like a football, petting its head absently.

"Harry, please," she said, desperation clawing in her gut. "I'm not above begging."

"Listen, hon," he said, "I didn't cut you off just for your Auntie to break my door down after your next OD. You may not value life, but I sure as hell value mine." Dishes clinked softly in the room behind him, and she realized she'd interrupted dinner.

"I don't even need a lot," she reasoned, wrapping her arms around herself as the evening chill set in. Her hair was still damp, and her swimsuit had soaked through her T-shirt. "Just a little hit. Like, a baby one. Teeny tiny. It'll help me sleep."

"If you need something for sleep, I can whip up a million other things. Bliss is nowhere on that list."

"I've had a hell of a day. Please." She needed to get out of her own head, her fucked-up brain. Forget about Ryland. Forget about Seb.

Slide into the dark and let it steal her away for an hour or two. Find somewhere better than this.

"Preaching to the choir. I said no."

"You're the only alchemist I trust down here." A lump was forming in her throat. The rest of her contacts were still down in San Diego, but Harry had moved back to LA a while ago. She'd met him at a party while he dealt potions, and then he'd set up shop here when one of the LA altas, Helena, had approached him about a business venture. A hunters' club.

It was utter insanity, but that was Harry. High risk, high reward, never missed an opportunity that came his way. The pitch was this: Helena would use her neuromancy to plant the idea in the heads of a few hunters. And she knew it would only work if she'd let them stay on their shaky moral high ground, imagining they were letting off witches who would've otherwise been dragged to prison.

The hardest part—getting one of the brass to keep his people in line—had already been solved. Rumor was she'd been having an affair with an ACE Commander for years. But for him to stay on board, she'd needed to "allow" his men to follow her employees after-hours, keeping tabs.

In reality, she was only planting false memories and erasing potentially incriminating ones. That delicate balancing act likely required an absurd amount of magic to maintain, but Helena wasn't the youngest alta in their coven for nothing.

No telling how many lives she and Harry had saved with the leads they'd gathered since. But how long could they keep it up?

"And thank the Goddess for your weak-ass network," Harry said. "Otherwise I'd be helping Auntie scrape you off the pavement again. Now, if you're done with this nonsense, I'm going to finish my dinner." And he shut the door in her face.

Standing beneath the anemic porch light, Cora fought the urge to bang on the door again and considered just waiting him out. He had to let his little dog pee at some point, right? How long would that take? There must be something she could say to make him listen.

She really was freezing, but...nope, she could do it. She could sit here for a bit.

As she sank to the concrete, back against the banister and knees pulled into her chest, Harry drew aside the living room blinds and mouthed GO HOME.

She just rested her forehead on her knees and closed her eyes.

Suddenly, someone was shaking her awake. "Hey, Cora. HEY."

Cora jerked her head upright. Her ass had fallen so fully asleep, she couldn't feel it. Shivering, she looked up into familiar eyes—Quinn's eyes. They were never the same color two days in a row, but she knew them, alright.

Goddess spare her.

"Hey!" Quinn tapped her cheek gently, not quite a slap. "What the fuck are you doing?"

With cold-numbed fingers, Cora used the metal banister to drag herself to her feet. "What? Why are you here?"

Quinn, upon closer inspection, wore a full face of makeup, a crop top, and heels, and she smelled like alcohol. She must have just come from a shift. No—too early, Cora realized, checking her phone. She'd left midway through.

"Gee, maybe has something to do with the hysterical call I got from Mindy, saying you were passed out on your drug dealer's porch."

"Harry called Mindy?" Disbelief and humiliation dovetailed in Cora's chest.

"Actually, Harry called Helena for Mindy's number, and Mindy thought I might be able to knock some sense into you. For fuck's sake, Cora. What happened?"

"I'm fine." Cora shook off the pins and needles in her legs. "I was just leaving."

Inhaling like she was trying to sniff her out, Quinn frowned. "Have you been drinking?"

"No." Cora's indignation echoed in the stairwell as she descended. Her anger wasn't all for Quinn, not in this moment, but she made a convenient target for it. "I haven't been."

"Don't get all pissy." As Quinn followed her down, she stopped by the tiny rectangular pool that sat in the middle of the U-shaped apartment block. Their voices echoed across it, and she lowered hers. "It's a reasonable assumption, considering how I found you!"

"I only fell asleep!"

"You need to be honest with yourself—"

"This is none of your business."

"My friends *are* my business," Quinn said after Cora, who turned and headed towards the high metal gate that led to the street. "I care about you, Cor, and I care about the work we do, even if we don't always agree on how to do it."

Cora kept walking, still hugging herself and shivering. She'd been hoping to avoid this confrontation for a bit longer.

Quinn plowed forward through Cora's silence. "I'm sorry that I panicked and put us all in danger, but you weren't behind that wheel. You don't know what that felt like. You can't."

To Cora's surprise, Quinn's voice cracked. Cora stopped and turned.

Quinn was fighting back tears. "I'm scared too, you know."

The hard knot of anger in Cora's chest loosened. "Why?"

"I'm scared of how good it felt." Quinn moved closer, words quivering. "To finally give the hunters what they deserved. I was drunk on the power of it afterward. I didn't want to be, I shouldn't have been, but I was. And then...the way you looked at me, after...like I was a monster..."

"Oh, Goddess." Cora reached out and grabbed Quinn's hands, looking down at them. "I just...needed a minute. The patients I get...the violence is over, you know? If they go, it's in a bed or the OR. And if they're lucky, their families are with them." She swallowed hard and looked up again. "I can handle blood. I can handle death, but the stuff that gets them there? That's not my wheelhouse."

"It's not *mine* either," Quinn shot back, hurt plain on her face. "But don't be so sure you would have reacted more reasonably. If you'd been in my place, you'd have done anything to get those people to safety."

She was right. Cora hadn't been put in the same position, and so they'd never know. She yanked Quinn down and wrapped her arms around her, tears pricking behind her eyes. "I don't think you're a monster. I don't. I just...reacted. I'm sorry."

Quinn squeezed her back, not caring that Cora's clothes were damp. "I was so worried when Mindy called me, and so furious at you for not coming to me, not telling me you were struggling again..."

"It came on pretty suddenly," she said, unsure how much detail to give. She didn't think she had it in her to retell that story right now.

Quinn pulled away but kept her hands on Cora's shoulders. "I don't understand, though. You're a nurse. *A nurse.* Nobody knows better than you what this stuff does to a person."

Knuckling away a tear, Cora smiled ruefully. "It's funny. That's what makes it so easy. You think you're...somehow more able to handle it, control the need, because you know so much about how it all works." A laugh bubbled up her throat before she could stop it. It felt all the more ridiculous now that she'd said it aloud. "You convince yourself you're different than every other person whose stomach you've pumped, or that because it's magic it's better."

Quinn let her hands fall to her sides, deciding whether to tiptoe. "Do you want to talk about...what brought it on?"

Cora shook her head and gazed down at her damp clothes. "Maybe once I've had a hot shower. And some tea. And some sleep." She wrinkled her nose as her stomach growled loudly. "And some food."

Quinn nodded and didn't push, instead walking Cora the rest of the way to where Lucy was parked. "I have a jacket in my car. Benny's Tacos? You can shower at my place."

Cora felt that yawning darkness around her recede just a little. Fatima had been onto something.

CHAPTER NINE

"You're out of it today." Ricky peered at Theo through bloodshot eyes from behind the glow of his laptop screen. They were working out of their suite across the street from INN|LA, recording guests' comings and goings.

Except to be by Harris' bedside, Ricky hadn't allowed himself any time off since the accident. He was the one who assigned Harris and Thompson surveillance duty the day Thompson died, and it clearly weighed heavy on him.

And with Harris yet to wake up, they couldn't get his version of events. They only had one license plate reader camera to go on, which identified the third car involved as Ezra's Mustang.

Sweeping the scene made it no easier to pinpoint how the tire blew. Both cars had spewed debris in every direction. Harris was obsessive about the care of his Camaro, which suggested something was off, but they had no proof. Still, the uncertainty and guilt dogpiled on Ricky and fueled his push to pin whatever he could on Ezra. To Theo's relief, Fletcher made it clear he wouldn't let them just storm the guy's house—but hell if Ricky's need to blame someone didn't make it harder to back off.

"Sorry," Theo said absently.

"I've never seen you like this, dude."

"I've just been thinking about...you know."

"What?"

Theo regretted bringing it up. He didn't have the energy for it. "Never mind."

"Wait, that girl again? Seriously?"

At least she'd shown more self-control than Theo did at Manhattan pier the other day. His grip on that was tenuous at best. For a brief and terrifying second, he'd wanted to close the distance. Crush her to him, breathe her in, like the moment they'd had in Boardroom.

Where the hell had that come from?

He'd been replaying that day in the surf shop over and over, when Cora's face lit up and she ran to him, throwing her arms around him. The way she'd felt against him as he spun her around, the way her hair had smelled...and the gut punch of her realization, of the grief and mistrust that followed, like someone had given him the sun and then immediately blotted it out.

Theo looked blankly at Ricky, who waited for a response to some question Theo hadn't heard. "What?"

"You're fucking unbelievable."

The ring of Theo's cell saved him from digging that hole any deeper. He'd never been so relieved to be on-call. "Ryland."

"Confirmed Principal Arcane Disturbance, Koreatown," the dispatcher said. "You might want to put on your big-boy pants for this one. The media's out."

The heart of Koreatown was a bustling, polychrome maze of karaoke joints and cafes, peppered with the musical clatter of dinner dishes through thrown-open apartment windows. At least half the businesses displayed signs in Korean first, offering secondary translations in both Spanish and English, but the one above the restaurant they headed to just read "BBQ."

It was a joint Theo had come to years ago with Ricky, and it hadn't changed—unless you counted the blown-out front windows. Most of the patrons had fled—those whose paths were blocked crouched under tables.

LAPD landed first on the scene, blocking the street and intercepting curious onlookers until ACE arrived. Dispatch briefed them on the way over—a domestic dispute gone bad over dinner.

Theo sensed it before they stepped out of the car. If the emotion behind arcane energy was potent, Theo felt the shape of it—and those threads of magic in the air writhed in rage.

Even though he always did his best to minimize bloodshed, Theo had been a TAC Specialist long enough to know not every standoff was your typical Crash-and-dash. With Ricky still angry about Thompson, he had a feeling this could go south quick.

As furious red telekinetic wards crackled along the building's shattered façade, they prowled around back, through an unlocked door that led into the kitchen. From their vantage point by the serving window, they could better see the two men who were—well, arguing was too tame a word.

One was worse off than the other, his medium-brown skin streaked red by a gash on his temple. He'd flipped a table to shield himself from the second man, whose rage they'd felt outside.

"—again, Antoine, after I moved halfway across the country for you!" Tears streamed down man number two's face, and his entire body shook. His blonde hair stuck up in all directions.

"I saved you from the Dallas mobs, I didn't drag you here against your will!" said Antoine. "She'll always be part of my life; we have a fucking daughter! If you can't handle that, I don't know how you thought this would work—"

Anguish poured from the second man: hot stabbing threads. He gestured toward the wall, and the overturned table slammed backwards, dragging Antoine with it, pinning him beneath its weight.

Antoine cried out in pain, his magic rippling as he tried to keep it contained. He refused to raise a hand to his partner, no matter how much abuse he took.

Theo was oddly moved by it.

Without a clear shot through the service window, Theo signaled Ricky before moving toward the swinging door. In one fluid motion, he burst through it to tackle the telekinetic, who heard Antoine's warning too late to duck. But as Theo rammed him into the linoleum floor, the witch wrestled the syringe from Theo's hand and sent it sailing across the room.

A crash behind them announced Ricky through the kitchen door. Blasting Theo backwards with a surge of energy, the telekinetic went after Ricky.

As Ricky opened fire, magic pulled his bullets in erratic paths, lodging in the wall above Theo's head. Stunned, Ricky hesitated for a half-second more than the telekinetic needed to twist the gun from his hands.

A gunshot cracked through the air, and Ricky was down, clutching his thigh with a howl. Theo's ears rang as his barrage of Crash darts glanced off the telekinetic's shield.

Ricky dragged himself behind an overturned table, and Theo joined him. "Gotta be tapped soon," Ricky wheezed, barely audible as the whine in Theo's ears receded. "Wouldn't have gone for the gun otherwise."

Theo didn't bother replying, knowing Ricky's own hearing was doing the same slow return. He was right. No witch could sustain all those wards and fight the two of them off forever. They'd need backup unless he exhausted himself in the next few minutes.

Wrenching Antoine out from underneath the table, the telekinetic pressed Ricky's gun to his head, shoving him in front like a human shield. Still, Antoine refused to use magic—he squeezed his eyes shut, sobbing about his daughter, Leila.

His partner wasn't moved. "If you don't call off the LAPD and ACE," the telekinetic said, "he dies."

Ricky made a strangled noise halfway between a laugh and a cry of pain. He pressed on his thigh with one bloody hand, the other hand too mangled to be of any use. "We don't negotiate with fucking terrorists. It's no loss to us."

But Theo balked as he watched the scene unfold.

Antoine hadn't lifted a finger the entire fight. That knowledge was a fist around his heart, tightening its grip. The love and grief and betrayal in Antoine's expression, the restraint he showed in the face of his partner's fury...Theo couldn't look him in the eye and make that call.

Or look himself in the mirror later, either, if he made that call.

He also couldn't neutralize the other man without the risk of killing Antoine. But as Ricky bled out beside him, upturned face asking what the fuck he was waiting for, he also knew he didn't have a choice.

Holding his breath, steadying his aim, Theo fired.

The wards dissolved as the back of the telekinetic's head splattered against a beautiful painting of a Korean woman, dressing her in patches of crimson and bits of brain. He crumpled to the floor next to Antoine, who was too terrified to open his eyes and see the truth of it for himself.

His hands shook, drifting skyward. "Please, I'll cooperate."

Theo signaled out a shattered window. The LAPD rushed in to secure the scene while a uniform helped Ricky to the ambulance waiting outside, and the guests trapped inside the restaurant spilled into the street.

Theo holstered his gun and uncapped his last needle full of Crash, approaching Antoine across a jagged sea of glass and debris and shattered plates of food. "This will help you relax."

Antoine swallowed, nodded. "I know what it is. Just get on with it."

Theo grabbed his hand, and Antoine came out from behind the table, stepping over the telekinetic's body. "I'll make sure they know you cooperated." Theo pressed the needle into Antoine's arm. "With any luck, they'll put you with the nonviolent offenders."

Antoine's eyes widened just before they began to flutter closed. "Why would you do that?"

"We're not all monsters," Theo said, more to convince himself than Antoine, and the man slumped forward in his arms.

The EMTs took Ricky to the closest level one trauma center. After Theo summoned a car for Antoine, handed him off to the transporters, and signed the paperwork, he followed the sirens and parked near the ER.

The cheerful, pastoral oil paintings on the walls of stark white corridors did nothing to distract from the scent of antiseptic and death. Really, why even bother?

Waiting for Ricky to leave the OR, he grabbed himself a cup of what passed for coffee here and figured he might as well update Fletcher, who picked up on the first ring.

"Santana went down, sir," Theo said without preamble. "He's in surgery now. Bullet to the thigh. Perp was hemorrhaging magic, managed to get Santana's gun from his hands. I'll let you know when he's out."

"What's this I hear about you requesting clemency for the second guy? You'd better not be going soft on me, Ryland."

Theo chose his words carefully. "Any of those videos will show he kept his magic bottled. Thought it might be a...teachable moment."

"In what way? This shit is exploding all over social media. I've got shaky cell phone videos from every angle, and we need to make an example of him."

"Spin it. We could make a follow-up statement. Witches stand a better chance of surviving if they cooperate, that kind of thing."

Fletcher grunted and paused. "Maybe." He hung up.

Theo wasn't sure what that meant for Antoine's chances, but supposed it was better than a "no."

Another hour passed. He called Ricky's mother and sister to fill them in while he waited, reassuring them he'd stay until they arrived. Finally, the doctor came to fetch him—a slight, red-haired woman with a pixie cut. Her face wasn't the kind of grim he'd expect from bad news, and he exhaled in relief.

"The bullet missed Ricardo's femoral artery," she said. "He came through surgery fine." Scribbling something on Ricky's chart, she led Theo into the recovery room. "He's awake now."

Theo knew Ricky had seen him hesitate back in the restaurant and expected he'd get called out for it. Those precious, wasted seconds meant the difference between life and death in the field. He had to get out in front of it, diffuse it.

"Hey, the doctors just told me about what they found. I'm so sorry."

Beneath the haze of painkillers, Ricky's eyes widened. "The hell do you mean?"

Theo sat next to Ricky's bed and held his hand, face stoic, voice somber. "That you have a bad case of being a whiny little bitch. Said there's no cure."

Ricky stared at him blankly, then began to wheeze as he snatched his hand away, and Theo realized he was laughing. "Fuck you."

"How are you feeling?"

"Like microwaved mierda." Grimacing, he shifted to adjust his pillow. "They told me I lost a lot of blood." *No thanks to you*, he didn't say.

"I'm sorry about what happened back there." Theo scrubbed a hand over his beard. It wasn't a lie, even if his next words were. "I've been out of it. Losing focus, not trusting my instincts."

"You need to get your head right." Ricky narrowed his eyes. "Whatever your problem is...this isn't like you. If you can't talk to me, at least talk to someone. We got that department shrink. "

Theo almost laughed. "Maybe." Not a chance he could talk this through with anyone ACE employed. His thoughts drifted to Helena's advice from the other day—to talk to Cora—and he shoved it away.

Definitely not.

"You just worry about getting better, alright? I need you back out there so you can put me in my place."

Ricky's attempt at a smile came out a grimace. "Count on it."

When Ricky's mother and sister finally showed up a bit later, Theo excused himself. At least the bullet would put Ricky out of commission for a few weeks, keep him from breathing down Theo's neck, and the relief in that realization was nothing less than a betrayal.

So why didn't it bother him as much as it should have? If he could so easily blunt the edges of the guilt, what kind of a friend, a partner, did that make him?

He didn't have time to ruminate on it, because as he slid into his car, the key exploded into a tiny ball of light.

Theo cursed and jerked backward into the seat, adrenaline spiking through him. The colorful blob flowed up the dashboard, and as two glowing eyes formed within it, he got the sense it was laughing at him.

Blues and pinks and oranges and silvers swirled through its body like—liquid? Smoke? It was truly impossible to tell. And magic hummed off of it, but it wasn't the usual pins and needles. It was different...an echo in his bones, not altogether unpleasant, but...ancient. Like nothing he'd ever felt.

He knew about sprites. Every TAC Specialist did, in theory. They were little aberrations of magic, rarely revealing themselves to anyone but witches. Perhaps his sensitivity counted for something there.

This sprite bent its upper half slightly, like it was cocking its head at him, curious. Could it understand him if he spoke to it? Did he want it to?

And then memory slammed into him. He'd seen one before, hadn't he? The night he...

"You were with Cora."

Why was it here? And how had it gotten here? He'd seen it leave with her, but...

"Did you follow me home from the beach, when I ran into her? Were you with her then?"

Almost in shame, it pooled outward a little.

"You can't stay here, you know."

The blob twisted to look at the little Lakers bobblehead on his dashboard and turned into an exact replica of it with a soft pop.

Great. That was answer enough. What was he supposed to do now? And...where were his actual keys? Damn it.

"Listen, I have a weird favor to ask."

The bobblehead didn't move.

"Please?" Was he really going to have to beg this sprite for help?

Sitting at that impasse, Theo remembered something else he'd read—that they liked shiny objects. He reached down and rummaged in a cup holder for some spare change, his thumb passing over the shape of a quarter. He buffed it on his shirt and held it up, waiting.

The sprite morphed back into a blob, its little eyes going big and round. Two tiny lumps Theo assumed were arms reached out to grab the coin, then it folded the quarter into its body—ate it? Put it into a pocket? Who the hell knew?

As the sprite leaned toward him, waiting for him to ask his favor, Theo blew out a long breath. "Do you think you could turn back into my car keys?"

CHAPTER TEN

Cora jerked and bumped her way into a narrow parking spot in front of Ryland's apartment. She wasn't sure how long she sat there, gripping the peeling leather of the steering wheel cover, staring at the neon sign of Moradian's.

Even if she couldn't remember which unit was his, the café next door was branded in her memory. A display of pastries invited passersby, and a jumble of signs in competing typefaces advertised varieties of coffee and tea. Lacy curtains framed the windows, reminding her vaguely of her grandmother's kitchen.

Maybe she'd grab a quick bite, a minute to defrost. To gather herself. Then she'd go up there and get Pip.

She yanked the keys from the ignition and closed the driver's side door, which cheerfully sprang back open. "Piece of garbage." She kicked it shut again, adding yet another dent to its collection.

A male voice carried from the sidewalk. "If you turn your head sideways and cross your eyes a little, this scrape looks like a penis."

Her chin jerked up. Ryland stared at her across the roof of her car, the ghost of a grin on his lips. Where the heck did he come from? "Don't do that. You scared the crap out of me." A pause, then: "Which one does?"

"This one." He pointed at the rear bumper, and she rounded it, turning her head sideways and squinting at the long, white scrape on the passenger-side door.

"Huh. Would you look at that."

This was laughable, their attempt at civil conversation. Tiptoeing around the reality of where they'd left things in that argument at the pier. Having time to cool down didn't mean all those feelings weren't still simmering just beneath the surface.

She was just here to fetch Pip. It was going to be fine.

And the flip-flopping in her stomach had absolutely nothing to do with the way Ryland looked in this light, or how his curls were still wet from the shower, or the fact that he'd showered at all in anticipation of her coming.

He raised an eyebrow, studying her. She resisted the urge to squirm. "You got my message, then?"

"It sure threw Marlo for a loop." The manager of Boardroom had come to her that morning with a sticky note. Apparently, someone named R had called to remind her he "owed her a Sprite."

Pip had been gone a bit longer than she was used to—sometimes he took a full day to resurface from wherever he'd been hiding—so she'd been relieved to hear he hadn't gone back through the ley lines. And then immediately nauseous at the prospect of having to retrieve him from Ryland.

Even more so, because she knew the sprite could travel anywhere he damn well pleased. Pip could just come back to Mindy's, and she had half a mind to wait it out. The other half of her imagined all the ways Pip might get himself into trouble, and the idea of hunters trapping and studying him made her sick.

"So, where's Pip?" she asked, hands on her hips.

Ryland's eyes sparkled with mischief. "He's...otherwise occupied."

Goddess help her. "I don't have the patience for games right now."

He held his hands up. "It's not me. Pip's the one who won't come down."

"Why not?" Then it clicked. "What is he?"

Ryland's grin widened. It had been so long since she'd seen him smile fully, it completely disarmed her. He looked so...harmless. Approachable, even. "A piano."

Cora closed her eyes briefly and said a silent prayer for patience.

"I tried to get him to shift back, but nothing I offered was good enough. Even my cuff links." It wasn't quite an apology. "He's very taken with it."

"Well, I'm not sure if you've noticed, but I can't fit a damn piano in this car."

"Fair enough." Ryland stuffed his hands in his jean pockets. "What now?"

106

"I didn't know you played the piano," she said before she could stop herself. She hadn't noticed one in his apartment last time, but she also hadn't seen the office alcove. It was an odd thing to imagine him doing, sitting at the bench, fingers on the keys. A soft thing that didn't at all reflect the hard edges of him.

Of course he'd take up new hobbies. Letting that simple fact blindside her felt ridiculous. No matter how different he was now, she still hadn't gotten used to learning new things about him, each one a reminder he'd lived half a life she wouldn't know.

But...the more she considered it, the more she realized it suited him. Piano was also deliberate, precise. Infinitely complex. It demanded both sides of the brain equally. It left little room for doubt and hesitation.

There was a strange comfort in connecting those familiar dots.

A shrug was his only answer. "You could wait if you wanted. Maybe he'll sense you're nearby and have a change of heart." He glanced up at his balcony, then back at her. "Come up."

Cora balked. She wasn't ready to continue the last conversation they'd had, and going up there meant she wouldn't have a choice. She also wasn't thrilled at the prospect of returning to the place she'd escaped from.

It helped that she had, at the very least, told Quinn where she'd be. Quinn had put up a fight, and when that hadn't worked, insisted on coming with, but Cora had stood firm. She needed to do this alone. Quinn's emotions weren't a variable she wanted to have to account for—not when she could barely keep her own in check.

But one thing was certain: she wasn't leaving here without Pip.

"Or," he said, reading her hesitation and pointing at Moradian's, "stay down here. See if he decides to investigate."

It was coffee. Just coffee. Not the end of the world. A public place would be better, anyway. Cora shifted her weight, considering. "I guess that could work."

A bell above the doorway chimed as they entered, and a slightly hunched, grey-haired woman in a floral apron beamed at them as she rounded the edge of the counter. She extended both arms toward Ryland. "Barev, my Theodore! Intcbess es?"

The energy in the room shifted. Another witch. The woman kissed Ryland on both cheeks, but her focus lasered on Cora. Her perfume, heady and floral, mingled with the smell of yeast, coffee, and something else...rosewater?

The witch Cora sensed had to be her—the place was deserted. Did he know about this woman, or she him? Cora wasn't about to out either one, so she sat back on her heels and waited for an introduction.

"Shad lav, Mrs. Moradian," Ryland said. "Merci. This is my friend, Cora."

Cora's chest flooded with unexpected warmth at the few Armenian phrases he seemed to have learned purely for the bakery owner's benefit. Reaching out to take the woman's hand, Cora was instead yanked downward and kissed on each cheek, same as Ryland.

Mrs. Moradian leaned away and squeezed both of Cora's hands in hers—pointedly enough to confirm Cora's suspicions—then shot Ryland a meaningful look. "Come, eat!"

Her genuine enthusiasm made the tension easier to bear as she served them coffee and halva. How would Ryland treat Mrs. Moradian if he knew what she truly was?

When she finally left their table and returned to the kitchen, they settled into silence.

Sitting across from one another, coffee between them, was a bizarre kind of normal. Stranger still was how they'd spent so many nights on the roof outside her bedroom window, talking about everything and nothing, and Cora still couldn't find a single word to say to him now.

After a bite of halva, Ryland broke the ice. "I thought sprites were mostly myth."

"They don't like to be seen," she said, releasing a nervous breath. "Pip is...different, I guess? Transforming into things is how sprites understand the world, but Pip also likes watching people react to different behaviors. Learning cause and effect in a way most sprites are too skittish to do."

"It was Pip. That night in the alley." Ryland wasn't asking.

Cora folded and unfolded her napkin. "Yeah. He scared that guy away. I was taking out trash bags, and I was distracted and..." she looked up at him.

"Angry with me, from earlier," he finished. His face was impossible to read. She noticed, absently, that he'd trimmed his beard.

"Yes."

She couldn't stand it. Couldn't stand having him so near to her while the years stretched between them like a chasm they had to yell across.

"How are your parents?" she blurted.

When Ryland's eyes widened, she got the sense people didn't manage to surprise him often. "They're fine. We don't talk much."

"Still in California?" The question was innocuous enough, but they both knew what it really asked.

Could they bear to stay?

"Up in Simi Valley now." Folding his arms, he sat back. Cora thought he'd end it there, but after a beat, he kept going. "They lived near the base until I graduated at eighteen. I spent weekends with them, but the rest of the time I boarded with the other kids in my class."

"They...let you do that?"

"Once the brass was sure we understood the consequences of running away, the rules eased up a bit. My first field training assignment was in the South Bay, near the base, but my parents didn't stay." His eyes darkened. "The memories they had of that place were enough to drive them north once they thought I didn't need them anymore."

Cora's heart sank. "Just...back to normal?"

"Wouldn't call it normal. They overcompensated for the lack of it, pretended nothing happened. Still do. And you know what? If that's what they need...fine." He sighed, a shoulder lifting and dropping. "It was rough for them. They couldn't protect me. It was made clear to them that coming with me, seeing me, was a privilege that could be revoked. They weren't willing to give that up."

Her hands fisted around the napkin in her lap. "Did you have any idea what was about to happen, before they took you?" *Before the night you almost kissed me*, she wanted to say. *You could have said something, anything.*

He hesitated. "My parents were acting strange. My mom was always on the verge of tears. My dad spent his days shut in the den. I was afraid they were getting divorced."

He'd never mentioned that. She would have remembered.

Ryland uncrossed his arms and leaned forward. His gaze may as well have been a lit cigarette stub on her skin. "I wanted to tell you. I wasn't ready yet. Putting words to it made it real. And when they told me what was really going on, I wasn't sure which sounded better."

His parents had known what it would cost them. They knew about her mother's magic, about Cora and Sebastian. His mother had to choose between never seeing her son again, or watching ACE train him to become the very thing that would hunt her closest friend down two years later.

No wonder his mother had wanted to forget. "I'm sorry," was all she could think to say.

He waited for a "but," for a qualifier, but she didn't have one. She truly was sorry. For him, for his parents. For herself.

"It's just me and Mindy now," she said, compelled to offer him something in return for the wound he'd laid bare. "She's all I have. Dad's never made an effort to contact us—me," she corrected herself, unable to hide the pang it sent through her.

"When were they taken?" Ryland's voice was soft, but there wasn't pity in it, and she was grateful. She didn't think she could stand pity. Not from him.

Swallowing against the lump building in her throat, she pushed the halva around her plate. "I was sixteen. They came to the house, they..."

Why was she telling him this? Why was she so desperate to be able to? She shook her head, and before she realized what was happening, he'd reached across the table to grab her hand.

The contact sent a jolt through her, and she instantly forgot everything she'd intended to say. Her pulse jumped beneath his thumb. She should have snatched her hand back. She almost did.

Instead, she looked up at Ryland and saw the boy she'd known peering out from behind the eyes of this rugged, scarred, bearded man.

Here sat the last, jagged remnant of a life she thought she'd lost to time completely. A glitch in the Matrix.

An impossibility then, and even more so now.

Ryland opened his mouth but closed it again when a blast of cold air hit them. A duo of men stumbled through the door, reeking of liquor as they elbowed past the table. Whatever it was they sang fell into a key only the neighborhood dogs could appreciate.

Instantly on alert, Ryland straightened and released her hand. Now Cora understood why he'd insisted on taking the seat facing the door.

Her fingers burned where his had been, but she didn't have long to contemplate it.

"Hey lady," the largest one slurred at Mrs. Moradian, who'd come back to the counter when she heard the bell. He adjusted his beanie over cold, reddened ears. "Gimme a...one of those." He pointed to a pastry in the glass display. "Actually, gimme both."

The second, the skinnier and darker of the two, barked similarly inarticulate orders at Mrs. Moradian. She looked annoyed but complied. They weren't far from the Arts District bars; this wasn't her first rodeo. "$14.50," she said, handing a pink box over.

Grubby hands grabbed, crumbs flew, mouths chewed without closing, and nobody handed her the cash. "$14.50," she repeated, narrowing her eyes.

Skinny inspected the baklava he'd already half-eaten and spoke with his mouth full. "Are these gluten-free?"

Mrs. Moradian wrenched the box from Beanie's hand. "No money, no pastry."

"Whoaaa whoa whoa! That bitch fucking assaulted me!" yelled Beanie, turning to look at them. "You guys saw it, right? You saw her assault me?" He whirled back around and tugged the box toward him. She dug her heels in, and then he let go with a shove, sending her stumbling into the shelf behind her.

"Hey!" Ryland crossed the cafe in three long strides and swung his fist into Beanie's face.

Cora yelped, leaping to her feet as Beanie crashed into the pastry display. It shattered around him, jagged edges ripping the down from his puffer jacket. Mrs. Moradian moaned softly from where she'd fallen but didn't stand up again.

Beanie regained his balance and mopped the blood from his nose, while Skinny stepped over Mrs. Moradian to rifle through the register. Cora didn't think, she just moved, scrambling to the woman's side. Skinny, preoccupied with the cash in hand, barely noticed them underfoot.

Meanwhile, Beanie—who had now lost his namesake in the scuffle— steamed with rage, and though Ryland might have outmatched him in skill, Beanie's fists had the benefit of inertia that only a two-hundred-fifty-pound man could wield. He lunged. The men fell headlong into the table Cora had been sitting at moments before, sending plates and glasses crashing to the ground.

Cora checked Mrs. Moradian's pupils, airway, and looked for blood— deciding she was okay to move, helped her scoot into the corner furthest from the fight.

Ryland stumbled sideways and ducked another swing, but the next one caught him in the nose with a sickening crunch. Still dazed from the first tackle, he broke his fall by seizing a nearby chair and brought that down too.

Beanie saw his opening. He bent down and grabbed the collar of Ryland's shirt with one hand, connecting fist and jaw with the other. He reared back to do it again and again, each time harder than before, painting the floor in flecks of blood spatter.

Ryland's grip on the meaty hand clutching his shirt was growing slack, and panic hummed in Cora's gut. She rose on shaky feet.

"Stop it! Stop it, enough!" she yelled, snatching a platter off the counter and rushing forward to smash it over Beanie's bald head. That gave him pause. He shook his head and let go of Ryland, standing up—up, and up, and up, to face her. His confusion morphed into anger again, and she knew she only had one choice.

She tapped into the ley line deep in the ground beneath her feet, drawing up new threads of magic. They unraveled and speared into the man's flesh and bone, searching, probing for a weakness, an old injury, a—

Snap.

"JESUS FUCKING CHRIST!" Beanie roared in pain and lurched forward, catching himself on outstretched palms. He rolled onto his back and grabbed his leg, close to sobbing now, and Cora realized in horror that the jagged shin bone had ripped right through the skin and muscle of his calf.

It took a lot to make her queasy—she had seen everything there was to see in the ER. But knowing she'd caused those screams, that blood... was something else entirely. Nausea roiled within her, and she grabbed the wall for support.

Until now, Skinny had watched the tableau from the dubious safety of the register, but he hadn't signed up to lose, and certainly not like this. Clutching the cash and grabbing another eclair as an afterthought, he dashed out the door without a backward glance.

Behind her, Mrs. Moradian was coming out of her shock, and Cora handed her a napkin full of ice from the drink dispenser. "You'll be okay. No blood that I could see. Keep this on your temple, and I'll be right back."

Shifting to Ryland's side, cupping his battered face and trying to block out Beanie's sobs, she asked, "Are you okay?" One eye opened fully; the other was already swelling shut. The good one darted around for a moment, unfocused, before landing on her. She pried open the bruising eyelid to examine his pupil, then sat back. "How many fingers am I holding up?"

"Eleven." He grinned, a flash of bloody teeth. "If I'd gotten him on the floor, I'd have had him. I tap out guys his size in training all the time."

Rolling her eyes, she moved behind him, grabbing his shoulders to help him sit up. "She's okay," Cora said as Ryland's head turned toward Mrs. Moradian. "Just a little banged up."

"Fucking assholes." He swayed to his feet, using the chair he'd tipped over as leverage. She stepped back when he waved her off. "I'm good. I'm good. Just give me a second." He finally realized what had happened to Beanie, who was still moaning on the ground. "What...what the hell did you do to him?"

"Later. Not here. Do you have Crash on you?"

Ryland blinked at her. "What?"

"Crash. Please. If you have it. It's a sedative, yeah? I need to put him under." She held out a hand impatiently, then added, "Can you close the cafe, pull the blinds?"

Ryland still stared down at Beanie through the haze of what was no doubt a nasty concussion, and she snapped, "Now, Ryland!"

He fumbled through the pockets of his jacket and eventually found a spare dart round, though clearly unsure about handing it over. She could thank the concussion for his compliance there, too. Before he could change his mind, she plucked the dart from his outstretched fingers.

As he shuffled away, slightly off-kilter, she knelt by Beanie's tear-streaked face.

"What the fuck did you do to me?" he ground out through clenched teeth.

Cora didn't answer. "You're going to fall asleep now, okay? You'll feel much better when you wake up."

He didn't have a chance to argue, because she peeled back his puffer coat and pierced the dart through his shoulder. Only once his breathing evened out did Cora assess the leg, prodding the torn muscle and shattered bone. An old sports injury, maybe? Skiing, football? Hard to say, and it didn't really matter. She'd fix it, regardless. He might be a piece of shit, but she'd just needed to incapacitate him. Not cripple him for life.

Though a glance at Mrs. Moradian made her think twice about it.

Ryland closed the last of the blinds and turned to the old woman, crouching beside her to murmur something, and then disappearing into the kitchen. Cora heard a clatter, and he came back into her line of sight with a first-aid kit.

Cora got to work herself, reaching toward the magic hum of the ley line, plucking threads of power and feeding them through her, then weaving them outward again in a warm rush.

Golden energy worked its way across Beanie's lower leg, and the bone began to rebuild, cell by cell. She could feel the heat leaving her body, spilling into his, knitting together sinew and flesh. The old scar pieced itself back together, and she resisted the urge to return the bone to its original, unmarred state. This asshole could just deal with a little ache here and there when it decided to rain.

There was no avoiding the fact that Mrs. Moradian could see, and Cora hoped she would pretend to be a grateful, nonmagical civilian for Ryland's sake. Cora turned toward them, and they both stared—the old woman with admiration, and Ryland in raw, unsettled fascination.

For his part, he'd meticulously dressed the scrapes on Mrs. Moradian's elbow and knee and cracked open an instant cold pack from the kit to replace the weeping napkin full of ice. Cora beckoned him over and he came, murmuring, "She's promised to keep quiet about all this. She's just grateful we were here. I've known her for ages, and she's always as good as her word."

Cora nodded and stood, nudging Beanie with her shoe. "This one though. He needs to wake up in a bush somewhere." She wiped cold sweat from her brow. Her body temperature always dropped during a healing, but more intense wounds needed more of her own life force to mend. "He needs to think he passed out and dreamed it."

Ryland looked the man up and down. "Doubt I can move him far, heavy as he is. But I'll get him out of here at least. His buddy looked blacked-out to me, so it may not be a problem that he saw the whole thing." He grunted and lifted Beanie from beneath his armpits, slowly working his way around the counter and toward the back door. "Even if he...remembers enough...and has the balls to...report it," he said, straining, "I'm the one...they'd call to...investigate...so...we're fine."

As he propped open the back door and hefted the man outside, Cora turned back to Mrs. Moradian. "Please, come with me and let me have a look at you," Cora said, helping her to her feet.

"No, no, no." Mrs. Moradian waved Cora off. "I am myself a healer and can manage."

"But you might have a concussion. You should—"

"My dear, the hunter needs tending more than me. Go to him." Mrs. Moradian smiled, the crinkles around her eyes deepening. "I was not born yesterday. I see what you are doing, and I think to myself, 'That is a witch who has not given up.' Keep going. He is a nice man. We kill them with kindness, so they do not kill us, yes?"

A lump formed in Cora's throat, and she pulled her into a hug. "Yes," Cora said over her shoulder. "Sometimes that's all we can do."

By the time they made it up to Ryland's apartment, it was well past midnight.

His adrenaline had worn off, and Cora knew he was now keenly feeling his injuries, but he seemed determined to suffer in silence as they climbed the last flight of stairs. He didn't speak until the front door was shut and their coats were tossed on the couch, until after he'd sauntered to the sink and leaned over the running faucet.

His voice was clipped with pain and fatigue. "You going to make me ask, then? What that was?"

Leaning on the kitchen doorway, Cora weighed her response. In his eyes, she was now a liability. Maybe he wasn't losing sleep over letting her go because he knew she couldn't reanimate the dead, or accidentally burn a house down, or do any of that big, flashy magic the media had a hard-on for, and this was the nail in her coffin.

The knowledge that if healing could be done, it could also be *undone.*

It wasn't like it was widely taught. Mindy had only shown her how to do it as a way of defending herself, and even still, they never spoke of it. It went against not just her oath as a nurse, but her oath to her coven, to the magic governing the natural order of things.

Whatever lay between Ryland and her right now—a ceasefire? something else?—felt so tenuous and fragile, she knew keeping it intact depended solely on what happened next. If he couldn't trust her, there would be no coming back from this, no matter what she said to him. The only way forward here was honesty.

And...not only because she felt a twinge of regret about blindsiding him.

It was because Cora had begun to understand how earning his trust might be the difference between the survival of the Whitefall Runners and their dissolution. Knowing about Ezra had helped save the McDaniels and those other families. What if she could manage to prevent another Nell? Another Oscar? There was no telling what she could learn from Ryland if she stuck around, and she was willing to swallow her pride long enough to find out.

Ryland swished tap water in his mouth and spat, repeating until it ran clear instead of crimson. She approached the sink and kept her voice soft. "Let me help you. Please."

His head lifted. Water dripped from his beard as he caught sight of her on his periphery. "Am I gonna walk away with my legs intact?"

She sighed, fighting the pull of exhaustion on her limbs. "Come on. I can see you're in pain. Stop being such a stubborn ass and sit down."

"Only if you explain how you did it." He pushed off the counter and grabbed a cold pack from the freezer before settling on a high stool at the breakfast bar. His good eye fluttered shut as he pressed the ice into the other one.

"What do they teach you?" Cora asked. "About magic, I mean. So, I'm not rehashing what you already know."

The ice he held to his face muffled his words. "We're taught the basics. Ley lines, different schools of magic, what they do. But most of what we know comes from witches who turned before covens put safeguards in place to keep people from talking. They're not as...forthcoming as they used to be."

Cora knew. She'd taken a blood vow, too, not to expose the coven's secrets. The vows differed from region to region, in language and severity of the consequences of trying to break it. Most altas forced vows of silence only, but some altas had become particularly wary of traitors in recent years, and Cora had heard of a Minneapolis coven that compelled its witches to rip their own tongues out if they tried to reveal anything.

Cora had special sanction to reveal how her healing magic worked, because she'd had to enlist the help of a surgeon at her old hospital if she ever hoped to get away with helping people in the OR. He'd demanded to understand the process before he'd let her use it, and he hadn't been the only one since then, either.

"You won't need this yet." Cora sat on the stool next to him, gently prying the ice from his face and prodding a finger near the cut on his cheekbone. It wasn't deep, but the bruising everywhere else was settling in. She tried her hardest to separate herself from the intimacy of her hands on his skin, telling herself he was just another patient.

"Also," he said, wincing, "we know some magic needs synergy: ritual, or an object of power to focus on, like a wand or a crystal. Potions, for example, or warding stones—you need an incantation to seal the magic. Tougher for our arcanometers to detect that, you know." He opened his eye and met hers, pointedly. "They work by sensing the *movement* of magic, not the raw presence of it."

Goddess, she was mining gold without even trying. He must really be concussed. Cora opened her mouth to speak, decided how to edge around the blood vow.

"That's all pretty much true," she said, feeling the shattered ridge of his nose. "So, healing magic uses something called cell memory. When I run my magic through your body, it understands what's out of place by comparing it to what existed before. I can't fix problems you were born with, because that's all your body has ever known, but I can force an injury to remember what healthy looked like."

She did that as she spoke, weaving threads of gold across the bone and cartilage, and his swollen eye shot open when he realized what was happening.

"Jesus, are you—?"

"It's already done."

He reached up to touch the underside of his nose and traced a thumb down still-crooked line of his bridge. Cora handed him the compact mirror from her purse and said, "The opposite of that is also true. I can find old scars and make them fresh as the day you landed yourself in the ER."

He opened the mirror and turned his head from side to side. "You didn't straighten it."

"I can but didn't want to assume. You seemed to...like it the way it was."

He looked up at her in surprise, like he'd expected her to see it as something that needed fixing. The sincerity in his voice threw her off. "Thank you."

She tried to ignore the way he looked at her as she brushed a thumb along the bruise blooming across his cheekbone. She wound her threads of magic tight, tighter, cutting off the blood flow from the damaged capillaries, then released them to break down what had pooled beneath the skin. His eyebrow lifted as the mark began to fade. "Like right now, I can see exactly where you broke your left rib about two years back, or the scar on your femur from what must have been a nasty stab wound. Also, your back right molar is an implant, and your right rotator cuff is acting up again."

Ryland stilled, every muscle in his body going taut. "You can see all of that?"

"If I'm looking for it." Matter-of-fact. She couldn't give him any room to doubt her, to suspect she was holding back something that would bite

117

him in the ass later. "Your assailant down there had a bad spill years ago, some kind of sports injury. All I did was undo the hard work his leg had done to forget that."

She framed the swollen tissue of his eye with her thumb and forefinger, and he winced, shuddering when the throbbing mass receded. "*Now* you can ice this. I'm pretty drained, and I want to save what's left to make sure you can still think straight. May I?"

She stood, bracketing his temples with her palms, threading her fingers into his hair. He hesitated, then nodded and closed his eyes. His entire body tensed. Goddess, was he...*afraid* of her? She didn't realize he had it in him to be afraid of anything.

"Hey," she half-whispered, dragging her fingers over his scalp in small circles meant to calm. His eyes opened again, and he frowned at her. "I'm just going to ease the inflammation and shore up the damaged nerve cells. Get some blood flowing so your body can do the rest. No surprises."

Something like gratitude passed over his face, but he shrugged it off. "Go ahead."

As she closed her eyes and worked, she was hyper-aware of his knee pressing against her outer thigh, of his hand brushing her elbow, and the swift staccato of her heartbeat. She kept massaging his scalp, not because she needed to, but because he'd made an involuntary, satisfied little noise, and it shot through her like lightning.

When she finished and opened her eyes, he was staring at her, an expression on his face she couldn't begin to decipher. Against all reason she let her fingers wind deeper into his hair. They stood there, flushed, longer than was comfortable.

What the fuck was she *doing?*

Then they both spoke at the same time.

"Why don't you—"

"Let me just get—"

Cora slipped into the living room, where Pip was sitting patiently on the back of the couch, tucked into the folds of her coat. "Nice of you to join us." How long had he been there? He was getting better at imitating human expressions, and almost looked smug. He disappeared into her pocket as she rammed her arms angrily into the sleeves. "We'll talk later," she grumbled. Then she looked up at Ryland.

He crossed his arms and leaned back against the counter, the picture of unruffled arrogance. Like she'd imagined all of it. "Thank you."

118

She paused, hand on her purse. "What would happen to you if they found out what you did? What you're still doing?"

He remained expressionless. "You let me worry about that."

Right, because it was as easy as just turning off her worry switch.

Suddenly, Pip startled into the air, and she realized her pocket was vibrating. She pulled out her phone as Pip settled back onto her shoulder, and Quinn didn't give her a chance to say hello.

"It's Fatima," she said. "She's in labor."

"Oh." Cora's eyes widened. All her fantasies of a long, hot shower and a soft bed evaporated. "Okay. I'll head right over." Mindy was making a house call up in Santa Barbara, so Cora was on midwife duty.

"There's just one teeeeeensy, tiny problem."

Her heart sank into her stomach. "What?"

"She's hemorrhaging raw magic. And she's a chronomancer, so half the damn street is in stasis."

"She's...what?" Cora's eyes met Ryland's. He frowned at her shift in tone.

A pause, a muffled voice, and the phone was handed off. Ghislaine's stern hiss came through the other end. "You'd better have a very good reason for being where you are right now."

Cora stopped breathing. "Fucking *Quinn*—"

"Oh, no," was Ghislaine's easy reply. "She didn't need to say a thing."

Cora cast her eyes to the living room window. One step, then another, and then she was flying to the glass, cupping her eyes to reduce the glare from the overhead lights. The street was quiet, still, but that meant nothing. "You're having him watched."

"Of *course* I'm having him watched, idiot girl. Have you abandoned your senses as well as your loyalty? Using magic openly and leaving witnesses?" She said *witnesses* in a way that implied that they'd already been taken care of, and a shiver worked its way up Cora's spine.

Her hands fell and she backed away from the window, drawing the curtains in a violent jerk. Ryland was on his feet now, eyes blazing with unasked questions. She held up a finger and her voice found an edge of its own. She may not know Ghislaine well, but she knew her type—and showing her belly wasn't going to get her anywhere with this woman. "What do you want?"

"I'm abjuring the time dilations as they appear, and I've left some households frozen entirely, but this is bound to draw attention sooner or later. Prove you are worth the trouble you've caused this evening and tell your pet hunter to keep the rest of them off us."

"But I can't tell—"

Ghislaine's voice was serpentine, silky, and full of venom. "I temporarily release you from your vow of secrecy, Miss Somerville. I trust, and your *coven* trusts, that you will use that freedom wisely."

Click.

Cora stared at the screen, dread slithering into her gut as she felt her magic shift inside her to accommodate the permission Ghislaine had granted.

Stupid, she'd been so *stupid* and so wrapped up in herself not to realize they'd have someone sitting on Ryland. Did they kill the man she'd healed? Did it matter? Unless she made up for it tonight, Ghislaine would drag her in front of the other altas to answer for this. And she was wasting precious time.

She realized Ryland was in front of her, still waiting for an explanation, and she looked up at him. "I...I need a favor."

CHAPTER ELEVEN

Theo and Cora drove the thirty minutes it took to reach Redondo in loaded silence, save for the five it took to call Special Agent Mason, who had the run of the South Bay.

He had to fight to keep his voice casual, especially since Cora looked like she was going to throw up, and he really, really didn't want her to do it in his car.

"Mason? It's Ryland. Listen, a friend of mine asked me to check out his ex's place down there. He's three sheets to the wind, but I'm humoring him because he's taken the breakup pretty hard."

"No problem," Mason said. She sounded distracted, and he could hear music and laughter in the background. "Whereabouts?"

"North Lucia Avenue. If you get any calls from around there, it's probably just him again, so save yourself the trouble. The man's belligerent."

"Thanks for the heads up. Vengeful exes, man. Never have anything better to do."

That taken care of, he turned to Cora, who looked more nauseous than before. "You told them *exactly* where we'd be?" she squeaked.

He shrugged. "She needed a reason to ignore any tips from dispatch for that area. I gave her one."

She sank forward, leaning her elbows on her knees, and put her head in her hands. "I thought you said you had a plan."

"I did. That was it. Calls wind up being nothing but paranoid raving all the time." He resisted the urge to explain himself further because she was going to argue either way. This really was their best shot at keeping other TACS away because he happened to know that department had just graduated a bunch of officers from field training, and they were all out celebrating before they got official assignments next week. If anyone else got a call from dispatch, she'd be right there to tell them not to bother. Assuming they answered their phones at all.

"This is ridiculous," she said, lifting her head. "I can't believe we're letting lives ride on that."

He tried to unclench his jaw, but annoyance was winning. "And you asked me to help you because you had a better idea?"

"There has to be one! We should—"

Theo yanked the wheel and pulled over, tires screeching. He leaned across the center console, and she shrank away from him, eyes wide. "We? No, no. You came to *me*, remember? You wanted my help. You don't get to then dictate what form it takes. You either trust me to do this my way, or you're on your own." He hadn't felt the anger sneak up on him, but he was practically vibrating with it now. She'd bet he wouldn't refuse her after she'd healed him, and she'd taken advantage of that.

The worst part was he knew, in his gut, that half his anger was turned inward. He hated that he *wanted* to protect her. The why of it didn't matter—she wasn't likely to give up on this woman no matter what he told her to do. As long as that patient was vulnerable, Cora would be. And damn it, he hadn't come this far with her just to let her get arrested again.

So, he'd help her alright, but he didn't have to be happy about it.

Cora stared, and only nodded in response.

Looking back to the road, he eased away from the curb, following the traffic downhill and into the thickening marine layer. They leaned into a turn and rumbled down a quieter street, passing the tame squares of yard and single-family residences of suburbanite clans. Here was a neighborhood that tucked in at a reasonable hour and began its morning with a friendly wave across the lawn.

He couldn't imagine anything worse.

Pulling onto N Lucia, a surge of energy prickled over his amygdala, and he was instantly on alert. Chronomancy was one of the rarer schools of magic, and he'd only come across it twice. From what he understood, witches couldn't time travel per se, instead shifting the passing of time within a finite bubble, called a dilation field.

As the car slowed, his brain caught up with his eyes, and he began to understand what he was seeing.

Many of the houses were dark—it was close to 2 a.m., after all—but an orange cat had paused mid-jump between a hedgerow and the eaves of a roof, suspended in midair. Further down, the leaves of a sprawling tree rusted into reds and yellows, then browned and dropped, then reversed course back to spring flowers: an entire season passing and rewinding, over and over again, in the space of seconds. The fog coming off the sea had frozen around several bungalows, while the rest of the mist appeared to disperse in random patches where time was ticking faster. It felt like a fever dream.

In the middle of the street stood a tiny figure, and as they approached, Theo realized she wasn't frozen—her arms were raised, and she was holding back the temporal anomalies on either side, allowing them to drive through unaffected. "That's Ghislaine," Cora murmured. "She's an alta. Abjurer, telekinetic, leyweaver."

Leyweaver.

He hadn't heard that term since the Academy. He'd never encountered one, either, or at least one he'd known about. Leyweaving was the hardest kind of magic—threading raw power directly from the ley lines, making it possible for a witch to learn magic they hadn't inherited an affinity for. Most witches could do it to some degree, a few cantrips at best, but to call yourself a leyweaver meant something.

That said all he needed to know about how dangerous she was. He certainly wouldn't have made the assumption from her height (or lack of), her wide-eyed, bespectacled gaze, and the loud zebra-pattered blazer beneath a veritable scarf of gaudy necklaces weighing more than she did. She lowered her arms and folded them.

"Stay in the car for a minute," Cora said. Theo opened his mouth to protest, but she shot him a withering look.

Admittedly, he wasn't keen on introducing himself anyway.

He read determination in the set of her shoulders as she walked through the headlights of the idling car and approached Ghislaine. They seemed to be arguing, and Cora gestured back at him a few times. Ghislaine stood preternaturally still, not giving an inch. Finally, she dipped her chin.

Cora turned and motioned for him to come. He killed the engine and got out.

Closer now, Theo could see streaks of silver in the short black bob cut blunt across Ghislaine's forehead, and opalescent zebras weighing down her earlobes. She appraised him slowly, and Theo wasn't sure how she managed to look down her nose at him from that height. "You're the hunter."

Years of cigarettes had given her faint French accent a rusty tenor, and her eyes held the intensity of an apex predator who'd just caught sight of their next meal. "TAC Specialist," he corrected her uselessly, and then as an afterthought, "Ma'am."

Her eyebrows disappeared under her bangs. "Only you would manage to bag the hunter with *manners*, darling."

Before he could clarify he'd been "bagged" by no one, Cora grabbed his hand and led him across the street. "Come on, before she changes her mind."

They followed the stone path to the front door of the tiny stucco cottage. It wasn't as nice as some of the others on this block, and the neighborhood was clearly being built up around it, but it had its own kind of dilapidated-beach-shack charm, with a garden to boot. Cora raised her fist to knock, but the door opened before she brought her knuckles to it.

A woman Cora's age stood before them, tall enough to look Theo in the eyes. Her black hair had been pulled into buns on either side of her head, and she wore a cropped t-shirt with rhinestone rainbows directly over each breast. "No," was all she said, and he realized her irises were...pink?

"Quinn—" Cora began.

"No."

"Quinn!"

"No! He is not coming in here." Then she folded her arms. And squinted. "Wait. Don't I know you?"

Theo peered back. He didn't think he'd seen her before, but...

Quinn blinked. "Oh shit, I remember you. Broody Broodsalot...from the night you...Goddess, that was *the* night, wasn't it?"

"What was what night?" Cora glanced from one to the other.

"Your hair was different," Theo said realization dawning. It had been short and pink. "You remember that? I didn't say a word to you."

"I remember people who tip fifty dollars on a twenty-dollar tab."

124

He grunted. "I was glad you left me alone."

"I should have pushed you off the roof instead." Quinn turned to Cora, hugging herself tighter. "He came to my bar the same night he kidnapped you. Or had you forgotten he, oh, I don't know, *kidnapped* you?"

Cora cut in. "Now wait a second—"

"That's the only logical reason I can give for why you'd pull up here, in his fucking car. I thought you were just going to get Pip—"

"Quinn—"

"Because surely," Quinn continued, eyes flashing with hurt, "you'd have confided in me if there was any other reason for the two of you to—"

From somewhere behind Quinn, a woman's cry pierced the air, cresting along with the waves of magic crawling over Theo's skin. Suppressing a shiver, he tensed, and Cora shoved past them both with an impatient noise. "I don't have time for this. From either of you. Quinn, if Ghislaine's stuck doing damage control outside, I need your help. How many centimeters dilated?"

Quinn looked from Cora, who was setting the kettle to boil in the kitchen, to Theo on the doorstep, back to Cora. "Just because we're not talking about this now doesn't mean you're not going to explain yourself—and him—later."

"*Quinn!*"

"Nine and a half? I think? I only watched a video on how to measure it so I'm not—" the door slammed in Theo's face, muffling the rest. The lock clicked.

He stared at the blue wood an inch from his nose. Could've gone better, could've gone worse. He was the one who'd insisted on coming in case someone else showed up, so he'd just have to deal with it.

As he collapsed into one of the Adirondack chairs on the front patio, something warm tapped the crown of his head. Theo didn't even blink this time—Pip drooped down the side of his head like a cracked egg, solidifying on his shoulder and nuzzling his ear.

Knowing Theo hated it only encouraged Pip further, so he tried his damnedest not to react. Near as he could figure, that's what Pip was after, anyway—another chance to observe him, like Cora had explained. The less interesting he was, the more likely Pip was to leave him alone.

Or so he told himself.

Pip slunk to Theo's other shoulder and reached a tiny, jellylike appendage out to touch his beard—a mission quickly aborted after a dose of withering side-eye—then dribbled down into Theo's coat pocket.

Behind Ghislaine's misty silhouette under the streetlamps, the shifting tree was hypnotic, going from season to season and back again. It was the standout aberration of the bunch because Ghislaine had easily negated other time rifts that had opened while they'd been arguing on the porch. No, he figured that tree was there for her. He'd bet she hadn't touched it yet because if she was going to play temporal whack-a-mole all night, she'd damn well have something pretty to look at.

Watching that tree on loop, Theo knew sitting down had been a mistake. By the time the thought was fully-formed in his head, though, he was already drifting off.

A while later, he became aware of a heavy blanket draped across his lap. It was still dark out, no sliver of pre-dawn light in the sky, so he mustn't have slept long.

Ghislaine held a go-cup of some hot beverage but was still more or less where she'd been before. The tree sat permanently in autumn now, like the rest of them, without any evidence it had ever looked otherwise. "I offered her a camping chair," Cora said from behind him. "But she wasn't interested."

Theo turned to where Cora stood in the open doorway, her eyes bloodshot. She'd pulled her long hair into a haphazard knot at the crown of her head. A few limp curls escaped to frame her face, and she'd stripped down to a white tank top that showed off her toned, freckled arms and a loose-fitting pair of jeans. She was also barefoot. Her toenails were painted pink. Why was that so disarming?

A bead of sweat trickled down her neck, and he followed it past her collarbone, down, down until she cleared her throat. "You're staring," she said flatly, taking a sip from the steaming mug in her hand.

"Nobody's driven down this street?" he asked, as if that was the most burning question on his mind.

"It's..." Cora looked at her phone. "Four in the morning. But she also placed some deterrent wards at both ends of the block."

"She's been at it for hours."

"She's not an alta for nothing. It helps that some of these houses are in stasis, though. Each time a rift opens, she decides what's worth closing.

126

Easier to keep a finger on the pause button and focus her energy on things that could actually cause harm."

"I meant the labor. That's a long time to expend magic like this."

Cora nodded, sipping. "It's mostly tapered off, but we're keeping watch just in case."

"How are things going in there?" He jerked his chin towards the house behind her.

"Won't be long now. Quinn's got her for a few minutes. I needed some air." She leaned down, crouching by the arm of his chair to peer at his cheekbone. Only the earthy base notes of her perfume remained, but it still brought him back to the surf shop when he'd first smelled it, and the memory dug into his chest. "I never did get around to this cut here."

He snatched her wrist as she lifted her hand to examine it. "You never quit, do you?"

Her cheeks flushed at the contact—or maybe just from how warm the house had been. "It'll scar. I don't have magic to spare right now anyway, but at least let me Steri-strip it."

Some people collected antiques; he collected visible imperfections that said *don't fuck with me*. If it scarred, all the better. "It's fine. You, however, are not."

"I've worked nights before," she said, but her exhaustion was only emphasized in the unflattering porch light. She finally pried her wrist from his grasp. It didn't escape Theo's notice that she let him hold it longer than necessary.

She had a quiet strength about her, even in this vulnerable moment—what was happening around them didn't matter. It came from letting go of the things she couldn't control, and focusing everything on what she could: bringing this baby into the world.

He understood that kind of calm all too well. He'd relied on it to get him through those first few years with ACE, accepting the fact that they owned him, giving up his dreams of civilian life so he might be able to concentrate on those little moments where he *could* affect change. Like he'd done with Antoine in Koreatown. Like he'd done with so many others he could never tell her about.

"Have you eaten?" he asked. "Besides the halva."

Cora blinked. Theo had even surprised himself with the question. It was such a simple way to care about someone, asking if they'd eaten, but usually it had been Cora who'd asked him. She knew he'd preferred her mother's cooking to his mom's affinity for takeout after working late.

The meaning of that question wasn't lost on Cora, either, if the conflict in her eyes was anything to judge by. "I had some cereal."

He was on his feet before he could talk himself out of it, folding the blanket. Cora stood too, frowning. "What are you doing?"

Fuck if I know. "Quinn might want to geld me, but if you haven't eaten then I'm willing to bet she hasn't either." He tossed the blanket on the chair and stepped past Cora into the house, beelining for the kitchen. "And this might just win me enough points to stay in the warm."

Cora followed him inside and shut the door as a low moan sounded from one of the bedrooms down the hall. He could hear Quinn's voice, muffled, and another man's. Every hair on Theo's arms stood at attention while the wave of magic washed over him, and he shifted uncomfortably.

"You're going to cook at four in the morning?" she asked, watching him open cupboards indiscriminately and take stock of what was in them.

"It's not entirely selfless." His own stomach was beginning to protest, and he wouldn't mind having something to do. The fridge had the basics: eggs, butter, some vegetables. "What would you say to an omelet?"

Cora opened her mouth to respond, but he'd stunned her into silence. She tried again. "I'd say...Thank you. For all of this. I'd say it's more than I deserve from you. You were right, earlier, what you said about being used. It wasn't fair of me to put you in that position."

"I chose to come," he reminded her. It hadn't been much of a choice, but he'd made it all the same. And the weight of that settled in his chest, unfurled a root. He tried not to think too hard about what it might mean.

Quinn's voice carried across the room. "What is he doing in here?" she asked, folding her arms and leaning against the mouth of the hallway.

Ignoring her question, he held up a block of cheddar. "Cheese or no cheese?"

"What?" Quinn stared at him, then the carton of eggs on the counter, and the pat of butter already sitting in the pan on the stove. It took as long for the butter to melt as it did for her to put together a coherent response.

"Cheese," she said angrily, and disappeared back down the hall.

He grinned at Cora and began grating.

———— ∽ ————

Don't push during this contraction, okay?" Cora said from behind Fatima, who was crouching on all fours in front of the bed. Fatima gripped the edge of the duvet as her next contraction took her, releasing a soft keening sound to get through it. "Baby's crowning, but you need to breathe, we don't want to go too fast. Wait until the next contraction comes...you're doing so well..."

John stood next to the bed, sweating as if he was the one giving birth. He looked like he might send the omelet Ryland had made him right back up the way it'd come.

She still couldn't believe he'd cooked for everyone but was too grateful to consider it overstepping. It had been exactly what she'd needed to get through this last hour, and there was no denying Quinn's mood had improved—although she'd made it clear Cora was still on thin ice.

They'd been able to take a few breaks and talk some, but it was clear Quinn didn't just feel sidelined—she was actually *jealous*. As if this friendship from Cora's past might threaten theirs. And that hurt ran deeper than either of them was willing to dig right now, so they let it be, instead focusing on helping Fatima through the home stretch.

"This is the one, okay?" Cora said, rubbing Fatima's back. "You can do this...ready, and push!"

The noise Fatima made began as a soft trill and rose into a howl of anguish. Cora motioned at John to crouch alongside her on the waterproof mat they'd laid down, and she held his hands outward to catch baby Ronan as he came out.

John breathed a sound of joy and relief, and all around them, the thick bubble of Ghislaine's recanting field popped—she could feel the very second that time resumed in all the households next door.

They'd done it. They'd gotten through the night. And Ryland had helped make it possible.

Fatima sat back on her heels and took the bundle John handed her, crying together with the infant, and Cora blinked back a few tears of her own. Nursing was unpredictable, and even with magic she'd still had ER patients she couldn't save, but delivering babies was something she'd always love. Something that filled her heart with hope, no matter what she'd endured.

That Ronan was born a free witch instead of in a prison camp somewhere meant even more.

A short while later, after everyone had cleaned up and Quinn had collapsed facedown on the living room couch, Cora found Ryland and Pip back on the front porch.

Ryland's cigarette glowed in the predawn light, and Pip watched the smoke curl upwards in fascination. She sank into the chair beside him, grabbing the blanket he'd set aside earlier, and they sat in silence like that for a few minutes. Birds were beginning to awaken, and the sprinklers had ticked on across the street.

It was so...peaceful. *She* felt peaceful. Maybe that was because she didn't have the energy to be anything else.

"I didn't know you smoked," she said, pulling her knees to her chest.

"I quit."

"I can see that."

"Over two years ago."

"Mm-hmm." She played with a loose strand of hair. "Do you remember when Sebastian stole a cigarette from the neighbor kid and hid it in the shoebox under his bed that he was *so sure* mom didn't know about?"

He ground the stub of cigarette under his shoe and raised his eyebrows. "I gave him his first Playboy to stash in there."

She elbowed him. "I'd wondered where he found that!"

"And your mom waited, didn't she? To say anything?"

"She did!" Cora laughed. It felt good to laugh with him. "She waited until the day he tried to smoke it in the backyard. She watched from the sliding door while he choked on it then threw up in the bushes, and she goes, 'Had enough?'"

Ryland grinned, shaking his head. "She always had a way about her."

And then her laughter died abruptly, as if all the air in her lungs had gone. She didn't want to ask, didn't want to know, and yet it was the only thing she'd ever wanted to know. It hummed in her gut, begging for an answer she wasn't sure he could give her.

He turned to her, and she couldn't keep it in. "You'd tell me if you knew anything, right?"

Surprise flickered across his face. "About...?"

"About them." Her throat constricted. "About what happened to them."

Ryland stilled. "You thought I'd been keeping it from you this whole time?"

"Honestly, how should I know?"

He got to his feet, put some distance between them. "Maybe the fact that I'm here, with you, with my ass on the line might give you a clue."

"Why *did* you come?" she asked, half to wind him up, half out of genuine curiosity.

"You're...Jesus, you're unbelievable." He paced away from her, then spun back around, like he couldn't decide where he wanted to be. "It's because despite all my best efforts not to, I give a shit about you." He stepped closer to her and grabbed her shoulders, pulled her to her feet. "I've accepted that you used me tonight. I'm not an idiot. But don't insult me even more by acting like I'm some kind of monster. Like I could stand here and look you in the face and not tell you what I knew."

Relief flooded her, then guilt, then another wave of exhaustion as her rigid shoulders went slack. He didn't deserve this, and she was letting weariness unravel her by the minute. She closed her eyes and leaned forward, deflated, resting her forehead on his chest.

He tensed, but then his grip on her shoulders softened, and she felt his arms tentatively pull her closer. She breathed him in, then out.

"I'm sorry," she sighed into his coat. "I'm so sorry. I don't know what to think, about any of this." She didn't want to trust him, but every instinct in her body rebelled against that logic. Her arms snaked around his waist, and he stroked her back, her hair. The soft weight of his hands on her bare shoulders had her shivering, but he mistook it for cold and grabbed the blanket she held, wrapping it around them both.

Goddess, it felt good to just pause here, to let him stand between her and the rest of the world.

"I'm so tired," she said. "I'm tired of being angry all the time. And I'm tired of not having answers, or closure. If they're dead..." she trailed off. "But if they're not, I could..."

He leaned back and stared down at her. "What, find them?"

She looked up. They were so close, their breath mingled in a single, visible cloud. "No...I don't know. Maybe."

"You can't be serious." Irritation crept into those words, low and thick, mixed with something else she couldn't name.

"Why not?" She couldn't keep the defeat from her voice. "Seb's my twin, my other half. He was your friend. Always brave to a fault, like...like he leeched it from me in the womb. I know he'd have figured something out by now."

"You don't have to be him, Cor."

131

"He'd do it for me. I know he would."

"Do what?" Ryland asked. "Even if you knew where they were, it would only drive you crazy."

She exhaled, confident that if he let her go her knees would simply buckle beneath her. He had a point. There was only one way into those places, and as far as she knew, nobody had ever found a way out. "Maybe."

But as she let him hold her, a small, unwelcome voice in the back of her mind whispered something that would replay in her head later that night, and the next, and the next.

What if, after all this time, she *could* find a way to save them?

CHAPTER TWELVE

Cora and Mindy puttered down the highway, away from the low-hanging desert sun. They'd taken Mindy's SUV because Lucy needed an oil change soon, but really, who was Cora fooling? The car wasn't long for this world either way.

GPS gave them a couple of miles to Joshua Tree, where their coven was gathering to celebrate Samhain. Cora always met it with some measure of trepidation. Not because of what the holiday represented—the thinning veil between the worlds of the living and the dead—but because of the people she was afraid to encounter each year.

With no other way to contact her family, the telltale silence was cold comfort, but still better than knowing nothing at all.

Before they'd disappeared, she'd spent each Samhain wondering if she'd meet her father for the first time—that she could remember, anyway. He'd been gone by the time she and Sebastian were three. Her mother hadn't talked about him. Cora knew she'd regretted marrying so young, but it had been too painful to tell her kids about the circumstances that led to him leaving.

He'd been a witch, though. That much she knew. Probably a healer, if Mindy's own magic was anything to go by.

And her mother had met Mindy first, then started crushing on the older brother, no matter how many times Mindy warned her away. But would Cora really look for Arthur Somerville if she knew anything else about him? She wasn't sure. Both her mother and Mindy were above poisoning the kids against a man they had no memory of, but that didn't mean Cora couldn't resent him for making Robyn Kearney raise two young children alone.

Rocky desert hills drifted past and revealed the edge of town, such as it was, nestled in the valley below. The long drive had finally forced the two of them to address both elephants in the room—the night Cora had fallen asleep outside Harry's, and the night of Ronan's birth.

She'd avoided her aunt successfully since then, a thought which only dredged up more guilt.

Cora was supposed to have come back to LA for her, to be *there* for her, and instead, she was anywhere but. Out getting herself kidnapped, looking for drugs, using magic where she shouldn't. She'd thought it would be better for Mindy not to know, not to worry, but wasn't that exactly what she'd been pissed at Mindy for doing with the news about Nell?

"I've been an asshole, Min. I'm sorry. I haven't...felt like myself lately, and I shouldn't have made that your problem."

Mindy wasn't angry, but the sadness in her eyes made Cora wish for it. "I've treated a lot of addicts in my day. I've learned not to take it personally."

Goddess, she knew she deserved it, but it didn't make it any easier to hear. "I'm not trying to make excuses for myself. Amends aren't something I can just make once and then forget about. I promised you a long time ago that I'd stop cutting you out."

And then she gave voice to the one thing they both had never admitted aloud. She'd barely admitted it to herself. "I wanted to move back so I could work on rebuilding our trust. But I told myself it was Oscar because I wouldn't have had the courage to face you otherwise. I needed a fire lit under my ass, and I'm sorry that that's what it took."

Mindy's long-suffering sigh said enough. Her shoulders slumped, and the shadows under her eyes seemed deeper in the late afternoon light. Cora had done this to her, and she hated herself for it. Finally, Mindy said, "Ryland's a trigger for you, sweetie. Everything else aside."

"I know." Cora had known it the second she drove away from him at the Manhattan Pier, as soon as she made the turn that would take her to Harry's instead of home. "But so is the whole damn Westside. I can't run from every trigger."

"You don't have to make it harder on yourself, though."

"That's the thing," she said, watching clusters of cacti fly past her window. "Every time I've relapsed, it's been loneliness. Yes, guilt. Yes, fear, but always on top of that is this crushing sense of 'nobody sees me.' And there are so many reasons why he and I shouldn't build this bridge, but one thing he's always been able to do is *see* me."

A fact that both comforted and enraged her.

She wanted someone to see her as desperately as she hated knowing anybody could; knowing she could be laid bare at all.

Before him, especially.

Mindy's grip on the steering wheel slackened. She sounded so damn resigned, and Cora couldn't blame her. Mindy had long ago realized her company wasn't enough on its own, and their argument about that had taken a while to come back from. An old wound that was still healing.

"A lot has changed since you knew one another," was all she said.

Cora chewed on the inside of her cheek. "Exactly. A lot has changed. And while I love you both so much, neither you nor Quinn can really understand what it was like growing up together."

No matter how badly Mindy wanted to that was something nobody else could touch. "If I can forgive him, if we can be friends again, I feel like I have the chance to..." Cora's voice broke. "To take it back. To do it over. I don't know."

"To own what they took," Mindy said softly, "and prove it doesn't own you."

Cora didn't trust herself to speak.

"Well, let me just say this." Mindy took a swig from the tall can of iced tea in the center console, as if steeling herself. A little fire had come back into her eyes, and it was a relief to know she hadn't completely given up. "I'm not your mother, and you're a grown ass-adult, so salt my advice to taste. But you need to understand Teddy is also a grown-ass adult. He is not simply a vestige of your childhood." When Mindy got deadly serious, the Georgia in her came out. "You might think you can leave it there, but ignorance does you no favors right now. You take my meaning?"

Cora's face heated. More than shame, there was a spark of anger in there, too. That anyone could easily boil down the complexities of their friendship, past and future, to that single truth—to the way his arms had felt around her. "We were only ever friends. I'm not dumb enough to open that can of worms."

Liar.

"Men have made me plenty dumb; I tell you what." The corner of Mindy's mouth twitched as the car began to slow. "You either go in with both eyes wide open and both feet firmly on the ground, or you're going to regret everything you do from here on out. You owe yourself that. Because anything less is gonna send you into a spiral of self-destruction when it inevitably ends badly, assuming you're still alive to do it."

Her eyes swam above that grim smile. "You've come so far, baby girl. I've seen you drag yourself out of dark places I know you don't want to revisit. Don't let that little voice in your head convince you any different."

As she set the car into four-wheel drive, Cora reached over to squeeze her hand.

They began rumbling down the dirt path into the hills, and an inkling of dread took root in her solar plexus, like bad heartburn. She couldn't promise Mindy that she knew what allowing herself to trust Ryland again would mean.

And she wasn't sure she wanted to know.

Their destination was a campground only by the loosest definition of the word. It had more in common with the yurt cities of Coachella: clusters of massive white canopies winged outward from a central bonfire pit, which, during the daytime, would sit in the shadow of the massive rocky outcropping that arced around them on three sides. That outcropping gave the site of power its name: Crescent Vale. Nestled here, they'd be shielded from view, but more important were the massive warding stones anchored within the hills themselves.

Witches had come here for centuries, and the warding stones were older than anyone alive could guess. To be allowed through, you had to feed the rock a bit of magic, so they were strengthened by the collective power of those who made the pilgrimage.

Cora couldn't see any of this yet, though she knew it was there. As they pulled up to the hill, sand crunching beneath the wheels of the car, their headlights found a boulder shaped vaguely like a squatting cat. It stood sentinel at the mouth of the tiny vale, which lay empty and silent beyond the wind whistling through.

A blast of brisk, dry air slapped Cora in the face as she shut the car door. She pulled her windbreaker tighter around herself and trudged up to the boulder-cat, which she'd nicknamed Salem as a kid. Their family had come up every year together, and then Cora and Mindy had every year since. It was nice to be able to bring Pip this time, and she sensed he was enjoying the view from his current perch atop her head.

Mindy left the car running and came around the other side, placing a hand on where Salem's head would be, and Cora reached over to his back.

Magic threaded through her in an instant, flossing through her insides with a quick jerk, and she imagined this was how it felt to be a cog in a sewing machine. She hadn't even reached for the ley line, but didn't need to—at this nexus point, it stretched up through the earth and fountained through everything, like a tap punched directly through the earth's crust.

Ley lines converged and branched off without much rhyme or reason, and many of them hadn't been mapped, but you could often follow them through history. Magic wielders had never strayed far from them, but people without magic still tended to settle along the main currents without knowing why, and so cities were built up around them as time passed. And since magic was drawn to magic, sometimes a new current would unfurl towards an old one, creating a new nexus point that amplified the magic even more.

It had diminishing returns, though. The larger the crossroads, the harder the magic was to contain. The veils between realms thinned, and if you spent more than a few months here, you could easily forget yourself. Forget what time was. Forget what it meant to be human.

Sites of power like this one were rare and ancient and sacred, a convergence of as many as twenty ley lines. Possibly more. The warding stones in the hillside weren't just there to keep unwelcome visitors out—they were there to keep everything else *in*.

Just as abruptly as Cora's magic had been siphoned from her, it was done. She stumbled back a step, her vision blurring and sharpening, and everything they hadn't been seeing and feeling slammed into them both all at once.

The thrumming power of those hills found an answering echo in Cora's bones. The sounds and smells of camp, the music and laughter and chaos, the wood smoke and roasting food, all of it came into sharp focus as the tents appeared before them.

There might have been hundreds of witches there, though not all of them were from Cora's coven—some had likely traveled from chapters in San Diego, Santa Clarita, San Bernadino. Theirs was an easy alliance, with many families spread between several, but the Los Angeles altas generally ran the show when they all came together.

"You go on ahead and find Quinn," Mindy said, shaking off the sensory overload. "I'll pull around and park."

Pip was practically buzzing as Cora wandered into camp, overnight bag slung over her shoulder. It wasn't fully dark yet, but the central bonfire looked like it had been going for some time. Groups of kids clustered here and there, playing games or darting after clusters of sprites that had spilled through the veil to play. Smaller fire pits created gathering places between groups of tents to grill over or meditate around.

A blush crept across the twilit skies above them, pink and orange and purple, mingling with the desert haze to form a murky gradient. They'd be able to see the stars clearly later, and a few people had set up telescopes.

But the most urgent pull came from beneath her feet. Anchoring everything was that primordial hum in her bones, her lungs, like being cradled in the very palm of creation itself.

She stopped and listened. The heartbeat of the earth. She could feel it here, the way she used to be able to with Sebastian, and it was like popping her ears after a bad cold. The deluge of magic filled her to overflowing, and with it, every bit of the land around her spoke in a language she finally let herself hear.

The ancient rocks whose stories had been shaped by wind and sand, the warrens carved by scorpions, the massive networks of root systems beneath the Joshua trees and Creosote bushes reaching for water. Creatures who burrowed to escape the heat of the day were beginning to stir the soil, and cacti were slowly opening their pores to the cool night air. Some plants wished openly for moisture, but these were a hardy bunch, and prideful too—most were quiet, stoic. Deliberate and conservative in their growth. They were true survivors.

She'd cut herself off from all of this years ago, because it hurt too much. Reminded her too much of Sebastian, and her mother's garden. Here, she didn't have a choice but to feel it.

Pip dribbled down her shoulder and bounced away as a trio of sprites sparkled past, falling in with them. Did sprites have families? Pip seemed more solitary, preferring the company of humans, but she didn't know much about the ones who stayed in the spirit realm.

Even leywalkers' accounts left a lot to be desired, but that was because passing between realms did a number on the mortal brain.

Few could physically do that kind of magic, and fewer wanted to.

Further into camp, Cora spotted Quinn on a folding lounger next to a smaller fire pit, and Harry next to her, sharing a blunt. Quinn's eyes were ice blue today, the same color as the streak in Harry's undercut, and her ponytail was a soft lilac. She laughed as she directed the breeze to morph his smoke ring into a phallic shape. Cora was surprised to feel a pang of something like jealousy at how easily they'd struck up a friendship, but quickly squashed it. She didn't need more reasons to feel alienated from Quinn today.

"Hey." Cora dropped her bag next to a camping chair. "Mind if I...?"

Quinn didn't immediately answer, just stared at Cora dreamily, and the size of her pupils said that blunt held more than weed.

"If you're okay to be around it, sugar," said Harry, his voice slow and thick as smoke curled from his nose.

A heady petrichor hit her, one she recognized as Nova. That hallucinogen never had any particular draw for her, not after a bad trip in sophomore year, but she hardly wanted to be the sober one in this trio. She turned, glancing back in the direction of Mindy's car. "It's fine. I'll leave you guys to it."

"Wait." Quinn eased off the lounger, like a fawn testing her legs for the first time. Cora raised an eyebrow as she sauntered forward with a giggle, placing delicate hands on either side of Cora's face.

"I finally get it," Quinn breathed with conviction, running her fingers up Cora's temples and into her hair. "We're all afraid of *connecting*. You know?"

Quinn's irises transformed again in the fading light, swirls of yellow bleeding into the blue, a reminder of the Great Horned Owl she preferred to shift into. Shifters often chose forms their other magic could support, so as an aeromancer, wings made the most sense—but it had more to do with that freedom only the sky could give her.

She'd probably take flight later tonight. All the magic pouring through them practically guaranteed it.

139

Quinn continued with a soporific, musical whisper. "We shouldn't be. We're all part of something *amazing*." She sighed skyward, closing her eyes. "There must be a reason your paths crossed again."

Cora had been ready to smile and nod with polite dismissal, but those words rooted her to the spot. She was talking about Ryland.

Quinn kept going, her hands falling to Cora's shoulders, her long-lashed eyelids fluttering open again. She swayed to music only she could hear. "I am a short burst of consciousness, the tapestry of the universe understanding itself. Do you know what that *means?*"

"I'm sure you'll tell me."

"It means *we* teach *it!*" Quinn pulled back, flinging her arms wide, spinning in a slow circle. "And I want it to understand how much I love you. I can't do that if we hurt each other." She frowned and pointed a finger at Cora. "I don't want to teach it the wrong things."

"Is this...are you forgiving me for the other night?" Cora glanced at Harry uselessly, as if he could answer for her. His eyes were half-open, staring into the small fire, and he was a million miles away.

"I *get* it," Quinn repeated. "Every connection has purpose. Every thread. That's what the goddess Leyra taught, right?" Quinn fell back into the lounger and smiled up at the few stars beginning to blink into the sky. "We have to reach for each other, or we *forget*."

Boots crunched through the dirt behind Cora, and Mindy's voice sounded over her shoulder. "What on the Goddess's green earth has that girl been smoking?"

Cora turned, unable to bite back her laughter any longer. "Nova."

"That'll do it, alright."

"Here, let me take that." Cora reached for Mindy's bag and picked up the one she'd set down, leading them both toward a nearby yurt. "I hope she remembers this in the morning, because it's the easiest hatchet we've ever buried."

"What'd you go and piss her off about?" Mindy ducked into the tent behind her. It was the size of a studio apartment, much larger inside than out, with a queen-sized bed, a sofa, plus a kitchenette with a mini fridge and a hot plate, both of which were enchanted to work without electricity.

"Same as you. Not being honest about Ryland. How much did this reservation cost, Min?"

"Don't change the subject." She lowered her voice a tick and winked. "But I got upgraded from last year because I helped one of the Samhain committee members after a botched nose job."

Cora snorted. "Aren't you full of surprises."

"And aren't you reaping the benefits? Hush and come along, we can unpack this later. I've got a few things Helena asked me to bring for her."

Cora did as she asked, following Mindy over the aisle of wood planks that stretched from the mouth of the vale to the center of its arc. Paper lanterns floated overhead, winking on as the last of the light left the sky, and drifted in clusters over the flat stone dais between the altas' tents.

An old altar sat in the middle, a smooth block of stone jutting out at waist height, where they'd once performed sacrifices in centuries past. Now it was used to burn incense and lay flowers, food, and other offerings for the restless spirits joining them.

Ghislaine was easiest to spot, waltzing. Ghislaine never walked. She floated, strutted, or waltzed—from person to person on impossibly tiny feet. Today they were stuffed into orange pumps matching the ornate pumpkin fascinator perched on her head. Large spider earrings weighed down her earlobes, and her vest of bright skull prints screamed over top of a shapeless black shift.

"My dears!" she sang at Mindy and Cora, arms wide. "Happy New Year!"

"Happy New Year," Mindy said, kissing the alta's cheek. "Great turnout despite everything, don't you think?"

"I was just chatting with our head of security." Ghislaine kissed Cora's cheek as well, like she hadn't threatened to drag her in front of the council the last time they'd interacted. "We've placed more wards a kilometer out in every direction, but even so, there is no safer place to be. I can't imagine anyone moving against a gathering this size in a place this powerful. Utter madness."

Her laugh raised the hairs on Cora's arms.

Behind Ghislaine, a dark-skinned woman with a curtain of tight, dark curls emerged from one of the tents. She was impeccably dressed, wearing her waxed canvas jacket, jeans, and lace-up leather boots like most folks would wear a designer suit.

But that smile of hers made every other detail fall away. It would have been warm on anyone else, but paired with the predatory gleam in her eye, her ramrod straight posture...Cora had the distinct feeling of her skull being cracked open and picked through, all of her dreams and fears laid bare at this woman's feet. What's more, she *wanted* to give those things to her.

"Samhain blessings to you. I wondered when we might meet." She looked Cora up and down, appraising, and Cora became self-conscious of the baby hairs escaping her loose French braid, of the old flannel and beat-up hiking boots she'd chosen to wear. "I'm Alta Helena."

Neuromancer, Cora realized too late.

She reeled backward in her mind, slapping the long-fingered hand that reached and sifted through the most secret parts of her. Alta or not, it was incredibly rude, and she shot Helena a glare that said as much.

Helena barked a laugh. "Just checking, my dear."

So *this* was her. Most of what Cora knew about Helena, she'd heard through Harry, who idolized and feared her with equal measure. Easy to see why, especially here. Ghislaine's presence dominated every space she occupied, but Helena's stance was a pointed rebuttal. It said *This dais isn't big enough for the two of us.*

It wasn't a question of being brave or stupid. She was just *sure*, and that was that.

Cora turned her glare to Ghislaine. "Still questioning my loyalty, are we?"

"Cora," Mindy hissed, elbowing her.

But Helena's smile only widened. "My little birds have many interesting things to say about you."

Cora swallowed. As the coven's spymaster, Helena no doubt knew everything there was to know about Ryland. And then some. Responding felt distinctly like walking into a trap, so she remained silent.

"Your hunter has certainly made an impression," Helena said. "I trust he'll continue to be...useful."

Just like that, the heat rising in Cora's face flowed out of it, and a tiny fist of nausea shoved its way into her diaphragm. Threats were already on the table, then. "He will be," she parried back, her voice miraculously steady.

She hadn't anticipated the tiny ember of indignation flaring to life in her chest, the urge to get defensive on Ryland's behalf. It grated even as she reminded herself what he was, who he worked for.

No part of her felt settled when it came to him, and she hated it.

"Oh, here you go!" Mindy said quickly, handing over a grocery bag full of herbs. "Just cut from my garden this morning. The ones I said I'd bring." She prattled on about how well the arrowroot had propagated, and how potent the lavender was, and some other things in a bid to diffuse the tension, but Cora wasn't really listening as she scanned the gathering crowd for Quinn and Harry. Anyone who could feasibly save her. Groups would begin their meditations soon, but she didn't expect to see those two among them.

When Mindy and Cora finally descended the dais together, Helena's gaze like a flame at their backs, Cora whispered, "You wanna tell me what that was?"

"I was afraid of this," Mindy grumbled.

"They can't seriously want—"

"They want whatever they can get away with having. They're altas, hon. You can't dangle an asset like Teddy in front of 'em without some consequences."

Cora gritted her teeth. "I didn't *dangle* him. I went by his place to get Pip back, and then everything happened, and Ghislaine threatened me—"

"Caving to her was your first mistake. If you wanted to keep him out of it, you should've sucked it up and let her drag you in front of the council. She outplayed you the moment you proved he was willing to lie to ACE for you. If he hadn't been, that would have been the end of it."

Cora stopped in her tracks and stared at Mindy, who shrugged. "If you'd looped me in, maybe we wouldn't be having this conversation." She held up a finger as Cora opened her mouth. "This isn't me trying to guilt you. I know why you held back. I do. This is me just saying I know these women, and they will hang your ass out to dry. You don't know what kind of game you're playing."

"Fuck." Stupid, stupid, she'd been so *stupid*. And now not only did she have to worry about dodging Ryland's hunter buddies, or them figuring out he was lying—she had to worry about what the altas might do to Ryland if he outstayed his welcome.

He deserved to know.

But when she thought about how she might tell him, she balked. It wasn't fear. Not this time. It was something else, something even harder to pin down.

As she and Mindy found seats around the bonfire, she realized she wanted to give him the freedom to choose. *Needed* to give it to him.

If she didn't, she'd never truly know where they stood. And she wasn't so sure she could live with that.

It didn't take much longer for everyone to gather. Murmuring voices fell quiet as Ghislaine and Helena were joined by Alta Maria, the most senior of the LA altas, and a handful coven elders from the smaller chapters.

The title of alta or altus was held for life, and when one crossed over, the remaining two would use the coven medium to consult with the spirits of the previous altas and nominate a witch to succeed them. The entire coven voted to confirm the succession, but that was a formality. Cora hadn't been around when Helena had succeeded Alta Wynne, but she remembered Mindy's call about the controversy it had stirred—she was the youngest alta to be nominated in two generations. Ghislane had taken particular exception to that choice, and it was no secret they didn't get along.

"Thank you, brothers and sisters, for gathering with us tonight," said Alta Maria, a stooped Mexican-American woman with salt-and-pepper hair secured by a floral calavera hairpin.

She stood behind the altar, lighting the candles there with a wave of her hand, and the lanterns above them flared brighter along with them. Her voice carried easily, amplified by magic and the rock formations circling them. She began in booming Spanish, then repeated what she'd said in English: "Many of you have traveled far, and we are grateful to have you here."

"As we observe Samhain together, observe the rhythm of life and death in nature, its cadence is a grim reminder of what we have lost in this war. A war against those who would silence our magic rather than celebrate the Goddess's miraculous Gift."

She paused to wait for murmurs of affirmation to die down and continued on in Spanish before repeating what she'd said in English:

"Here, upon the altar our ancestors used to offer their thanks, and generations of ancestors before them, we honor the currents of magic that the Goddess wove in a tapestry across the world. She has many names, many depictions, though we call her Leyra, and each of her entropic threads binds us to the nature beneath us and the cosmos above us. Every time you reach for her thread, you wind yourself tighter into that tapestry, into this miracle. That is Leyra's Gift. We celebrate Samhain at this nexus of her miracle."

As she switched to Spanish again, Cora looked at the wide-eyed children scattered around the great fire, on laps, on blankets. She remembered the first time she'd heard this speech, back when Alta Maria had just ascended. The tone had changed since then, darkened as they'd put more years of bloody history behind them.

"Tonight, we set aside our indignation over our suffering at the hands of the living. Instead, we welcome the spirits of our loved ones while the magic linking us to their realm is the strongest and appreciate the sacrifices that allow us to continue our way of life—sacrifices we will continue to make for one another, no matter what happens."

The bonfire roared higher, the lanterns above them flared, and the wind stopped altogether. The vale was blanketed in a thick stillness, and every hair on Cora's arms stood on end.

That was their dismissal. Spirits had begun to come through the nexus.

Mindy's hand found Cora's, and their eyes met. She nodded. She could do this. She'd done it a dozen times. Around the bonfire, witches began settling in, closing their eyes, reaching out with their magic. Cora crossed her legs and did the same, melting into herself, brushing up against the gossamer veil on the edge of her consciousness.

The sounds of the world around her retreated, muffled.

Something cool touched her spine. That chill crept upward as she focused on the veil and the whispers behind it.

She directed tiny threads of her magic toward it in greeting, inviting the connection, seeking a response.

Seconds, hours, days passed, there was no way of knowing—not in this state. The only thing grounding her was Mindy's hand. Time ceased to be a measure of anything as the whispers grew louder, curled around her, sighed like spectral breath in her ear.

There was a tug on the thread. Her body flooded with warmth.

A familiar hand rested on her shoulder.

Goddess, no. No, no, no. She can't be here.

Don't let it be true. Please.

Cora tasted salt as tears fell to her lips. She couldn't speak through the veil, but they were linked until she released her end of the tether, and she clung to it for dear life. Through it, she sensed her mother's smile and felt her pride, felt everything she'd wanted to tell Cora but couldn't all these years.

145

Grief carved through Cora's gut, but her mother's presence blunted the edges. And then as surely as she knew her own name, Cora knew how loved she was. Her heart was so full she thought it would burst, and the raw crash of emotion towed her under.

It was a mix of relief, the relief of knowing—finally—but also the guilt of not having been there, and the selfish gratitude that she'd been gifted this precious moment with her mother regardless of the horror that made it possible.

She was here, and that could only mean she was dead.

Who did this to you? Cora wanted to ask. *How did this happen?*

Her mother pressed back against the image Cora conjured of what she'd been made to suffer, wrapping it in overwhelming peace and calm, making her understand that whatever she felt now...whatever she was, now, couldn't be touched by human cruelty. It was enough to slow Cora's ragged breathing and steady her hiccupping sobs.

I need you, mom, Cora said. *I don't know where to go from here. I'm so fucking lost.*

She opened her eyes, and the world was gone. In front of her, a single peony bloomed. Then more unfurled beside it, and a tree wound upwards from the earth, its branches weighed down by clusters of lemons. A fountain sprang forth. A heavy key.

Her mother's secret garden.

Take it back, it seemed to say.

What? "What does that mean?"

The sound of Cora's own voice woke her from the trance—she'd yielded to the pull of the physical world. She blinked, slowly remembering where she was.

Pip had found them. He was a soft weight nestled in her lap; those tiny glowing orbs narrowed with concern. Mindy had been holding Cora close while she cried, stroking her hair.

Cora sat up, rubbing her smeared makeup away with her sleeve, still coming down from the emotional whiplash of being yanked out of meditation. Mindy dabbed her own eyes and answered the question in Cora's. "I didn't feel Oscar."

Hardly a confirmation he was alive—not every spirit came through the veil on Samhain—but it was better than nothing. "No Sebastian either," Cora said, still gripping Mindy's hands. Her own wouldn't stop shaking. "She's..."

146

Mindy leaned forward, pressing her forehead to Cora's. "She's free."

And she was, wasn't she? Free from that awful place, wherever it was, whatever had been done to her there.

Free. What a thing to finally be.

"Do you think...he was with her? At the end?" They both knew Cora was talking about Sebastian. Her voice broke. "Do you think he got to say goodbye?"

Something she would never get to do, not really. She hoped he was allowed the dignity of that.

"I want to believe it, baby," Mindy said into Cora's hair, pulling her in again. "And so that's what I'm going to do."

Mindy rocked her for a long while, saying nothing more, even as the heady magic in the air began to thin. Other witches were up and moving again, while some sat deep in their grief. Smaller fires had flared up in the surrounding pits, and groups were splintering off to eat or reminisce, or like Quinn, shift and let the wild out.

Cora sat up again, cradling Pip in her hands. He nuzzled her thumb.

Mindy spoke first. "There was something else."

Alarmed, Cora looked up at her. "What did you see?"

"My grandmother." Mindy's voice was soft, reverent.

Cora had never met her, but she'd heard plenty of stories over the years. Great-Grams and Mindy had been close. "What did she say?"

Mindy's eyes widened, something sparking behind them. "I need to find paper. And a pen." At the incredulous look on Cora's face, she said, "I...finally know her recipe for blackberry jam cake."

Cora stared blankly, stunned speechless.

Almost sheepish, Mindy dabbed her cheeks again and elaborated, somewhat uselessly, "I've been searching for it for years."

An odd pressure began to build in Cora's chest. It bubbled up, and up, and spasmed out of her as a giggle before she could even realize what it was or take it back. She covered her mouth as the tears continued to come, feeling completely ridiculous, like every emotion inside her was competing to burst forth all at once.

Mindy's own tearful snort joined hers, and then they couldn't stop, clutching each other and giving themselves over to the sheer absurdity of the moment—laughing as they cried, crying as they laughed, and not caring who around them happened to see.

After the drive home the next morning, Cora spent the rest of the day wallowing in bed. Mindy's grief manifested in the other extreme—she deep-cleaned the house, top to bottom. Trash bags of old clothing appeared in the sitting room, along with boxes of shoes and whatever else she'd pulled down from the attic to donate.

Mindy had also made the blackberry jam cake, which was every bit as magnificent as she'd built it up to be. Cora had the feeling it was all her mother's idea—something to distract them, to comfort them, to perhaps keep Cora from itching for a little something else to get her by. Goddess knew the urge was there, stronger than ever.

But when she awoke the morning after, remnants of a sleepless night swirled in her mind. She kept seeing the peonies, the lemon tree, pieces of the garden still hidden in that old house.

She hadn't been back since the day she ran.

Her earliest memories of OC were her best ones, long before people began disappearing, long before the technology to create arcanometers and Crash was viable. When Sebastian could play harmless pranks on his teachers, or Cora could skip rocks with Ryland and heal ladybugs in broad daylight.

Her mother sat them both down one day, before any of that, when they were barely old enough to understand. "Do you know what a secret is?" she'd asked. "It's something really important, that nobody else knows except us. You two are special, like Mommy and Mindy. And some people might not understand. They might be afraid. So we have to be careful, okay?"

Later, the tone of those sit-downs changed. Later, they were about survival. But kids think they're invincible. Who's to say they hadn't gotten a little too comfortable playing in the yard, thinking they could trust their neighbors, thinking nobody was paying attention?

Was it the Adres, who had the barbecues? The Sandlers, with the awkward daughter Cora's age and the trampoline? The Guerreros, that young couple with the newborn who had moved in just months before? Crotchety old Mr. Adam, who complained about the toys left out on their driveway?

Who could do that to a family and still lay their head down at night?

She sat up and swung her legs over the side of the pullout. Pip lay curled on the cushion next to her, looking affronted when she jostled him. "Let me fold the bed away, you. Shoo."

So saying, she spent the next hour tidying the room to calm her fried nerves. She had the bad luck to catch sight of her face in a mirror, swollen eyes the only evidence she'd been crying in her sleep. After lighting sandalwood incense to stave off negativity and invite good luck, she took a deep breath and reached for her phone.

Ryland's number sat in her contacts, glaring up at her on the bright little screen. She'd gotten it from him at the McDaniels', in case Pip needed retrieving again. Or so she'd told herself.

Seven attempts later, she pressed SEND.

[11:12am] C
Hey.
[11:15am] R
Hi. Everything ok?

She blew out a breath, unsure how much to put in writing.

[11:17am] C
Something happened the other night.
[11:17am] C
I need to go see the old house. Wondering if you wanted to come with.

The "typing" icon appeared, then disappeared. Then appeared again. Then disappeared. Finally:

[11:21am] R
Wow. Haven't been back to oak manor in years.
[11:22am] R
I'm already down in westminster for a memorial. Could meet up after.

Cora swallowed. She wondered if the memorial was for the hunter they'd killed.

[11:23am] C
I'm sorry for your loss. No worries if you're busy.

[11:24am] R
I didn't know him well. Just supporting the squad.
[11:24am] R
I can get out of here by 3.

His reply all but confirmed it. That there was no body to bury suggested he was still being studied, probably for traces of magic. They wouldn't find any, but...maybe she could find out what they did have.

[11:25am] C See you then.

Cora tossed her phone on the couch and headed for the shower, trying to unclench the fist of dread gripping her chest tight, tighter.
No backing out of it now.

CHAPTER THIRTEEN

Cora headed south on the 405 towards Irvine but stayed under seventy. Any faster and Lucy began to shudder. Fine by her. The longer she took to get there, the more time she had to reconsider.

Her corduroy jacket was too warm. Her jeans were too stiff. Her ponytail was too damn tight. Every exit off-ramp taunted her.

Springdale St.

Brookhurst St.

MacArthur Blvd.

Turn around. Turn around. Turn around.

Emotion was a fist in Cora's throat. She wasn't sure *what* she was supposed to feel. There was a difference between thinking someone might be dead and knowing, between easing your grip on hope and seeing the last grains of it run through your fingers. And even as relief wound its way into her heart, the relief of not having to wonder, so did the guilt of feeling it.

Not to mention in those rare moments when she thought she might be okay, the guilt for *not* grieving.

And it was a struggle to balance the hope Sebastian was still alive—could be spared her mother's fate—with the crushing helplessness of not knowing how to do it. Of not knowing where to start.

You do know where to start, that voice said. *You start with Ryland.*

Which Ryland? The one she owed nothing to, who had spent a lifetime locking up in his neat little box of "enemy"? That was the one she could use and discard.

Or was it Ryland who'd been forced into a life he hadn't wanted, who'd risked more than she probably realized to help the McDaniels, who'd subscribed to the hunters' narrative to survive and just needed to grant himself permission to find a way out? Who had held her the other night? Who she, despite all the reasons she knew she shouldn't, was trying to make excuses for?

That was the one she couldn't sell out to Helena.

Cora had just wanted to stay a step ahead of the raids; she hadn't known mining him for information would seal his fate. She'd been too distracted to give the altas the credit they so clearly deserved.

But she didn't have the headspace for this guilt right now. That was valuable real estate. Mostly taken up by the skipping record of *turn around, turn around, turn around.*

Her focus narrowed to it. If she kept repeating it, it almost didn't sound like real words anymore. What was that called? Semantic satiation? It took the teeth out of it until it was just syllables, a jumble of noise, a nonsense mantra that hilariously gave her the courage to *keep* driving.

She didn't realize she'd been idling on Oak Manor until a knuckle tapped her window.

The knuckle belonged to a hand that belonged to a forearm, which had the jacket of a dark funeral-appropriate suit slung over it. And the forearm belonged to Ryland.

He peered down at her through expensive-looking sunglasses, and he'd managed to tame his riot of curls with some kind of hair product.

She rolled down the window, trying not to think about just how damn good he looked with his tie loosened just so. "Nice suit."

He shrugged. "It does the job."

Does it ever.

But now that she was on that street, with him, she wasn't sure she could do this. Her fingers twitched. She could just keep driving. Make this whole neighborhood disappear.

The sun baked down through stagnant air, like even the breeze had reconsidered getting involved.

Ryland leaned down close, rested his elbows on the door, and pulled down the sunglasses. Looked her right in the eye. "Hey." His voice was soft.

She tried to breathe. "Hey."

"We'll do it together," he said. "Okay?"

Together. A tiny jolt shot through her. It was such a loaded word. But she chose to hear the encouragement in it.

Cora could only nod. Her fingers pulled the keys from the ignition, then opened the door. Her feet moved to the pavement, and her legs forced her to stand, and her elbow nudged the door shut.

Somehow her body did all those things, in that order, and she was here. The only thing left to do was face it.

They'd parked closest to Ryland's, so they walked towards it first.

The yellow stucco was burned into her memory, the orange tile roof, the little arch above the garden gate. A UC Irvine bumper sticker was plastered across the window of the old Jeep Cherokee out front. "Good car," Ryland murmured, looking it up and down. "Always wanted one of those. In green." Then he surveyed the house next door. "That's still Rob's car, there. Guess they got that fence he was always going on about."

"Look at the size of Buster," Cora said, jerking her chin towards the ficus towering out front. "He was just a baby."

"Why'd we call him Buster?"

"Beats me." Then Cora squinted, dredging up a memory. "Didn't Sebastian bust his teeth on that thing? Ran into it with his bike?"

"Ah. A skateboard, I think."

"That's right. Fucked his elbow up, too."

"He was showing that scar off for weeks."

"Trying to impress this one girl at school. Steffy, Sophie something..."

Goddess, how was it suddenly this easy with him? She'd missed it, so fucking much, and the easier it was, the more it hurt. The more she remembered it couldn't be that way anymore.

He'd gone quiet, too, as if mirroring her thoughts. Then: "I'm not sure what I expected to feel, coming here again."

"What *do* you feel?" She asked it half for herself, for all her swirling emotions, trying to pick one out as being 'right.'

"It's going to sound odd," he said slowly, untangling the words in his mouth, "but it's like a movie backlot. Like it was all a set built for the stuff in my head." He sighed, looking up at Buster the ficus, at the bird's nest in its branches. "I don't think there's much left of me here."

"Disappointed?"

He turned to her, stuffing his hands in his pockets. "Don't know what I was hoping for. Clarity, maybe." He shot her half a smile. "A younger me to pop open a window, tell me something profound about who to be."

That struggle didn't show on his face the way Cora knew he could read it on hers. But the solidarity of that feeling still narrowed the chasm between them. Just a hair.

Then his smile faded. "You said something had happened the other night."

Their safe little bubble of memory popped. Cora glanced down the street, where her old house waited to the left of the bend. Her eyes flickered back to him. She opened her mouth, but no sound came out. He stepped closer, and she tried again. "The garden," was all she got out. "I came to see mom's garden."

"Then let's go," he said, frowning at his childhood home. "I think we're spooking the folks who live here."

Sure enough, when Cora followed his eye line, a hand quickly released a curtain in the upstairs window. "You could ask them, you know. To see it. Say you used to live here."

Ryland shook his head. "I was never here, anyway. Not really."

No. Because he'd been at her house. They'd always been at her house.

They set off, walking in silence, and rounded the corner. She forced one foot in front of the other. She focused on Ryland next to her, matching her stride as the brass mailbox came into view.

The last time she'd seen it, she'd been running away.

Hers was a single-story bungalow, smaller than Ryland's, despite housing more people back then. It had been cozier, he'd said, than the big, empty rooms of his parents' place. They'd always been working. Cora's mom had, too, but with her landscape design business, she'd been able to work out of her home office.

The bougainvillea had doubled in size, creeping up and over the garage, and the paint on the siding was new. Not fresh, just new to her—someone else had lived there long enough to let it chip in a few places, long enough for a tricycle and a basketball hoop and some stubs of chalk to accumulate in the driveway. Long enough for a whole different life to grow in place of hers.

The blue paint shielded her from the crush of memory, just a little. She could almost pretend she didn't remember what it looked like underneath.

She took a few steps up the front walk, imagined knocking on the door and asking if they'd let her see inside. The owners before them had done it, driving by one day on their way back from their granddaughter's graduation. They wanted to see the place where they'd raised her. Cora's mom had loved showing them the new deck she'd put in.

But Cora looked back at Ryland and shook her head, instead walking through the grass to the side of the garage. He followed behind, giving her space, but making sure she could see he was there. They'd be hidden enough in this spot—Cora's mother had picked it to be discreet.

She dropped to her knees and felt around beneath the bushes for the flat, heavy rock, her heart kicking a little when her fingers brushed the edge. Prying it upwards and moving it aside, she grabbed a fistful of earth and the old brass key hiding within.

The soft grass tickled her ankles as she sat back and turned the key over in her hands. Alone it wasn't anything special—it belonged to a trunk they'd kept in the attic. She was looking for the gate her mother had enchanted it to open.

Cora turned, meeting Ryland's eyes. A silent question.

He dipped his chin and knelt beside her in the dirt. She'd shown him how to get in once before. As she brushed the soil from the tarnished brass, plucking a thread of magic from the ley line. The leaves and branches of the bush snaked aside to allow them through.

At her hesitation, Ryland whispered, "I'm right behind you."

Cora pulled air into her lungs, forced it back out, and crawled forward into the past.

The secret garden was exactly the same, like it was suspended in time. She shouldn't have been surprised the enchantment still held after all these years—her mother had been a master terramancer. The canopy of leaves and flowers was tall enough to stand in, creeping over a spread of grass broad enough for a wooden swing and a small pond with a fountain. Flanking that, fragrant star jasmine rambled up white latticework, and clusters of wild strawberries sheltered beneath the lemon tree—not because they needed shade, but because Cora's mother had wanted them there—and there were herbs for alchemy and ripe red tomatoes and all sorts of wild and beautiful things that shouldn't all bloom together but somehow did.

The peonies, though, were her mother's pride and joy, a spray of impossible colors that never wilted. She used to spend hours here reading or meditating, and Cora could always smell them on her. Peonies and lemons—she'd take them from the little tree and pick strawberries to make strawberry lemonade. Whatever she plucked up grew right back the next day.

The scent of them now was a gut punch, and she sank down by the pond's edge. She dug her fingers into the grass, reaching for some way to anchor herself to the present. If she wasn't careful, she'd forget when she was.

In fact, she'd almost forgotten Ryland was there. "Samhain," she explained, her voice quivering. "She came to me on Samhain."

The sound of the fountain's trickle stretched between them as he realized what she meant. Then his footsteps were soft over the grass behind her. He sat down on her left, by the pond's edge, and stared into the rippling water.

"I'm sorry," he said, those words twisted with emotion she couldn't begin to unpack. Like he was apologizing for a hundred things at once.

"You wanna know the most fucked-up thing?" she asked. "I think...I think I'm angry at *Sebastian*."

He leaned back, resting his elbows on his knees and searching her face. "Why?"

"I wish I'd had more time with her. And part of me is jealous that he did." She let out a shuddering breath, still holding in her tears. "It's so stupid. Comes from such a place of fucking privilege, right? I shouldn't think that, but I can't help it. That's not fair to him. Or to mom. I've had a real life, and he hasn't."

"There's no should or shouldn't, here." Ryland said. "There's no best way to field grief. Hard to build rules around something that never makes sense."

Cora drew her knees closer. "I could never really resent either of them for having that time together. I just wish...you know. Sometimes I think a prison might not have been so bad if both of them were there. If we could still have been a family."

Ryland stilled beside her. She continued, feeling small, "I've...never admitted that before. But you think about the way a life should go, and you picture the people you love in every part of it, no matter how sideways things get. It's just what you do."

He said nothing for a long moment. Neither did she. Then he shifted, kicking off his loafers, peeling off his socks, and rolling up the cuffs of his slacks before dipping his feet in the pond.

He reached down and grabbed the sole her left sneaker, too, pulling it towards him. Eyebrows rising, she extended her leg into his lap as he untied the laces, pulled it off, and unrolled her sock to reveal pink-painted toes. He did the same with the right one before setting her feet in the water, too.

It was such an intimate thing. Too intimate, she thought. Just like she'd done for him, the first time.

She'd brought him here after his grandfather died. Ryland had retreated so deeply inside himself, she wasn't sure anything could bring him back out. He'd been closer with his grandfather than his own dad. So, in a desperate bid to get him out of bed, she'd promised to show him something she'd never been allowed to show anyone. Something she made him swear to take to his grave.

Here, now, the sensation of the water gave her a more concrete focus, something to help pull her out of the depths of her own head. She felt the fist of emotion around her throat loosen just enough to say, "Thank you for coming with me."

He lay back on his elbows, then all the way, folding his hands under the back of his head, and she knew he was in that memory with her. She lowered herself backward, too, staring up at the canopy of vines overhead and the sunlight glimmering through them. "Of course," was all he said.

They lay side by side in the grass for what felt like ages. It was a kind of peace she hadn't known in so long, just the sound of the water, the rustling of the breeze, the heady perfume of the flowers.

"I guess I get why people have funerals," she finally said. "You want to give someone a proper send-off. You want to...mark it somehow."

"We could say something, here, if you want."

She started to shake her head but stopped. The corner of her mouth curved upward. "I suppose you're dressed for it."

"I suppose I am."

Cora splashed her feet in the pond, thinking. The bottoms of her rolled-up jeans were wet, but she didn't care. She could stay here for hours, days, even, just like this. Settled into this tentative...*something* with him.

The Cora and Theo Demilitarized Zone.

"I'm not sure how to do this," she said.

"Just talk to her."

Cora turned her head, the grass tickling her ear. Ryland's eyes were closed. He made it all sound so casual. So easy. And to her surprise, it helped.

Inhale, exhale.

"Hey, mom." It felt silly, especially in front of him, but his eyes were still closed, giving her that space, and she kept going. "I'm not sure if you can hear me, but...I just felt like this was where you'd be if you could be anywhere. If you could spend forever somewhere."

A bird was singing. A bee buzzed nearby.

Inhale, exhale.

"I'm sorry I couldn't..." Her throat closed. She blinked back tears. "I'm sorry I couldn't be with you. When it happened. I'm sorry I couldn't do more. I'm sorry for everything."

The key was a warm, steadying weight in her hand. She tried to focus on the feel of it. "I miss you, Mom. I love you." She was out of things to say.

Ryland waited to see if she was done, then spoke. "Thank you, Robyn," he said, opening his eyes again, "for treating me like a second son. Even when I didn't deserve it." He paused. "Especially when I didn't deserve it."

The knife in Cora's ribs twisted, twisted. She could hardly breathe.

As she lay there beside him and wiped her eyes on her sleeve, she had the distinct feeling of letting go of a string tied to a future that might have been. A balloon, getting smaller and smaller against the sky.

Fear was an interloper. Theo thought the Academy had beaten it out of him. But in the week that had passed since he'd revisited the old house, it began to sharpen the edges of his temper, to eat away at his ability to sleep a solid eight, to make him reach for cigarettes again.

He couldn't afford to feel it. Couldn't even remember the last time he'd been this worried about someone else. It rooted itself in his chest like a nasty cough.

He wasn't sure what it might mean, this thing he was about to do. What it would mean for their tenuous truce. What it would mean for him if ACE found out.

That his uncertainty wasn't enough to keep him from doing it...it said more than he was willing to process right now.

Because when she'd looked back at him before crawling into that garden, unafraid to let him see her unravel—trusting him to steady her, against all reason—he knew he couldn't let her live in limbo forever. If he had the power to give her closure, he'd do it.

So he'd wound up here, at the base, pulling up next to the guard gate. He flashed his ID, and they waved him through to the next security checkpoint.

Theo headed through the TACS bullpen of cubicles and straight to the office he never used. He did most of his work in the field and only came here to catch up on paperwork because the Vanguard database didn't support remote access. A file lay open on his desk, and a photo of Antoine Roy stared back at him. The witch from the Korean BBQ joint had been the last Theo apprehended himself.

He forced himself to meet the sunken stare in the man's intake portrait. It captured a shadow of the man he once was, his boyfriend still splattered on his shoes. Death might have been a mercy, but that wasn't for Theo to decide.

Except Antoine, he remembered, had something left to live for. He'd spoken of a daughter from a previous marriage. He thumbed through the folder until he found a one-sheeter on his ex-wife. Lana Kaplan-Roy's current whereabouts were unknown, and someone had made a note in the file about Montreal. She was untouchable there, and some tension melted from Theo's shoulders. If her daughter was with her, then the kid would be untouchable, too.

But she wouldn't have been told Antoine's fate. And from the sound of it, she and Antoine were close enough for her to wonder. For her to be afraid for him. Theo had the power to give her closure before she became another casualty of a system designed to make her one.

He scribbled down her contact information on a sticky note and pocketed it.

Then he pulled up the file on Ezra's case, beginning the long slog through the report. Pressure from the brass was mounting, and Fletcher needed an update, so he'd do his best to say as little as possible in as many words as possible. Maybe take the heat off Ezra a bit longer while Ricky recuperated.

Two hours and three cups of coffee later, he figured he had come up with something passable.

"Ryland."

Theo didn't jump; he'd heard the muffled footsteps across the carpet. His face betrayed nothing but casual curiosity as he stood and nodded at Fletcher. "Commander."

"How goes the Ezra Foster probe?" Fletcher had a massive binder in his arms, dressed for a day of meetings. The police commissioner would be on-site today, Theo remembered. They'd sent out an email about it.

Theo didn't have to feign weary frustration. "Hitting dead ends left and right. Searched his hotels for spikes, his bars. I think either someone tipped him off, or he really is clean. After meeting the man myself, I'm inclined to believe the latter, but I'm hoping I can get close enough to find out more."

This next part was the one he had to be careful with, and he kept his tone casual, even as his heart thundered. "I've been pursuing a lead on a friend of one of Ezra's employees, and while I don't think the friend has specific knowledge of any illegal goings-on, the employee's a gossip. It's detailed in the report I was about to send over." If anyone looked too closely at who he'd been with, it gave him a reason for hanging around Ezra's inner circle. The best lies were always peppered with a bit of truth.

"Good. I'll look at it." Fletcher grabbed the sheaf of papers Theo had printed off for him. "Santana doing okay?"

He was referring to Thompson's memorial. Ricky had been out of the hospital for days now but was still leaning on a single crutch. He'd been silent and stone-faced throughout the service, two things Theo had never known the man to be, even in grief. "Doesn't help that Harris' condition hasn't improved," Theo said.

"I feel for the kid," Fletcher said. "He stopped by here afterward and grabbed his notes, even though I told him to focus on his recovery. Maybe you can talk some sense into him."

"Respectfully, sir, I don't think sense is something he's got on a good day."

Fletcher snorted. "All the same." He held up the binder and turned on his heel. "Better get to it."

Theo watched Fletcher retreat until the elevator doors whispered shut, and then waited another excruciating minute before he was convinced the coast was clear. Only then did he sit and log in to Vanguard, the ACE intake database.

It covered all the reports from southern California, a region feeding three major internment facilities: The Beach, The Grove, and The Farm. Names intended as a cruel joke, a stark reminder of everything they weren't.

The Farm was their Supermax, home to everyone from demon worshippers to necromancers to blood magic cults. Witches who'd made enough of a public scene could wind up there, too. If Antoine's boyfriend had survived, they'd have sent him there. Antoine's own file showed Fletcher kept his promise and sent him to The Beach instead, which Theo was relieved to see.

Theo hadn't exactly lied when he'd told Cora he didn't know anything about her family, but he hadn't given her the whole truth, either. He'd had years to look them up in the database but couldn't bring himself to do it no matter how many times he stared at the blinking cursor in the search bar. Because once he knew their fates for sure, he couldn't take it back.

Now, though, he stood at that threshold, fully prepared for the weight of that knowledge. Robyn had gone back to her maiden name, he remembered. Kearney. He typed it in, took a breath, and hit 'enter.'

The harsh lighting of the intake photo in front of him did little to detract from Robyn Kearney's button nose and kind, round face. Eyes swollen from crying were still hard, determined. He'd seen that same look in Cora's eyes before, that same slightly downturned mouth.

There wouldn't be a full report on her tenure, not here. Only general information—known addresses, aliases, dependents. Date of birth. Location. Status.

Name: KEARNEY, ROBYN LAUREN [SOMERVILLE, ROBYN KEARNEY]
Facility: 034M "THE BEACH"
Case Number: 0017863A **Status:** DECEASED

He pulled up Sebastian's file next.

Theo had last seen him when Sebastian was fourteen, but by the time this photo was taken, he'd grown more into his height, filled out. His jaw had begun to square off, but he hadn't shed those boyish freckles. He was trying hard to look brave, not quite hitting the mark.

Theo's heart pounded as he read the words below the photo.

Name: SOMERVILLE, SEBASTIAN JAMES

Facility: 034M "THE BEACH"
Case Number: 0017863B
Status: IN RESIDENCE

Theo exhaled slowly.
In residence. *Alive.*
And he was right there in Morongo Valley.

CHAPTER FOURTEEN

[6:43pm] T
> I need to talk to you.

Theo paced back and forth in front of the drawn blinds of his downtown studio. If the altas were going to have eyes on him at all times, he wasn't about to make their job easy...

[5:47pm] C
Hi to you, too. What's wrong?

[5:47pm] T
Where are you?

[5:48pm] C
You're scaring me. I'm with Quinn at Bungalow

[5:48pm] T
Stay there. I'll meet you in 40

[5:48pm] C
???????

The phone vibrated again, but he didn't want to put any of this in writing, so he ignored it and grabbed his motorcycle helmet. It wasn't worth driving to the Westside in rush hour unless you had a bike, and boy, did he have a bike.

His motorcycle was the envy of every commuter he roared past on the 10. Anyone who'd felt the rush of wind like this, creeping under the cuffs of their jacket and whipping across their neck, knew witches didn't have a monopoly on magic. His mom would be horrified to know he'd bought the damn thing, would tell him all the ways he could die on it, and he didn't have the heart to tell her that's why he rode it in the first place.

He'd shut down for so long. To get through the Academy, to get through his field training, to get through those rare weekends at home with his parents. He'd been so angry that they hadn't done more, even knowing the time for running was far behind them, and then they had the nerve to *pity* him for it.

It didn't help that at sixteen, those raging hormones and cynicism and angst were begging for an outlet, and he was more than content to blame the only support system he had. The people who were supposed to protect him. Possibly the only people who could have anchored him through the worst years of his life if he'd let them.

Driving that wedge between them sealed his fate. One by one, he slammed doors on all the things that made him vulnerable and shut down for long enough that he'd forgotten how to do more than just exist.

The bike had once been the only way for him to feel anything at all. He'd had to invite death in every once in a while, just to remind himself he had something to lose.

As he breezed along the HOV lane, a call came through the headset built into his helmet. He half expected to hear Cora's voice, demanding answers, but it was Ricky. "You wanna grab a beer? I'm stir crazy as hell and thirstier than a bitch in your DMs."

Theo grinned. "Shouldn't you be on a cocktail of pain meds?"

"No, mom. My script ran out. Tryna numb the world in other ways."

"I would, but I can't. I'm meeting someone in Venice."

"Someone?" That piqued Ricky's interest. "Any someone I know?"

"Nope."

"That was a mighty quick answer."

"Only answer I can give you."

"It's her, isn't it?"

164

Theo nearly swerved, remembering too late that Ricky knew about the 'mystery woman' from his childhood. That hesitation was all the ammo Ricky needed.

"I'm fucking right, aren't I? Where you headed? Candlelit dinner? Sunset cruise? Romantic walk along the—"

Still rattled, Theo said, "Fuck off. It's not like that. We're just going to Bungalow." As soon as the words left his mouth, he regretted them.

Ricky huffed a laugh. "Oh, come on! I can tag along to the goddamn Bungalow. I gotta meet the woman who's got your panties in a twist. I'm so fucking bored, T."

"Another time. Tonight's not—" The rest of his sentence didn't matter, because Ricky had hung up.

For fuck's sake.

For fuck's *sake*.

Cold dread slithered down Theo's spine. Ricky couldn't meet Cora. He'd seen those security photos, same as Theo. They were grainy, and from a shitty angle, but Cora's hair wasn't something you could just forget. Those long waves, that deep chestnut—you might not be able to hunt her down on those photos alone, but if you knew her? If she was at that bar with Ezra? You could certainly put two and two together.

He tried calling her. No answer. He tried again, without any luck, as he rumbled along and found a spot on the street outside the hotel.

Ricky lived nearby, but Theo had a few minutes on him, and that might buy enough time to get to the roof and warn her. Helmet tucked under his arm, he made his way through the sleek lobby, rode the excruciatingly slow elevator to the top floor.

The Lazy Nomad on the roof of Bungalow was just as he remembered it—esoteric art, funky light fixtures, and a jungle of potted and hanging plants. He zigzagged through the fire pits and low-slung lounge seating across the smooth concrete terrace, scanning for Cora, hating how impossibly crowded the restaurant was.

"Whoa! Where are you going in such a hurry?" said a familiar voice, and Theo pivoted, remembering to look down as an afterthought. "We have a table right over there."

Cora peered up at him in concern. She'd worn a long, flowing skirt, and her hair was a tumble of loose curls she must have tried hard to make look accidental. He knew these things about women.

"You have to leave," he said, grabbing her elbow and leading her toward the elevator. She yanked away from him, sloshing some of her—was that water or vodka?—over the edge of her glass.

"What the fuck is your problem?" In the brighter light by the elevator, he could see she hadn't slept well. "You send me this cryptic text, scare the crap out of me, and now—"

"It's my partner," he said calmly, too calmly. So calmly he was likely scaring her more than if he'd panicked.

"Your what?"

"My coworker, Ricky. He's on his way here. I told him not to come, but he insisted."

Cora's eyes widened. "Another hunter? Here?"

"He's seen the photos. The ones with you and Nell. You can't be here when he arrives."

Cora's freckles darkened against her paling skin. "What about Quinn?"

Theo frowned. "What about her?"

"If any traffic cameras—" And then she stopped herself.

Theo's confusion crystallized into realization, his entire body tensing. "Why," he said slowly, "would Quinn be worried about traffic cameras, Cora?"

She looked like she was going to be sick. "Never mind, forget it—"

"*Why*," Theo repeated, "would she be worried about traffic cameras?"

Cora was close to tears. Her voice was a whisper. "It was an accident."

Jesus fucking Christ, help him. He scrubbed a hand over his beard, pacing away from her, then back again. "We don't have time for this."

She looked back at the table she'd abandoned, where Quinn and Ezra warily watched their exchange. Theo hadn't realized Ezra was with them. Ricky was going to lose it.

"You have to go," he repeated, out of things to say.

"Ry—"

He grabbed her shoulders and steered her to the elevator. She let him, giving Quinn an apologetic wave as Theo nudged her in front of the opening doors. Ezra was already on his feet, stalking over to them, but he stopped short.

Theo followed his eye line. They were too late.

Ricky limped out, one crutch under his arm, and Cora stood there like a deer in the headlights. He raised an eyebrow and sidestepped her, motioning for her to get on the elevator, and she jerked forward. "Oh! Sorry. Thank you."

Then he saw Theo and grinned, leaning in and clapping him on the back. "Hey man, what's up? You get stood up or something?"

The elevator dinged shut behind Ricky, and Theo let out a long, slow exhale. "She can't make it. Just texted me."

Ricky looked Theo up and down, noting the tension in his shoulders and the muscle clenching in his jaw. "Take it easy. You look like you could use a drink more than me, and that's saying something. Why don't we—" As Ricky leaned left to peer at the bar, he noticed Ezra standing behind Theo, and his face went through the whole gamut of emotions before settling on rage.

"YOU!" Ricky sputtered, pointing, Theo forgotten. He shoved aside a waitress, whose tray went crashing to the ground. Glasses shattered, a burger flew, and Ezra stepped forward. Quinn was already on her feet behind him. "I was hoping I'd catch you here, mamaguevo."

Ezra stepped between Ricky and Quinn, eyes flashing. "Listen, man, I don't know you, and I don't know who you think you are, but—"

Ricky reared his fist back and caught Ezra in the jaw with an expert left hook. Ezra stumbled backwards into Quinn, nearly taking her down with him. Somewhere, someone gasped. "What the fuck is your problem?" she said, helping him to his feet. Other patrons backed away, wanting no part in it.

Where the hell was security?

"I'm not too proud to start a fight with a cripple, if he's stupid enough to pick one," Ezra growled, grabbing the front of Ricky's shirt, shoving him backwards. He crumpled as his weight shifted to his bad leg, falling into a table and sending more drinks to the floor.

Ricky waved away Theo's offered hand and struggled to his feet with a grunt of pain. He dragged himself forward, every wiry muscle taut. "You killed a good man and put another in a coma. They had families, they had lives—"

Theo met Quinn's eyes over Ezra's shoulder, and her face turned the same shade Cora's had.

Great. Just perfect.

"What are you talking about?" Ezra squared his shoulders and closed in on Ricky. "If you think you can just come in here and threaten me in my own restaurant—"

"Yeah, I think I can, you piece of shit."

"Stop it! Stop it, both of you!" Quinn shoved between them, and hotel security threw open the door to the stairwell by the elevator. "If you're gonna accuse him of anything, take it to his lawyers, or get the fuck out of here."

Ricky's nostrils flared. Security grabbed him and forced him to the elevator. "I bet you're in on it too, bitch," he spat.

Theo picked up the abandoned crutch and shot a look of apology at Ezra and Quinn before following Ricky down to the parking lot. His partner cursed the whole way, writhing against the security guards, who half carried, half dragged him down eight flights of stairs. By the time they reached the bottom, he'd lost a little steam, but not a whole hell of a lot.

Ricky hobbled outside and collapsed on a curb, muttering a colorful string of curses as he prodded his thigh. Blood seeped through his jeans where his stitches had reopened.

Theo crouched next to him. "You just going to sit here and bleed out, then?"

Ricky winced through the glare he shot at Theo. "I'll make that hijo de gran puta wish he was dead."

"If he presses charges, Fletcher will do the same to you." What would Theo say right now if he was actually trying to bag Foster? What would he be maddest about? "Now you've tipped the guy off, and you've tipped off whoever's been helping him. If you think this won't send them to ground, you're an idiot. You just made this job a fuck ton harder."

Ricky's jaw twitched as he tried to bottle his fury. "This is fucking bullshit. *He* is fucking bullshit."

Theo ducked back inside to poke around for a first aid kit and came out wielding a roll of gauze he'd pried from the begrudging fingers of the desk clerk. "Here. Don't be a hero about it." He tossed it at Ricky, shaking his head. "Call yourself a cab. You're not ready for the field. Not even close." Ricky wound the gauze around his thigh angrily, tying it off with a haphazard knot. His fingers shook with rage, and anything more precise would've been impossible. He sat back, sucking in a breath. "When does it stop?"

"What?" Theo wasn't sure if the question was directed at him.

"When does it stop?" Ricky repeated bleakly. His eyes were unfocused, settling on something in the middle distance. "This anger. This...disgust. I look at people doing shit, unimportant shit like grocery shopping and filling up their gas and bumming a cigarette, and I don't understand how they can just go on living normal lives." Now he looked at Theo. "How you can."

Theo's gut twisted. This, at least, he didn't need a lie for. "You ever ask yourself why I don't field train anymore?" Ricky grunted noncommittally.

"It was years ago, before we were partners, but I had a rookie. Selena Guimarães." Theo's throat threatened to close. He never talked about Selena. He hadn't even talked to the ACE shrink about it, after.

A shadow passed over Ricky's face. "Why didn't you tell me?"

"Because I was ashamed." Because she had loved him, and that had gotten her killed.

The worst part was he couldn't love her back. He'd done his best to let her down easy, and she'd still leapt in front of him when that electromancer lashed out with a bolt of raw lightning, taking it right in the chest. He still remembered the smell of the singed hair on his arms, the sharp heat from his wristwatch as it branded him with burns.

She'd given him just enough time to fire off a round of Crash, and then the witch was down, but so was she.

He'd gone through that call, over and over, thinking of all the things he could've done differently. It had seemed like such a routine run, some squatters in an old, foreclosed house. A beat cop with an arcanometer had noted a minor magical disturbance. Theo hadn't sensed any emotional pull, anything to indicate the need for more backup.

Selena had lived in a very full household, a multigenerational family whose grief he had blocked all memory of. That whole time period was hazy in his mind, dreamlike, like his brain begged him not to recall it. He just knew they couldn't have an open casket funeral.

"I couldn't be responsible for anyone anymore," Theo said, loosing a sigh. "I told them I was done."

"I wish I could stop feeling so fucking helpless."

Because he hated lying to his friend in one breath and comforting him in another, Theo could feel himself shutting down again. Slowly but surely, he was forcing himself to put distance between them, so he wouldn't have to face the truth of his own actions.

Their friendship had been a pillar of Theo's last few years on the force, forged in life-or-death scenarios that demanded the highest level of trust. Shared trauma had brought them together and kept them together.

But what tied Cora and Theo together was something else entirely. He couldn't easily define what made them make sense, but the closest he got was this underlying sense of family, an anchor to a world he hadn't been forced to belong to. Lying next to her in her Robyn's secret garden, needing to sweep her into his arms as she cried but innately understanding her need for space...

Ricky would kill Cora if he had to. Without remorse.

Theo had gone so long without her in his life. And now it felt like she had never left. He couldn't let her go again.

Not for anyone.

Checking his phone, he had four unread texts from Cora, the last of which mentioned she was hiding in Ezra's personal suite. A new one pinged.

[7:02pm] C
Let me know when it's okay to come up

[7:02pm] T
I'll come to you. Too many ears up there

[7:03pm] C
Can you at least bring my purse? Quinn has it

[7:03pm] C
Wasn't done with those tater tots either :(

When Theo headed back inside to return to the roof, the concierge who'd found him the gauze waved him back over. "You're Mr. Ryland?" The short black woman kept her hair natural, and her expressive eyes confessed she had a million and one questions she'd like to ask him but thought twice about it. Her name tag said Tali.

Theo nodded, though it had been a long time since he'd heard "Mister" precede his name. Tali leaned forward on her elbows, sparing a glance at Ricky on the curb outside. "Is he going to be alright, or do I need to call someone?" It was half a threat, like she wasn't sure if implied ambulance or the cops.

"He won't cause you any more trouble. I promise."

She eyed him through narrowed lids, unconvinced. "Ezra told me to send you to his office when you came back in. It's just back there, third door on the left." She jerked a thumb for emphasis, but she'd gone back to watching Ricky warily.

"Thanks," Theo said and rounded the desk to follow the corridor behind it.

Ezra's office was all sleek, ashy wood, with a longboard and a fish board propped against one wall. From the grey of the wax coating them, they were well-loved. He probably rode out from here in the mornings, when he had the time for it.

The man himself sat back in an old Herman Miller lounger, clutching a bar rag full of ice to his cheek. Quinn perched on his desk, falling silent when Theo entered and shut the door.

"Sorry about that," he said. "I told him not to follow me here."

"Is that why you shoved Cora into the goddamn elevator?" Quinn asked. "Who the fuck was that?"

"That," Theo sighed, folding his arms, "was my partner. I was worried he'd recognize her from the security footage. From the night your cousin was taken." He nodded at Ezra, who set down the ice and moved to stand.

"I guess it's time we were finally introduced." Ezra surprised Theo by reaching out. "I'm Ezra Foster. You must be my...mystery benefactor."

"Theo Ryland." He grasped the offered hand, felt the strength in it. It was as much of warning as an olive branch.

"Keep your buddy on a leash, and we'll be fine. I can make things difficult for him."

"Maybe so, but you're smarter than that." Theo spared a nod at Quinn. "You don't want my CO poking around in this any more than I do." Nothing about this was simple, except their need to keep it quiet. "I hope we understand each other."

Ezra's voice carried a note of resignation. "I have enough enemies. I can live without adding another to the list."

"Good." Theo felt some of the tension leave his jaw, actively worked to relax his posture. "However that crash happened...he has nothing concrete on you. He only knows they were chasing your car. But his rookie died that day, and the other one hasn't woken up yet. He's not going to give up easy."

When Quinn's brows rose, he added, "Caltrans doesn't have traffic cams in Venice yet. They're tied up in city approvals. We checked."

"Lucky us," she muttered. She didn't offer any additional details about that day, but he figured he could get them out of Cora.

"Look," Theo said, turning to leave and grabbing the familiar leather handbag on the chair by the door, "if his man Harris comes out of the coma and remembers anything to implicate you or Cora, we'll have a real problem on our hands. Think about how you want to spin it."

Ezra narrowed his eyes to slits. "Let's hope he doesn't, then."

Cora paced in the very salmon-pink hotel room, waiting for her phone to ping again. It had been fifteen minutes since Ryland's last text, and Quinn wasn't responding either.

She'd tried flipping through channels on TV, but it was mostly background noise to keep her company. She couldn't focus on anything beyond that unnerving, deadly calm she'd heard in Ryland's voice.

At least she'd had the chance to talk to Quinn again since Samhain, since the night she'd collapsed by the fire and cried to her after making contact with her mom. Quinn had held her, but they hadn't spoken, mostly due to the fact that Quinn was half-stoned and very much struggling to form sentences.

A knock on the door had her nearly jumping out of her skin. *About damn time.*

She rushed over to the peephole, confirmed it was Ryland, and ushered him in. He had a takeaway box in his hands, and the fact that he'd remembered her tater tots made her chest tighten. "Oh, bless you, these are warm," she said, unfolding the lid. Her mouth was already full when she asked, "What the hell happened up there?"

"My partner gave Foster a shiner to remember him by," he said easily, grabbing a tater tot from the container and sinking into the loud, banana-leaf-patterned sofa. "Once he saw him, all bets were off. And he's one hell of a southpaw."

Cora sat on the other end of the sofa and passed him the little container of aioli. "What's his problem with Ezra? How do they even know each other?"

"His trainee died in that car accident, Cor. And the other still hasn't woken up."

Cora couldn't look him in the eye. Instead, she focused on a potted plant. "That's the funeral you went to."

"It was." His voice was still calm, but only just. "I need you to tell me what you know."

"It wouldn't change anything."

Ryland shifted, resting his ankle on his knee. "Ricky blames Ezra, and he's going to come after him any way he can. That includes the witches he's hiding." He paused, giving her a pointed look. "That includes anyone helping him."

"It wasn't his fault. He wasn't even in the car," she said, half a whisper. She'd figured the hunters would investigate, but she hadn't realized Ryland had such a personal stake in it. "He let us borrow it."

"Why?"

"The witch who gave birth? The one you helped? Quinn and I were moving her to that safe house when they followed us."

Ryland sat back, rubbed a hand over his beard. Cora could see the gears whirring behind his eyes, the understanding he'd not just aided witches that night, but aided the same witches who were involved in the death of his partner's trainee. He was in deep, and only getting deeper.

He said nothing for a long time, jiggling his leg. Then: "Ricky was shot on a call. That's why he was on a crutch. Staying out of the field has slowed him down, but he's not the type to stay put for long. Especially not with an ax to grind."

"There must be something we can do." Cora bit her lip. "Maybe a neuromancer could—"

"No." One word, with all the authority of a hunter behind it. "He might be a problem, but I'm not going to let someone mess around in his head. With his memories."

Cora's cheeks burned. She was so used to tossing ideas like that around, she'd forgotten he still had plenty of reservations about magic itself, even if his opinion of her had changed. "Right. Sorry." She picked up the container of tater tots again, desperate for a way to diffuse the tension, and offered him another.

To her relief, he took it. "We'll think of something."

The silence stretched between them again, even as the couch seemed to grow smaller. Cora finally asked, "What had you come here to tell me, anyway? Before Ricky arrived."

Ryland exhaled, long and slow. His eyes were shadowed by some emotion Cora couldn't read. "I looked into Sebastian."

Wait, what?

173

Cora paused mid-chew, her hand near her mouth, as all of the air left the room. A jolt of fear shot through her chest, sharp and hot. Had it always been so warm in here?

She fought down a swallow. "Looked into him? How?"

A muscle in Ryland's jaw ticked. "That's not important. But he's alive."

Alive.

He was *alive*.

"You're sure?" she asked, not daring to hope, not until he'd said it again and she could confirm she hadn't hallucinated it the first time. All the shame and guilt she'd felt moments before, every emotion not currently teetering on the precipice of incredulous joy, whooshed out of her.

Ryland nodded. "I'm sure. And I know where to find him."

"You know *where—*?"

The world seemed to tip sideways. Vertigo gripped her, then something giddier, lighter. She could almost float.

She had prayed, every day, that she hadn't seen him on Samhain because there had been no one to see. That he'd somehow made it this far, soldiered through, found a way to keep going in spite of everything. She thought for sure she'd be able to feel it if he was dead.

She'd been right.

She leapt to her feet, unsure what to do, raking her fingers through her hair. She wanted to dance and cry and shout it from the rooftops. Her cheeks were wet, and she was laughing as Ryland stood and began to say something else, and before either of them realized what was happening, she'd grabbed either side of his face and kissed him.

She supposed she might have kissed anyone in that moment, spilling over with grateful delight as she was, but the second her lips met his and his words died in his throat, she remembered he *wasn't* just anyone.

Her heartbeat wouldn't rush in her ears like this for just anyone.

Coherent thought wouldn't abandon her for just anyone.

And that wasn't just anyone's arms settling around her as he kissed her back on a ragged inhale, first slowly, like his brain hadn't yet caught up with it all, then deeper and more frantic, drinking in her joy without apology.

All she could be sure of was the tickle of his beard, the strength of his chest against hers, the last stubborn base notes of his cologne. Sluggish heat burned through her blood, like she'd awakened something lying dormant.

174

All the times she'd wondered, as a girl, what it might've been like if he'd kissed her the night before he left...it had never come close to this warmth and softness and hardness of him all at once, how her body had shut down any protests from her brain, how she wanted to yank away from him just as much as she wanted to stay.

But she did finally break from him, touching her lips and breathing short, ragged breaths against her fingertips. The clarity she'd hoped would follow, once free of his touch, didn't.

She wished he'd say something. Anything. A deer frozen in headlights, all her vulnerabilities cast into sharp, unforgiving relief, she finally opened her mouth to speak. "I'm...I'm sorry, I don't know what—"

"Never," he interrupted, their faces close enough for his breath to caress her cheek, "apologize for doing *that*." His words fell between them like bricks, each heavier than the last. He brushed a piece of hair from her face, following the line of her jaw, then tilted her chin up with his thumb and forefinger. "I am going to tell you where your brother is," he said, his voice impossibly even and calm despite the fire in his eyes.

"Okay," she managed, still coming down. The thought of Sebastian was more than enough to ground her again.

"I can't control what you do with this information. I knew that when I came here."

"Okay," she said again, a little steadier this time.

"But fuck if you didn't just make it harder for me, Cor."

She knew what he meant. She felt it there, too—a humming in her gut, knowing what he'd risked to tell her this. And he'd be standing there, wondering how he could be okay with all the ways she might put herself in danger because of it. Maybe it would have been easier to bear if there was the plausible deniability of their friendship, something giving them both permission to back away and let it be, enforce the emotional distance they'd tried so hard to maintain.

But that wasn't what faced them now. Not after that kiss, that simple confirmation of everything they'd never said to each other. They both had to make their peace with it.

"Tell me," was all she said.

So he told her.

175

CHAPTER FIFTEEN

Cora had been working in Mindy's garden since early this morning, but she'd passed the whole day on autopilot, her mind a whirlwind of thought, and her chest tight with emotion.

Seb was alive.

Ryland had kissed her back.

Sebastian was just hours away in Morongo Valley.

She and Mindy had driven right past there on their way to Joshua Tree. They'd been a stone's throw from him.

Ryland had kissed her back.

Nell might be in that prison. Oscar might be in that prison.

Ryland had kissed her back.

They knew where Seb was.

She couldn't begin to guess how she'd get Sebastian out of there. But it didn't matter yet. It wasn't enough to steal her giddiness away.

And when she'd come home and told Mindy last night, and they'd clung to each other like they'd fly away with joy if they didn't anchor each other to the world, it hadn't mattered, either. For now, they just desperately needed to feel something that wasn't grief. They'd allow themselves that much.

Cora sat back on her heels and looked at the roll of black landscaping fabric she'd use to replace the weathered one beneath the bed of gravel. She could've done this magically, but she'd wanted to feel the dirt under her fingernails, pound the dozens of little metal stakes into the ground herself, and soak her shirt through. There was a unique catharsis in it.

And until now it had hurt to let herself feel more. As much as she missed the breath of the earth, she hadn't been able to bring herself to reach for it without Sebastian here.

But going through the motions of it, building herself up to the idea, she could feel today was different.

Her family had lived in all those things, too, and she wanted them back. It was like losing her vision or sense of smell; the difference between just digging in the dirt and understanding it, hearing what it had to say.

She shed her gardening gloves and dug her fingers into the warm grass, opening herself up to the tiny patch of garden that lay securely within Mindy's masking spell. Down, down she went into the soil, fanning out through the roots of the old Australian Willow overhead, listening to the song of the wind rustling its long, fragrant limbs. There were squirrels in its branches, and it was happy to have the company. It was a sentiment the creeping passionflower vine shared, though its visitors ran more to the hummingbirds stopping by on their way further south, and bees who hadn't yet been sent into hibernation by the November chill. It would stop flowering soon, and Cora encouraged its blooms to stay open just a little longer, fed it just enough magic to keep those creatures happy for a few more weeks yet. Selfishly, she loved watching them, and knew Mindy did, too.

A buzzing, buzzing, *buzzing* at the base of skull snapped her out of it. Someone had crossed the perimeter, and not someone Mindy had attuned the wards to. Cora withdrew her magic and bottled it, abandoning her tools in the backyard and dashing into the house.

A knock echoed through the foyer as she slid the sliding patio door shut and locked it. She grabbed a knife from the block in the kitchen and silently moved to the peephole, her heart pounding. Pip, who'd been moonlighting as a coffee-table book on aerial photography, bounced at her heels. Mindy wouldn't be back for a few hours yet, so that was a small comfort, but—

It was Ryland.

Holding...flowers?

Cora swung the door open and peered up at him, taking in the knit cap over his dark, wind-tousled curls, the muted flannel beneath his saddle leather jacket. She'd forgotten it was chilly out, after the hours she'd spent working in the yard. His black eyes were warm, though, as they found their way to the serrated bread knife still in her hands. "Greet all your guests this way?"

Pip bounced upward and into Ryland's collar. He yelped as Pip wiggled down his shirt and popped out his left sleeve in what Cora guessed was an enthusiastic hello. Cora swallowed, lowering the knife. "How did you know where I live?"

"I don't know where you live. I know where Jennie Sinclair lives, though, with her aunt Mabel. Would be a pretty shit TAC Specialist if I couldn't figure that out."

"You brought..." She finally acknowledged the bright yellow blooms in his hands. "A kalanchoe." It wasn't a bouquet of cut flowers. It was a living plant.

He'd remembered.

He'd remembered that she hated cut flowers because she couldn't hear them. Because she just saw them as tiny, withering corpses.

"For you and Mindy." He shrugged. "Thought maybe I could...soften her up a bit."

Cora didn't know what to say. A little ember of something ignited in her chest. She realized he was still standing on the doorstep. "Um, here, come inside. Thank you." She took the plant from him, and he stepped into the foyer. "This will probably come across as rude, but..."

"...why am I here?" he suggested, slanting his lips.

"I just meant...is everything okay?"

"Does it have to not be, for me to appear unannounced on your doorstep?"

"I..." She suddenly became aware of her sweat-soaked shirt, her gym shorts, the dirt under her fingernails, her hair escaping wildly from its loose bun. "I wish you'd warned me, that's all." Goddess, he was looking at her like none of that mattered anyway, and she felt completely exposed. "Mindy's not back yet, but I'm sure she'll love this," she said, changing the subject as they headed toward the kitchen. "The yellow ones are her favorite."

"That looks painful," he said, following her to the island counter.

She set the kalanchoe down and turned to him, frowning. "What does?"

"Your neck. The back of it. Tomato-red."

"Oh, for fuck's sake," she said, twisting as if that would help her see it. "I always forget to spell my damn neck."

"Too good for sunscreen?"

"Very funny. Honestly, I don't even think we keep it in the house anymore." Cora sought refuge from his gaze in the walk-in pantry as she rifled through the various jars of concoctions Mindy kept around. Why was this so damn awkward? Why did a plant have the power to turn the world on its head?

She found the salve she was looking for and turned back to the door, but Ryland was blocking her exit, leaning casually against the wall. "What's all this?"

"Mindy's apothecary," she said with a sweep of her hand. "Everything a witch could possibly need, and plenty you probably never will." She turned a mason jar around, label facing front. *15-minute nap serum* had been crossed off with a permanent marker and above it read *52-minute nap serum*. That, too, had been crossed out, with a note: *OLD RECIPE, UNSTABLE, DO NOT DRINK.*

Ryland pulled a jar off a shelf and swished it around, holding it up to the light. A tiny, preserved anole lizard floated inside, behind the vague label: *USE THIS ONE, NOT THE OTHER ONE.* "She certainly has her...system," he murmured, and put it back. "You sure whatever you've got there is safe to use?"

Cora looked down at the jar of burn salve, which only had a date scribbled on it. "Hasn't failed me yet." She moved to leave the pantry, but he still filled the doorway, still smiled easily.

Her stomach fluttered. They hadn't talked about the other night at all. They hadn't even texted a casual "hello."

Goddess, she wished she'd had time to take a shower.

"You want help?" he asked, breaking the spell.

She put a hand on his chest and shoved past him, under no illusions she would've been able to do it if he hadn't let her. "I can handle it, thanks."

"Why not just heal yourself?"

"Healing takes work. I've been working all day. And Mindy," she said, opening the jar and using a spatula to scoop some greenish goop out, "already did that work for me, bless her." She hissed as the cool paste made contact with the back of her neck, goosebumps rippling up and down her arms. "Now tell me why you're really here. Besides to make nice with Mindy."

Clink, clink, clink.

179

Three small, amber glass vials sat on the counter when she turned around. Ryland frowned at them, as if half-considering whether to put them back in his jacket.

"What are those?" Cora fitted the lid back on the jar and set it down, palming a vial when he didn't immediately answer.

He watched her hold it up to the light, rolling it between her fingers. "Crash."

She froze, lowering her hand.

"I want you to take them," he added, as if it would clarify things.

Unease and dubious excitement churned together in her stomach until she couldn't tell which was which. "Why?"

Ryland settled onto a barstool with a slow exhale. "I took a call. Years ago. Old storage unit someone had been keeping magical contraband in. They'd managed to get their hands on some Crash, too."

"How?"

"No idea. They wouldn't reveal their source. But we *were* able to get them to confess they'd been micro-dosing it, trying to figure out if they could build up some sort of immunity."

Cora was tracking, and the excitement in her stomach became less dubious. "Did it work?"

"Officially, no."

She heard the unsaid 'but.' "Unofficially?"

Theo drummed his fingers absently against the granite. "Unofficially, there was an incident at the prison they were sent to. I don't know more than that because I don't have the clearance. But there were certainly rumors. It was a big deal at the time, some kind of breakthrough magic. Begs the question, doesn't it?"

Cora looked back at the vial in her hand, suddenly floored by what she held. He'd given this to her because he was afraid of what she'd do with the knowledge of Sebastian's whereabouts. He wanted to truly give her a fighting chance. "You don't want me on your conscience."

"I don't want you helpless. That's different."

It didn't matter. It was an opportunity to level the playing field. Anything else it meant, anything else he felt...

"Amber glass," she finally said, nodding at the other two vials. "Does it degrade?"

"With UV rays. And reacts badly with certain plastics."

"Expensive to make, then." She set it down. "Is there enough to share?"

"I can requisition a little more without raising eyebrows. Larger quantities are harder, restricted to prison orders. But I'm not even sure if this will work. I want to test it with you."

"What? Right now?"

He smirked, eying her gardening clothes. "You have somewhere better to be?"

"I did, in fact, have a hot date with the shower." If he was going to stick around for a bit, that was where she drew the line: clean clothes.

His scarred brow lifted. "Fine, then. Don't let me stop you."

Cora took a longer in the shower than she'd meant to, but she needed the time to gather herself. She wasn't sure why the gesture had surprised her so much—it wasn't the first time he'd helped her. Maybe the feeling bowling her over right now was a real thread of trust taking root.

This wasn't just her dragging him to the safe house or inviting him to see their old street again.

Sebastian's whereabouts, the Crash...he'd brought this to her doorstep on his own.

As she stepped out of Mindy's master bathroom, toweling off her hair and pulling on a sweater and jeans, voices floated in from beyond the bedroom door.

Shit, shit, *shit*. Mindy was home. And Cora hadn't thought to warn her with a text.

Cora found them facing off over a plate of steaming shepherd's pie. "I insist," Mindy was saying from across the kitchen, and it wasn't *quite* warmth in her voice. Hearing the bedroom door open, she said to Cora, "Did you hit your damn head, woman?"

Cora stopped short, tracking from Ryland's uncertain face to Mindy's steely one. "I—no?"

"You didn't suffer amnesia? Forget your manners completely?"

Ryland cut in. "It's no problem at all, really. I'm not hungry."

"Men are always hungry," Mindy grumbled, scooping more pie from the Tupperware she'd opened. And next to it: two more plates. Three sets of cutlery in a pile on the counter. A few cans of La Croix.

Goddess help her, Mindy invited him to stay for dinner.

Ryland swallowed. He seemed to realize this was a test. The microwave's hum and timer beep filled the silence as Cora fetched napkins, at a loss for anything else to do.

As she sat, she had the distinct feeling of having been sent to the principal's office, and the set of Ryland's shoulders said the same.

"Now, then." Mindy brought the reheated plates to the table and doled out flatware. Her voice had a keen edge. "This is nice, isn't it?"

It was an effort not to choke on her first bite, no matter how good it was. Cora swallowed and said, with a curious indifference she didn't at all feel, "How long has it been since you two saw each other?"

Ryland was better at this than Cora was. "Was it Catalina?" He paused, then shook his head. "No, that Fourth of July. You brought the most incredible peach galettes." He took a bite, then leveled a fork at Mindy. "Those I'll never forget."

Mindy wasn't swayed by the praise, though she looked tempted. "Got yourself into a bit of trouble since then, haven't you?"

"It has a way of finding me."

Knowing exactly the kind of trouble he'd gotten into with Cora, and also knowing he knew that *she* knew, Mindy decided not to waste time rehashing. "Like that scar there." She gestured to the one dividing his eyebrow. "You didn't always have that, did you?"

"Sure didn't."

"It must have a story?" Her eyes gleamed with interest.

Cora froze mid-chew. Mindy was playing a dangerous game, asking those kinds of questions. "Min, don't be rude—"

Ryland held up a hand. "It's okay. Really."

"You don't have to answer," Cora murmured to him.

"I said it's fine," Ryland repeated with finality, grinning now. Cora kicked him under the table. What the hell was he doing?

Mindy sipped her drink. "Regale us, dear."

He shifted, sitting up a bit. "Well, Cora's probably told you how I got taken to the Academy, and all that." Mindy nodded, and he continued, "I came in as a minor, so I was in Pre-Academy until I turned eighteen, which is when they send you over to live in the actual training barracks. A witch joined our class not long after I moved in, one who'd turned. An older guy called Richie."

"Turned?" Mindy asked, leaning in. "Do you know why?"

"Far as I remember, he was already military when he was outed. Some kind of special ops. Too dangerous to keep around, too valuable to lose. The choice to turn wasn't exactly a choice for him, so I heard." He absently folded the corners of his napkin, eyes darkening. "A pregnant girlfriend who'd outstayed her visa, and a veiled threat to send her back to Honduras where the cartels had a price on her head. They'd met when he was down there doing...something or other."

"Tough break," Mindy said, and Cora knew the emotions warring on her face—sympathy for the traitor, guilt for the sympathy, anger for the injustice of it all.

"Don't feel too bad for him, now." Ryland winked, expertly sidestepping the unease rolling off her. "He was an insufferable smartass. He'd done Basic years ago, since he was enlisted, but he still had to do all the TACS training. You can imagine that didn't go over easy with a decorated combat vet, let alone special forces. Having magic didn't do his ego any favors, either."

With annoyance giving way to curiosity, Cora leaned forward a hair. This had been such a big part of his life, and she knew almost nothing about it. She wanted so badly to fill in the blank pages of him.

"Now the Academy instructors ran a tight ship." Ryland was settling into himself, allowing the dynamic to shift. A few moments ago, Mindy had owned the room—now it was his. Even Pip had abandoned whatever form he'd taken in the pantry, squeezing out between the crack in the door to listen from among the salt and pepper shakers on the table. "They'd never dealt with a witch in the LA Academy before, because the program was still young, so they were always wary of Richie. He thought it was time to mess with them. Too good of an opportunity to pass up."

A grin tugged at Ryland's lip. "They caught him slacking one day, and it just happened to be one of the six days per year it rains down here. So, the drill sergeant got creative with his punishment, sent Richie outside with a broom to clear the rain off the sidewalk."

Mindy's brow rose, but she clearly had no desire to interrupt.

"You can imagine this exercise in futility didn't sit well with Richie, but he made a show of going to do it, anyway. Guess what he did next."

"I couldn't possibly," Mindy said.

"Ten minutes later we hear Sarge bellowing outside, and we all run out there. Richie is standing there going, 'Sir, I've completed the task you assigned me and made sure the sidewalk is clear of rain, Sir.'" And we look around, realizing that while the rain's coming down, it's not actually hitting the sidewalk. It's just bouncing around it, flowing into the grass or the street."

Mindy gasped an incredulous laugh. "He didn't!"

"Sarge had a conniption. Once Richie was out of the brig, we got him good and hammered. He needed it, too, because they'd threatened punitive discharge, which in his case would mean a one-way ticket to the prisons. I doubt they'd have really done it, because they weren't exactly up to their ears in magic-wielding volunteers, but they sure scared him straight."

Mindy asked, "But the scar?"

Ryland's lip quirked. "Same night, I face-planted into the corner of a table after having a few too many. Of all my injuries on the force, it's the least exciting one."

Mindy sat back, chuckling, staring into her drink. "I don't know what to make of you, Teddy."

"How so?" he asked, leaning back to mirror her.

"I know there are lines we draw. Certainly feels like this should be one of 'em. But you've given us a reason to hope, and that's no small feat right now." She fisted her napkin, and Pip slouched over, pressing against her hand. "You found Seb. You saved Cora. And you risked your hide to bring those here." She glanced over at the vials of Crash. "Regardless of what you believe, of the things you've done, I can at least look you in the eye and tell you I'm grateful for that."

Ryland looked down at his plate as the silence settled. Then he said, "There's a lot I'm not proud of. But this family has always been good to me."

It wasn't a plea for forgiveness. And perhaps that made it all the more genuine to Mindy.

Pip had been fascinated by this whole exchange, but in the heady quiet that followed, the Crash vials caught his eye. He swirled and bopped his way over to them, poking one. It tipped over, rolling away from him, and he plucked it up again with a formless limb, carefully rearranging the vials back into a line.

As they watched Pip, something Ryland said earlier percolated in the back of Cora's mind. "What did you mean," she said slowly, wheels turning, "before Mindy came home, when you said 'prison orders' of Crash? Of Recantanyl? Where does it come from?"

Both sets of eyes snapped to her. Ryland frowned. "It's manufactured in a secret facility somewhere—there are a few. I don't have the clearance to know specifics. But the conditions are precise, controlled." He scratched his beard thoughtfully. "I'd guess prisons are sourced by their nearest plant, same as us. Why?"

"Have you ever seen how it's shipped?" Adrenaline zipped through her gut.

"It's delivered to our base in trucks, marked as produce or something innocuous. I've seen them unload it before."

"In plain sight," she breathed, seeing the exact moment Mindy realized where she was headed.

"You thinking of stealing one?" he asked, concern creeping into his voice.

"Not quite." Cora stood, kicking back her chair, too jittery to keep still. "Just...commandeering. What if we swapped out the drug? Planted *fake* Recantanyl in that delivery truck?"

Mindy stared at her. "A delivery of a harmless, useless placebo to a prison," she said, working through it. "And they'll use it, none the wiser, on those witches—"

"—who can break themselves out when their magic returns," Ryland finished. Mindy and Cora both turned to him, waiting for more. He chewed on it for a solid minute. Finally: "It's...not the worst idea. In theory."

He was struggling with it, she could tell. The idea of a bunch of witches he'd put away just back on the streets in an instant. But he had to have known this was a possibility when he'd given them Sebastian's location. She let him work through the discomfort, until he finally said: "The Beach is Tier 1, minimum security. Lot of folks there who don't deserve to be. Wrong place, wrong time. Wrong friends or neighbors. Kids there, too. That's where the Academy pulls them from if they can."

He leaned forward, his face stony. "Tier 2 gets a little more nebulous. Tier 3...those are the ones I'm invested in keeping where they are. And frankly, you should be, also."

Mindy stilled, staring him down, like she was steeling herself for a fight. Cora jumped in before it could derail. They were so close to figuring this out. So fucking close. "Is this even workable, with The Beach? Beyond 'in theory?'"

He pulled at his beard, body tense under the heat of Mindy's glare. "The manufacturing, the routes, the schedules are all need-to-know, and I don't have clearance to. If Command catches me digging, it's game over."

"Let's say they didn't," Mindy said. "Let's say we found the routes, knew where the truck would be and when. We...what, pull a roadside heist?

Somehow unpack all of that shit, swap it out, re-pack it without anyone noticing that truck is off schedule?"

He stood, restless now. "More to consider: what reinforcements would the feds send in if they tried it? How far would the prisoners get without outside support?"

"And how would those witches know they could use their magic after so long living without it?" Cora added. She was willing to bet most of them had given up on trying.

"That one's not a problem," Ryland said. "Nell's there, too. And her parents. I could make an appointment at The Beach to question the Tesauros about Ezra, as part of my investigation, and tell them what they need to know."

"We'll need help from the outside," Mindy mumbled. "A lot of it. Those people are going to need somewhere to go."

"Min," Cora breathed, realization dawning, "That prison is built just miles away from a ley convergence. *Our* convergence."

Mindy stared at Cora. Theo stared at Mindy.

"You're fucking kidding me," Theo said.

"Leyra's left tit, you're absolutely right," Mindy said, ignoring him. "We'd just need to power up a couple leapstones to send 'em there. We could even get a few people to move in, draw the guards away...but how would we know when? We can't communicate with anyone inside."

Cora walked over to the island counter, and Pip spilled into her hands. He nearly vibrated with excitement, picking up on the energy in the room. "Maybe that's not true." She stroked his head. "Can I ask a favor, Pip?"

Pip sat up as straight as he could while wobbling to and fro. Cora grabbed a scrap of paper from a kitchen drawer and scribbled a happy face on it, then rolled it up tight and secured it with a shiny paper clip. She turned back to the sprite. "Could you give this to Theo for me?"

Pip reached for the paper and examined it, deciding the paperclip was sufficient payment, and folded the note into himself. After a long second, he seemed to remember he'd been given instructions, and drifted over to Theo's empty plate.

Theo stared at him, waiting, but nothing happened. Pip sat there patiently.

Then he understood. Theo reached into his pocket and fished around, procuring a gleaming penny. Pip bounced up to relieve him of it and pulled the note out of wherever it had been hiding. It unfolded slowly on the table.

"Baby girl, you're your mother's daughter through and through," Mindy said with pride, looking sharply at Cora. "I'll bring it to the altas. See what kind of trouble they want to get into."

———⟨∞⟩———

Cora supposed she'd had worse family dinners. At least this one had ended with a half-baked plan for a prison break.

She and Theo now sat in the living room with the shades drawn against nosy neighbors, staring at Cora's nightcap on the coffee table: a syringe and a vial of Crash. Mindy had given them some space, turning in early, though Cora was willing to bet she'd sleep with one eye open.

They'd decided to try practicing with small doses and see what was possible. Theo uncapped the vial and syringe, pulling a few milliliters from it and squeezing a drop from the tip of the needle.

"If you're hit with this," Theo said, crouching next to her, "you'll still go down from the sedative. The good news is whoever shot you won't immediately realize the Crash hasn't worked. When you wake up, their guard will be down."

"And the bad news is I'm out for hours."

"We can't avoid it. TACS never carry pure Recantanyl; only prisons do. For now, you'll try to break through in small increments, and we'll work up from there."

He was much gentler than the first time, but she still flinched when the tip of the needle pierced the soft flesh in the back of her arm. A wave of drowsiness crested through her, warm and heavy, but she fought through it.

She closed her eyes and fell into a meditative trance. The ambient sounds of dishwasher churning in the other room fell away until all she heard was the thrum of her own heartbeat. She reached down into the earth, digging toward the ley line, groping for the edge of a string to tug. Instead, she found a slick black mass of tendrils writhing around it, cutting her off.

Everything about it felt wrong. It was a sour note on an instrument; a bite into something too cold, singing through her skull. Reaching toward it made her skin crawl. Everything inside her screamed to pull back—it pulsed, dark and angry and awful—but she shoved through the fear and grabbed hold of it.

She recoiled, yanked back to the present. A shiver rode through her. He wasn't going to like what she was about to tell him.

Theo frowned. "What's wrong?"

Cora waited for the next shiver to pass, then took a deep breath. "This isn't just chemical. This wasn't just created by scientists."

"What, then?"

In his eyes, she could see he already knew. "Crash is alchemy. It's made with corrupted abjuration magic."

Theo's expression shuttered.

The silence thickened, curdled.

Cora scrambled for a way to diffuse it. "Recantanyl abjures magic in the body, at the source. It cuts me off from the ley lines, makes those threads slippery. They don't respond to the passive magic in me, seek it out. But it does something else, too. It keeps you from *wanting* to really fight it. And that's high-level neuromancy, not just abjuration."

He ran his hand across his face, jiggled his leg. "Fuck." He jerked to his feet and walked over to the window, back again, muttered a string of curses under his breath.

"Are you really that surprised?"

His eyes flashed. "I wish I was. I'm angry that I'm not."

"They don't tell you?"

"Of course not." Fury built within him, rolled off of him as he paced. "Witches who turn, they can deal with. They can say, look how noble our cause is, even the enemy's on board. But if people knew about this?"

"Their moral high ground would be destroyed," Cora said sourly.

He ran a hand through his wild hair. "The irony is, if they'd just come out from the get-go and told everyone we could only fight magic with magic, nobody would hold that logic against them. Instead, they spent years building this image, this brand, internally." He scoffed as he said, "Good old-fashioned hard work and ingenuity made Recantanyl, they tell us. We're better than magic. We don't need it. It's wild. It's dangerous. It could set little Timmy's hair on fire for no reason at all. You don't want to set little Timmy's hair on fire, do you?"

Yeah, she could see it. Was that how he he'd felt, as a recruit? "People with power sell that lie because they're scared," Cora said. "They're afraid of losing control. They're afraid of being less. You can't work hard to become a witch; you can't throw money at someone to make you a witch;

you can't schmooze your way into becoming one over a game of golf at the country club or by rubbing elbows with the right people."

Theo nodded, an incredulous laugh riding through his words. "All the power, influence, and money in the world but you'll still think someone's got it better if they have magic and you don't. What's left, except using that to keep the scales tipped? If they copped to using magic, they'd be admitting they're afraid. Their egos won't let them."

"So, they sow fear in others instead," Cora finished for him. It made so much sense, she didn't know why she hadn't seen it sooner.

It was such an individualistic thing, that fear. Because you could walk around with a license in Oslo, or Patras, or Seoul. If you declared your hydromancy, you could work in agriculture, or if you were a healer, you could get special dispensation to work in a hospital; on other hand, diviners had to put their investments in a blind trust, or if you declared your pyromancy, you needed extra insurance.

It didn't matter that many witches didn't declare and license themselves; the seeds of acceptance had been planted. The option was there. It had been there even before all those governments weighed in, when everything went to hell in the US, and made it their official response to the chaos.

Would it work? Was it sustainable? Nobody knew. It was the world's greatest experiment. Everyone was watching, waiting for something terrible to happen. Progress was slow, like the witches there were emerging from a long sleep, yawning, looking out the window, deciding if they wanted to take that first shaky step into a legitimate existence.

Cora understood the caution. There was power in being an unknown quantity, a secret. There were still protests in those places, just a different flavor, a new kind of prejudice.

And back here, the news networks owned by the media oligarchs whose egos were some of the very ones in question dragged those countries through the mud every day, and everyone kept locking each other up.

Theo pinched the bridge of his nose and steered them back to the issue at hand. "Is it possible to break through it? Does that mean it's a waste of time to try?"

"No." Cora chewed her lip. "I mean no, it's not a waste of time to try. Every witch has passive magic—it's how we connect to the ley lines—not in our active magic reservoir, but in our cells, our DNA. It doesn't do anything, really, it's just kind of there, but I might be able to tap into it. Let me go back in and give it a shot."

As her eyes fluttered shut, she sank back down into her mind, into limbo, until she found the inky mass again. It contorted, quivered, crawled over itself. But she saw it for what it was now and faced it down, ignoring the warnings her hindbrain screamed. She bottled her revulsion and reached out.

She pushed against her passive magic, sent a ripple through it. Pushed again, sent another. Her head throbbed in time with her pulse, a bead of sweat followed the slope of her nose, but she shoved aside her physical discomfort. A gentle tide rose and fell, lapping at the edges of the wrongness, gathering momentum with each nudge of her will against it.

She could feel her muscles contract with each push. No, that wasn't the way. She relaxed into it instead.

Passive magic couldn't be forced to listen. She had to move with it, flow with it, not fight it. She had to be the ocean. Be the waves. Wear it down.

After what felt like hours—there was no way to know, time moved differently in this state—a chunk of the eroded Crash loosened, broke away.

A golden thread wriggled, sensing freedom. It slithered loose. A second one followed.

She seized and pulled, unraveling and unraveling, spooling magic into herself as if she needed a reminder that she could. As if she could banish that awful wrongness from memory just by wrapping herself in power again. Then she rose up and out, spilling herself back into the present and the soft lamplight of the room where Theo was dozing.

"Theo! I did it!" she squealed, not caring that she'd jolted him awake. "I broke through!"

Theo jerked upright, blinking, like he'd forgotten where he was. Then: "What? It worked?"

"It worked!" She looked back down at the syringe he'd left on the table, and realized she was shaking with exhaustion. "It's possible. I know you hardly gave me anything, but...with a little practice...enough time..."

When she looked back up at him, there was something familiar and sad in his eyes. It fell short of relief, fell short of hope, like he was afraid to let himself feel them.

She understood that fear all too well. A million doors had flown open between dinner and this moment. Maybe one or two would lead to a future they'd all survive to see.

It'd be so easy to pick the wrong one.

CHAPTER SIXTEEN

"What time do you get off? You wanna grab dinner from that new vegan place down the way?" Quinn had used her break to pop down to Boardroom when Cora had told her about the kiss and had stayed to catch up on everything that had happened at Mindy's the other night. Cora was indulging her between customers, swapping out price tags for their fall sale, and looking for Pip amongst the skim boards.

Today Quinn wore a sleek side-shave of icy blue hair and long, pearlescent white nails. Her irises were veined with purple. Shifters collected a library of different forms over time—they started off with the ability to change aspects of their human appearance and went from there. Transforming into an animal meant spending hundreds of hours bonding with it first, understanding it. Quinn had once spent an entire summer sitting by the Great Horned Owl enclosure at San Diego Zoo.

It was easier, and much more practical, for her to change up her look and call it a day—but she did occasionally take flight.

Cora considered. "Holiday hours haven't started yet, so we could swing it. I skipped lunch today, so I won't balk at lab-grown meat."

"That's actually not vegan."

Cora opened her mouth, frowned, and then closed it. "It's not?"

"Well, it's still meat."

"You can't possibly believe that."

"I've heard they do a mean portobello steak, though."

"See, here's my problem," Cora said. Quinn rolled her eyes and mimed handing her a soapbox. "You can't just drown a mushroom in A1 and call it steak. Why do the mental gymnastics for the steak fantasy? Why not be satisfied with the mushroom?"

"I trust the chef. His restaurant in New York has a Michelin star." Quinn wrinkled her nose. "Come to think of it, you probably need a reservation. Like, a month in advance."

"A month's wait for plant-based cheese. Will wonders never cease?"

"That's *Michelin-star-adjacent* plant-based cheese."

Cora watched the lone customer linger at the front of the store for a moment longer. The moment they left, Quinn picked up where she'd left off before anyone had come in. "A fucking roadside hijacking, Cor? Are you insane?"

"I thought you'd be excited! That's right up your alley."

"Right, let me just pencil it in between my two o'clock train robbery and four o'clock jewelry heist."

"Mindy already ran it by the altas. They have a plan."

"Those altas are not your fucking friends, Cor. You learned as much on Samhain."

"I don't need them to be! I just need them as invested as I am in making this work."

Quinn sighed, knowing this was already out of her hands. "Okay, what's this grand plan of theirs?"

Even without customers in the store, Cora lowered her voice. "You know Helena's club? The one Harry works at?"

"Malleus? Yeah. That place sounds like a trip."

"Helena told Mindy Theo's *commander goes.*" Cora paused to let that sink in. "His fucking commander!"

"No way."

"Yes!" Cora leaned closer. "She used his clearance to get the shipping routes. She's already planted the instructions in his head, and she's just waiting for him to come back with them."

"What? So fast?"

"I guess he came in the other day, and she made the call right then and there. Ghislaine was *pissed* when she found out. They'd had a whole meeting set up to discuss the way forward, and she ripped the rug out from under all of them."

Quinn whistled. "Helena better watch her back. Ghislaine will turn her into a toad."

"Worse, if she can get away with it."

"I love alta drama. It's so much better than mine."

A companionable silence fell as Cora began re-folding shirts.

After a long moment, Quinn said, "I...still can't believe it. About the Crash."

Cora couldn't, either. "I think it really fucked Ryland up." But maybe it would give him the ability to forgive himself, too—to understand he wasn't just betraying the hunters. Because they had betrayed him first.

"What the hell goes on in those labs? I'd bet my left tit they're not just using volunteers to make the stuff."

A macabre image took shape before Cora could stop it: an assembly line of alchemists, abjurers, and neuromancers, in a sterile, lightless bunker somewhere. All with guns to their heads.

Or guns to the heads of their loved ones. That felt more like the hunters' style.

"They'd need a lot of them," Cora said. "I wonder if they source from the prisons."

Quinn opened her mouth to respond, but a commotion from down the street drew their attention to the display window. They could hear shouting—no, more rhythmic, chanting—though it was difficult to tell what was being said. From the mouth of where Market Street intersected the boardwalk, they caught glimpses of the marching crowd.

It wasn't the usual mix of eccentric artists, tourists, and skateboarders—it was more organized, and marchers carried everything from hastily-scrawled upon hunks of cardboard to professionally printed signs. WITCHES, KNOW YOUR RIGHTS, said one.

Bless her. Bless anyone with the courage to put a target that size on their back.

"Did you know this was happening today?" Cora asked.

Quinn shook her head. "I didn't see any of it coming up this way, but I've been here for like..." she checked her phone. "Half an hour. Usually if something's scheduled, Ezra knows about it. Maybe they started in Santa Monica." The front door chimed as she opened it, looking down the block in the other direction, and froze. "But *they* sure didn't."

Cora saw what drew her up short. A clump of angry-looking people with signs of their own were moving towards the shop, en route to intercept the marchers down the way. She read them, one by one.

WE CAN'T FIGHT WHAT WE CAN'T SEE

MAGIC PUTS OUR KIDS AT RISK
YOUR MAGIC IS MY PROBLEM

Quinn was already on her phone. "Hey, Ez? I think things could get messy down here." As she filled Ezra in, two women clutching folded-up signs had peeled off from the boardwalk marchers, ducking into the door Quinn still held open. They were somewhat out of breath and wide-eyed.

"Hey," Cora asked the one who wasn't on her phone, "What's this protest for?"

"This lawyer started it from her office in Santa Monica," the other one said. "She announced her firm would do witch cases pro bono."

Brave, brave idiot. She wouldn't mean criminal cases, because once witches were taken by hunters, due process flew out the window. But civil cases—defamation, wrongful termination, suing for custody—those happened plenty. Folks threw accusations around all the time, and from what Theo had said, hunters dealt with their more than their fair share of bullshit.

Cora dragged Quinn inside as the second group passed by. They watched from the window as both sets of marchers crushed into one another on the boardwalk, bringing everything to a halt. A police cruiser blocked off the intersection to the left, another joining it shortly after. She allowed a small bud of relief to bloom in her chest.

It was a mistake.

When the first shots rang out, it took a moment for Cora's ears to communicate with her brain. For all the violence she'd witnessed on the news and the internet, she had the privilege of never having been shot at. The reality of that pop-pop-pop sound was deceptively innocuous. For a brief, suspended-in-time moment, she thought someone had set off a firecracker. Then screams erupted from the crowd and the illusion shattered.

The marchers broke form and spilled into the alleyways. Some of them screamed as more pop-pop-pops echoed, and people flowed past the store like an erratic river. It was impossible to tell where the shots had come from, or who.

Cora didn't speak, didn't think. She just grabbed Quinn's arm and dragged her behind the register counter. The two women bolted out the front door before Cora's mouth could catch up to her brain and yell at them to get down.

Quinn dug her iridescent nails into Cora's arm and peered around the edge of the counter. Cora followed her eyeline: outside, glass shattered. Someone had broken the façade of the T-shirt shop across the way. The orange glow of flames licked up the wall, and they spread as another Molotov cocktail was lobbed inside.

She weighed their options. The thought of getting hit by a stray bullet was less unpleasant to Cora than being trapped in a burning building. "We need to go, now," she said, and jerked her thumb behind her. "I parked Lucy back that way, just a block down. Take my keys, pull around, and I'll lock up, for all the good that'll do." Anyone could throw a brick through the glass, but a lock would still deter some.

If the building didn't go up in flames, anyway.

"Done. Be back in three." Quinn snatched the key fob Cora tossed to her and disappeared out the back.

Cora hit the lights after taking care of the front door, emptied the register, and grabbed her purse—which Pip was trembling inside. "It's okay, buddy," she said, reaching in to give him a reassuring stroke of her thumb as she closed the grate on the alley door. "We just have to—"

A strong hand clasped over her mouth, yanking her backward and smothering her yelp of surprise. Something sharp pricked her shoulder. Her vision began to swim. Then the shadows swept her under, bleeding together until she could see nothing but dark.

———— ∽ ————

On any other day, Theo might have been replaying that moment in his head, the one where Cora had said his name.

She'd called him Theo. Not Ryland.

He wasn't sure she'd realized she'd done it. But he definitely had. He just couldn't devote headspace to figuring out what it meant, because he was too busy navigating the pre-sunset crush of pedestrians on Venice boardwalk, swimming upstream toward the orange barricades.

A pair of skateboarders clipped him, and a cop shouted at them, flagging them down. More police were clearing the paths and shops, telling people to go home, as orange flames glowed in the distance behind them. TACS in uniform prowled, too, though none he recognized.

The muffled bangs of homemade fireworks echoed through the night, and trampled signs littered the street, their words bleeding together as they lay in puddles. The smell of damp, charred wood clawed at the back of Theo's throat.

Ezra stood in front of an ice cream shop, just past the barricades, talking to a few police officers. His dreads were pulled back into a ponytail, and he'd thrown a sweater on over his board shorts, like he'd just come in from last glass and didn't have time to change.

When the call came through, it had taken Theo a solid minute to figure out how Ezra could have gotten his number—he finally remembered leaving it with the concierge after Ricky's meltdown, in case the idiot decided to come back. Ezra had just said, "There were shots fired at a protest near Boardroom. Quinn called and said some shit was happening, but she's not answering now."

He'd never been more grateful for his bike and California lane splitting laws.

Theo flashed his badge as he crossed over, returning Ezra's nod. "Anything?"

Ezra shook his head. "Still not answering. Speedway and Pacific are blocked off. They wouldn't let me down to see Boardroom, said there's still activity over there, but—"

"I can get us through." Theo patted his badge, flipping it around so it was visible on his waistband. "You carrying?"

"Excuse me?" Ezra's eyes went wide, and he stopped dead in his tracks. "You...know that shit ain't normal, right? That's not a thing people just...do, at least outside MiliTactiLand or whatever fresh hell you come from."

"Point taken. I have a clutch piece you can use if it comes down to it."

Ezra's eyes went wider, and he shook his head. "Never held one of those in my life. Ain't about to start now. Not to mention this place is crawling with cops just looking for a reason—"

"Suit yourself, but we're wasting time. Curfew's at nine."

Dusk had fallen, and the bike path was eerie as they moved north along it. Side streets sat empty beyond the bright red cast of emergency vehicle lights and the shattered glass that reflected them. Residents smoked from condo balconies, and hotel guests peered through windows, many sets of eyes scanning the darkness between the anemic streetlights. Ezra grabbed an orphaned pocketknife off the concrete as they walked, flipping it shut and fisting his hand tightly around it.

As they turned off the bike path at Market Street, they passed a liquor store, blackened on the left side only, escaping the worst of the neighboring T-shirt shop's fate. The front window gaped, a jagged, empty maw. Their shoes crunched over the remains of it on the sidewalk.

Parking meters blinked red, many of the cars there having outstayed their welcome. Theo recognized one of them, especially the phallic scrape on the side of the passenger's side door. "Wait. Come back, Ezra. This is Cora's car."

As Ezra circled back to him, Theo walked around the front and peered through the driver's side window. He pulled at the handle. Locked. "Well, I suppose that means they're on foot."

"Ezra!"

They both whirled at the sound of Quinn's voice. She dashed around the corner, and Theo had never seen her look anything less than artfully disheveled, but here she was in all of her haggard, panting, sweat-slicked glory.

Ezra closed the distance and crushed her to him, burying his face in her blue hair, murmuring things Theo couldn't hear. By the way they parted suddenly after, staring like they were seeing each other for the first time, he'd guess neither had expected that greeting.

"Where's Cora?" Theo asked, eyes darting to the shadows in the front window of Boardroom. It looked deserted.

Quinn's face was flushed, though he couldn't decide what from. "I don't know."

Dread shot through him. "Wasn't she with you?"

"She told me to pull the car around from a few blocks over while she locked up. I'd left my phone in there, I didn't realize. When I got back and she didn't come out, I went to see what the holdup was. I couldn't get back in, and I found this." Quinn unclasped her fisted hand so he could see.

In her palm sat a broken otter keychain from Monterey Bay Aquarium. He'd seen it before on the ring that held her Boardroom keys. The tiny metal hook atop the plastic had been yanked open.

"Where?" Theo asked, wrapping himself in deadly calm. "How long ago?"

Quinn spoke over her shoulder as she led them around back, to the dumpster by the door. "I ran all up and down Pacific, looked into every shop that wasn't already closed. Maybe thirty, forty minutes, I looked. It took longer because I had to dodge all the cops. I would have shifted, but I couldn't find a safe place to do it. I thought she'd gone searching for me, and we'd just missed each other, but..."

Theo shined his phone light on the ground, stepping slowly from one end of the alley to the other. They walked with him, matching his pace. He didn't know what he was looking for until a few long minutes later, when he finally saw it.

He knelt on the pavement, feeling the weight of both sets of eyes on his back as his fingers brushed over a small plastic cap.

His heart dropped into his stomach as he held it up. It couldn't have been there for long—it was clean, glossy, and clear.

And it was the right size. The right shape. He already knew, but he took out the Crash syringe in his jacket anyway, holding it out for Quinn and Ezra to see. The cap on his own syringe was the same.

They were speaking, but he couldn't hear.

Someone had planned this.

Somebody knew.

Had the unrest just been an opportunity? Had they been sitting on her, waiting to get her alone, jumping at the chance to take her under the cover of all the chaos?

"...scrying to locate her," Quinn was saying. "I'll head to Mindy's. Maybe you guys should come."

"What do you think?" Ezra asked.

Theo looked up, realizing that had been directed towards him. "What?"

"About waiting for them to scry."

"It won't help." He looked back down at the syringe cap. "They won't find her. Not if she's Crashed."

"So, we sit around, then? Do nothing?" Quinn was on the verge of tears. Ezra looked like he was going to be sick—Cora was two for two on being kidnapped near this alleyway. *His* damn alleyway.

Theo stood, pocketing the useless hunk of plastic, mind racing. Quinn would slow them down like this. That was just a fact. They needed to move, and she was breaking down. "No," he lied. "No, you're right. Maybe you'll pick up on something we can use. If it wears off, or she pushes through it..."

She wouldn't. She'd barely gotten through an eighth of a dose the first time. But a little hope shone in Quinn's eyes, and he hated to squash it.

"I'll take her car," she said. "I've already got her keys."

"I'll stay with you," Ezra grunted, nodding at Theo, understanding settling there. Whatever they were about to do, he didn't want Quinn to be part of it. Ezra pulled out his keys, letting her back into the store to grab her phone, and held her close when she emerged again. "Be safe, okay?"

"You, too," she said. "I'll call if we find anything." Then she was gone.

Distant sirens murmured on the breeze as the two men faced one another, alone now. Whatever Ezra had to say to him, it wasn't something he'd thought Quinn should hear.

"You think it's him," Ezra said, his voice low and dangerous. It wasn't a question.

"If he recognized her at Bungalow, he didn't let on. But Ricky's the only one who makes sense."

Betrayal gnawed in his gut, betrayal he had no right to feel. He'd done the same to Ricky, choosing Cora. He couldn't fault Ricky's loyalty to his men.

Loyalty that had once been his, too.

But fuck if it didn't sting, to think that was it. The death rattle of a friendship that had gotten him through the Academy, then rekindled when they'd become partners years later. Someone he'd trusted with his six. Someone who had saved his life more times than he could count.

He didn't have time to wallow in it. He'd unpack all this shit later, or maybe never. He'd have to shut it down, like he always did. Shove it away.

Find Cora first.

"I don't think he was working with anyone, though," Theo said, swallowing hard. "If my CO had sanctioned this, I'd be in cuffs already. They'd court-martial me in an instant."

"Why would he do that?" Ezra asked. "Why not just let them put you away for...treason, or whatever? Wash his hands of it?"

"Could've been too angry to do the rational thing. Or he's still building a case for it. Probably the latter, if he has Cora. Maybe he thinks he can get something out of her." Theo didn't want to imagine how. Ricky could be a downright ruthless bastard.

"There's...something you should know. It might be related."

Ezra's tone set off alarm bells. Theo raised an eyebrow, spread his arms. "Such as?"

"This morning I made sure Harris wouldn't be an issue anymore."

Theo went very, very still. Ezra's entire body tensed, like he sensed a predator had spotted him.

"What did you do?" Theo hissed.

Ezra didn't answer, and hot rage bubbled up inside Theo as he grabbed the front of Ezra's shirt. So much for shutting it down. Heat became frost, and he bit off every icy syllable. "*What* did you do, Foster?"

"What I had to."

"Oh, for fuck's sake." Theo let Ezra yank away from him. "You idiot." He really had underestimated the guy. "Skittish around a gun, but you'd end a man in a coma? Not just an idiot, then—a coward, too. *Jesus.*"

"What would you have done in my place?" The vein in Ezra's temple bulged. "What would you do to protect Cora?"

So that's what this was about.

"I'm doing it, aren't I? And somehow, I've managed to keep her out of the line of fire until you decided *you* knew better." Theo prayed for patience. "You've fucked us. All of us. I had to walk Ricky off a ledge for you, and that was when he thought Harris still had a chance. What do you think he'll do to Cora now that he has nothing to lose?"

"They can't tie it back to me. I made sure of that. If Harris woke up, it wouldn't have just been Quinn's ass on the line or mine. Cora would have been in danger too!"

"That wasn't your decision to make!" Theo got back in Ezra's face again, sized him up. "Jesus fucking Christ, it doesn't *matter* if nobody can tie this back to you. Ricky's on the warpath, and he already blames you. You think he cares what evidence says?"

"You don't know what I've lost," Ezra said through gritted teeth.

Theo did, but this wasn't the time or place to drop that bomb. "I don't need to. It doesn't make you fucking special. It doesn't mean you can do whatever the fuck you want. Now two TACS are dead instead of one, and you'd better pray Ricky won't give us a reason to make it three."

Those words rang in their ears as they stood in that alley, neither willing to be the first to back down. Theo was half-convinced Ezra would take a swing at him, and he almost wanted him to. But something small and bright chose that moment to blink into existence, oozing its way out of Theo's balled fist.

Theo opened his hand, and where Cora's broken otter keychain had once been, sat a trembling Pip. He looked from one man to the other, as if trying to decide whether he'd still rather be that hunk of plastic.

"You," Theo breathed, "have no idea how happy I am to see you right now."

CHAPTER SEVENTEEN

Observations came to Cora in discrete, shattered pieces. A dripping sound. The smell of dust and fresh paint. Wetness on her face, pooling on cool concrete beneath her. The scream of every muscle, every tendon as she tried to move.

Her eyes fluttered open, and the world was sideways. No...she was sideways. She shifted upright too quickly, and her vision darkened before returning. With bound hands, she braced herself against the cool concrete floor when vertigo washed over her.

She was in a building under construction. The dust on the floor was thick enough that permit or budget issues might've halted work on it. Unfinished drywall lined one side of the room, opposite a lone window on the other. The rectangle of glass was high and small. Basement, she guessed, craning her neck upwards.

Water leaked from the exposed ceiling, and a droplet hit her squarely on the forehead. Her ankles were taped together, so she wriggled away from the puddle forming beneath her as best she could.

How had she gotten here? The last thing she remembered was...

Heavy footfalls sounded on the basement steps, and she inched backwards until the wall made it impossible to go any further. A light shone down from above, swaying, and she realized whoever it was carried a lantern. Their silhouette filled the doorway, and then they grabbed a chair, scraping it across the floor until it was mere feet away from her.

They set the lantern down with a clank, and then her eyes had finally adjusted. She'd seen this man before.

Ricky sat and leaned toward her, elbows on his knees. His brown eyes searched hers, expressive brows furrowing. The lamplight exaggerated the shape of them. "You don't look like much."

Cora swallowed against the sandpaper in her throat. "Who the fuck are you?" She had no clue what he knew, but she could guess why he'd brought her here. And it was best to play ignorant if she was right.

"You don't remember me?" He pouted a little, leaning back and folding his arms. "I remember you. I didn't at first, but something nagged at me, after that night at Bungalow. I would have missed it if I hadn't been holed up at home with a bum leg, bored out of my mind, going through the Ezra Foster files again and again and again."

She took care not to let any recognition show on her face. "What are you talking about?"

"This," he said, and unfolded a photo he'd pulled from his jacket pocket. Cora already knew what it was, but it still twisted her gut to see Nell there, holding her bag, holding on to a little bit of hope. "It was the hair that caught my eye. Real pretty shade, what do you call it? Auburn or some shit? And real long, too. Distinctive."

Cora shook her head. "You're out of your mind. I don't even know where—"

The impact of his hand sang up her cheekbone, jostled her brain inside her skull. She didn't realize he'd smacked her until she was looking to the left wall, eyes watering involuntarily. "Drop the act, bitch," he hissed, grabbing a fistful of her hair and yanking it back until she cried out. "We both know you're Ryland's ghost."

"Ghost?" What did that mean?

"The way he looked at you...how scared he was that I'd seen you...that was when I knew. I just didn't *want* to see it. I didn't want to believe he had it in him." Ricky released her and stood, began to pace. "That motherfucker protected you for nothing. How does it feel to know none of the shit he did for you mattered?"

He seethed, trying to rein in his erratic breathing. "He threw away this partnership, this friendship, just to be left holding the bag for some chick who *never* had his back like I did! Nobody *ever* was there for him like I was. I woulda taken a bullet for him, any fucking day." His voice cracked. "I did take a bullet for him. It's still in my fucking leg." Rounding on Cora now, getting in her face again, he yelled, "Don't I deserve an explanation? Anything?"

She could see tears on his face, hear how hoarse he was, and just thought of Ronan. Ronan, Ronan, Ronan. That free witch born in a world he'd only see a corner of. Cora knew her words were a mistake the moment they left her mouth. "You'll get what you deserve."

Ricky made a strangled noise and grabbed the metal chair, flinging it to the other side of the room with a crash. She shrank away from him. "Did Thompson get what he deserved? Did Harris? They were just...they were kids. They were fucking kids. Harris couldn't even legally *drink*."

Fear clawed its way into her chest and up her throat, closing it. Who were those people? His rookies?

For the first time, she actually thought she might die in there.

"You mighta had something to do with that, too. Maybe you didn't. But I don't fucking care." He flipped open a hunting knife, and the blade gleamed in the lamplight. "You're gonna tell me what you know about Ezra Foster, and how he's moving all those people. You're also gonna tell me how Ryland's been helping your coven, and maybe, just maybe, I'll send you to go see your little friend Nell Tesauro instead of dropping you in a shallow desert grave."

Cora's hands trembled as he fired up a small blowtorch and turned the blade within the flame.

He asked, "Do you know whose knife this was?"

She shook her head, her stomach rising into her throat.

"J. Harris," he read, showing her the engraving. "He died this morning. Sat in a coma since the accident, hanging on. He let me borrow this knife a few weeks back, and I hadn't gotten around to returning it. Now I never will."

"I'm sorry," she said without thinking.

"Don't you fucking dare," he hissed. "You don't get to be sorry. You didn't know them at all."

He tossed aside the blowtorch and grabbed her hair again, yanking her forward and then moving to settle his weight on her shoulders. As he pinned her facedown on the concrete and ripped away the panel of her sweatshirt, cold air swept up her back. "You didn't know them, but I'm gonna leave this name all over you so you don't forget. And if at any point you decide you feel like talking, give me a thumbs up, mmkay?"

A scrap of her shirt was pressed into her mouth.

Then the man on top of her pressed the flat of the scalding steel between her shoulder blades.

She'd never felt anything like it. A scream erupted from her, and she writhed, trying to buck him off of her. Coherent thought splintered. The sear of the blade towed her under, and then again, in a different spot, and then again. The smell of burnt flesh filled her nostrils; bile rose with it.

How long would she last? How long before she broke, before she begged him to stop? What would happen if she didn't? She couldn't bring herself to wonder if he'd do more, do worse. She didn't want to imagine what it looked like, but she'd treated all kinds of burns; it was hard not to recall them in awful, vivid detail now.

Her entire world narrowed to the places he pressed that scalding metal. There was nothing else but pain, the heat, the smell, and the helplessness of knowing it would come again, even during the short reprieves when he paused to reheat the blade with the blowtorch.

Eventually she dissociated, sequestered in a far-off place in her mind where nothing else could touch her. A place she didn't want to come back from.

When the weight finally lifted from her shoulders and the strip of cloth was pulled from her mouth, she didn't move. Her tears were falling freely, snot had dribbled from her nose, and her vocal cords were raw from screaming. Ricky nudged her with his boot. "I gotta hand it to you," he said, admiring his handiwork from above. "I didn't think you'd let me do your entire back."

Cora said nothing, just stared at the unfinished drywall, so he walked around to crouch in front of her.

"I think I went about this all wrong, though. You think you're something of a martyr, don't you? Helping all these people go down the coast, hiding them from ACE. You'd do the honorable thing. You'd never give them up just for yourself, right?"

Cora wished he'd die.

"I wanna play a game," he said softly.

His tone sent off alarm bells. She imagined, in great detail, all the different ways he *could* die.

"I've gathered a lot on Foster, on your little operation. All stuff that Theo never brought to our boss, even though he said he did. I've also got a lot of juicy stuff on Theo, and what he's been up to these last few weeks.

Enough to cause a lot of problems for everyone, even if it's not a slam dunk just yet."

Cora shifted, trying to sit up, and cried out when the skin on her back protested. Her vision blurred from the pain.

"I'll give you a choice," he said with a cold smile. "You can either tell me everything about you and Theo, flesh out some juicy details I'm missing, or you can give me Foster and friends, and your whole little smuggling ring. Whichever you choose...I'll let the others walk free. How about it?"

What?

He'd really...?

The reality of that choice kicked her right in the teeth. She'd have to give up Theo or give up the Runners.

Give up Theo or give up Ezra and Quinn.

"He betrayed me for you. Now you've gotta decide if he's worth betraying the people *you* care about." Venom threaded his words. "It was an easy enough choice for him. Just kicked me to the curb. Not the same for you, huh?"

No matter what, someone would waste away in a prison cell. And without Theo, the risk of maintaining the Runners might be too high, not with so many eyes already on it. She might be condemning them all either way.

She almost wished Ghislaine hadn't temporarily lifted her vow of secrecy the night of Ronan's birth. It would've been a dubious comfort to let that make the decision made for her, by way of not having one at all.

"What if I don't choose?" she asked, trying for anger and landing somewhere between panic and dread.

Ricky leaned closer. "Oh, that's the really fun part. You see, I've got everything I know packaged up all nice and pretty, ready to send off to ACE. If you don't choose one, I'll just send it all over, and then everyone's equally fucked. Nice and fair, you know?"

Cora's chest was caving in. She could barely breathe. She could barely think. "I'm going to kill you," she ground out. Her eyes had no tears left. "And if it's not me, it'll be Theo."

"You don't want that, either. If I die, it all gets sent anyway." At the horror on her face, he grinned wider. "Cool little thing called a dead man's switch. Saw it in a movie once."

"You're a fucking lunatic."

"And you have twenty minutes to decide. Setting a timer..." he tapped something on his phone. "Now."

Cora strained against her bonds as he pulled out a box of cigarettes and lit one, the orange embers glowing bright against the shadows cast by the lantern. She followed that orange dot as it limped towards the staircase and up, disappearing around the corner.

Thank the Goddess for that small reprieve, the weight of his eyes off of her as her mind raced, her breathing shallowed. The panic attacked loomed, chest growing tighter still, and she couldn't see well enough to count anything but the beats of her thundering heart.

One. Two. Three. Four. Five. Six.

Her back felt like it had been doused in gasoline and set aflame.

Seven. Eight. Nine, Ten. Eleven. Twelve.

She inhaled deeply through her mouth so she wouldn't have to smell the lingering stench of burned flesh.

Thirteen. Fourteen. Fifteen. Sixteen. Seventeen. Eighteen.

Slowly, slowly, she regained control of her lungs, pressed back against the suffocating specter of her fight or flight response. Her pulse was still rapid, blood rushing to the burns on her back, but at least she should think again between the thumping.

Nineteen.

Twenty.

Twenty-one.

She tried to channel her ICU calm, that feeling of standing in front of a dying patient and taking inventory of injuries, prioritizing, delegating.

Could she look at this objectively? Could she really say that giving up one person to save an entire group of refugees was just math? One for two of her friends, and who knew how many others?

She thought about Nell again, about Fatima and John and Ronan, about everyone else sitting in a holding pattern trying to make it further down the coast to Whitefall. About the people who might be waiting for them when they arrived. About the families who might still be reunited there.

Yeah. She could. *But.*

Setting aside how she felt about Theo (its own terrifying question mark), would giving him up really guarantee the Runners' safety? The hunters would just interrogate him anyway, maybe find a neuromancer to dig out the answers he refused to give.

There was also the fact that she couldn't trust Ricky as far as she could throw him, and his word meant jack shit. And assuming he *didn't* turn Theo in if she gave him the Runners, she was willing to bet he had all sorts of other ways he'd like to exact revenge that didn't involve officially court-martialing him. The sting of that betrayal clearly ran deep, and that wasn't something a man as loyal as Ricky would be able to walk away from.

If she gave up Theo, she might be saving his life by sending him to prison.

But if she gave up Theo, she'd probably condemn the Runners anyway. They'd still have to pause operations and pivot, this time without the benefit of knowing what the hunters knew. They'd probably have to reroute from using LA as a base of operations altogether and go through other coven territory.

Other covens that might not be as keen on taking on that risk. Covens whose people they couldn't implicitly trust.

Giving up a *strategic* piece of the Runners...was that a possibility? Contain the damage, like a tourniquet, so that when the feds acted upon it, her coven would know exactly what had been compromised?

Fuck no. Too risky. She didn't think that once she gave them a piece of it, they'd be satisfied. They'd just have somewhere solid to start.

As far as Cora was concerned, there was only one choice. She had to find a way out of here, incapacitate Ricky, and get help.

Cora closed her eyes, fighting the urge to slip under and give into the black. It was probably too soon after her injection, but she had to try. She controlled her descent, reaching down into herself, into the earth through the cold concrete beneath her cheek, and grasped for the ley line. If she could release her magic, and anyone was scrying, at least they'd be able to home in on her location.

The sticky clump of black cutting her off felt like solid steel compared to what she'd faced before at Mindy's, and she grimaced as she leaned into her passive magic again, trying to erode it away. A thousand tiny knives shoved into the sensitive flesh behind her eyes, but she fought through them, trying to wear the Crash down and away.

Sweat rolled down her brow. Nausea rose again, and she swallowed against it. A sharp pain sang through her skull, but she ground her teeth and worked through it, fighting against every instinct in her body that begged her to back off.

Long minutes passed, minutes she didn't have. She was banging her fists against that black clump now, exhausted and desperate, unable to relax into it anymore—and then like a great, crashing wave had come to tow her under, she could no longer stay conscious against the agony from the raw, open wounds across her back.

"He's smoking a fucking cigarette," Theo observed from behind the bush he, Ezra, and Pip were crouched behind. "Like he's got all the time in the world." He wiped sweat from his brow, having shed his jacket long ago.

Ezra flipped his pocketknife open and closed, eyeing the way the light glinted off its sharp edge. "How do you want to play this?"

From their vantage point behind the boxwood hedge in the park across the street, they had a clear view of the construction site where Ricky was keeping Cora. There were no lights beyond the embers from his cigarette and the streetlamp on the corner, so it was hard to tell if there might be another way in. If they wanted to check, they'd have to wait for Ricky to go back inside so they could cross without him seeing.

Pip trembled on Theo's shoulder, itching to get to Cora. He'd been like this the entire way, practically buzzing with frustration. At first, it had taken a moment for the sprite to stop wallowing in what Theo quickly understood as shame. Theo got the impression Pip had tried to pull Ricky off of Cora and failed.

But when Theo reassured him he could still help, Pip was off like a shot, pinballing from tree to sidewalk to mailbox, bouncing and flowing so quickly he and Ezra had to run to keep up. They'd gone for blocks and blocks—a few miles, at least—and lost him a couple times, since he'd popped in and out of sight to avoid being spotted by passersby. Eventually, though, they wound up in an old neighborhood on the edge of Mar Vista and Inglewood. Theo recognized the sign outside as belonging to Ricky's cousin's construction company, because Ricky had a habit of pointing them out whenever he could.

Theo was limping on blistered toes, since he hadn't been expecting to run so far in these damn boots, and poor Ezra only wore a beat-up pair of Birkenstocks, but it was the last thing on anyone's mind as they caught their breath. Most of Theo's thoughts ran to violence: primarily, the things he'd like to do to Ricky once he got his hands on him.

"If she's not here in five minutes, we go in anyway," Theo said. Ezra had called Mindy once Pip slowed, and she'd stayed back to scry with Quinn just in case the sprite had it wrong, sending one of the other altas in her stead—whoever had been closest.

"That won't be necessary," said a familiar, musical voice. They whipped around, Theo leveling his gun at a figure that leaned casually on a parked car behind them.

Both Theo and Ezra relaxed at the same time, recognizing the impeccable posture and long, tight curls of Helena Prescott—then turning to each other. "You've met?" Theo asked.

She moved closer and came to a crouch beside them, raising an eyebrow at Pip. "Interesting company you've both been keeping these days."

Then it clicked. Helena was an alta. One of Cora's altas.

Of *course* she was. He groaned. "I knew it. I knew Malleus was a fucking honey trap."

Ezra just grunted at Helena. "I told you he wasn't as dumb as he looked."

She smiled humorlessly and peered over Ezra's shoulder, watching Ricky crush the butt of his cigarette under his shoe. "This one, hm? It was only a matter of time before he snapped." She turned to Theo. "Not very by-the-book, is he?"

"It's possible he's trying to get information out of her before he hands her over, but..." Theo's skin crawled just thinking about it. "*Dingus* here—" he looked pointedly at Ezra, "killed his man, the one in the coma, this morning, so he's probably taking that out on her, too."

Helena's eyes narrowed. "And you were going to run in with *that*?" She nodded at the sidearm Theo held. "Goddess help me. Do you think another hunter disappearing is going to take any heat off of you?"

He hadn't, really, but he also hadn't seen another option. In fact, he'd mostly seen red. "We didn't know we'd have a neuromancer as backup until five seconds ago. I'm guessing you have a better idea?"

From the furrow in her brow and the tingles up and down his arms, he figured Helena was already working on it. "I am just going to keep him out here a little longer," she murmured, "while you tell me more about what he knows."

Theo's grip on his sidearm tightened as he realized what she intended. "You're going to alter his memories?"

"Really, my dude?" Ezra hissed. "That's where you draw the line? You were gonna run in like Rambo, but the minute we have a magical solution to this shitshow you balk?"

"It's not like that," he said. "I draw the line because I want to wring his fucking neck myself. And I'm tired of wasting time out here. Cora could be..." he swallowed the rest of the sentence.

"Then *tell me*," Helena hissed, "what Santana knows. I can lure him over here with magic, but I cannot rewrite or remove memories without physical contact. Before I do so, I need to understand what he is *supposed* to know, and what he isn't."

Theo exhaled, rocking back on his heels. "He knows Ezra rented the apartment Nell was found in. He saw the security footage of Cora and Nell. He knows his men died tailing Ezra's car, knows that Cora is friends with Ezra's employee, and that Cora works at his Boardroom. But he didn't know for sure that it was Cora in that photo until he saw her at Bungalow a few days ago. He acted like he didn't put it together then, but he must have. He wouldn't have taken her otherwise."

"Do you think he acted alone?"

"Unless we find anyone else in there, I'm inclined to say yes. Look at him," Theo said, and they turned back to Ricky. "His limp is a lot worse than when I left him on the curb at Bungalow. If he'd had to drag or carry her to his car without help, that would've aggravated his leg, so it makes sense."

Helena considered for a long moment, tucking a curl behind her ear, then said, "This is what I'll do." Theo felt the magic around them thicken. "He'll forget everything from the restaurant to now, except the death of this man this morning, The rest will be a blur of grief that he won't particularly want to remember, but I'll nudge him out of the anger stage so our dear friend Ezra here can sleep at night. I can use more of a hammer than a scalpel, as it were." She grimaced. "The latter requires materials we don't have and nuance we don't have time for."

"Fine," Theo said, watching Ricky crane his neck in their direction and reminding himself that Helena was the reason for it. His spine went rigid as Ricky sauntered over, crossing the street with hands in his pockets, so casually. Close enough now to the hedge that concealed them that Theo could leap out and tackle him if he wanted to, beat his face to a bloody pulp. Ezra's hand on his arm steadied him.

Helena waited for Ricky to get closer, closer, and then she stepped out from behind the hedge and clapped her palms to his temples.

Ricky didn't have time to do more than grasp Helena's wrists. Now he simply stood, slack-jawed, as Helena rifled through his head. Theo couldn't see it, but he could certainly feel that magic dancing across his skin, and he tried not to picture that hammer and scalpel analogy too literally.

"Go," she said to the men through gritted teeth, and they didn't need to be told twice.

Theo and Ezra crouched as they crossed the street, sticking to the shadows for the neighbors' benefit. Most windows were dark, but you never knew. The home's exterior was more or less built, so they did have to use the front door, but inside, all bets were off. Rebar stuck out in odd places, walls were just frames in some spots, drywall in others. The kitchen had been half-tiled, and the sink hadn't yet been installed—it wouldn't ever, considering it lay on the floor in two pieces. Pip floated just in front of them, giving off enough light for them to see by, and stayed with them as they cleared rooms one by one.

Finally, off the laundry room, they did discover a flight of stairs leading down with soft light filtering up through the mouth of it. Pip made a noise Theo had never heard before—had Pip *ever* made a noise?—and zipped down there without a second thought.

They'd kept quiet on the first floor in case anyone or anything was waiting down there, but as it turned out, they needn't have bothered.

Theo flew down the rest of the way after Pip, falling to his knees beside the shadow on the concrete that was Cora's crumpled body. "Cor," he breathed, tilting her face up. Her eyes were closed, but she was breathing. A bruise bloomed across her left cheekbone. "Cor!"

The sprite zipped around her head in panic, grabbing a strand of hair, the tip of her nose, the lobe of her ear. He finally settled on her bruised cheek, running down one side of her face and making that same soft trilling sound over and over again.

Theo didn't have a weak stomach by any stretch of the imagination—he'd seen way too much to claim that—but nausea roiled within him as he took in the thirty-odd, blackened outlines on her back. They sat in three precise rows, stretching from her hips to her shoulder blades. Most of them were solid, slightly tapered shapes, though here and there he could make out some kind of writing. Then his eyes fell on the hunting knife beside her, and the engraving on its blade. *J. Harris.*

"Jesus H. Christ," Ezra murmured as he picked it up, then noticed the blowtorch on the ground. "He branded her. He..." Sweat beaded on Ezra's forehead as his face turned ashen.

"Call Mindy." Theo's voice shook with rage as he flipped out his own pocketknife to begin sawing at the tape on Cora's legs and arms. When Ezra just stood there, rooted to the spot with shock, he roared, "Get Mindy here, *now!*"

CHAPTER EIGHTEEN

Cora...

The word pressed into her mind, urgent, snapping her attention away from the novel in her hands. She peered across the backyard through the open stitching of the hammock, suddenly on alert. Her mother could leyweave, but only just. She rarely spoke mind-to-mind, unless...

Cora, run! GO!

There was fear in her mother's voice, thick and acrid and real, and Cora didn't waste another second questioning it. She tipped out of the hammock and ducked behind the trunk of the thick tree it was tied to, searching the bay window at the back of the house for movement.

In the living room, a man dressed in black slung her brother over his shoulder. Sebastian was limp, a rag doll, mouth lolling open. Dread spiked through her gut, and her heartbeat ramped up and up and up.

They'd been found.

Someone had told, and they'd been found, and she was next if she didn't move right fucking now.

She dove into the neighbor's yard and dashed across it, through their thorny bushes, zigzagging across lawns, vaulting fences. Lucky, so crazy lucky she'd insisted on gymnastics camp with her friend Lilly for the last two summers. The squeal of tires followed her, but those men didn't know this part of town the way she did.

Splinters bit into her fingers as she climbed another fence, and then she broke into a wide-open field, the soccer pitch for the local YMCA. She flew past some kid's birthday party, not realizing in that moment that she'd never have another one with Sebastian; she turned down a street leading onto UC Irvine campus, and only once she'd taken refuge in a parking garage, collapsed, dry heaving on the pavement.

She was still holding her book.

Limping her way into the throng of students was as good as disappearing. Along the way, she commandeered a student ID someone had dropped. Maybe it had money on it—she would need food. A place to spend the night. Was it even safe to contact Mindy? The twenty-four-hour library beckoned, a haven for all-nighters and the students who slept through them.

A lost-and-found bin sat behind the turnstiles at the entrance. She grabbed a maroon sweatshirt with the college mascot, three sizes too big. Big enough that she could hug her knees to her chest, zip it around them. She sank into a stale-smelling couch and prayed nobody would notice she was too young to belong there, reading a book the library probably didn't carry.

-------⟳-------

Cora jerked awake with tears staining her cheeks, sweat dotting her brow. A few things became apparent to her at once.

Her back was wet.

Something smelled musty, earthy.

She was lying on her stomach, and someone was holding her down.

Panic splintered through her, and she bucked against them with a strength she didn't know had returned to her yet. She thrashed, and her fist caught them in the throat.

Theo doubled over, gasping. She jolted upright, recognizing the familiar rows of books lining the white shelves in Mindy's den. A draft of cool air swept across her sternum. She was naked from the waist up.

"I'm...Goddess, I'm sorry. I'm so sorry." She grabbed a throw blanket from the back of the pullout couch and clutched it to her chest.

"It's...okay..." Theo wheezed, holding up a hand. "I was just...trying to keep...you from making a mess."

Her galloping thoughts slowed. "Mess?"

Theo pointed at the sheets, which were now smeared with a bright green paste. "I was dressing your back while you slept. Mindy gave me this." He held up a mason jar filled with the stuff.

"It's just...I was held down while..." A brief flash of memory wound its fingers around her throat, and she couldn't say more. But she didn't need to. He understood. "You're safe, Cor."

Safe.

She didn't think she'd ever feel that way again. Not truly. She swallowed, her throat like sandpaper, and he pressed a glass of water into her hand before she could ask for it. Cora didn't even thank him before gulping the whole thing down.

Pip took that moment to burst into being, bouncing up from where he'd been moonlighting as one of her pillows. Eyes wide, she let him sit cheerfully in her palm. Theo said, "He never left your side. Not for a second."

He'd become her pillow. Her *pillow*. So he could stay by her. Tears welled, and she blinked them back because she had a million things to ask before she let herself dissolve. It felt like she was trying to think through molasses. Pieces of the previous night began to surface in her memory, and she shoved them down. She wasn't ready for them. Not just yet.

One question desperately wanted out, though—one she was almost too afraid to voice. "Is it...bad?" In response, a vein in Theo's forehead formed a hard ridge. When he didn't answer, she said, "I want to see."

He forced out a weary breath. His eyes were sunken, bloodshot, his beard unruly. How long had he been awake? "You should wait until Mindy can finish. She was able to close you up, but you had gone into shock, so it took a lot out of her to stabilize you. She also had to reverse any infection. She's resting now so she can do another round."

"It...doesn't hurt. Is that...?" She pointed at the jar.

"For the pain. You're still inflamed, at about first-degree burns right now."

"You saw?" she asked. "What he used?"

He paused. "Yeah, I saw," was all he could manage to say between gritted teeth.

Goddess.

What he must be going through, this man.

What he'd done for her. What he still might do.

"I'm sor—" she began to say.

"No." His eyes glittered with rage, and his voice was thick with it. "Don't you shoulder that guilt. Don't you fucking do it. He wasn't the friend I thought he was, but I didn't want to see it."

"Grief can turn us into people we don't recognize."

Abruptly, he stood. His fists clenched at his sides like he wanted to break something but couldn't find anything deserving enough in Mindy's happy abode. "It's not your job to make me feel better about this. This is my shit, okay? Not yours."

Nobody understood that feeling better than she did. And while she couldn't make his hurt go away, she could distract him from the helplessness. Give him something concrete to fix.

She let him regain control of himself, let him pace to the window and back again before asking, "Will you finish putting the salve on my back?"

He exhaled. The tension in his shoulders released by small measures, but still he didn't look at her. "Of course."

Theo helped her up so he could strip the ruined sheets, stuffing them in the wash before grabbing an armful of towels from the linen closet and lining the mattress. He'd made himself at home in the day she'd been out. She settled on her stomach again, gingerly, inhaling her aunt's laundry soap in the terrycloth. Theo pulled the desk chair to the edge of the bed.

Neither spoke as he dabbed the salve across her shoulder blades. She closed her eyes. This was a thousand shades more intimate than that kiss in the hotel room if she was willing to admit it to herself. His fingers trailed along her skin and goosebumps followed, sending a jolt through her chest and her belly.

She listened to his breath. It became shallower, shallower, caught when he brushed across her lower back. His touch was feather-light, but it burned through her, and she tried to relax into it, meditate through it.

"You need to sit up." His voice jolted her from her doze and her eyes fluttered open. He held gauze in one hand and a roll of bandages in the other.

She pushed up to sit, crossing her arms over her still-naked chest. He met her eyes deliberately and gestured for her to turn away. She did, crossing her legs and twisting her long ponytail up into a messy knot, out of his way. Every hair on the back of her neck stood at attention as she held her arms away from her sides.

216

Theo pressed the gauze into her back and began wrapping, strong arms circling her to pass the roll across her abdomen and around again. The air between them was charged; he took his time across her rib cage, muttering an apology as he accidentally brushed a thumb just below the swell of her breasts.

Her own breath was shallow now as he came around one last time, under her left armpit, compressing her chest, then over, and he was done. "There." His voice was strained as he fastened the bandage to itself. He cleared his throat, tried again. "You can wear a shirt now if you want."

She twisted back to face him, saw the fire in his eyes as he stood. She didn't want him to walk away. She almost found the courage to say it, but he spoke first.

"Rest a little longer. You've really been through it." He was already closing the door.

For a second time that day, Cora jolted awake. The last bit of low November sun was slipping through the blinds to cast long slants on the wall. It was getting dark so early these days, so she couldn't have slept long. The smell of food meant Mindy must be up and about, and Cora's stomach reminded her she hadn't eaten all day.

But food was the last thing on her mind. She knew, now, what had made her so unsettled in sleep. What her cotton-stuffed head had let her shove away without second thought, because she hadn't wanted to face the trauma of it.

She rummaged through her clothes, which she'd finally gotten around to cramming in the tiny closet, and winced as she pulled on a dark, gauzy T-shirt that hung loose over the dressings down her spine. She wished, badly, for a shower, but figured that wasn't on the docket as long as her torso was bandaged.

Cora drew up short as she ran into the kitchen.

Theo had commandeered the TV to watch a Lakers game, a sight so normal it blew her away. He was in his socks, the sleeves of his cable knit sweater rolled up to his muscular forearms. A half-finished beer sat sweating on the counter he was leaning over.

"Bullshit!" he hissed under his breath. "That was a clean hit!"

"Ref needs his damn eyes checked," Mindy grumbled, puffing on a joint in one hand, flipping a pancake on the stove in the other. Honey and banana and peanut butter. Cora's favorite comfort food. And she must have been stressed if she was toking in the house; she usually did it outside for Cora's benefit. "Every bad call so far's been his. Hand me some paper towels, will you?"

Theo did as she asked, not taking his eyes off the screen.

The whole tableau was...disarming. Like a parallel timeline she'd never let herself imagine, because it was too painful to wonder what this could have been like.

What it might have been like with her mother standing there, alongside Mindy, eating peanut butter straight from the jar like she always did when she made them "HBPBPs."

With Sebastian and Theo yelling at the screen as someone ran the ball down the court, and Seb crushing a beer can on his head like he always did with 7 Up.

She'd forgotten Theo cared about basketball. It was such a small detail, but it itched. She wanted to nourish this fledgling universe of trust somehow opening in the space between them all in the kitchen; to stay here in the slice of time that had created it.

Instead, she had to shatter it.

"What happened to Ricky?" she asked, panic rising in her voice.

They both turned. The batter bowl slammed down hard, like it had half-slipped from Mindy's hands. Her aunt dropped the joint in an ashtray crossed the kitchen in three long strides, only remembering not to pull Cora in for a hug at the last second, and Cora wrapped her arms around Mindy instead, inhaling her perfume and shampoo. The familiar scent grounded her, but not by much.

"Oh, baby girl. I am so glad you're safe." And then Mindy choked up, looking back at Theo. "I'd better hope this man doesn't come to collect the debt I owe him, because we'll be out on the damn street."

Theo watched them both, a strange look in his eyes. "Those pancakes are payment enough; I saw what you put in them."

Mindy's brows pinched at the fear Cora wore plain on her face. "You're safe, honey. Nobody can touch you here."

Safe, safe. That's what everyone kept telling her. "You don't understand. I *need* to know what happened to Ricky."

"What's wrong?" Theo stepped slowly around the counter, beer forgotten.

"He had a...he called it a dead man's switch." Cora shook her head, bringing her fingers to her temples, trying to recall exactly what Ricky had said. "He told me he'd send them everything he had on us, on you, if something happened to him."

Theo stood up straighter. "He what?"

A pancake was burning. Mindy stepped back, letting Theo lead Cora to a seat at the kitchen table as she went to rescue it.

"Tell me everything you remember," he said in that deadly calm, brushing a strand of hair from her face, and she did. She told them about the choice-that-wasn't-a-choice Ricky had given her, breaking down again as she worked through the logic of it, describing how she'd fought to get to her magic and couldn't. By the time she'd finished, Mindy's face was pale as death, and Theo was practically vibrating with the rage he was trying to contain.

"What happened to Ricky?" Cora asked again slowly, not because she wanted to know, but because she needed to.

Theo and Mindy's silence was a living thing, working its way into Cora's lungs and making it harder to breathe. Finally Theo said, "His memories from the last few days were rewritten."

Her initial relief at his being alive quickly twisted into horror. "So whatever he was doing to keep the information from being sent—"

"—isn't something he'll even remember to do," Theo finished, running a hand through his hair and letting his face settle into his palm.

Fuck. Fuck fuck fuck *fuck*. This was bad.

Cora turned to Mindy, mind racing. "Could we reverse the neuromancy?"

Mindy's lips pressed a thin line. "Not the way Helena did it. She muddled things up, shook up his memories like a snow globe and let the pieces fall back in a way that vaguely made sense. Trying to pick something so specific out of his head now would be damn near impossible." She set the stack of pancakes on the table between them, but everyone seemed to have lost their appetites.

Theo looked up, gears whirring. "Whatever it was...could have been an email account set up to send everything in it after not logging in for a while. Anyone can set that up nowadays. But paranoid, like he was? Could be someone he trusted with the paper files, with instructions to bring it all to Fletcher if he doesn't call by a certain date. Could have just hidden it somewhere he knew they'd look if he was dead."

"And we don't know when D-Day would be," Mindy grumbled.

"No. Could be twenty-four hours. Could be days. Could be weeks. Every moment we spend chasing down the wrong lead is a wasted one. This is a zero-sum game."

Cora peered at him, tapping her fingernails against the table. There was something he wasn't saying. "But you have thoughts."

Theo sighed, looking over to Mindy, then back to Cora. "Nothing worth betting on."

"Teddy," Mindy huffed, "You're all we *have* to bet on. Out with it."

He kicked his chair out and stood, walking over to his beer and downing it. After a long, slow exhale that seemed to give him a better grip on himself, he said, "Ricky's damn smart, but he's one scatterbrained sonuvabitch. If he set up a dead man's switch, it sure wasn't something he'd have to refresh every day. Every week? More likely, but I'd say the sweet spot is two."

"Why's that?" Cora asked.

He didn't like talking about Ricky, she could see it. Especially not to lay bare a bunch of details only a good friend would know. "He had this thing he liked to do to help him remember stuff. He'd bundle tasks, you know, always call his sister on his way to the grocery store, always take the trash out when he walked the dog. They were all situational, except one. Every two weeks, like clockwork, he'd send his abuela a letter, because he knew she loved getting mail. That's also how he remembered to drop off and pick up his dry cleaning, because it was right next to the post office."

Cora shoved down any shred of respect that made her feel for Ricky. He could love his abuela and still be the man who branded her last night; those things weren't mutually exclusive.

"I think it's safe to assume he'd try and 'bundle' this, too. If he had to remember to log into something, or call somebody, he'd make sure he didn't forget."

"Do you know when he last sent her a letter?"

Theo considered. "When he got blood on the shirt he wore to Bungalow, he was mad about it just having been dry cleaned." He counted backwards. "Five days gone. If I'm right about this, that gives us nine to figure something out."

"If you're right," Mindy said, finally grabbing a pancake on principle and stabbing it with her fork. "And we won't know if you're not, until it's too late. So I say you two, and Quinn and Ezra, and whoever else, post up in a safe house yourselves. At least give an old lady *that* peace of mind."

"You're not old," Cora said, aware that she was missing the point entirely.

"I'm serious," Mindy said, mouth full of pancake. She jabbed her fork at Cora. "The Runners will put you up, not in one of Ezra's places, but someone completely unattached to him or any of us."

"And what then?" Cora's voice wavered, but she couldn't help it. "Do we come out ever again? Do we go to Whitefall?" The last word stuck in her throat like a chicken bone. She'd been a waypoint on dozens of witches' journeys down to the secret city, but she'd never imagined having to end up there herself. It was just so...final. "I can't just...abandon all the work we've done."

Or abandon all the people who might still need her help. Or let go of the only thing that had given her a sense of purpose, that had helped her find the strength to wade through the darkest days of her addiction. How much use, if any, could she be on the other side of Whitefall's wards?

And she couldn't ask Theo to give his whole life up, either, to go with them. Even if staying here was looking less and less like an option for him.

They both looked at Theo to tip the scales in someone's favor. His eyes widened, a deer in the headlights. "It's...not a terrible idea," he conceded to Mindy, and Cora's face heated. "What?" He shrugged, folding his arms and leaning back against the island. "It's not."

Sifting through the knot of emotions inside her, she plucked a thread of anger, because that would be the easiest to bear. She stalked over to Theo, poking his chest. "And I suppose you'd still try and get into The Beach, to get a meeting with the Tesauros, even with this anvil swinging over your head."

He leaned down, his face inches from hers. "And I suppose you'd still insist on helping hijack the Crash truck, knowing the same."

"That's different. You'd be walking right into their territory. They'd know you were coming. If the heist goes the way we want it to, they won't know we did anything at all."

"Can we just agree you're both stubborn idiots?" Mindy said from behind them. "As far as I'm concerned, the safe house is a non-negotiable part of this, nine days to find the switch or not."

Nine days. It could be enough time to figure out how to stop the information from leaking, but... "We don't necessarily need to find the switch if we get Theo in and out of The Beach before it goes off."

Theo pinched the bridge of his nose and sat down at the kitchen table again. "Not if we're just attacking the prison. But we're still leaving everyone's asses out to dry, ours included." He lifted his head, and his eyes were unfocused, settling somewhere in the middle distance. "I knew this could happen, though. I can make my peace with having to find somewhere to go, if it comes to that."

Cora raised her eyebrows at Mindy. He didn't get it.

"And just where do you think you'd be going?" Mindy asked, keeping her tone casual.

Theo shrugged. "Vancouver, maybe? I have a cousin up there. ACE would try and extradite, but—"

"Teddy, hon, there's a place for you in Whitefall. If you want it."

He blinked. "Sorry?"

"Apology accepted."

He blinked again, glancing at the half-smile that had crept on to Cora's face to match Mindy's. "I don't understand."

"We'd have to make your case, but hon, anyone who helps orchestrate a damn prison break is gonna have a place in Whitefall."

He opened his mouth and then closed it, running his fingers through his beard. Cora realized they'd actually stunned him speechless. Then he just said, "Oh."

"Yeah, 'Oh.' Anyway, that's if you want it. So just give it a think. In the meantime, we have to get you two somewhere safe." Mindy scooped pancakes onto the two untouched plates and shoved them in front of Theo and Cora. "Eat first. I don't care if you're hungry. You're gonna eat, and then you're gonna pack, and we'll have someone escort you, Teddy, to grab some stuff from your place. Cor, you and I are gonna finish those burns on your back, 'cause I know you must be dying for a shower." She stood and took her own empty plate over to the sink, talking over the running water now. "Tomorrow morning we'll get the altas together and decide the next move. Roger?"

Cora stared at Theo. Theo stared back, then at his plate, still speechless, probably wondering when he'd lost control here.

Finally, he managed a hoarse, "Yes, ma'am."

CHAPTER NINETEEN

Theo and Cora stood with their suitcases in front of the safe house that the Runners had provided for them. His eyes roved over the chipped stucco exterior, the rust stains below the gutters, and the iron security bars over the windows without really seeing any of it.

Everything had flown so far off the rails in the last forty-eight hours that Theo couldn't begin to unpack it.

Once the fear and rage of finding Cora on that basement floor had burned off, he'd only had guilt and disgust and hurt left to wallow in. He knew some of that disgust toward Ricky was half a projection of his own self-loathing, of the shame that he'd had it in him to betray his friend. But he'd tried to keep Ricky out of this, whereas Ricky had deliberately gone after Cora, and that was the line between them.

Didn't make it sting any less, though, to know Ricky could have that much hate in his heart, let alone want to direct it his way. Knowing someone he'd once called a friend had been driven so far off the deep end by shit he'd done.

Ricky's actions were his own. Logically, Theo knew it. But logic didn't make the end of their friendship any less of a weight in Theo's stomach. It didn't change that Ricky had lashed out in anger not just because of what Cora and Quinn had done to Thompson, or what Ezra had done to Harris, but also because of what Theo had been hiding from him all this time.

There was that—the betrayal itself—and then there were the brands.

224

He was glad Cora hadn't been able to see them. As a nurse, though, she'd probably been able to guess. He'd never forget what they looked like as long as he lived.

He'd also never forget how it had felt to sit there next to her and wait for Mindy to arrive, or the sound Mindy made when she saw Cora, or the fear in her voice when she'd told him Cora had gone into shock. He'd had some medical training himself—it was part of the job—and he knew how easily things could have gone south.

If Helena hadn't come, Ricky would be rotting in a gutter somewhere, and Theo would be able to sleep a hell of a lot better.

Looking at Cora had been difficult this morning. Talking to her, even more so. He'd been silent most of the drive here, and Pip had given him wide berth, clinging to Cora's shoulders instead. In fact, they'd both wordlessly understood his need for space and given it without question.

Even now, as he and Cora rolled their bags up the front walk, she stayed a few steps behind him. She only nodded when he held open the front door for her, moving past him with a tight-lipped smile.

He hated it. He hated this. But he didn't know how else to be right now.

Crossing the threshold, Theo drew up short. They might as well have gone through a portal to 1995. Heavy crown molding atop warm, sponge-painted walls, blocky maple furniture, glass tabletops, and plastic plants. The thick brocade curtains were pulled tight and brushed against jade green carpeting. "What's that smell?" he asked, locking all three deadbolts behind them.

"Mothballs." Cora snorted, and it broke the ice a little. "I feel like Blanche, Rose, and Dorothy are going to jump out at any second."

He'd felt the same, but hadn't wanted to seem ungrateful, so kept it to himself.

"There's a tube TV in here," she called from the kitchen. "With a VCR!"

"Just missing some Lladró figurines and bad—" he stopped in the arch of the kitchen door, surveying the awful floral print that bellowed across the walls. "...wallpaper."

Cora pointed to a shelf in the breakfast nook. "Does a wave of galloping horses count?"

True to her description, six porcelain horses spilled out of a cresting ocean wave in a sculpture as long as Theo's arm. "That doesn't even make sense."

She stepped back, considering it. "I think it's perfect."

He returned the small smile that was curving her lips, thankful she'd been brave enough to try and bridge the growing distance between them.

They moved down the hallway that led to the back of the house, looking for a spot to dump their bags. The rest of the house was in a similar state, with worse striped wallpaper in the single bathroom, and a tiny office outfitted in more of that pink-tinged maple. The final door, then, had to lead to the bedroom.

Inexplicably, the carpeting in only this room was a deep maroon, featuring an old cane rocking chair with a huge stuffed teddy bear in residence. The bear looked constipated.

Beside it sat a single, king-sized bed.

"Oh." Theo coughed, trying to dislodge something in his chest that wasn't strictly physical. "I thought Mindy said this was a two-bedroom."

Cora sounded as surprised as he felt. "Maybe they changed it? Turned one into the office?"

They exchanged a horrified look. The only thing worse than imagining this place hadn't been redecorated in over two decades was the idea that it had been.

He couldn't help it. A laugh bubbled up from somewhere inside him, and then he couldn't stop.

It was the only thing that made any sense. If he couldn't laugh about all of this, he'd shut down completely, and he couldn't let himself do that. Cora had put on a brave face, but she had monsters of her own to fight. He wouldn't let her face them alone.

Especially when he'd created one of them.

And it was better, at least, than stewing in all the things he wanted to do to Ricky, all the images of Cora's burns that lived rent-free in his head, and the idea that he might never go back to his studio ever again. He hadn't let himself really say goodbye to it last night, not wanting it to feel real. That might have been a mistake.

He never imagined, not in any of his wildest dreams, that he'd wind up under the witches' protection. It was so fucking absurd, and had all happened so fast, and in the oddest possible place, that there was nothing left to do but laugh.

Cora, after a shocked pause, had found herself laughing along with him, and they both looked and sounded a little bit unhinged, but there was a mutual understanding there, a complete lack of judgment. Just the knowledge that they weren't alone in this whole bizarre experience, and that there was still a little light to be found in all the dark.

"I can't deal with that bear," Cora gasped when their laughter had tapered off. "This thing is going in the closet."

"You really want it there? Where it'll sit all night, scheming?"

She wrinkled her nose. "Fair enough. Goddess, who the hell owns this place?"

"I'm not sure I actually want to know."

They both fell silent as they stared at the bed again, and Theo noticed a blush creeping up Cora's cheeks. "Listen," he said, "I'll grab the living room couch so—"

"No way. You're not sleeping on that couch." Her words had a surprisingly sharp edge to them, and the frustration he'd left on simmer all morning rose to meet it.

"Well, neither are you."

"Theo, you've given up so damn much." Her voice caught as she turned back to him, and her eyes glistened with sudden, unshed tears. "More than I bet you ever expected to. The least I can do is give you the bed. I should never have—"

"Don't. Don't you dare. I chose to do what I did," he said, jabbing a thumb into his own chest. "I decided where my priorities lay. That call was mine."

And hell if something didn't click into place within his chest when he said it aloud.

"I can't just be okay with that," she said, throwing her hands into the air. "You don't understand what it was like to...to lie there in that basement and try to weigh the fucking pros and cons of giving you up to save the Runners. I had almost convinced myself that turning you in could save your life, because Ricky would likely try and kill you anyway. That's where I'd gotten to."

That's where this guilt was coming from? That she'd considered letting Ricky take him? His next words were gruffer than he intended them to be. "You *had* to go there, Cor. You had to be cold and step back and look at the whole picture. That's wartime triage. That's what the situation demanded. I have to do that all the time."

227

Her voice climbed into a higher register as it wavered and broke. "I can't do that with you. I can't." She paced away from him, raking her fingers through her hair, and turned back. Her fight-or-flight response was in turmoil; he could see it plain across her face. "I was so tired of being afraid to let you back in. Afraid to want everything that letting you in would mean."

She took a shaky step toward him. "And I fooled my ass into believing it was possible not to, early on, but it didn't matter. Because I'd never let you go in the first place."

Something within him shifted as she said it. She put her fingers to her lips, like she hadn't meant to give it voice, but it was out. It was there, hanging between them.

His heartbeat thundered in his ears. He didn't know he'd crossed the room until he was already there, yanking her into him, crushing his lips to hers, and tasting the salt that had dripped onto them.

There was no closing the door that admission had just opened. His mind was a wild jumble of nothings that couldn't begin to approximate coherent thought. He pulled away for half a breath, staring at her, and she didn't miss a beat as she grabbed a fistful of his shirt and dragged him down again.

It was an answer, sure enough.

What passed between the warm slide of their lips was everything they couldn't say to each other; a frenzied realization of need as much as want. It was a mutual submission to whatever had dogged them over the last few weeks. It was his tongue slipping into her mouth; her hands gripping his hair, their bodies pressed against each other with nothing to hide.

She clung to him like she'd float away if she didn't, and he was more than happy to ground her, to be that rock, to remind her what was real as they tumbled onto the bed.

Theo rose over her, kissing the tears from her cheeks, kissing her jaw, and then lower, grazing the soft skin of her neck with his teeth. She arched into him, her pulse leaping as his mouth trailed down her collarbone. He filled his hands with the soft curves of her, loving every inch of what she was giving over to him, floored by the trust it implied, wanting more.

But he had to let her set the pace. She'd been through trauma so recently that she might not know her triggers yet, might not be able to anticipate her reactions to them. And hell if he didn't know what that was like.

He couldn't let her feel trapped beneath him. He pivoted as she wrapped her legs around his waist, pulling them both upwards to sitting, and then they were both shedding their shirts, breaking their kiss to toss them away.

She stopped, her hand on his chest. Her eyes went wide as she traced the jagged scars she found there, and he breathed through the vulnerability of it. She didn't ask, thank god, just came back to him, kissing him slower now, her long skirt riding up as she ground against his lap.

He slipped his thumb beneath that skirt to trace the outline of her, cursing under his breath at the heat and dampness he discovered there. As her bra joined the pile of clothing on the floor, he drank her in, savoring the thrill of her bare skin against his and the way her own need made him need her back twice as badly.

He unzipped, lifting his hips to pull his pants down, and she lifted with him, but he only got as far as his thighs before her patience ran out.

Slow and deep, she sank down to take all of him, gasping and driving her hips to meet his. Half-dressed, her mouth found his again, all warmth and purposeful movement, letting him know she was in control. He dug his fingers into the flesh of her thighs, wresting a little bit of that control back from her.

Some long-buried piece of him resurfaced as he drove into her. Now their movements were faster, more desperate, punctuated by the little breathless noises neither of them were able to silence. A spring tightened, twisting and coiling. He had the distinct impression she was stealing back something she'd lost in the past few days, and when the hairs on his arms tingled, he knew for sure.

She set her magic free, and Theo came alive, came apart.

A primal noise rose out of him as threads of raw magic rippled in air and snaked through his body. A strangled cry marked her relief and stoked fire in his own as she clenched around him. He held her for several long, heaving breaths as she slumped forward to rest her head on his shoulder, letting the aftershocks roll through them as they slowly drifted back down to earth.

He had shattered. Pieces of himself clamored to find their way back together again. Thoughts fought to surface through the haze of satisfaction.

They didn't speak. Even if they'd been able to form words, and string those words into sentences, and build those sentences into a meaningful exchange, it wouldn't matter. It wouldn't capture whatever had just passed between them.

That was now raw and real and out in the open, laid bare on the ugly floral comforter of the strange bed, in an even stranger safe house, somewhere in a suburb of Torrance.

———— ⌒∽⌒ ————

Cora hadn't slept.

It wasn't for lack of trying. But for all that her clean, organized lines had blurred and reshaped between those sheets just hours ago, one thing remained vivid and constant behind her closed lids.

Ricky.

She didn't expect he would just go away. She knew he had now settled in her head, nice and cozy, next to those hunters she'd run from as a girl. It had taken years of therapy, and for a while, a lot of drugs, to make those men disappear. They'd come back, though.

Sitting at the kitchen table by the light of the old tube TV, watching soundless 3 a.m. infomercials, she wished her sponsor was still alive. She was itching for a drink.

No, that was wrong. She was itching for more than that, but knew Harry wouldn't indulge her anymore, and she couldn't very well just walk into a dispensary or ask Mindy to bring some of her weed, so she would have settled for a drink instead. Mindy's sleeping draughts might stave off the nightmares, but they did nothing for her once she woke.

Theo had, though. He'd realized his mistake when he pinned her, that her racing heart wasn't just because of him. Lying beneath him had triggered something new in her that she didn't quite know how to face, and he'd simply rolled with it, giving her the reins instead.

She'd never been so consumed by need, so willing to trust someone else with the power to unmake her. And she'd never had someone so easily walk her off a ledge she didn't know she'd been standing on.

Their thirst for one another was wild and uncomplicated in this strange, safe new place between his skin and hers, between where he ended and she began. It wasn't just a passing fever of wanting and having; it was another language only they could speak.

230

It had given her the strength to face all three altas at dinner, when they'd come by with Mindy, Ezra, and Quinn, and walk through the delivery schedule Fletcher had unwittingly given Helena. They'd already put together a team to pull off the swap, and the next truck was due in two days' time. It was either that, or wait another three weeks, which clearly wasn't an option.

Two days. That was it. That was all they had.

Theo made his appointment to see the Nell's parents, the Tesauros, at The Beach the day after, just in case things went awry. It would be cruel to get the inmates' hopes up if they weren't able to make the swap after all, so it was better to have that time buffer if they needed to pivot. But they couldn't spare more days than that on the off chance Theo was wrong about the switch's timetable. The earlier they all got in, the better their chances of getting out.

Their chances of getting out. What were those, anyway?

The room suddenly felt too close, too warm, and she got up to open the window in the breakfast nook. The security bars cut the moonlight into neat rows on the table as she let the cool November night in. This was just the beginning—once they'd made the swap, the real work began. And it was up to the witches inside.

Did Sebastian think she'd given up on him?

Did she want the answer?

She jumped, heart like a fist in her throat as Theo pressed against her back, wrapping his thick arms around her shoulders, resting his chin on top of her head. He was naked from the waist up, but the way he held her against him was more possessive than sexual. She softened into him. "I'm sorry. I didn't mean to wake you."

"Don't apologize."

On TV, they watched a lady in an orange dress gesture grandly at *Chop Wizard! Never cry over onions again!*

Cora finally said, "He wouldn't have run like I did. Sebastian."

"Is that what you were dreaming about?" Theo's beard tickled her forehead. "He wouldn't have but not because he was brave. He wouldn't have done it because he was stupid."

"He was both when it counted."

"You were a child. You wouldn't have stood a chance against ACE."

"Even still." She drew her bottom lip between her teeth and turned in his arms, looking up at him. His dark eyes glittered in the moonlight. "What scares me the most is...he's lived nearly half his life in there. It'll never be like it was, the two of us."

"No," Theo agreed. "It won't. But it wouldn't be that way even if you'd grown up together, Cor. You'd still have changed. You were becoming your own people, not just two halves of a pair."

"I...don't know if I can handle the reality of him as a stranger to me. Someone I'll have to get to know all over again." They hadn't just been part of each other's lives. They'd been part of each other. And she'd had to learn who she was without him, grow and compensate for all the things she'd relied on him to be for her. She was still learning.

"You want to know the weirdest part?" she asked. "He hasn't aged at all in my mind. I saw on a crime show once how when a kid goes missing, the parents keep their room exactly like they left it, sometimes untouched for years, hoping they'll come back. I've done that but in my brain."

"Makes sense to me," he said. "That's how you knew him."

She turned, looked up at him, traced the crooked line of his nose with her finger. His curls danced in the breeze, a boyish thing so at odds with everything else about him. "I guess I don't have a choice."

"We all have a choice." They both knew he wasn't just referring to Sebastian.

Cora pulled away in the silence that followed and sat again, handing him half of her PB&J. "Here. Take some."

He sank into the chair next to her. "You sure? You haven't eaten much since..." He took a bite instead of forcing himself to say it.

She turned sideways in her own chair, pulling a knee up so she could rest her chin on it. "It's...the smell. Of cooking things." Her voice lowered to a whisper. "Especially meat."

Theo froze mid-chew, looking like he regretted that bite after all. His voice was soft. "I didn't even realize." He swallowed hard. "Jesus, Cor, I wish you'd said something. I made those pork chops earlier and everything—"

"I was embarrassed," she said, swallowing against the memory. She felt like crying but didn't want him to shoulder any more guilt than he already had. She hated that Ricky had taken this from her, too. "You couldn't have known."

"I should have." He put the sandwich back on the plate, pushing it towards her. "I've seen a lot that would put anyone off food for a while, but I guess I got used to it."

"How did you cope, early on?" she asked. "They must have—I don't know, shrinks, I guess—at the Academy?"

"At the Academy, sure." He sat back, folding his arms over his broad, bare chest. "You're still dealing with kids. Once you're assigned to a unit, though, you realize they were never there to help you. They were there to normalize things, gaslight you into being afraid to speak up. But on a few occasions, nobody could convince me what I saw was par for the course."

Those dark memories had probably never seen light, and she didn't want to hear them, but steeled herself to ask anyway. He looked like he needed to unburden himself but refused to add to her nightmares. "Like what?"

"Don't."

"I can handle it." She straightened a little. "Lots of people believe what they do because their experience of the world shaped the way they behave in it. Not because they woke up one day and chose to. I want to understand them."

Not that Ricky particularly deserved her understanding, but she was desperate to make some sense of what he'd done.

He stared at her, then scrubbed a hand over his face. "Most with the luxury of deciding whether to join...they're so afraid of magic their only solution is eliminating it. No half measures, no 'learning to live together.' This became a war because in their minds, it never could've happened any other way. But Ricky's not one of them."

"What is he, then?"

Theo blew out a breath. "He doesn't hate magic. Not really. He allows it when it suits him and fights it when it suits him. He didn't kidnap you because he thought it was real justice—he did it because he was hurting. People like him, people like my old CO... they benefit from the toxic culture others before them created, and just perpetuate it."

"Your old CO?"

"He had a mean streak a mile wide. He picked on sensitives because he didn't have the gift for it. I was the only one in his unit, so I had a target on my back."

"What did he do?"

He receded into his thoughts, gaze focused nowhere in particular. "We got this call, maybe a week after I was assigned to his unit. He dragged me to a house where someone had summoned a demon, and it went south. The neighbors called it in. Cleary—that was his name—thought it was a good idea to send me in first. Said it would put some hair on my chest."

His Adam's apple bobbed. "It was worse than a massacre. The bodies were...unrecognizable. It took weeks for a team of medical examiners to piece them back together and ID them. Everything had been...removed, you know, and swapped. The pieces of them. This person had that person's eyeballs stuffed in their sockets, and so on."

Cora shoved the image away. "It must have been..." She couldn't even find a word for it. Didn't want to reduce it to one.

Theo spoke faster, the memory spilling out of him. "The attention to detail was meticulous, the stitching, and the bodies were days old—the man whose mind was infected by that demon, he lived in that house while he did it. He fed on whatever was there. He'd regressed mentally when we got to him, speaking like a child, sometimes speaking in tongues. Our best demonologist had trouble translating—we had to call in someone from Delaware."

"Cleary grabbed my shoulders and forced me inside to 'take a good whiff,' he said. Made sure it was burned into my brain. And when I stumbled outside and vomited, he stood over me and laughed." Theo's hand fisted on the tabletop. "I hated him for a lot of reasons. He was a sociopath and a murderer. He became a witch hunter for sport; the badge was just a way to get paid for it. But for the longest time, Cora, I was grateful to him for showing me what witches were capable of. The anger fueled me for years."

Weeks ago, she would have been disgusted, gotten defensive. Now she just did her best to listen. "What changed?"

"I investigated the South Side Slasher."

"*You* worked that?" Cora had heard of him. Everyone in California had heard of him. A serial killer active about four years ago had earned the moniker after murdering twenty people in the space of a week. Their bodies were discovered peacefully lying in their beds, wrists slashed, exsanguinated—with the blood itself nowhere to be found. Until a few days later.

When intricate red murals began popping up in the same neighborhoods the victims had died in.

"They brought me in to consult. But when we finally caught him, he wasn't using magic. He was just batshit." Theo rubbed his beard. "He saw himself as an artist. You read what he said in those articles. How he thought he'd elevated his victims in those murals, made them immortal. Made their lives mean something they never would have otherwise."

Cora was tracking. "And he didn't need a demon. His own mind was enough."

"Yes. His own mind was more than enough."

"I'm sorry," Cora said into another long silence. "I shouldn't have..."

"No, don't." Theo got up to close the window when he saw a shiver roll through her. "I'm sorry. I made this about me."

She stood, watching him, and slid back into his arms when he flipped the latches closed. "I asked, didn't I?"

He wrapped himself around her and buried his face in her hair, breathing deep. "It's like that story has been lodged in my throat for years."

The raw truth in his admission—the vulnerability in it—felt new and strange and wonderful.

"I hope," she said, searching for the right words, "one day, when you're ready, you can tell me more about that life. And I might be shocked by some things or need a little time to unpack my own thoughts, but I can promise you I'll listen with an open mind and try my hardest not to judge." For whatever that was worth.

He pulled her closer, and she leaned into it, melted into him. They stood like that for a long time.

How had she gone her whole life without this? Without knowing what it felt like to be held by him?

"Would you let me try and give you better things to dream about?" he eventually murmured into her hair, pulling her with him toward the bedroom.

"You'll have your work cut out for you."

"I like a challenge."

Well. When he asked so nicely, how could she say no?

CHAPTER TWENTY

Clouds of desert dust danced across the highway as the shadows receded under the afternoon sun. They were somewhere on the 10 outside Eagle Mountain, which was little more than a modern-day ghost town founded to work a now-defunct iron mine and steel mill.

Two cars made an inconspicuous caravan: Quinn, Cora, and Theo in Quinn's SUV, while Ghislaine, Helena, and two other witches from the coven took the other. They'd brought on eccentric siblings Dustin and Viv in the stead of Alta Maria who was, in her words, "not cut out to be doing roadside heists at her age."

Cora recalled seeing them at Helena's Samhain gathering and knew they were celebrated pyromancers. Their Fourth of July fireworks were famous, though nowadays they had to go out into the middle of nowhere to do them. Dustin also had a secondary talent for illusions, which would come in handy.

Both in their mid-thirties, their bright blue eyes held a certain wildness you'd expect from people who enjoyed playing with fire. Viv's hair was a long, unnaturally red river to her waist, shaved clean off on one side of her head, while Dustin's brown buzz hugged his skull and bounded an intricate tattoo lacing down the back of his neck. Had a fiery mishap preceded those hairstyles?

Helena left one of her people in Phoenix to follow the truck from the lab in a rented car, calling with periodic updates on its location. Right now, he was twenty minutes due east of where their caravan had pulled off the highway, setting up to pretend one of their cars had broken down. With luck, any good Samaritan would see the second car and assume someone already stopped to help them, rather than get in their way.

Time slogged by as they waited for the spring water truck, and whenever a tall silhouette poked over the horizon, Cora's heart tripped over itself.

Quinn sat next to her on the rear bumper of her SUV, wearing pink-rimmed sunglasses and popping some bubblegum. Today her hair was a deep navy braid with tiny silver star hairpins.

"How's Ezra taking it all?" Cora asked.

Quinn's smile was humorless. "We just told a self-made businessman he might lose everything he's worked for and has to leave the community he's invested so much into building up. How do you think he's taking it?"

Cora grimaced. "Fair enough."

"No. It's not fair. It's fucking tragic."

"I didn't—"

"I know what you meant. I don't blame you Cor, don't worry. I'm just..." She exhaled, long and slow, playing with the end of her braid. "My heart breaks for him. He always knew this was a possibility, just like I did, but...if I'm being honest, I don't think he ever planned on leaving if shit went down."

"Really?"

"Would you?" Quinn popped her gum again. "He didn't start with nothing, but his dad cutting him off sure made it a hell of a lot harder. He'd built up a small nest egg flipping houses, doing most of the contracting himself, but he did it for the South Side. He did honest work and sold homes back to families at reasonable prices, turning down cash offers way over asking from developers left and right. It was fucking hard work, but he saw the wave of gentrification coming, and he wanted to do what he could to keep the spirit of those neighborhoods alive."

"I had no idea."

"Yeah, he doesn't talk about it. When the opportunity came along to buy Ember, that was his first real business, and things just exploded from there. It was condos, then it was INN|LA, then Boardroom, but he always, *always* helped people as he went. He never forgot the people who gave him the means to get there. LA is his town. I think he always expected he'd die here one day."

Cora's stomach turned over. She couldn't imagine what it felt like to be so entrenched somewhere, so woven into the fabric of it, and have to face leaving all that behind.

Her eyes roved to Theo, who was chatting with Dustin by the other car. He might not be staring down the barrel of the choice Ezra was, but he was still leaving a lot behind, too.

An entire way of seeing the world. A system, a kind of structure, that he'd found support within when his own family had failed to protect him, no matter how wrong or misguided it was. Untangling yourself from that was no small feat; neither was rebuilding yourself from ground zero or having the grace to admit how sideways you'd gone in the first place.

And still he seemed so unshakable, so...grounded. Practical. Like tackling one thing at a time, focusing his energy on tangible problems, would all add up to something that he could square with, in the end.

Quinn sniffled, and Cora realized she was crying behind her sunglasses. "The only reason he's even entertaining the thought of leaving is because of me. Because he wants me to be safe, and he knows I won't go if he doesn't."

That was news to Cora. "You won't? I didn't realize you two...that things had..."

"It's not that. I mean, fine, maybe a little that. We're just not...anything specific. I don't know, it's fucking nebulous. Whatever. The point is, I can change my appearance at will, Cor. It wouldn't be hard to get away with. I'd just need a new ID. But if I'm with him, and he's got the feds on his back, or whoever else...it puts me in the line of fire if something goes down. They could use me against him. But I'm not going to leave him to face this shit alone."

"What's the worst they could charge him with?"

"I'm sure as fuck not a lawyer, but...aiding and abetting? Obstruction? They could seize any asset he hasn't moved to his shell company... He was already in the process of shifting ownership of some things, but that shit takes time."

"I'm sorry, Quinn." And because anything else Cora could say would feel woefully inadequate, she just grabbed Quinn's hand and squeezed.

Suddenly, a green sedan passed them, honked twice, and Helena nodded at the group. "This next one. Get ready."

Adrenaline spiked in Cora's chest. She and Quinn leapt off the rear bumper and made their way over to the rest of the group.

"Just overheat it," Dustin was telling Viv. "We don't need anything exploding like last time." Cora caught a hint of the deep south in his voice. The two were transplants.

"You're one to talk." She narrowed her eyes at the truck in the distance. "Or did you hit your head and forget your Vegas mishap? I bet the poor Bellagio doorman's still growing his eyebrows back."

"Everyone's a critic," he grumbled.

The box truck heading toward them spewed smoke from its engine, and the driver kicked on the hazards as he slowed. He puttered off the road a ways downhill from them, and Helena beckoned at Dustin and Cora to follow. The rest of the group would stay with the cars—it'd be no good to spook the driver and give him the chance to call for backup. Theo had warned them he'd probably be armed and trained to use whatever he had, so it helped that Helena was beautiful enough to pause a finger on a trigger.

"Hey there, man!" Dustin plastered on a neighborly smile and called out to the driver climbing down from the cabin. "Need a hand?"

"I never had no trouble on that hill before." The driver's hair was more salt than pepper, and he carried some extra weight around his middle. He didn't reach for the handgun on his hip, but the bulk under his shirt suggested a ballistic vest. Cora didn't feel the pull marking him a witch.

"Yeah, we had a little trouble ourselves. Picked up a nail on our last rest stop, but those folks were kind enough to let us use their jack."

"Road trip, huh? Where you headed?"

Helena inched forward, closing the distance between them. "Joshua Tree. A little hiking, a little camping, you know."

The man looked her up and down. Even in her dusty boots and flannel, Helena seemed better suited to poolside cabanas than the great outdoors. "I see. Well, enjoy yourselves. It's gonna cool down a little, and you'll have—"

Helena reached out to grasp his temples. Before he could go for his gun, his eyes rolled back and the surrounding air shimmered. A breeze swept dust into Cora's eyes, and she shielded them, watching in awe while Helena planted the new orders in his mind.

Just as suddenly, Helena broke the connection and stumbled away, steadying herself with a hand on Dustin's shoulder. It was the only time

Cora had seen her look any less than a picture of poise and grace. The driver's expression relaxed, blank, and he saluted before climbing back up into the cab and waiting there.

They hopped into the cars and circled off the road to park next to the truck, shielding them from the scrutiny of passing traffic. Helena would still guide curious eyes away from the scene with a nudge of her magic, just in case. Dustin's illusion hid them within a mirage, but he couldn't hold it forever, so they needed to work fast.

Viv focused her power on the complicated lock on the back. "It's magically sealed. Goddamn hypocrites."

If only she knew.

Propping open the door, they handed up jugs of Harry's placebo serum, which went considerably faster with Ghislaine's telekinesis than it would have by hand. Inside, they found pallets of stacked boxes packed in polystyrene and wrapped in plastic. To Cora's relief, each box contained large, amber glass bottles instead of the small syringes Theo kept on him, which were better suited to lab use than field use. He checked over all the labels as the bottles were emptied and refilled, tasked with ensuring everything had gone back in the proper order. Reapplying the seals was just a matter of letting Viv add heat to the glue that had kept them in place.

Even Pip was helping unwrap pallets and saved a bottle from shattering on the ground when it slipped from Quinn's sweaty hands. He seemed thrilled to be there and did his part to keep spirits up.

It took nearly an hour for them to dump out and replace all but three pallets. The serum evaporated off the warm pavement, leaving no trace of what they'd done. They were getting the last jars settled when a voice crackled on the driver's CB radio, demanding to know his status.

"Engine seized up around Eagle Mountain, sir. Letting her cool down a bit and I'll be 10-8 again."

"You need assistance? We can have an escort sent out of Indio and be there in no time."

"Negative, sir. I'll get us moving in no time. 10-7."

Cora marched through the dirt toward Helena, shielding her eyes from the glare of the sun overhead. Helena frowned as she scanned the stretch of road along the shimmering horizon.

"Penny for your thoughts?"

Helena smoothed an errant baby hair escaping from her ponytail. Beads of sweat gathered on her forehead. Cora hadn't known she *could* sweat.

"When we sorted through that mountain of paperwork, we discovered each one of these shipments is insured for $2.5 million."

Cora coughed on some dust. "Say what now?"

"I would guess," Helena continued, "whomever this man reports to would rather not leave such valuable cargo sitting on the side of the road, no matter what his driver says. I am also not in the mood to wait around and see if that is true."

Crap. "We should hurry," Cora called out to Ghislaine through the still afternoon heat. She'd remembered to cast the charm against sunburn, at least. "Get this wrapped up. Dustin, how's the mirage holding?"

He leaned against the truck in the shade, eyes closed, arms folded over the lean muscle of his chest. His brow furrowed under a fine sheen of sweat. "Getting there. Got maybe ten minutes left in me."

"Folks in the truck, how long for those last pallets?"

"Twenty?" Theo yelled back.

Helena's brow gathered. She shook her head. "Pushing it."

Cora stuck her head back in the truck. "Forget it. Leave it, there's no time. We might have company soon."

"Make sure everything looks exactly the way you found it, *exactly*, especially the tamper seals, then fix that lock," Ghislaine told the others behind her.

The next few minutes were a flurry of movement. They swept any evidence out of themselves out of the back of the truck and Viv crouched by the padlock, turning it over in her fingers. "It'll take a second to replicate the magic used to lock it. Better get the cars running and be ready to scoot."

They piled in and did just that, the knot in Cora's stomach twisting with each passing second. Pip vibrated with anxiety on the dashboard as the engine idled, and then turned into a Lakers bobblehead she'd never seen before. She popped out of Quinn's moon roof with her binoculars, keeping an eye on the road out of Indio, squinting against the glint of sunlight off the cars edging over the hill.

An involuntary shiver took her when she spotted a trio of black vans about a mile and a half away. They couldn't wait any longer. "Viv, in, NOW!"

Dustin released the box truck from his mirage but kept it wrapped around the vehicles. Viv hopped in the second car and slammed the door. Quinn roared back onto the highway, crossing the median to take them in the opposite direction of the approaching vans. An oncoming car narrowly missed them, and Cora promised herself it was the last time she'd let Quinn drive.

As they sped off, Cora reached into the earth behind them and asked the roots of the sparse brush to shift the top layer of dirt over their tire tracks, which they did happily.

Theo, slick with sweat in the seat behind her, cursed under his breath. Quinn let out a hoot, laughing as they roared past the black vans. "Guys, did we just do that shit?"

His eyes were still on the black vans, and when he was finally satisfied they weren't following, lay his head back against the headrest, eyes closed, still panting.

Quinn set the A/C on full blast, and he finally smiled, basking in it. "Yeah. We did that shit."

Cora watched the vans grow smaller and smaller behind them and sent up a silent prayer to whoever might be listening.

Please, let it be enough.

Theo's goodbye kiss to Cora was hard and quick, not wanting to give the moment any more weight than it already had. Do that, and they'd be tempting fate.

Fletcher had sounded normal on the phone when Theo organized the meeting before the roadside swap. No more comment than usual when he took time off last-minute to 'see his sick mom.' If his CO knew anything, he hadn't let on, and Theo generally had a knack for reading people.

Theo chatted with Ricky, too, and had done his best to bottle the rage that bubbled up at the sound of his partner's voice. Ricky's story tracked with Helena's: that he'd been pretty out of it and slept most of the week, thought he might even be getting sick. Theo had told him to hang in there, to let him know if he needed anything, all the while visualizing his hands around the man's throat.

But today was a different day, and Theo knew better than to blindly follow his confidence that the other shoe hadn't dropped. He was a soldier before anything else, and that meant calculating risk. Hell if he'd let Cora see his uncertainty when he pulled away from that curb, but it didn't mean his gut wasn't churning with it.

After all, this had never been their best idea. It was just their *only* idea.

242

Part of calculating that risk meant when he'd volunteered to go into the lion's den, he knew he might not come back out. But he was surprised it didn't bother him more. A kind of atonement, he supposed, for everything he'd done to put so many in there in the first place. It was the only way he could look Cora in the eyes and promise her anything—hell, it was the only way he could look himself in the damn mirror at the end of the day.

Was he playing the martyr? Maybe a little, but just for himself. A small relief to know that after all these years of shutting down, an ember of conscience still flickered in that hardened heart of his.

It was that feeling he'd chased so often on his bike, or on the mat, or doing this damn job in the first place. Coming so close to the edge, kicking up that adrenaline, and reminding himself his life was fucking worth something. Except this time, he wasn't just feeding the animal in him that had made it possible to survive all these years. This was something else— something that if he nurtured it long enough, might actually have the strength to fight back against that beast when it counted.

The trip into the Mojave was a familiar one now, but he nearly missed the turn-off, concealed as it was in the brush along the highway. It wasn't paved, just a stretch of packed dirt that his Pontiac could barely clear, and he narrowly missed high-centering the damn car on a jutting rock. Navigating back was going to be near-impossible if the sun set on him.

Eventually, the dirt road found another paved one, far enough from civilization that the highway he'd come from was barely visible in the haze. This took him through a rocky pass and then spat him out on a slice of desert that was barren of anything other than what he'd come for.

There it was. The Beach.

An airstrip shimmered in the afternoon sun, its old hangar unassuming and battered by the scrape of sand carried on the wind. But the double barbed-wire fencing and armed-to-the-gills guards at its perimeter undercut any effort the rest of it made to look inconspicuous.

He knew it sat on layers of subterranean prison that had been intended as a nuclear fallout shelter for the Los Angeles elite, but those plans were abandoned three-quarters of the way through construction. It suddenly occurred to him that everyone in there had gone without sunlight for years.

Before him, now, a guardhouse loomed. He'd bet the man inside had looked more cheerful before the hair on his head decided it'd rather move down his back and arms.

"Identification?" the guard barked. His ID badge said *Lee.*

Theo handed over his badge. "Specialist Ryland. I have a meeting with the director."

Lee made a show of peering at a clipboard. Through bulletproof glass, Theo spotted a combat shotgun resting casually in the corner of his hut.

"Please step out of the car, sir, so I can inspect your vehicle." He opened the door on the side of the hut and peeked through Theo's windows, popped the trunk, checked the underside. Careful. Thorough.

He passed over everything again with an arcanometer. If anyone tried to hide something under an illusion, they'd be outed before they made it past the perimeter.

But the second Lakers bobblehead on his dashboard wasn't even a blip.

Lee lumbered back inside and pressed a meaty thumb on a buzzer, waving him along. Both layers of fence crept to the side, and cameras swiveled to follow his car as it pulled away.

Finally through, he could take better stock of the defenses inside the compound—watchtowers bounded either end of the hangar, one sniper poised in each. Massive flood lights framed the perimeter. He counted the cameras and guards, spotted the loading bay. A service elevator sat behind a stack of old pallets. More cameras there.

But what really drew his attention were the two armed escorts waiting by Visitor parking sign, flanking a man in mirrored sunglasses. Fletcher was here.

He'd done onsite interrogations before. Usually they sent out one escort, maybe two, but it's possible Fletcher wanted to oversee this personally. It was his case, after all. That would make it tough, though not impossible, to get his message through to the Tesauros. Theo would just have to be smart about it.

Theo stepped out of the car and approached with a small salute. "Hey. Didn't know you were coming down for the onsite, but I'm glad you're here. We can good cop/bad cop it."

But he halted as the escorts shouldered their weapons, barrels trained on him. Theo bristled as Fletcher said, "Sorry, Ryland. There's been a change of plans."

Cora watched planes take off into the setting sun for as long as she could bear it, walking through the waves that rolled along the stretch of beach just under LAX. Green half-circles burned into her vision, but she didn't care.

Around the neck of the bottle of Macallan 18, her fingers were numb with cold. So was the rest of her, but the cold had nothing to do with it.

Theo was gone.

He was gone, and maybe it wasn't her fault, but it sure felt a whole hell of a lot like it was. She knew he'd made his own bed, but he'd made it because she was there, and that was more or less the same thing.

They'd come so excruciatingly close. The Recantanyl had been swapped. The strike team had been cast. But Theo hadn't been able to meet with Nell's parents, so the damn witches wouldn't know their magic was free. Every witch in that prison was a weapon they couldn't afford not to have.

She'd lost Theo and Sebastian in one fell swoop. All that hope ripped out from under her in an instant. The whiplash of it had sent her reeling all the way to the top shelf of the liquor store. She knew better than to go begging Harry for a hit of anything, so Macallan was the best she could do

If she was tossing out her chip, she wasn't about to waste it on Jack fucking Daniels.

And it had been far easier than she thought to undo all of her progress. First, she lost the battle with the threshold of the corner shop, which her traitor legs walked her to. Then, she lost the shelf standoff. With that momentum, the cash register didn't stand a chance. A handful of moments that, individually, she usually had the strength to walk away from.

Not now. Not in this reality. They weren't checks, here. They were just hurdles standing between her and some kind of oblivion, which was infinitely better than facing the day sober.

It wasn't fair that it was so easy when everything else was so damn difficult. A tiny part of her had wanted to just walk into the waves, slip silently under the water out there, let it draw her out to sea.

Earlier, when she'd begged the altas to find another way into The Beach, they'd stonewalled her. A risk they couldn't afford to take, on the chance that Theo might sell them all out. It didn't matter what he'd done for them, for her, already.

It was another reality she had to face, that even now, she didn't know what he was enduring just to protect her. But it never crossed her mind to doubt him. And she wasn't just driven by the need to make his sacrifice mean something. She knew, from the eyes they had on The Beach, that he still hadn't come out. If they found another way in, they could save him, too.

Now well on her way to tipsy, Cora could only think of one.

So she sauntered into the post office, grabbed a blank card from the spinning display, and addressed a hastily-scrawled letter to Mindy's house. A text or an email ran the risk of getting read immediately, and Cora needed to be safely at The Beach before Mindy knew about the shit she was getting ready to pull. Then she typed Ricky's address into the rideshare app on her phone.

She hadn't known where he lived, but she knew the Runner they had tailing him, and the reminder of favor owed was all it took.

Now, standing out in front of the small stucco triplex, her balance far worse than it had been before she'd gotten in the car, she knew this was a terrible, terrible idea. And that was exactly what drove one foot in front of the other. She'd nursed enough self-loathing in the past twenty-four hours that not a single part of her imagined a fate she deserved more.

Forgive yourself, forgive yourself, forgive yourself. Bullshit, bullshit, bullshit. It wouldn't change anything that had happened. It wouldn't bring back what they took.

As she walked into the courtyard, the world was tilting, or maybe she was—hard to say. She leaned on a concrete planter for support and bellowed, "Ricardooo Guillermoooo Alejandrooooo Saaaaaaantana!"

She'd heard Theo call him that once, on the phone. Well, she was pretty sure she had. Either way, she was committed now.

Her voice echoed into the night, and a dog barked in response, then another. "Come out here," she slurred, channeling Quinn's creativity with insults, "you...bag of dicks. You biiiiiig, crunchy old piece of shit."

A light flipped on in the window of number three, and her heart thudded against her ribs.

Got you.

She sang his name again as she stumbled up the steps. "Guillermoooo Ale...tana..." That didn't sound right. Oh well. "Riiiiiiiiicar—"

"Who the fuck..." And then he only had a second to duck before Cora chucked the half-full MaCallan at him. It shattered against the wall of the entryway and splashed amber liquid everywhere. A very, very expensive mess.

"You ruined everything, you fucking asshole," she said, the sight of his face sending her back into that basement, tears pricking her eyes, nausea roiling in her stomach. Before she lost her nerve, she swung at him, in the way she imagined one was supposed to, having never actually swung a fist at anyone before—realizing too late that she'd lost her balance and missed him completely.

What she had really wanted to do was rewind the bullet she knew was probably still in his thigh, make him endure the pain of getting shot again and again, but that would have landed her in a worse facility. She couldn't do that. She had to end up at The Beach. That much was clear in her mind, no matter what else was sideways and blurry.

He sidestepped her, letting her stumble forward onto hands and knees. He only had to pin her once she was down.

"Are you happy with yourself?" she hissed as he grappled with her, wrenching her left arm behind her. She gasped, tearful now, at the sharp pain that sang through her shoulder. "Did that magically solve allllll your problems? Did it bring back your little buddies and make everything better?"

She could have sworn she felt him shudder as he pinned her, leaning down so his breath tickled her ear: "No, but it'll help me sleep at night. Just like this will."

This time, when she felt that pinch in her neck, she was ready for it, welcoming the shadows that swallowed her.

———————∽◦∾———————

Theo paced. He sat. He slept. He ate when the food was edible.

There wasn't much else to do but brood.

He supposed it was too much to expect they'd allow him a lawyer or a phone call. Fletcher had made it clear his rights were few and far between. Didn't matter that he'd given them twelve years of service, and two in the Academy before that—the brass was not happy, and the ACE Tribunal was chomping at the bit to see him.

They had him red-handed on obstruction for the Foster probe, but the rest of Ricky's allegations were murkier. He'd made a case for accessory after the fact to the murders of Harris and Thompson, which even Fletcher had to know was reaching. And while he'd strung together enough evidence for them to hold him on conspiracy charges, there was still a lot they didn't know, which meant Theo had time to kill in here. If he could rely on anything, it was the wheels of bureaucracy turning at a glacial pace.

On his way down to this cell, he'd done his best to take stock of the layout and security. Two-factor biometric authentication, topside; twelve sub-levels, according to the elevator, and a thirteenth labeled "Labs." There were bulletproof glass vestibules around the elevator bay on each sublevel, with a guard stationed at each to swipe the badges of people coming and going. The vestibule doors were secured by maglocks, something an electromancer could probably short without a key.

The room they'd interrogated him in had been on sublevel two, a sleek warren of what looked like personnel offices. Everything was blinding white, minimal, sterile. Soft blue light leaked from long, geometric crevices carved in the concrete floor, and he'd noted a camera on the elevator entrance, two down the hallway. Definitely more he couldn't see. If they kept the offices here, he guessed they housed the security barracks upstairs on the first sublevel—the easiest place to cut off access to, and from, the rest of the compound in an emergency.

Now he was on sublevel three, his holding cell the first in a long corridor of similar rooms. In his cell, everything was bolted down—the sink, the toilet, the table, the chair, the cot. He had his own shower though, and that was a blessing.

Meanwhile, Pip was happy to turn into a Rubik's Cube or one of the tabloid magazines from Mindy's coffee table or even just make shadow puppets with him. Theo was grateful for the company, but somewhat at a loss. Despite asking Pip to find some pens and paper so he could get a message to anyone downstairs, the sprite had so far refused to leave his side. Sweet, but infuriating.

Lucky, too, that cameras weren't pointed into the individual cells. There was enough security in this place to make it redundant on the upper floors. They were probably more worried about the magic-wielders downstairs and for good reason.

Even if they had cameras on the cells, cameras are only as good as the eyes on them. How many people would they need to employ to keep watch twenty-four seven?

From tiny window and tray slot in the heavy steel door, Theo could still observe the main thoroughfare, the guards walking back and forth, the workers in lab coats that escorted inmates through intake. Some offices on this floor, too, but from what he could tell, less of the administrative kind and more of the practical-realities-of-running-a-prison kind.

When he'd asked why they didn't move him, Fletcher's answer had been a gruff, "Move you where? We need you alive."

Theo understood. He was a loose end the witches had every reason to want to tie off. If he were Fletcher, he'd keep Theo in the one place that might stand a chance of living through his trial. And Theo let him think it, even knowing Cora would never allow the altas to see that as an option.

That might not stop them from taking care of him behind her back, though. He'd seen enough from Ghislaine to believe her capable of it.

He lifted his head from his hands when footsteps approached from down the hall. He heard a male voice—a familiar one—exchange pleasantries with the guard stationed at the mouth of the corridor.

It took all of his willpower—and some he didn't know he had—not to launch himself at Ricky when his face appeared in that window. "Hey. I like the new digs," was all Ricky said, raising his eyebrows.

"Proud of yourself, huh?" Theo asked, fighting to keep his face blank.

"Funny. Cora asked me the same thing."

That did it. It hadn't taken much. *"Get her name out of your fucking mouth."*

Ricky grinned, resting his elbows on the tray slot and leaning closer. "Your girl has an addiction problem, my friend. Did you know?"

What?

Ricky grinned wider and fished something from his pocket, pushing it through the slot. It was a coin.

Theo leapt to his feet and stormed over to the door, relishing the way Ricky stepped away from him. He picked up the embossed metal disc and stared at it. The blood drained from his face.

18 MONTHS, it read. He flipped it over. This was a Narcotics Anonymous coin. Theo swallowed and looked back up at Ricky's punchable, punchable face. "This was hers?"

"Was. Won't do her any good now, since she got shit-housed and tried to punch me in the face."

"She did *what*?"

Ricky shrugged. "Day one all over again for her—that is, if she's sobered up by now. But she won't find a bottle in this place, so it might be good for her. Might be just as good as rehab, even."

Time slowed to a halt. He hadn't suspected, but...thinking back to Bungalow that night and what had been in her glass. Water, not vodka. And then the La Croix stash at Mindy's, the beer he'd picked up from the corner store and the way Mindy had hidden the six pack in the back of the garage fridge.

The coin dug into his now-closed fist, but his anger wasn't because she hadn't told him. No, there was plenty he hadn't told her, either, and he wasn't about to fool himself into believing sex would magically make it easier to. They'd spent years apart. Years that came with baggage, and baggage they'd need more than the last two months to unpack.

Instead, his anger came from watching Ricky revel in her vulnerability yet again, in something raw and personal she hadn't given that motherfucker any permission to know.

And fine, maybe it grated a little that he'd found out before Theo did, whether either of them had the right to know or not.

Ricky's grin widened. "Yeah. Bummer, huh? After all that work you did to find her, too. Doesn't that helplessness just mess with you? Knowing that someone you trusted went behind your back and destroyed the life of a person you care about?" The smile disappeared, and his voice lowered to a hiss. "How does it feel, you piece of shit?"

He knew Ricky was trying to get a rise out of him, and he almost let it happen—but the coin in his hand steadied him some. Just enough to allow him a deep breath, give him the self-control to pivot and walk back to the table, letting Ricky's curses bounce off his back. This little piece of her was all the armor he needed.

He lay the coin on the metal tabletop, knowing Pip was eyeing it from wherever he was hiding, and focused on it until Ricky kicked the door and stormed off. What did it mean that she was here, at The Beach? Had she really risked everything just to take one good swing at Ricky?

Maybe Ricky was self-important enough to indulge that thought, but Theo didn't believe it for a second. She was fucking traumatized. Terrified of him. She never would have sought him out without a damn good reason. Without a plan.

Theo smiled to himself.

He'd never been so proud of someone he wanted to strangle so badly.

CHAPTER TWENTY-ONE

Cora dreamed of airplanes: crashing ones, ones flying over alien landscapes, ones waiting on the tarmac indefinitely with flight attendants that wouldn't let her leave to use the bathroom.

The images swam in blurry white, and she slowly became aware that she was lying face-up on a table. Her ankles and wrists were restrained. The room around her came into focus, and she filled and emptied her lungs, praying for the pounding in her head to quiet.

"Oh, the Somerville clan." A voice to her left drew out her name like she was a game-show prize. A woman in a lab coat typed something into the computer beside her. She was easily over six feet, skinny as a board, with heavy blonde bangs and thick-framed square glasses that didn't suit her. "An elusive one, you are. The first note in your file was made over a decade ago. When your family joined us, minus the eldest daughter." Long red fingernails tapped the desk.

Cora seethed but didn't respond.

The woman flashed straight, white teeth. She was far too cheerful.

"That you, sweetheart? What do I win?"

"Technically, I'm only the eldest by two minutes."

"Technical is all I do up here. I'm Dr. Greer, by the way. Now let's see..." She scrolled down, typed some more, scrolled again. "Oh, right. This is where I get to tell you you've been found guilty of the crime of witchcraft, blah blah et cetera..." She kept scrolling, mumbling. "...something

something, here until you're no longer a threat to yourself and your community, and so on...Sorry, I don't usually work intake, I'm just covering for someone."

Who the hell *was* this crazy bitch?

"Oh, here we go. Says here that you threw a $500 bottle of scotch at Special Agent Santana's head. Wowza." She wrinkled her nose. "Personally, I would have gone for the Macallan 12. Don't think any man is worth the 18, but you do you."

"The 18 was for me," Cora said, glowering. "I had no intention of sharing."

"Clearly, according to your blood work here. BAC of 0.17 a few hours ago. How's the hangover?"

As if in answer, Cora's stomach lurched, and she shut her eyes briefly, just grateful to be lying down. "I'll manage." Not that Greer actually cared.

Greer scrolled some more, typed some more. "That reminds me. That drug in your system? It's called Recantanyl. Does a fun thing where you can't use your magic, and you'll get an injection every day. Some side effects, headaches, nausea, suffocating existential dread...or maybe that's just this place." She wiggled her eyebrows, not taking her eyes off the screen. Then: "Oh! *This* is interesting."

Cora couldn't help herself. "What?" If this woman was going to use her as a guinea pig for her tight five, Cora might as well try and squeeze some information out of her. She shouldn't have been surprised to find someone so clearly off the deep end working at a place like this, and yet...that she could be so blasé about the whole thing was a level of sociopathic Cora couldn't comprehend.

"Oh, I don't know. I really shouldn't tell you." She typed some more, considered. "But I just feel like the intake staff really get to have all the fun, so I probably will anyway. First, though, we should see if you can sit up now. The sedative will have worn off. Just try not to puke on my floor."

Greer released the straps holding Cora down, and she sat up slowly, trying not to let her stomach win this rout. If she wasn't careful, she'd get the spins. She noticed a pile of gray clothing on the edge of the table, and Greer nudged it over to her. "Strip and put these on. You smell like a walking distillery."

Sifting through the pile, Cora found a jumpsuit and several sets of undergarments, socks, and shirts. She didn't really care that Greer was watching as she changed, but a new wave of nausea hit when she saw the bar code tattooed on the underside of her wrist. The surrounding skin was angry and inflamed. "You've got to be fucking kidding me."

"I joke, but I never kid," Greer said with a smile.

Cora clenched her jaw as she pulled on the white cotton panties and donned the long-sleeve shirt under the jumpsuit, hoping to banish some of the chill that had seeped into her bones while she lay unconscious. The slip-on shoes were a half size too small and pinched her toes, but she had a feeling Greer wouldn't give a shit about that, either.

"Stand against the wall." Greer adjusted a small camera hanging off the monitor of her computer.

Lovely. They'd document this wonderful hair day for all of posterity. Cora pressed her back to the concrete blocks and gave Greer her widest, toothiest, fuck-you-est smile.

"So," Cora said casually as Greer continued typing, "You said you don't usually work intake. What do you do, then?"

"Oh, I'm a researcher," Greer said back just as casually, not looking away from her screen. "I am just *fascinated* by the kind of shit you guys can do. Biiiiig no-no to say that topside, but I can tell you there are hordes of scientists just chomping at the bit to study how magic works in the human body. When I scored this job, I won the fucking lottery. My colleagues at Berkeley practically shit themselves. I kinda wasn't *supposed* to tell them, but could I really pass up that chance?"

"What the fuck?" Cora said, mostly to herself. She should have known this kind of thing would be going on, but she hadn't given it too much thought. Of course they'd want to study magic—and what better place to do it than an underground bunker with an endless supply of test subjects? Her heart dropped into her stomach. What kinds of experiments were they running? How were they planning to use what they learned?

And what horrors had she just signed herself up for?

Greer finally turned back to her and grinned. "You and I? We're about to get real cozy. You know how many sets of twins we get in here? Like, none. I think you and your brother are the third pair total, first since I took this gig. I have *so* many things I wanna try. The nature vs. nurture conversation *alone—*"

Cora's ears were ringing as she tuned out Greer's rambling. She'd come to rescue Seb, and she might have condemned him to something even worse, just by completing their duo.

What had she done?

———————∽———————

Two armed guards shadowed them down the hallway, as Greer herded Cora into a sleek, stainless elevator, which she opened with a swipe of the badge pinned to the pocket of her white coat. They were on the third floor, and she pressed the button for sublevel nine.

Cora was afraid to know what was on the other floors. She was afraid to know anything else at all. But Greer answered her questions even as they hung there, unasked. "Your block leader will show you around. Families with children up to sixteen are in blocks four, five, and six, plus classrooms for the school-age kids. Rec room, cafeteria, library, are seven. Eight and nine are women, ten and eleven are men. Twelve is medical, which connects to the labs on thirteen. That's where you'll usually find me."

Cora didn't want to find this bitch anywhere. She fought to control her breathing, her nausea, her pounding head. It had been almost nineteen months since her last hangover, and her body was not happy. Never mind the lack of tolerance—pushing thirty meant her days of bouncing right back from a night of drinking were over.

There was a comfort, though, in this brief moment of *never* wanting to smell or see liquor again.

The doors slid open with a cheerful ding, and they stepped into a small receiving chamber. Two guards flanked a frosted glass door, blocking inmate access to the elevator. A woman in a deep purple jumpsuit stood to the side, like a vivid bruise against the clean, stark white of the walls.

Greer and the woman exchanged a look full of...something. History there, Cora guessed. "This is Anita, your block leader. She'll get you set up." Greer turned to Cora and winked. "I'll be seeing you, babe." She swiftly disappeared back into the elevator, waggling her fingers as the doors whispered shut.

A roll of Anita's light brown eyes said that was nothing new. She had skin the shade of dark honey, high cheekbones framed by gray-streaked ringlet curls left to run wild. Cora put her somewhere in her late fifties, and though her face was free of makeup, she had a distinguishing beauty that transcended the need for it.

She nodded at Cora. "Follow me."

A guard swiped his badge and waved them through the frosted doors, which slid shut with finality behind them. The next area was a bustle of activity, voices, movement. Inmates appraised the newest arrival.

A labyrinthine sprawl of alcoves lay before them, two sets of bunk beds in each. The partitions between were an unforgiving concrete block, but a beautiful tumult of graffiti splashed down the center lane as far as Cora could see. Narrow panels of light veined the ceiling above, stretching from one end of the block to the other.

Anita led her past rows of alcoves until they came to an empty one—or at least, it looked empty, but upon further inspection one of the beds was already made up. A small drawing of a young boy peeked out from under the pillow of the top bunk. The other bunk was unmade, with fresh blankets folded in neat piles on the thin, lumpy mattresses.

"Gloria works the kitchens this time of day, but you'll meet her later," Anita said. "For now, just put your things down. You have a locker for your clothing and personal affects over here. Bathrooms and showers are down the hall. See that tattoo on your wrist? It's your ticket to everything. Scan it to start up the shower, and it's set on a seven-minute timer. You get one every other day."

"Who drew that?" Cora nodded at the picture.

"One of the ladies used to be a sketch artist for the FBI. She does commissions for folks. We're on a Jell-O for-hire system."

The reality of this place finally slammed into her. Jell-O as currency. She didn't know why that was the detail that did it—maybe it was just one little thing that brought her over the edge, but the walls were closing in, the air suddenly grew thick, and she couldn't get enough in. She struggled to suck in breath, her furious, quick rasps making her dizzy enough that her knees reconsidered holding her up. She slid onto the edge of the nearest bunk.

Oh, fuck. Oh fuck. Oh fuck—

Anita popped a squat in front of her and was saying things she couldn't hear.

I'm here. I'm stuck here. We are so deep underground. I might be here forever. I might be trading Jell-O for tampons for the rest of my life. What if there's an earthquake? Will the whole place cave in on us? What if the experiments go wrong? Will they just let us die? How did mom die? What if I can't get us out? What if—

Cora's cheek stung, and she looked into Anita's kind eyes, realizing the woman had slapped her. Not hard enough to leave a mark, but enough to drag her out of her own head. She focused on Anita's face, slowing her breath to match Anita's long, measured inhales and exhales. "Pobrecita, breathe with me. That's it. Breathe with me. In, out."

When she could speak again, Cora wiped her eyes and said, "Goddess, I'm so sorry. Thank you. I just..."

"No need." Anita waved a hand and passed her a crumpled tissue from her pocket. "Everyone needs a moment. It's just a matter of when it hits you. You got that out of the way, and at least it won't happen in the middle of dinner."

"That bitch Greer didn't help," Cora grumbled, taking the tissue and dabbing her eyes. "She's a piece of work."

"They all are, in their own way. You'll get used to it." Anita rolled her eyes, though. "She's definitely a special case."

Cora didn't want to get used to it, but she reminded herself why she was here. Who she was here for. It helped her sit up a bit straighter. "Do you have any idea where I can find Sebastian Somerville?"

Anita's brows gathered. "Sebas..." Then her eyes widened. "Oh! You mean James? James Somerville?"

"Who?" Was Sebastian not here? That couldn't be right. Theo had said he was here. She felt the brief flutter of panic and then—"Oh." James was his middle name. He'd started going by James? "I...I think so. He looks like me, right? We're twins. Fraternal, obviously." She was rambling as she processed it all.

"Oh, god." Anita blinked. "I knew you looked familiar, but I couldn't place you." She hesitated, awkwardly placing a hand on Cora's shoulder. "I should tell you..."

"I know," Cora said before she could go any further. "I know about my mom already."

A flicker of relief, gone as soon as it had appeared. Cora couldn't blame Anita—she wouldn't have wanted that responsibility, either. "Then I will just say I'm...sorry for your loss. Robyn was...a light."

"Um, thanks." Cora looked at the ground, sifting through her brain for something better than that. "It's a comfort to know she had friends. People who cared."

Anita nodded, tight-lipped, and dropped her hand. "James goes upstairs with his friends to watch TV about now, if you want to wait for him there. I can show you the rest on the way."

"Sure. Thanks," Cora said, sniffling one final time and getting to her feet. She reeled with that new info, picking it apart. Seb had *friends*. There was TV. This woman knew him well enough to know where he'd be around this time of day. She'd known Cora's mom, too. Been friends with her, from the sound of it.

Anita rose with her and squeezed her hand. "Come on. Follow me."

Anita led her back into the narrow passage, toward what Cora guessed were the bathrooms. "Each cubby manages a week-long rotation of custodial duties for the entire floor. It's near to the front of the block right now, so yours won't get it for some time yet."

Past those, a heavy fire door with a small window spat them into a concrete-block stairwell. "This connects each floor, starting on sublevel four and going down to lab level. But your tattoo will only get you access to this floor, the other women's floor above us, and the seventh, where the communal areas are." They began ascending, and Cora peeked through the window of the next floor. It was identical to their own, with different art on the partitions.

Anita rattled off instructions while they climbed, scanning her wrist outside the next door they reached. A wary guard watched them from the opposite end of the landing as a bolt clicked open. She pushed the door ajar with some effort and led them through the sterile corridor beyond. "Each block has designated time slots for meals, but you're free to use the library and rec room from seven in the morning to ten at night. Lights out is ten-thirty, no exceptions. If I catch you up and about past then, I'm obligated to report you...but I won't. Usually a guard will be the one to catch you. You don't want that."

They passed a large, open room devoid of furniture except a few tables and chairs. Another guard stood outside, and Cora began to sense a pattern. "What goes on in there?"

"A few ladies host a yoga class twice a week," Anita said. "There's also a TV, but it only gets local channels, news, a few daytime soaps. Sometimes we'll get lucky, and a holiday movie will be on, but that's rare."

"They don't censor the news?"

Anita shrugged. "It's not like we can do anything about it. I think they get some sick satisfaction from giving us a little hope."

Pairs of eyes followed them down the stretch of hallway—some gaunt, others wary, hopeful, dismissive. New bodies meant new trouble for some, new company for others. A shift in the culture of their grey-jumpsuited microcosm. Not that she felt unwelcome, but she didn't feel the spark of camaraderie she thought she should. They marked her for an outsider and made sure she knew it.

"Left is the kitchen. Further down is the cafeteria. Our block eats with block eight, the women's floor above us. Breakfast is at six-thirty. Lunch is at noon. Dinner's at six-thirty again. We have half an hour, and if you sleep through it, you're out of luck. The families eat after us, and the men after them. Don't linger past your time slot. Injections are after dinner, always."

"Here's the library on your right. You'll find a lot of decent reading in there, actually. We have a sign-out system to keep track of who has what. Oh, I forgot to mention. If you need the infirmary, you come to me first, and I'll see you're taken care of. You don't want to go down there if you can help it. You'll spend enough time in those labs as it is."

Well, that wasn't ominous. "Greer had mentioned something about that."

Anita pulled Cora through the door into the stacks, out of earshot from the nearest guard. "You do not want to upset her. You listen to me, okay? You do what she tells you to do, and you will make it out of there alive, but plenty of people have not. I say this not to scare you, but so you understand."

Cora swallowed hard. "I knew there was something deeply wrong with that woman."

"You look at this place and you ask yourself, why is this not a work camp? What do they gain from us being here? Yes, the children go to the Academy, but what else? It's because *we* are the resource. *We* are the product. Do not forget that."

Cora's hand found a nearby bookshelf, just in case her knees made good on their threat to buckle.

"And this goes without saying...but stay away from the guards. You talk back, you touch them, you look at them funny...I can't protect you. They're just as quick to use real bullets as they are Crash, and we're never sure which they're in the mood for. Do you have any questions?"

Hundreds, but none that Cora could stomach the answers to. She shook her head. Anita saw it in her face and motioned to a beat-up armchair in the corner. "Why don't you sit for a minute? I can tell James you're in here. It will be a more private place for a reunion, I think."

"Thank you," Cora said hoarsely, walking over to the chair and sliding bonelessly into it. She needed a moment to gather herself before she saw him, anyway.

Anita left Cora alone in the stacks.

The next five minutes were the slowest of her life, so she scoped out her surroundings. The stacks spread from the concrete floor in regimental rows and clean, unembellished lines. They, too, were molded in concrete, but the crowding of books broke that uniformity, a cheerful jumble of colors and shapes, and the smell of parchment and leather was a comfort. Reading nooks scattered throughout the maze, circling simple pendant light fixtures.

The prisoners took care of this space, maintained its dignity with the cautious affection of a child afraid its favorite toy might be taken away.

She was flipping aimlessly through a book on bird watching, the irony of doing so in a windowless building not lost on her, when she heard the old nickname.

"Cor?" She jumped.

The timbre of his voice was unfamiliar, deeper than she'd last heard it. When she turned to look at Sebastian, he wore a strange man's face cast from the template of the teenage boy she remembered.

He wore his shoulder-length auburn hair in a ponytail, and the top of her head barely reached his collarbone. An eight o'clock shadow framed a faint dusting of freckles along his carved cheeks and strong slope of nose they shared, but his freckles weren't as pronounced as hers. Lean muscle roped along his arms, but he was too skinny, his chin too sharp, his elbows too angular. He had the hollow, thousand-yard stare of a war veteran instead of the laughing eyes she knew.

All these observations crashed into her at once. And all that came out was, "Goddess, what are they *feeding* you?"

Tears blurred the stranger in front of her. "It's you," the blurry silhouette said, his voice sharp and resonant, a little deeper than she'd last heard it, but without the undercurrent of laughter it had always carried. He'd always sounded mischievous, like he was in on a joke you weren't supposed to know, and that thread of him was nowhere to be found in the stranger before her. "You're real."

"I'm real," she said softly, and then suddenly he was there, sweeping her up in a hug so tight she thought she'd shatter in it. The ground fell away from her feet, and she marveled at his strength in spite of his obvious undernourishment.

"I can't fucking believe it's you," he said, pulling back, hands tight on her shoulders, just far enough so he could look her up and down. She did the same, each trying to reassure themselves the other was actually there. Then ten thousand things tumbled from their mouths at once:

"I'm so fucking mad at you, Cora—"

"You're so *tall*—"

"—letting yourself get stuck in here—"

"—there's so much we need to—"

"—the hell were you *thinking*—"

"—when did you start going by James?"

"You're real. Fuck, you're real," he kept repeating, moving his hand from her cheek to her hair and back again, and her throat swelled too much to do more than croak, "I'm real, Seb, I'm here."

"Here, come sit." They moved out of the stacks toward a free table and chairs out of earshot from the other inmates. Still reeling from the clash of adrenaline and relief and giddiness and fear, she wasn't able to do much more than let him lead her. Her hand shook within his, and he squeezed it.

She was glad he asked the first question, gave her galloping thoughts a focus. She wouldn't have been able to string words together otherwise.

Sebastian lowered his voice to a whisper. "How did you get caught?"

Cora glanced around, matching his volume. "Is it...can we talk here? It's safe?"

He shrugged. "Safe as anywhere else."

"So...no, then."

"Depends on the guards, on the day. Mendoza's here now, so we're fine. He gives us our space. Duncan, O'Connell, Gonzalez, all good. You'll learn their rotations."

She would, and the reality of that slammed into her. "I'm not here by accident, Seb." She reached for his hands. They dwarfed hers, even more pallid next to her tan. A jolt flowed through her fingertips on contact: the validating click of one puzzle piece into another. Every observation of him felt like a story she'd been told, coming to life in front of her.

He threaded his fingers through hers. "I don't understand."

261

She scrambled to pluck a coherent train of thought from her racing mind. "I saw mom on Samhain."

Cora didn't think Sebastian could get any paler, but he managed it. His palms became clammy against hers. "So...you know how..."

She shook her head. "You don't have to tell me now."

He ground his teeth together. "What does she have to do with you being here?"

"She...okay, let me back up even further." Cora's own hands were shaking, and every time she tried to speak, her tongue tripped on the words. "Ryland. You know, Theo. This started with him. He's a hunter, Seb. He was conscripted by them, the night he disappeared, and put into training."

"Wait, what? *Ryland*?" He'd said it a little louder than he meant to and dialed his voice back down again. "Ryland's a hunter?" The whites of his hazel eyes showed, anger taking a brief backseat to shock.

"Yes, but—"

"Nintendo bedsheets Ryland?"

"*Yes*, but—"

"No-crusts-on-my-pickle-sandwich Ryland?"

"*Listen* to me!" She swallowed a laugh. It felt so good to want to laugh with him. "He's with us. He's going to get us out of here."

"How?"

Right. There was that part. "Well...actually, we have to get him out of here, too."

"Is it too much to ask for any logical progression in this story?"

"If you'd just stop interrupting me—"

"Sorry, sorry. This is a lot to take in." He shook his head. "Damn it, I did it again."

She waited, and he gestured at her to go on. "So," she said, "*How* we managed to secure his help is a long story for another day, but he's been giving us Crash to study and I've been training with it for...well, not long, but I can shake off a full dose maybe an hour or two before it wears off. It gets more...pliable, I guess, as time goes on."

"Cor, no offense." His tone suggested the opposite. "Do you really think one person's magic is going to be any use against an army of trained hunters?"

She narrowed her eyes. "Lucky for you, I've grown a few new brain cells since we last saw each other. We got our hands on some reports we shouldn't have and intercepted a drug shipment on its way here. Did a little roadside switcharoo and filled every container with a placebo that looks and behaves like the real thing. I'm here to tell our team on the outside when it's circulating."

"When it's circu...what? You did *what*?" His volume crept up again, and he forced himself back to a whisper. "How?"

"A day will come when the drug doesn't work. For everyone here. You'll be able to reach your magic again. And we'll have a team waiting outside to send us to safety in Crescent Vale—you remember that place, don't you?"

"Who are you?" He felt her forehead, tugged her hair. "You look like her. You sound like her. Not so sure about the massive balls you're dragging along behind you, though. Don't remember those."

She swatted him away. "Come on. This is serious."

He jiggled one leg, made a thoughtful noise in the back of his throat. "Hell, alright. Put me in, coach."

"Tell me who we can trust with this. Someone on each floor, at least, who can rally their block once it's go time. Someone who won't breathe a word of this to anyone until I say so. What about the Tesauros? Sonya and Emilio?"

"How...do you know Sonya and Emilio?"

"Not personally, but I was supposed to..." Cora swallowed. "Their daughter, Nell. Before she was caught, I was helping take her to Whitefall. They're cousins of a friend, Ezra, and...it doesn't matter. I'll tell you the whole story sometime."

But he'd grown solemn as she rambled. "You don't know what the people here have been through. You should if you want them on board."

She didn't like the shadow passing behind his eyes. "Tell me."

"The last time we had an escape attempt was...oh, coming up on five years ago, I guess. Everyone involved was gunned down on the spot or executed after questioning." He ran his hand roughly over his face. "Even the kids. It took days to wash the blood off everything. They had us do it ourselves. We were up to our elbows in it."

Cora followed. "And now the survivors...they'll want to know what makes this any different."

"Wouldn't you?"

She sat forward and took both his hands again. "Last time they didn't have outside support, or their own magic to defend themselves. You can tell them there's an entire team waiting, with all our coven's altas to boot."

"They might not believe you. It might not be worth the risk to them. You've been in here less than a day, and they've had their hope chipped away for years."

"But they'll believe *you*." She looked at him hard. A possibility occurred to her. "You don't believe me, do you?"

"Cor, I..." He exhaled long and hard, looked at the floor, looked back. "I do. Of course I do. I just...you came in here guns blazing, and I'm trying to reconcile the Cora I knew with the one I just met twenty minutes ago. All that time we had together...we just spent the same amount of it apart."

"You think I don't realize that?" Emotion swelled in her throat, and she didn't bother to whisper now. She'd had plenty more time, too, to build herself up to this moment. To worry about how different he'd be, about whether he'd even recognize her. "I mean, you're James now, for fuck's sake."

"I'm not saying that. I mean, shit, you had however long to come to terms with it before coming here. Just give me a little time, okay? I don't mean to upset you, but you've got to understand."

No, that was fair. She had no right to be indignant; she'd just gotten caught up in the adrenaline of seeing him. "I'm sorry. I can't blame you." Then: "Why James?" It was going to take her forever to get that one right. And it was just one more reminder of how much he'd changed, of the wedge this place had shoved between them.

He grew silent. She waited, giving him the space he needed to find the words.

Finally, he said, "There's so much you'll never get about being here." He swallowed, that faraway look in his eyes, and Cora's chest caved in at the sight of it. "For as long as I've been here."

She let him take his time.

"I didn't want to lose who I was, in all of that. Because part of that was you, too. It had always been Seb and Cor, Cor and Seb. It felt...unbalanced. It was always a reminder of what I'd lost. But James..."

Cora's cheeks were wet. She grabbed his hands in hers.

"He could *just* be James. He wasn't dragging you around—"

"—like a phantom limb," she finished for him. How long had it been since they'd finished each other's sentences?

264

"Yeah. He could let go."

Goddess, that fucking hurt. It felt like her heart had lodged permanently in her feet. He blurred in front of her. The tears dripping off her chin left dark gray dots on her jumpsuit. She sucked in a shaky breath and blew it out. "I'm so sorry," she said, her voice breaking. "I'm so fucking sorry, Seb."

She dragged him back to her in a hug so tight she thought she'd snap his skinny ass in half. "I should have come sooner. I should have done more, I should have—"

"Don't you fucking dare," he said into her hair, stroking it with one hand, shuddering like he was trying to contain his own tears. "You had to live your life, just like I did. I had to let you go to do it, and I shouldered that guilt every damn day." He pulled away and looked her in the eyes. Their mom's eyes. "Listen to me and listen good. Are you?"

She nodded, fumbling for the tissue Anita had given her.

"If I can forgive myself for that, Cor, you can forgive yourself too."

Cora just crumpled into his chest and sobbed.

CHAPTER TWENTY-TWO

At dinner that night, flashbacks to those first weeks of lonely lunches at a new high school followed her through the double doors into the cafeteria. Long, rectangular tables ran the length of it. A line had already formed alongside the serving bar.

Five guards prowled in body armor. Keeping to the center of the group, she was careful not to draw the gaze of Novak, one of the guards Seb warned her about.

Seeing Seb had absolutely wrecked her. Nothing, nothing she'd imagined came close to what it felt like to hug him and know he was healthy and safe and whole. To reassure herself he was real flesh and blood and not just a product of a teenage girl's overactive imagination.

She'd spent most of the rest of the afternoon with him, swapping stories and reminiscing and explaining how she'd ended up here in the first place. When the dinner bell rang for her floor, she'd almost insisted on skipping just for a few more minutes with him, but he'd insisted she go. She had to start introducing herself to people, earning their trust. Convincing them she was someone they could follow into battle. Because essentially, that was what she would ask them to do.

There was so much she needed to bounce off of Theo, and it grated that he was as close as he was out of reach. She hoped Pip would sense her nearby and try to visit her tonight; if they could at least pass notes through him, she could tell Theo she was here. What was he thinking right now?

Maybe he'd already tried to send a message to Emilio and Sonya Tesauro. She'd have to find them and see.

Cora slid her tray down the stainless-steel counter, filling it with whatever looked edible, then settled at an empty table. A stocky woman with waist-length black hair plunked down across from her.

"Um, hi," Cora said. What was the etiquette here?

The woman saved her the trouble of wondering for too long. "I am Lupita. I am here maybe three, four year. Your mother, I loved her very much." She squeezed Cora's shoulder. A heavy accent halted her words.

Cora froze mid-chew. "You...knew my mother?"

Lupita's eyes were warm. "I had no English, when they bring me. So then she is sitting with me in the library every day, finding books. I learn *El Gato Ensombrerado*. You say, *Cat in the Hat*. The day before she leave us—" Lupita did the sign of the cross in the air, "—I finish the *Cat's Cradle*."

Cora stared at Lupita. She'd gone from Dr. Seuss to Vonnegut. "She helped you learn English?"

"The words, they are harder to say, but on paper, I enjoy."

"Lupita here really missed reading. She was a journalist in Mexico before she came over." A middle-aged woman sat next to Cora, tucking white-blonde hair behind her ears. Her full lips spoke of an overindulgence in fillers. She couldn't have been here too long; her roots only showed a few inches. But she looked familiar.

"Wait...Gloria Greene?" Cora asked. "Meredith from 'Seven Widows' Gloria Greene?"

"Ah! A fan! The very same." Gloria winked. Her Memphis twang was authentic—she didn't put it on for the show. "Surprised you recognized me without the arsenal of hair product. But I'll tell you a secret—plastic drinking straws are great for curls, in a pinch. Your mama taught me that. She taught me most all my prison beauty tricks, now that I think about it. Smart woman, she was. Inventive. A real creative soul."

The tension left Cora's shoulders. "She must have been star-struck when you walked in. Did she tell you we used to watch you every Wednesday? It was the first 'grown-up' show she let me see, but she still covered my eyes during the sex scenes."

Gloria hooted with laughter. "Missy, even I cover my eyes during those scenes nowadays. These high-res TVs ain't kind to nobody with pores and cellulite, I'll tell you that for free. You know, if we could've put it in a job description, I'd'a paid anything to keep an illusionist on staff."

Suddenly Gloria's head snapped back, and she cried out. Scrambling off the bench, she followed the black-gloved hand gripping her hair. It belonged to Novak.

"Something funny?" He threw her to the floor, his color rising. Ambient chatter around the room died as Gloria tried to sit up. Novak knocked her down again. He pressed his boot on the back of her neck, digging his heel into the soft flesh. She began to sob. "Just having the time of your life over here, huh?"

"No, sir, I—"

"You know what I think?" He turned to the rest of the room, hooking his thumbs in his belt loops. "I think you're getting a little too comfortable here, is what I think. Having yourselves a grand old time, like it's all a joke. Well, this isn't some goddamn summer camp, you hear me? We're not gonna sing songs, or roast marshmallows, or braid each other's fucking hair."

Drops of spittle hit Cora's arm.

He stepped off Gloria, and Cora helped her up, squeezing her shaking hands.

"Thanks for clarifying that," said a brunette two tables down from them. "Here I was all ready to make friendship bracelets."

Nobody laughed, and Lupita made a noise in the back of her throat. "Oh, Penny, no," she whispered.

"You got something to say, huh?" Novak rounded on Penny and dug the barrel of his handgun into the back of her head.

When the steel met her skull, she began to turn, slowly, slowly. He kept the gun trained on her, and she sat forward, facing him now, pressing her forehead into the barrel. He looked unsettled as she stood, but neither backed off.

On her feet now, she was nearly as tall as he. "Just one thing. Your old woman should have done the world a favor and swallowed you, Mitchell Novak." And then she spat right in his eye.

Cora thought maybe he was just feeling important, maybe he was just trying to scare them into behaving, but the table in front of Penny was already soaked with blood and brain matter and whatever else, and she slumped backward into a puddle of herself, and only then did Cora realize she hadn't heard the gun go off. She only heard ringing, shrill and incessant.

She watched Novak wipe his face in disgust, watched his mouth move, but his voice didn't carry over the high-pitched whine filling her ears. He holstered his gun and hiked up his pants by the belt loops. The women around Penny were covered in bits of her, trays slowly flooding with crimson. One of them brought a shaking hand to her mouth and pulled in shallow, ragged breaths.

"Someone clean this shit up," she finally heard him say. He spat in Penny's direction and walked away, whistling.

"Why would she do that?" Cora whispered to Gloria, back in their cubby. Their other bunkmate, who'd been at Penny's table but made no effort to introduce herself, lay in bed staring blankly at the ceiling.

Theo's absence was a physical thing in her chest, burrowing deeper. She desperately needed to tell him what had happened, to explain it to someone who would have a normal damn reaction to the horror of it. She felt like she was going crazy. These women were numb, like the only way they could handle the reality of this place was dissociating. Only Gloria cried, and Cora suspected it was because she hadn't been here long.

"Some folks are so far gone, hope don't mean nothing. Penelope, she'd been here longer than your mama. Came in with Lupita, actually. And a regular victim of his, physically, mentally. Wanted him to end it, I suppose." Gloria dabbed her eyes. She'd aged ten years in the last half-hour. "Just like her to go out with the last word. Hell of a woman, and smart to boot. A professor at USC before all this went down. Ph.D., the works. Taught neuroscience."

Cora had to keep reminding herself to breathe.

What if her mother had been just like Penny, wrecked by abuse day in and day out, until she'd just lost the will to fight?

What if she thought she'd done her job, raised Sebastian as best she could, but still couldn't bear to stay and see him grow up in this place?

What if Cora couldn't keep the promise she'd made these people, and it all fell apart, and they had to spend another week washing the blood of children off the walls?

Goddess help her, the blood. There had been so much of it.

She'd treated gunshot wounds, sure. She'd watched doctors pry bullets out of mangled flesh. She'd stabilized patients with severed spines, collapsed lungs. She'd seen patients post-op with their abdomens left wide open, packed with gauze and plastic wrap to keep the intestines in, while trauma surgeons muttered about fragmentation over lunch.

None of that prepared her for Penny, whose face kept exploding in her mind again and again and again, or for the underlying hum of tinnitus that kept jolting her back to the cafeteria just when she thought she'd gotten a hold on herself.

If Penny had waited a week or two...

A wave of guilt crested, crashed, and Gloria kept on. Steadied by the simple fact of her rambling, Cora tuned back in. "That bitch up top, Director Haas? She don't care much what happens down here, long as none of it gets out. You can see we've made this place a home as best we can, and sometimes, it just maddens them, don't it? Ten, fifteen years just being someplace, and a whole new life takes root. Not like you can stop it. But Leyra knows they try."

A man's voice echoed down to the end of the block, and Gloria poked her head into the hallway. "Oh, look, there's Remy with the injections. Come on, don't be afraid. Just stand next to me, roll up your sleeve with the bar code on it. That's it, there you go. These needles are small. They go into the fatty part of the back of your arm. Like insulin, like my daddy used to do it."

All the women lined up, arms out. She sensed the incident at dinner made it a more solemn affair than usual. Nobody spoke. Nobody moved. Nobody breathed.

Except Gloria, bless her. As he moved down the line, she kept her voice low. "Remy, he's good with the needle, so don't you worry. Always gentle. Never leaves marks, which you can't say for all of 'em."

He had a small contraption to scan each witch's wrist, like she'd used for inventory at Boardroom. Some sort of tracking system, she guessed. It made sense to know who'd been given what dose when, especially if your life and job depended on it.

When Remy got to Cora, he squinted. "You're new, but you seem damn familiar."

She didn't know how to respond, so she settled for honesty. "You might know my brother, James."

"That so? Huh. Didn't know there were more of you running around."

"Well, not anymore," she said with a grim smile. He returned it, the bastard, and scanned her wrist. It gave a different beep than it had for everyone else down the line.

Remy frowned. "You're flagged to go down to the labs after this."

Cora's heart stumbled. "Already? Why?" Damn it, she thought she'd have more than a day before she had to see Greer's face again.

Remy shrugged before taking her arm, swiftly administering the Recantanyl, and moving on to the next cubby. "I'm just the messenger. Report downstairs in fifteen."

"You'll be okay," Gloria whispered to her, patting her shoulder. For an actress with two Emmys, she was mighty unconvincing.

Cora squared her shoulders. She wasn't about to let anyone see how terrified she was, so she'd draw on anger and spite to get through this. "You think I have time to squeeze in a shower?" she murmured to Gloria. She hadn't had time to since she arrived, and she desperately needed one.

Gloria raised her penciled-in brows. "I wouldn't go down there a minute earlier than you gotta."

That was enough to get Cora moving. If she was going to face Greer again, she was determined to do it with a little dignity.

She grabbed her towel and didn't look back as she moved down the center aisle towards the bathrooms, keenly aware of all the eyes on her as she passed each cubby—it was impossible not to be, as ambient chatter quieted and heads turned.

She felt a lot like a lamb going to the slaughter and wondered what everyone knew that she didn't.

Everything made sense.

Standing in the entrance to the lab was like ripping off a blindfold she'd been wearing for years. Even knowing there was magic in Crash, even understanding that those without power would do anything to get it, she never imagined just how deep and desperate the rot had become.

The ceilings of the concrete chamber stretched high above her, tubes and wires twisting along them like gravity-defying snakes. Glass shelves full of vials and bottles and odd things in jars sat in neat rows uplit by linear LEDs. Long desks rose from the concrete floor, single molded shapes designed not to be moved, holding microscopes and autoclaves and contraptions she'd never seen in any hospital. Screens covered every wall, reading out various measurements in real time, though what the numbers and abbreviations meant, she couldn't guess.

But what stopped her in her tracks were the wide glass pillars filled with liquid, rising from the floor to the ductwork, their bubbling the only sound aside from the whirring of and humming and beeping of everything else. Her fingers rose to one as her brain tried to make sense of the creature in front of her.

Curled in on itself, as if it were sleeping, it bore the arms and legs of a human child but the translucent pink head and tail of an axolotl. The resident of the pillar next to it was also some kind of hybrid, this one with a wolf's fur rippling to and fro in the water, claws beginning to protrude from short and stubby fingers. She kept going, looking down and down and down, to the lioness with a woman's head and breasts and hips, and the man with bird wings and the child with fox legs and then it hit her.

Shifters. All of them. Suspended in some kind of fucked-up, half-formed stasis.

Cora was going to be sick. She backed away and stumbled off the raised PVC platform, looking for a trash can to hurl in. Before her now, a corridor unfurled, long and lonely rooms built into some kind of strange crystalline rock. Cells made of massive hunks of the same green mineral kept the sprites contained. It crept up the walls on this side of the lab, an organic, earthy contrast to the stark, clean lines of the rest of the space.

Cora could see into the cell nearest the mouth of the hallway, see the curious face pressed against the clear crystal there, and then she really was sick.

Strong hands stroked her back and held her still-damp hair away from her face as she retched on the glossy floor. "It's okay," Sebastian was saying. "I'm here. Get it out. It's okay."

She didn't ask what he was doing here, just wiped her mouth with the tissue he handed her and sat back on her heels, gasping. If she was here, of course he was here. Wasn't that what Greer had said? She'd run tests on them together?

"Where is she?" Cora asked softly, and Sebastian helped her up.

"I'm not sure," he said, "but she'll be around before long."

"You've...spent a lot of time here?"

"And if I never do again, it'll be too soon."

Cora looked up at him, his vacant expression saying everything he couldn't. "How long have these people been like this?"

Sebastian shrugged. "Never more than a few months, usually. Some, because they don't survive longer than that, and some because she gets bored or wants to try something new."

"Are there others like her?"

"Babe, there's nobody else like me," said a familiar voice, and they both turned. Dr. Greer sat on one of the concrete desks, swinging her legs to and fro. She wore gold high-top sneakers with her lab coat, and Cora was surprised she hadn't noticed them earlier. "But yeah, there are usually a couple more researchers here with their postdoc minions. I'm just staying late because I am soooo excited to sink my teeth into you two. Figuratively." She grinned. "I think."

"What are you doing with them?" Cora asked, looking at the shifters behind Greer.

"Oh, don't worry about them. They don't feel a thing." It wasn't an answer, and she knew it. She rubbed her hands together and pushed off the desk. "Just look at you both, together at last. How long has it been? That's gotta be a trip."

Sebastian's hands found Cora's shoulders as she stepped away from Greer, leaning back into him.

"Already the protective brother! So cute. Okay, come on. I wanna show you something cool." Neither of them moved to follow her down the platform that ran between the pillars and the grid of screens, and she groaned. "You guys need to lighten the fuck up. Come here. I'll give you a damn lollipop afterward if it'll help."

Cora felt Sebastian nudge the small of her back, and she took a tentative step forward, sparing another glance back down that crystalline hallway. The window from before was empty now, but it didn't matter.

She'd seen Nell, and Nell had seen her.

They stayed several paces behind Dr. Greer as she led them around a corner, deeper into the lab. More shelves and machines and screens lined the walls, but this part looked like some kind of grow house, with herbs sprouting from containers, vines drooping from the rafters, and trays of dried leaves and flowers waiting to be put into slides for the massive electron microscope in the center of it all. They must be studying herb use in alchemy here.

Further down they went, passing pairs of armed guards at regular intervals. They edged along a water tank big enough to fit a dolphin, and large tiled rooms with nothing but drains and spigots—maybe they brought hydromancers in there to do Goddess-knew-what. On their right, another warren of crystalline cells housed hollow-eyed witches that watched them pass. "What is this stuff?" she whispered to Sebastian, and he shook his head.

"They mined it and brought it here, a long time ago. I remember when they were still building this wing of the lab. It's some kind of dampener. Doesn't cut you off from the ley lines completely but turns the faucet to a drip."

"Why not just build the whole place out of it, then?"

"The way they talk about it...I don't think there's much of it to go around. They call it stagnicite. The thicker it is, the less magic gets through." He pointed into the cell of a witch who lay curled on a cot, staring blankly at the wall. A shiny white clamp had been molded to the inside of the woman's wrist, embedded in the skin. "You see that fixator, there?"

Cora's chest hurt. She tried not to stare, but it was difficult. The clamp continued around the outside of the witch's arm, forming some kind of gauntlet over rows of tiny amber tubes. "What does it do?"

"It's a Crash pump. Works like an IV, controlled remotely. If any experiments they run in here get out of hand, they can shut it down. But they also set it to drip if anyone has to leave the stagnicite for any period of time. That way they don't have to wait for a full injection to wear off if they want to run tests."

The end of the warren spilled them into a circular room flanked by more guards. Examination tables sat beneath bright, low lights, and several were occupied—sleeping witches in hospital gowns lay hooked up to all manner of machines, with more screens behind them displaying vital signs. This looked like a post-op room, and Cora realized, and her eyes roved over the victims' scarred flesh. On the curved wall behind them, rows of steel thermoses fit neatly into some kind of clear honeycomb, each container clearly labeled.

"You're *harvesting* their organs?" Cora breathed, horror shuddering through her. Was this the fate she'd condemned herself to?

"Don't be dramatic." Greer rolled her eyes. "Nonessential ones, mostly. Who needs two kidneys?" She started counting on her fingers. "An appendix? A gall bladder? Tonsils, adenoids, spleen? And livers grow back. Bone marrow replaces itself. You can have a fairly normal life with one lung—"

Cora couldn't do it. She couldn't endure this woman for a second longer. Greer had worn her threadbare, and she'd been here less than a day. "Let me heal them," she said without thinking.

Greer cocked her head, and too late, Cora realized her mistake.

"Healer?"

It was almost a hiss, low and soft and curious, a sound so at odds with the rest of her behavior that Cora took a step back. She heard Seb curse under his breath, and understanding smacked her between the eyes.

Greer hadn't known what kind of magic she had, because Seb only had interest in honing his terramancy before he was taken. He'd never practiced much healing, so Greer thought Cora was just a terramancer, too.

Greer closed the distance between them in two quick strides, grasping Cora's wrist and twisting it until she cried out in pain. "You will not, under any circumstances, tell the director what you are. You will not tell any of the guards or staff outside of this lab. Do you understand me?"

"I don't...know why...I would," she gasped, and Greer bent to whisper in her ear.

"If the folks upstairs find out, they're going to take you. Do you know the going rate for a healer these days? Do you know what a fucking nightmare it's been for me to keep one here? I keep losing them to Congressmen and foreign oil barons and goddamn pharmaceutical company CEOs." She released Cora and stepped away, adjusting her glasses. "It's bullshit. The work I'm doing here is way more important than some billionaire having a personal fountain of youth at their beck and call."

Cora's brain was still processing the first half of that, and from the look on Seb's face, he'd heard it all. "The *going rate?*"

"The government's not in the business of selling people as a rule, but governments are made up of people, and everyone has a price." Greer folded her arms. "And, babe, magical slavery might seem like an easy way out of here, but I promise you it's only gonna be hell. The only thing folks fear more than witches is death. Once they know," she said, pointing a finger upward, "Everyone else will, too. You think the Kochs of the world will settle for being outbid if it means cheating death for another twenty years? Think again. You will never sleep with both eyes closed as long as they're looking for you."

"And you really wouldn't take that money?" Cora asked, still rubbing her wrist from where Greer had grabbed it.

"All the money in the world won't buy me what I want to know. That's why I'm in a fucking bunker in the middle of the desert. Knowledge," she said, grinning sweetly, "is *my* God. Now, do me a favor and sit up here, will you?" Greer stood between two empty examination tables, patting one with each hand. "We've got work to do."

CHAPTER TWENTY-THREE

Cora slept well past breakfast, which was fine because her appetite would take days to return, anyway. It wasn't just the image of Penny slumped over the table that stuck between behind her eyes; it was those half-formed shifters floating in sleep; Nell fogging up the window as Cora fell to her knees; Greer's grip on her wrist as she told Cora what her life was worth.

You will never sleep with both eyes closed as long as they're looking for you.

For all the screws that Greer had loose, at least Cora knew exactly where they stood. That kind of transparency was worth a lot in a place like this. And even after the horrific things she'd seen in that lab, everything she'd imagined that woman might put her and Seb through, the tests she'd done last night were pretty standard.

Greer had said she needed control readings, something to compare future data to, and so she'd checked their vitals, hooked them up to EEGs and EKGs, done urinalysis and taken blood—enough to make her woozy. The lumbar puncture to draw cerebrospinal fluid had been the worst part by far, but with those thermoses of organs sitting in such neat rows on the wall, she could only be grateful Greer hadn't added any of theirs to the collection.

They'd stayed downstairs well into the night, another reason she was slow to get going this morning. When she finally made her way to the common area, Gloria and Lupita looked relieved to see her up and about.

"We were afraid she'd put you through the ringer," Gloria said, pulling out a chair in the lounge for her to join them in front of the TV. A small group had gathered there to watch *Groundhog Day*. Fitting. "You okay?"

"Physically, yes." Neither of them seemed brave enough to ask her to elaborate. Not with the shadows in her eyes. She didn't sit in the offered chair. "Have you seen Seb around?"

"His floor just left lunch. I think he's in the library. We saved you a sandwich." Gloria handed her ham and cheese wrapped in cellophane, and she took it even though she didn't want it, hoping the gratitude still came through.

"Thank you." She turned it over in her hands, resolving to force herself to eat it later. "I need to find him, but I'll catch up with you in a bit." She felt their eyes on her back as she turned on her heel and left. She wasn't about to waste what little emotional stamina she had left on small talk. Her heart ached too much to pretend.

As she entered the library, she was struck by the *realness* of him again, sitting across the room. She didn't think she'd ever get used to seeing him and not just imagining him. And every observation she made about him— from the way his brows furrowed to his cowlick to his freckled arms—felt like a song she hadn't heard in years, only to find herself murmuring along to the chorus as it played on the radio, not knowing how long those lyrics had been buried in her memory.

The corner he sat in lay furthest from the guards stationed at the door, and beside him was an unfamiliar man whose hair was more pepper than salt. The man's wife, Cora assumed, by the way they gripped each other's hands, had frizzy, deep brown curls that brushed her shoulders and a strong nose that suited her sharp cheekbones well. The three of them looked up as she approached.

"Sorry to interrupt," she began, but the man looked at her with such intensity that she had the feeling they'd been waiting for her.

"You're Cora," he said without preamble, his grip tightening on his wife's fingers.

"I—yes," she said, eyes flickering over to Seb, who dipped his chin slightly.

"Emilio and Sonya Tesauro," Emilio said, turning to Sonya and back again. He stood, and before Cora knew what was happening, he'd crushed her against him in a hug.

He was a lean, willowy man, made even more so by this place, but still with the distinct kind of strength only a dad could have. It was an odd comfort—one she relaxed into, patting his back awkwardly. "You did so much for our Nell," he said, his voice beginning to break. "I know it didn't go the way we'd hoped, but we never thought...we never..." he couldn't finish, pulling away and resting his hands on her shoulders. "Just...thank you for trying."

For trying. Fuck if that didn't sting.

Sonya clasped her hands in front of her, perched on the edge of her armchair. "You went down there last night, didn't you? I heard them say you did."

"Sonya," Emilio said, but she held up a hand.

"Did you see her? Please, tell me that she's okay. We haven't been able to—" Sonya's lips pressed in a quivering line, and Cora finally found words.

"Yes, I saw her. Briefly. She's okay." It wasn't an outright lie, but it felt like one. Nell *had* been able to look out of her cell, and that meant she was alive and mobile. She wasn't suspended in a tank, and she wasn't on one of those tables with her organs in a jar.

Perspective was a hell of a thing.

Sonya made a gasping noise and sat backward in her chair, and Emilio sat back down, patting her hand. "I told you she'd hang in there, baby. She's got your stubbornness, that's for sure."

Seb nodded at the chair next to him, and Cora sat, realizing she'd crushed the sandwich in her hands. She set it aside, patting it back into shape while Emilio and Sonya got a grip on themselves.

Thank you for trying. Thank you for trying. Thank you for trying.

"You both know why Cora's here," Seb said, lowering his voice and leaning in. "I know you have your doubts. You said as much to me yesterday, but don't you think it's important to talk through them?"

Emilio's face had fallen into his hands, and he inhaled deep to exhale long and slow before lifting his eyes to them. "I think this is gonna get us all killed. I don't know what else there is to say."

Cora schooled her features into neutrality. *Treat him like any scared patient, show him you can keep your head on straight.* She lowered her voice even more, barely whispering. "Nell's okay for now, but how long do you really think she'll last down there? You haven't seen what it's like." She pointed at Seb. "He has. I have. It makes this place look like the Four

279

Seasons." She took a page from Anita's book. "I tell you this not to scare you, but to help you understand. You might think you're saving Nell's life by not rising up, but the life she'll have down there isn't a life. And I don't think Greer gives up her toys if she can help it, so the only way you'll get to see your daughter again is if you get her out."

Emilio's hands were trembling, and she leaned forward and took them. "You don't know me from Adam, and that's okay. I'm just the woman who got your daughter locked up and got herself locked up too. But I didn't come here by accident. And I didn't come here alone." She pointed a finger upward. "There's a hunter up there who's been hauled in because he helped me get to this point. A hunter who knows what this place is and what these people can do. He did it anyway, and he'd do it again, because he believes it's possible."

Talking about Theo choked her up a bit, but she needed him to see her as anything but scared. She had to stand on the shoulders of her mother to do it, but she'd do it. "And Robyn? She was a fixture of this community. She cared about all of you, very much, from the stories I hear. And I'm my mother's daughter, Emilio. I won't fail this time."

Hell, after that diatribe, she even believed it.

Tears were rolling down Emilio's face, but he just shook his head. "Those are pretty words, but for those of us who had to wash the blood of children off their hands...who had to line up those bodies in the hallway..." He pulled away from her and fisted his hands in his lap. His wife put a steadying hand on the sleeve of his jumpsuit. "I don't know. I just don't know."

And for all it frustrated her to hear, Cora couldn't blame him.

--------✺--------

Dr. Greer didn't send for her that night, and Cora hoped Seb had been able to dodge her, too. She didn't know which was worse—actually being down there, or waiting around to be needed, knowing her body wasn't her own no matter where she went.

Cora managed to trade her Jell-O cup from dinner for some pieces of paper and a pen. Pip must have sensed it wasn't safe to find her last night, but she had a sneaking feeling he'd be around after lights out. She didn't have anything shiny for him, but he'd understand.

With her comforter pulled over her head, she waited, trying not to fall asleep—and sure enough, after about half an hour, a soft *pop!* jolted her out of her doze.

Pip was a much-needed reminder that a world still existed outside the walls of this place. He had dimmed himself slightly, so the thin comforter tented around them better obscured the light he gave off. It was just enough to write by, and she snuggled him for a good few minutes before letting him fold the little note she'd written into his body. She gave him the pen, too, just in case Theo hadn't been able to find one.

Hi. Saw you get stuck, came to help. Long story, you'll have time to be mad later.
What happened? Holding up okay? - C

She sent him off with a pat on his tiny blob head and missed him immediately. A few minutes passed, then he returned, spitting the note and pen back out. A blurb had been added below hers, in messy, angular scrawl:

I'm going to kill you, you beautiful idiot.

Cora grinned, her stomach fluttering. Goddess, it felt so good to talk to him. Pip picked up on the little ember of happiness blooming within her and seemed to appreciate being the reason for it. "You might just be the best thing that's ever happened to me," she whispered to him, and meant it. She kept reading.

Fletcher knew, helped Ricky remember. Ricky came to gloat, haven't seen him since.
Needs time to build case. Left me here in case coven comes to tie up loose end. Better for us.
Don't forget me when you break out. How is Seb? Any word on the Tesauros?
Pip has been good company. Getting better at the Rubik's cube. - T

Cora grabbed the pen and squinted in the dim light beneath the covers.

I miss you. Lots to tell you. Good to see Seb, but long way to go with him. Nell, Emilio, Sonya all here. Dr. Greer runs research lab, crazy bitch. Even crazier experiments. Ever hear of "stagnicite?"

Worried about getting prisoners on board. Tried before, years ago. Lots died, kids too. Hard to forget. Not much fight left in them. Emilio hardest nut to crack. He's afraid for Nell. - C

Theo's next message took longer.

Stagnicite pretty new when I was getting started. People were excited about it. Hard to find, even harder to mine. Rationed it mostly to supermax.

As for prisoners, give them reason to follow you into battle. They aren't soldiers. Can't fall back on training or strategy. Make them believe again. You don't have all their baggage. Use that. If anyone can, you can. -T

Cora chewed on the end of her pen. Sebastian had said something similar—that their hope had been chipped away for years. It was easy to let that helplessness take root when anything else was beaten out of you. But she wasn't there. Not yet.

She clicked the pen back open and wrote, *I think I have an idea.*

When Cora wasn't working on breaking through the Recantanyl, she was sitting in Dr. Greer's lab with Sebastian.

She'd managed, consistently over the past few days, to fight her way to the ley line within the final hour before her next dose. The drug became more pliable as it wore off, so she'd carved out a small window of opportunity to use her magic if needed. And as badly as she wanted to break Greer's legs right now and leave her writhing on the floor, she was saving it for just the right moment. In case there were no second chances.

Greer had both Cora and Seb hooked up to a brain scanner whose like she'd never seen in any hospital. It reached down from the stagnicite ceiling on a massive metal arm, and they both wore cage-like helmets that wired directly into it. On top of that, a modified fluoroscopy machine fed a video of Seb's left shoulder into a nearby monitor, and a tiny surgical camera was strapped to Cora's forehead.

Seb had a bullet in his shoulder that had healed over, and Greer was forcing her to take it out.

There was a lot he hadn't told her yet, but the story of the bullet was one he finally had. It involved the guard Novak, and how he'd threatened Seb so their mother would go away with him. Each time she came back dappled with bruises, a faraway look in her eyes. As long as Seb was alive, the bastard could get her to do anything. So, he had stopped trying to get under Novak's skin, because he knew she suffered for it.

But once she was dead, it didn't matter if he took a swing at the guy or not. So he had. And Novak gave him that bullet, plus another that had gone clean through, and a month in solitary for it.

Not all his stories were like that. He'd traded ones about their mother for Cora's tales of Mindy, Quinn, and Theo, sprinkled with nursing school anecdotes and the undergraduate debauchery that came before it. He hadn't gone to college. Maybe he still would, he said. Maybe he'd become an artist. Or an engineer. Maybe he'd become a cannabis farmer, since the world had changed enough for that to be a thing.

He was up to speed on whatever came through their local news channel: the city riots, the astronomical price of gas, the latest "alarming new social media trends" which he of course, had no context for, since the last social media platform he'd used was long dead.

He'd read every book in the library. The biographies, the poetry anthologies, the medical encyclopedias, the steampunk romances, the Hardy Boys mysteries, the botany manuals. He told her how Panama disease decimated the Cavendish banana population and recited every Guinness World Record from 1987.

But he never had a complete picture of the world. Never enough to feel like more than an outsider to all of it, an observer on the fringes.

All of these things weighed heavy on Cora as she ran her fingers over the pink scar, no more than a year old. This was another thing that had changed him, irrevocably, pushing him further from the brother she'd known. "Any pain at all, when you move it?"

"Some stiffness when it rains," he said, and Cora snorted, fully aware he hadn't experienced weather in over a decade. Piece by piece, he was coming back to her, but they had such a long way to go. She hadn't had any real time to process that their bond as twins could never be what it was, and she certainly wasn't about to start now. They'd get through this first, unpack all that shit later. But seeing embers of that sense of humor she'd loved so much gave her a scrap of hope to cling to.

Cora's left wrist itched where the Recantanyl pump had been embedded, and she tried her best to ignore it. It wasn't as unwieldy as it looked, but it would take some getting used to. At least Greer wasn't keeping her and Sebastian down here full-time, though how long before the leash was shortened was anyone's guess.

Snoring crackled through Cora's earpiece, and Greer leaned toward her mic outside the stagnicite room. "Not getting any younger here, and James isn't getting any less irradiated by that fluoroscopy machine. If you care."

"This would be easier if you'd just give him a damn anesthetic," Cora grumbled. "I wouldn't be so afraid of hurting him."

"Nah." Greer crunched on a potato chip from the bag in front of her. "Drugs might affect the readings."

Seb locked eyes with Cora. "I can take it," he murmured. "Just get it over with."

Cora couldn't see the easy smile Greer flashed, but she could hear it in her voice. "See? He's fine."

This was fucking barbaric, but she kept repeating what Anita had said, reminding herself there would be other, more important hills to die on. It also didn't escape Cora's notice that Greer could have them doing far worse to one another and chose not to. She couldn't help but feel like the doctor was trying to endear herself to Cora somehow, and Cora wasn't about to take the bait.

Closing her eyes, she reached for the ley line. Her last Recantanyl dose had completely worn off now, so the only thing standing in her way was the stagnicite room. It didn't feel at all like the sticky black mass she'd run into before. No, this was more like a cloudy film, a veil, that she was pressing up against, feeling for an opening she knew was...right...*There.*

She tugged on the thread, unprepared to feel it tug back, a thrashing fish on a line. Pain shot through her brow. Distantly, she could hear beeping on one of Greer's monitors, and then the doctor's voice was in her ear, soothing her. "Slowly, slowly. Don't want to hurt yourself. You'll get used to it, but your body needs a minute to adjust."

She almost ignored the woman out of spite, but her head really *was* hurting, so she loosed her grip on the thread and let it spool into her gradually. It felt like trying to drink out of a pinched straw.

"I'm going to heal over the scar tissue, bit by bit," Cora said to Sebastian. "It'll push the bullet out. Better to do it this way than reopen the scars outright, because I don't know how quickly I'll be able to stop the bleeding with my magic slowed like this. Ready?"

Seb just nodded, closing his eyes and breathing deep, and Cora began.

She was grateful for the fluroscope, because it meant she didn't have to waste magic finding the bullet. But reversing the damage done was a slog like she'd never experienced. She had to beg individual muscle fibers to cooperate, beg the cells to remember where and how they'd once worked together to make a functioning shoulder. The chill in her toes and fingers barely registered as she worked, spearing each thread toward that bullet and reeling it in by millimeters.

Seb, try as he might not to tense, was only making it harder each time he flexed in pain. He was sweating, grinding his teeth together, but determined not to make any noise that might give Greer more satisfaction than they already were. "Don't be a hero," Cora whispered to him. "Every time you flex this damn shoulder, you push me back. If you have to scream, scream."

"Don't fucking tell me...not to be a hero..." he said through his teeth. His bare chest heaved, glistening in the bright lights. "You're shivering...you gotta take it easy..."

"I won't draw this out any longer than I have to," she shot back, even as a wave of drowsiness made her brace against the table Seb lay upon.

"Cor," Seb warned her, but then he couldn't hold it in anymore, and a strangled noise rose out of him.

"Almost done," she lied. "Just hang in there a bit longer." They'd probably been at this for twenty minutes, and the bullet needed twice that to get the rest of the way out. She knew, from her slurring speech and weakening heartbeat, that they wouldn't get there today, and Greer must have been able to see it, too.

"You should watch through the infrared camera, it's *wild*," Greer said. "Your body temp is at ninety-four degrees. This is fucking fascinating. Okay, listen to your brother. Live to die another day."

Cora released the thread and stumbled backward, the movement ripping out half the electrodes attached to her scalp. Seb breathed a heavy sigh of relief and didn't move—couldn't, since he was strapped down to the table. That had been something he'd asked for when Greer had refused an anesthetic.

The stagnicite door to the observation room snicked open, and Greer tossed Cora a mylar blanket before flipping some of the machines on standby. She nudged Cora back into a chair and unstrapped Sebastian, letting him sit up. "How do you feel?"

"Like rainbow farts and sunshine. So kind of you to ask."

Greer rolled her eyes. "I'm asking out of academic curiosity, dipshit, not the goodness of my shriveled heart."

"Ever given birth through a body part not designed for it?" He rolled his shoulder and grimaced.

"I'll add it to my bucket list," Greer said sweetly, and grabbed him by the elbow. "Come with me. I want to get some static X-rays. You," she said, pointing at Cora, "stay. I want your recovery on the thermal cam. And keep that pulse oximeter on." Greer mumbled something to the guard stationed outside the room and disappeared down the corridor.

Cora didn't have it in her to move even if she wanted to. The mylar crinkled as she wrapped it tighter around herself, and she rested her head back against the wall, shutting her eyes against the spinning room.

It could be worse, she reminded herself, wiggling her fingers and toes to ease some of the numbness. As if on cue, that image of Penny flashed behind her closed lids, slumped over the table, and Cora's eyes shot open again.

It could be worse. It could be worse; it could always be worse.

It took less than twenty-four hours.

One moment, Cora was trailing the rest of her block heading upstairs for dinner; the next she'd been dragged backwards by strong hands, one clamped over her mouth, and shoved into an empty classroom off the Pre-Academy wing in the commons.

The concrete floor rose up to meet her, skin scraping off the heels of her hands as they broke her fall. From behind her, the door clicked shut. Gasping, she scrambled to her knees, trying to get air back into her lungs

286

as heavy footfalls neared. She turned to face her attacker, crawling backward across the room.

Beady black eyes stared her down. Novak folded his hairy arms over a ballistic vest, his smile a crooked slash across his face. Scars and tattoos peppered his jaw and his neck. "Hello," he said, and she scooted further away from him as he laughed. An ugly, awful sound.

How many times had her mother endured that laugh? The thought made her sick.

"Haven't had a chance to be properly introduced," he said, stepping forward again. She used a nearby desk as leverage to stand, putting it between them. "You're the spittin' image of him, aren't you?"

"If you mean James, that tends to happen with siblings," she said, rustling up courage from a bright, raw new place inside her. "What the hell do you want?"

Novak took another step forward, and she put another desk between them, moving further into the row. "Secrets have a way of getting out in a place this small."

Panic fluttered inside her. She stared back—waiting for him to elaborate, fighting to keep her face neutral.

He gestured to the Recantanyl pump on her wrist, inert as it was right now. The only person who could trigger it was Greer. "Someone's been playing doctor downstairs."

Her panic iced over into cold dread. It was barely a relief that her other secrets were safe. Greer had acted like she trusted those lab guards not to talk, and clearly someone had. She wouldn't be happy when she found out.

Though by that time, Cora might be halfway to the basement of some media oligarch's summer home.

She couldn't let them take her away. Who else might he have told, if anyone? Maybe he was just confirming it first, looking for the truth of it in her eyes. He didn't seem like the type keen on sharing the finder's fee if he could help it. "I just do what Dr. Greer asks."

That smile widened. "For someone so goddamn smart, she has no business sense. I bet she told you all about where healers go, didn't she? Tried to scare you, talk you out of it?"

Cora swallowed. "She mentioned they're...in demand."

"You'd be freer than here," Novak said with a shrug. "Get to see daylight. Get to hear the rain. Eat better than this, probably."

"Tempting." Why was he wasting time trying to convince her? He could just haul her away, and that would be that.

"I wonder...can your brother do it, too?"

That got the reaction he'd wanted. "Don't you fucking touch him," she all but growled.

"Bet I could more than double for the pair of you. Wouldn't you like that? To stay together?"

"Don't pretend to give a shit what I think."

Novak leaned against the whiteboard behind him, assessing. "Easier for me if you go willingly. Fetch a better price for someone who knows how to show a little gratitude. Lotta people can kid themselves into thinking they're doing you a favor by getting you out of this place. Don't think for a second, though, that I won't find a buyer if you put up a fight." That sly grin reappeared. "And the folks willing to own the ones who fight? Well...it's your call, sweetie."

Goddess, how many witches had he trafficked this way? Where were they all now?

Would Greer know?

No. No. That was a fucking den of snakes, indebting herself to Greer. The doctor was not her friend, no matter how hard she tried to convince Cora otherwise. *Don't borrow trouble. Focus on the problem staring you in the damn face.*

Staring back, Cora made a decision. She'd been prepared to have to make it, but entertaining the thought of killing a man, actually doing it, and living with having done it were all very different things. It helped that she didn't have a choice, because letting Novak walk out of this room meant she and Seb would certainly wake up tomorrow in the back of a strange van. Not a snag she'd made a contingency plan for.

Cora rallied the threads of magic she'd been able to drag out from under the Recantanyl in the past hour. "There's just one teensy problem," she said, stepping towards him now instead of away, savoring the flash of uncertainty behind his eyes as she did so. Her magic threaded through him, searching, searching.

ACL tear, no.

Old stab wound, maybe.

Bad cirrhosis, not quick enough.

Well, well, well. Was that stenting from an *aneurysm?*

She looked closer. Yep, it seemed like Mitchell Novak had endovascular surgery at some point, been lucky enough to cheat death once. "The problem," she continued, heartbeat roaring in her ears, "is that I'm exactly where I need to be, and there's only one way I'm leaving this place."

She inhaled deep, steeling herself, and tore the aneurysm back open.

Novak cursed and slid down the wall, clutching his head in one hand and grasping at the nearest table with another. She watched his eyes widen at the resurfacing memory of the last time he'd felt that pain, and he opened his mouth to speak, to ask her something. No words came, just an aimless sound.

The hemorrhagic stroke she knew he was having would affect his speech, his motor functions. She watched him struggle to sit upright, waiting for the seizure that was bound to come.

Then: *Oh, Goddess.* She couldn't. She couldn't sit here and watch him die, no matter what he'd done.

Could she?

She had to.

She was losing precious seconds. If she wanted to intervene, she couldn't waste any time.

What would he do if she saved him? Was it enough just to threaten—

BANG.

The door burst open, and Greer stormed through it, white coat billowing, then pulling up short when she realized Novak was on the floor. Her eyes darted from his seizing body to Cora's look of horror, and back again. And then a squawk, a sharp laugh, found its way out of her mouth.

Too stunned to move, Cora could only watch as Greer crossed the room in three long strides and stood above him. "If you save him," Greer murmured icily, "I'll make sure you regret it. Not to mention whatever he'll do."

"Greer—"

For good measure, Greer stepped forward and leaned on his windpipe with a gold high-top sneaker. It almost didn't matter, because he was mostly gone anyway, but Cora winced at the crunch and nearly looked away.

"What, you have standards for how you murder? Convince yourself he was living on borrowed time anyway, is that how you justify it?" Greer cocked her head to one side. The rims of her glasses brushed the underside of her bangs, hiding her eyebrows completely and making her expression even harder to read. She knew, then. She knew how the reversal worked.

Cora shook with anger, even though it was mostly directed at herself. "He was going to sell my brother. Sell *me*."

Her fingers wound around angry, stubborn resolve. The promises she'd made. And it made the weight of what Novak had done to her mother, to Penny, to Seb, and so many others—including the ones he'd sold—bear down just a little bit less, ease up just enough to let her finally get a full breath in.

Satisfied that he was dead, Greer finally stepped off of Novak's throat. "I know."

"That's why you came up here?"

"Somebody talked. I bet it was Harlow, that piece of shit. I knew he was acting shady." Greer shook her head, then twisted a short lock of her blonde hair as she started pacing. "It's always the new guys. Fuck me, I'm so fucking *sick* of this." Greer whirled and kicked a desk, sending it crashing onto its side.

Into the tentative silence that followed, Cora said, "You...think they'll try again?" This was an odd sort of limbo to be in with Greer, having a mutual enemy.

The doctor slid into another desk, resting her chin in her hands and shrugging at Novak's body. "I don't know. Novak was always the guy. Harlow's just a set of eyes and ears, but it's too lucrative for someone else not to take his place." Her eyes snapped up to Cora's. "You're coming downstairs where I can keep an eye on you. James, too."

"You can just...do that? Even if I've...?" *Killed a guard,* she didn't say, but didn't need to.

Greer turned and flashed her a wide smile. "Babe, I can do whatever I want. This is a research facility, first and foremost. Other prisons do other shit. You think they let high-risk inmates use magic, even in a controlled setting? Fuck no." She leaned in. "There may be a woman in the ivory tower upstairs who calls herself Director, but below deck, my colleagues and I run the show."

Clearly there was some animosity there if the director had turned a blind eye to Novak. Cora didn't want to get in the middle of it. "I'll pass." But her stomach clenched. She still had so much to do up here. How could she organize an uprising from down in the damn labs? How could she convince everyone it was worth the fight?

"Good thing you don't have a choice," the doctor said cheerfully, grabbing Cora's elbow and yanking her to her feet. "Up you go."

Shit, shit, *shit.*

"Ease up, good god," Cora said as Greer dragged her from the room and back into the hallway. "Anyone ever tell you your bedside manner could use some serious work?"

"All the time," Greer said casually. "There's a reason I work in research, babe. Data doesn't cry. Or sue." She grimaced. "Or have family to placate."

As Greer steered them down the hall, Cora spied a group of seven women in gray jumpsuits stalking toward the door, led by Gloria and Lupita. They pulled up short when they saw Greer, and Cora's heart stuttered.

They'd been coming for her. They hadn't left her. They'd gone for backup, and they were about to rush Novak, to hell with the consequences.

Penny's death might not have been something they could prevent, and fear might've kept them silent while Novak abused her mother, but that shame was coming home to roost. They weren't about to let Robyn's daughter suffer the same way she had, even knowing it might be the last thing they ever did.

Pride. That was the feeling swelling in her chest, she realized. Something in them had snapped. Something important, something they'd need if they were going to survive the fight out of here.

And if Cora had won over seven, she could win over more.

She dipped her chin at them, and a few craned to look past her as the classroom door shut, wondering where Novak was. Greer yanked at Cora's elbow again, walking them up to the pair of guards stationed outside the TV room, ones she'd briefly made eye contact with as Novak dragged her away. "Excuse me," Greer said, loud enough that everyone in the atrium of the commons turned. Ambient chatter stopped.

The guards frowned down at them, only just now realizing three people had gone into that room and two had come out. "What?" the one on the left barked, and then added as an afterthought when Greer glared daggers at him, "Ma'am."

"I think Mr. Novak needs medical attention," she said sweetly, feigning concern as best she could. "He just...collapsed."

They shared a look and rushed into the classroom. Cora, Greer, and the seven women watched them go. Cora dared a quick glance at the group, one Greer wouldn't see, and nodded almost imperceptibly.

Nobody spoke. Nobody needed to. They all understood.

As she and Greer closed the rest of the distance to the elevator, Cora made eye contact with every prisoner she passed. She made sure each person saw the defiance coiled there, so there'd be no question about what she'd done. About what she was willing to risk.

Even if it made her sick to think about Novak sliding slowly down that wall, slumping forward, forming wordless shapes with his mouth.

She prayed that maybe now, they'd take her plan seriously. Cora needed that certainty. All she had was the descending elevator, taking her further and further from the people she needed to organize, to rally. She had allies up there to speak for her, but would they be enough?

Get a grip. This is what's happening now. Triage it.

The floor jolted as they stopped. Greer swiped her badge at the vestibule entrance. Maybe she could check in on Nell. Maybe she could...

"Dr. Greer," she said suddenly as the doors to the lab whispered closed behind them, hoping she wouldn't live to regret asking it, "What if I helped you?"

Greer stopped in her tracks, letting go of Cora's elbow now that they stood in the atrium. It was teeming with people at this time of day, all in white coats carrying clipboards, peering at screens, writing in notebooks. The din of murmurs and beeping, whirring machines was enough to mask Greer's lowered voice. "Helped me how, exactly?"

Cora took a deep breath, feeling very much like a mouse trying to bargain with a cat. "By your own admission, you hate direct patient care. That would be fine in the botany lab, but you research arcane physiology. Tough to avoid, no?"

Greer's brows might have been raised, but beneath those bangs, it was hard to tell. "I'm listening."

"I'm willing to bet some of your test subjects aren't doing so well. You might not care right now, but it throws a wrench in things when they die on you, doesn't it?"

"It *is* annoying," Greer conceded. "Stop dancing and make your point."

"Let me heal them," Cora said softly, "like I asked that first night I was down here. Let me do all the bedside manner bullshit you hate. Give them better quality of life, and you'll get more accurate data. Don't you want to see what they can really do? That fucking stagnicite makes it hard enough, without everything else getting in the way."

Greer's eyes narrowed, but she was thoughtful. "I'd need to reprogram your Recantanyl pump to a steady drip anyway." Right now, Cora's was just a failsafe since she'd been having regular injections upstairs. "What's in it for you?"

"These people need help," she said, and it was certainly true, if only half of the truth. She'd realized that evacuating the lab when the time came would be a big fucking problem. How many of them would be able to walk on their own, let alone fight their way to safety if they needed to? She needed them to be independently mobile, at the very least. Otherwise, if they took too long, reinforcements might arrive before they could all get out. "If I can do anything, even something small, to make life down here more bearable, why wouldn't I try?"

Greer leaned back against the nearest table and tapped her long nails against it, chewing the inside of her cheek. She snapped her fingers decisively, "Yeah, okay."

Cora blinked, confident she'd misheard. "What?"

"I said *okay. Do it*. I'm tired of waiting for people to recover from procedures, anyway. And it'll give me more opportunities to watch you work." She jabbed a finger at Cora. "Don't think this gets you out of working with James. I don't want your own recovery time to interfere."

"You're serious? Really?"

"What did I say? I joke, but I never kid. Now close your mouth before something flies into it. I don't know whether to be insulted or proud that you think so little of me." Greer did her best to sound wounded but didn't quite hit the mark.

Cora snorted. "I think you like that I'm just as transparent as you are, so let's not bullshit each other. We both know you don't care either way."

Greer was quiet for a long moment, studying the challenge on Cora's face, then bared her teeth in a grin that could only be described as feral. "I do like you, Somerville. And I'll be really, really bummed if I have to kill you one day."

Cora swallowed hard as she followed Greer deeper into the labs, knowing she meant every single word.

CHAPTER TWENTY-FOUR

Theo had felt it, earlier. It was a quick jolt, an angry flash of magic somewhere below, and then gone just as quickly.

Pip had felt it too, darting underneath the cot in surprise. In an instant, Theo was on his feet, forgetting he could only go as far as the door of the cell. Through its steel-framed window, all was quiet. He waited, strained to hear if anything might be happening down the hall.

It was her. It had to be.

Five minutes, the longest of his life, passed. Then somewhere nearby, a voice crackled through a guard's radio. Theo only caught "officer down."

Several minutes later, the guard on him hadn't moved. But to his left, a door slammed, and a raised voice echoed.

"I don't care what you *think* happened," a man said. "I don't pay you to think. I pay you to do your fucking job." A pause, garbled speech from another radio. Theo couldn't hear what was said, probably because the guard closest him was on a different channel. "What did I just say? You saw her walk out of there. Detain her ass until we know for sure!" Another pause, crackle. "What do you mean? Greer already took her down?" Static, crackle, garble. "My office, ten minutes. And bring some fucking coffee."

Theo stepped away from his door as a uniformed man stormed past, holding himself with the posture of a Captain. Behind him, more doors opened and closed, hushed voices murmuring, but nothing else clear enough for Theo to hear.

For fuck's sake, what had she done?

He loathed this feeling, the utter uselessness of being stuck in there. Waiting for something, anything to happen, and then not knowing what was going on when something finally did.

She'd taken his advice to heart, at least. Further than that if she'd killed a damn guard. He knew what it took to earn the kind of trust that sent you into the fray after someone—the kind of person you had to be to make people follow. Cora didn't have a soldier's instinct, or even a leader's, but she had a good head on her shoulders and a reason to fight. That much was obvious.

What wasn't as visible was just how much courage she had, all those months she'd spent hiding and ferrying refugees...not to mention the courage it took to stay sober, to make that choice day after day after day. He ran his fingers over her NA coin in his pocket, the weight of his respect for it grounding him.

She'd had to make them see it somehow. He just hoped that gamble paid off.

He was surprised he hadn't worn a path in the floor by the time they came to pick up his empty dinner tray. From just out of sight of the window, Pip watched him pace, unsure how to help. Eventually he transformed into a stress ball with the name and number of Mindy's dentist. *Dr. Luna Gives You More To Smile About!*

Theo begrudgingly lay back on the cot, bouncing Pip against the wall. He wanted to send the sprite to Cora but didn't know how closely she was being watched. Pip had taken point there, anyway, seeming to know when she'd be in a position to respond—there had been some nights where he'd flat-out refused to go, and Theo had learned not to press him.

Something tickled Theo's ear, and he froze. It was both cold and warm, liquid and cloud. He squeezed the ball in his hand, confirming Pip was still there, and quickly sat up.

At the head of his cot perched another sprite.

Pip took shape again, dripping through Theo's fingers to flow over to it. The second sprite was slightly smaller, the swirling glow within them leaning more towards deep twilight blues and purples than Pip's bright rainbow. They leaned toward one another, communicating in some shared language, and then the second sprite vomited out a pile of coins, buttons and broken, old brooches. On top of the pile lay a three-inch notepad and a pen no longer than his thumb. Pip's eyes grew wide.

Hi Teddy, dear.

Mindy's handwriting was tiny, elegant, and round, filling the first few pages.

Hope you're well, considering. This is Nyx. Brought Pip some goodies because I assume he's working overtime for next to nothing. We're all here at CV. Altas too. That took some doing, but you know how persuasive I can be. Please let me know how you and Seb and Cora are. Any news on the drug? xoxo Min

P.S. When you send Nyx back, let her take some buttons. I have plenty more, but she seemed very perturbed when I suggested they were all for Pip.

Nyx had made herself at home, swirling and bouncing in and out of the pockets of Theo's gray jumpsuit, and Pip chased her, trying to pull her out of view from the small window. They fled under the cot, and Theo had the distinct impression she was being scolded. She'd learn, as Pip had.

Theo smiled to himself, clicking the pen open and beginning his reply.

They'd come down to the labs to argue about throwing Cora into solitary, but she considered it a win. If the guards thought she was a threat, it only added fuel to the fire she'd lit under everyone else. At least here, Greer treated her well enough. Cora didn't delude herself into thinking it was anything other than pampering the golden goose.

She quickly found she could still chat with Theo through Pip, and hangman became a favorite game of theirs.

He'd told her about Mindy and Nyx, too, but didn't want to send Nyx anywhere but back to Mindy just yet. The other sprite didn't have the self-awareness Pip had developed, or his more nuanced understanding of the dangers they faced in here. Giving her any reason to explore before she was ready might be a recipe for disaster.

Pip now ferried messages to Gloria, too, which was how Cora learned about the new voices popping up in defense of her. It wasn't just Gloria and Lupita rallying more support from the other women's' blocks. Robyn and Penny hadn't been Novak's only victims—there had been wives, too, of men on the other floors, and daughters. Those men were beginning to win over some of the staunchest holdouts. Emilio among them.

Perhaps the biggest change, Gloria observed, was the guards' behavior. Novak had perpetuated a culture of corruption, reveled in his power, savoring the fear he saw in the eyes of everyone he passed. Eliminating that had left the guards on their back foot, looking around, waiting to see if that was still an accepted norm. Someone would step into that vacuum soon enough, but for now, their uncertainty evened the odds.

Little by little, Cora got used to the stagnicite, and her healing became more efficient. It was a good thing, too, because the inmates down there were in rough shape.

Greer let her share a cell with Sebastian, at least, citing the logic that it might deter anyone from coming to take them in the night. And during the day, she let Cora visit the others, roaming freely within reason. It became apparent Cora's magic alone wouldn't be enough to get them all in fighting shape, so she argued with Greer until the doctor let her put together a little cart and stock it with the basics. Saving magic on diagnostics sped things up a bit.

She started on those sleeping witches she'd first seen, the ones whose organs had been taken. Technically, Greer had been right when she'd said they could survive without them all, but some would pose more of a problem than others. The lungs and the livers she regrew first—the livers just needed a little push to get themselves going while she worked on the missing lung. The kidneys came next. She wanted to keep at it, but she didn't know how many more days she had before the fake drug circulated. She'd come back if there was time.

She didn't tell Greer, either, that she could regrow tissue if there was enough left to start with. Let her think they couldn't afford to lose another lung, at least until someone opened them up again.

Cora had finally gotten the bullet out of Seb, too, so the doctor had plenty of data to sit with in the meantime. The more there was for her to pore over, the less attention she paid to what Cora was doing. She'd still follow her around from time to time, taking videos and making her wear the ridiculous EEG helmet, and those days made Cora want to rip her hair out.

The inmates didn't quite know what to make of her. Most were willing to talk to her, to hear about what they'd planned, but a wary few weren't about to trust someone Greer had given privileges to. Cora couldn't blame them.

The one that hurt the most, though, was Nell.

Today was the third time she'd visited her, but the first time they'd been alone together. Greer had tagged along twice before, which was more than anyone else Cora had seen. Nell hadn't said a word, and Cora was hoping she might be more forthcoming when the doctor wasn't there.

"How's the hand?" Cora asked, turning over the girl's palm to examine her shattered fingers. Nell had punched the stagnicite wall in a fit of rage, and the lab technician got a nasty static shock when he tried to bandage it. At least she was letting Cora touch her.

Nell shrugged, staring off into the middle distance.

"Your parents and Ezra are asking about you. You want to tell them anything?"

Eye contact, finally. Nell's were hazel that leaned more amber than green. "Why do you keep coming back? I don't want to talk to you."

Cora lowered her voice to nearly a whisper. "Because I'm going to help get you out."

"Right, 'cause you were so good at that last time."

Cora didn't let her see how much that stung. Nell wasn't wrong. "This time it's different."

"Why the hell should I believe that?"

Cora rose from her crouch and sat next to Nell on the cot. "Because we have lots of help."

Nell scoffed. "Yeah, Ezra said that. But Poppy left me at that damn apartment. *Everyone* left me there."

Cora blinked back tears. She wouldn't understand, and they couldn't ask her to. "We have someone different. New." The whole time they'd been speaking, Cora had been threading magic through Nell's fingers, encouraging the bone back into place, slow and steady. Nell winced, and Cora said, "You want to meet her?"

She didn't wait for an answer. She just looked around, angling her back to the window. "Hold out your other hand. Your good one." Then Cora fished in her pocket for a silver hair clip she'd found on the floor and placed it in Nell's open palm.

"What are you doing?"

"Just wait. Don't react. We can't let anyone walking past here see." Then Cora whispered, "Nyx?"

Nothing happened. Nell raised her eyebrows, and Cora tried again, reaching out with a thread of magic. "Nyx, come here. We found something you'll like."

To Nell's credit, she didn't jump or scream when the sprite appeared in Cora's lap. Her eyes shot wide open, though, and stayed that way. "What the hell is *that*?"

"She," Cora said, "is a sprite. You've heard of them."

"I've...never seen one," Nell said softly, watching Cora stroke Nyx's head. Nyx leaned into the touch, solidifying and pooling slightly, the nebula of starry blues and purples swirling within her. "She's...wow."

"Look," Cora said, and they both watched Nyx flow over to Nell's open hand, reaching out to pick up the hair clip. Nyx turned it over, looked at it sideways, and then pushed it into her body.

Nell squeaked. "That's gross. Where does it even go"

Cora's toes were beginning to numb, but she kept working on Nell's fingers. "No clue. Pocket universe, maybe? She can turn into things, too."

"Like what?"

"My friend Pip—another sprite—turned into a piano once. But usually small things that go unnoticed."

"So...how is she going to help us? Turn into a gun or something?"

Cora snorted, fighting to concentrate on mending bone while imagining Nyx as a combat shotgun. "Not quite. That would be a dangerous thing for her to get wrong, anyway. She's been—"

Out of nowhere, Pip burst into being and slammed into Nyx. This time, Nell and Cora both jumped. He bounced around them, waving his tiny blobby arms, and pulled a hastily scribbled note out of his stomach. Cora unfolded it.

PHASE 1 GO. LOVE, GLORIA

Cora's breath froze in her lungs, but she choked out, "Like that. She's been doing that."

Nell frowned, peering at the note. "Who's this from? What does that mean?"

"It means...we're leaving." Cora swallowed hard, the letters of the note going blurry. "Nell, we're getting out of here. Tonight."

"Wait, what? Like, right now?"

"Right fucking now."

CHAPTER TWENTY-FIVE

The desert sunset slipped into night, and the lanterns of Crescent Vale roared to life.

The camp had sprung up slowly at first, then all at once. Coven volunteers from had been stockpiling medical supplies and water and warm clothing. Ezra had taken the reins there. He might not have magic, but he was determined to be useful, and he had the ability to source large enough quantities of it.

Mindy, meanwhile, was playing operator. She'd spent days coaxing sprites out from the rocks, longer still trying to teach the one that stuck around how to pass notes back and forth. Mindy had named her Nyx for the vivid nebula that bloomed inside of her, and now her tent was full of stacks of paper and extra pens and tiny notes torn from notebooks, all strung up on cork boards in order. Pip and Nyx had been bouncing back and forth, delivering hand-drawn maps and detailed accounts of the type of security Theo and Cora had seen, and the altas had used it as a war room of sorts, piecing together their understanding of The Beach note by note.

Ninety minutes after Pip brought word that the fake drug was in play, the ten-witch strike team assembled by a fire pit, taking stock. Shrouded in black, all wearing ballistic vests, three in particular stood out: Viv, with her waterfall of bright red hair, Harry, who'd dialed down the glitter but still wore black rhinestones fanning from the corners of his eyes, and Quinn, whose irises were already the bright yellow of her owl form.

Among them were an electromancer named JC, who carried himself with ex-military swagger, and Cait, a terramancer, who had a stocky gymnast's build and a tawny pixie cut. They both looked more than capable of handling themselves in a fight, a relief because Ghislaine and Maria, while powerful, looked like they'd fall over in a gust of wind.

Dustin, Helena, and Mindy completed the group. A small one, but they'd be quick, powerful, and efficient. Get in, draw out the guards, provide safe passage to Crescent Vale, and get out.

Harry, who had several potions clipped to his utility belt like grenades, bent and unzipped the duffel bag at his feet. He pulled out a quart-sized jar and sloshed a muddy potion inside it. "This should do the trick, but you must drink the whole thing. No good if you vomit."

Dustin raised an eyebrow. "*Should* do?"

Harry's eyes flashed. "I haven't had long to test it. This is the best I have. It will not totally kill the Crash, but it slows it down, keeps it from sticking. So let us hope adrenaline keeps you going if you are hit." He passed more jars around and lifted his own. "All right, ladies and gents. *Prost*!"

They drank, most stopping to retch halfway through. "Don't let it come back up!" Harry pleaded. "I don't have extra!"

"This tastes like fucking swamp water," Viv choked out. "If you're such a goddamn prodigy, why can't you make it drinkable?"

Harry flashed his teeth. "I had other priorities, sugar. You know, like making it work."

Viv chased her potion with a swig of whiskey from her hip flask, despite Harry's protests that he didn't know how they'd interact. After a moment's hesitation, Quinn pinched her nose and chugged in solidarity.

Ghislaine, Helena, and Maria sat next to two heavy, watermelon-sized lumps of crystal, together muttering a long, complicated incantation to make them glow from within. The glow brightened, and a tether formed between the two stones before winking out in an unnatural gust of wind. "These crystals are linked for the next three hours." Ghislaine turned to the group. "One will live just outside the base, and the other stays here. Feed it a small amount of energy, and it will send you to camp."

"If you don't get lost between," Quinn murmured to Harry, eying the crystals warily.

"These will hold," Ghislaine said with steely finality, and Quinn's mouth snapped shut.

They piled into two cars, one carrying the second leapstone and a very nervous Pip and took off through the dark slice of desert. Dustin hid their caravan in shadows, but the moon was bright as they pulled up about a half mile from the base.

From there, Quinn shifted soundlessly, a flap of wings the only indication that she had taken to the skies to keep watch. Mindy kissed Pip on the forehead and sent him back beneath to spread the word that Phase 3 was starting. Viv and Dustin moved through the darkness toward one of the three sentry towers, Helena close behind them, as Dustin's illusion shielded JC from sight so he could skirt around the fence closer to the compound.

They waited in tense silence until Helena pressed her voice into everyone's minds. *JC has overloaded the security feed.*

One sniper dropped from sight, out cold, then the other. Four more in two other towers quickly followed as Helena's magic demanded they give in to the heavy weight on their eyelids, collapsing into sleep. *Snipers out. Lights going in three...two...*

The massive flood lights shorted, bulbs shattering and blinking out. By the time the guards patrolling the tarmac realized what was happening, the entire base had been plunged into moonlit dark.

Viv beamed. "Let's kick the anthill." She and Dustin focused on the comms tower a ways behind the hangar, and for a long moment, nothing happened.

Then flames erupted into the night and sent debris careening through the air like small shrapnel rockets. The steel tower groaned and swayed, slowly twisting until it collapsed upon itself, its death rattle sending up a plume of dust and smoke. The ground shook with the force of it, and Cait used that momentum to crater the earth across the airstrip, shoving rocks up through the smooth tarmac to break the long, clean lines and crack through the helipads. If reinforcements did come, landing in itself would be a hurdle.

As more guards poured up from the barracks, only the orange glow of flames against the night sky lit the way toward whatever carnage awaited them.

It took all of Cora's self-control not to shake as she left Nell's room, avoiding the eyes of her armed escort. Having the cart to push was a blessing, and she was glad she had a long list of people to see today. As they walked, she discreetly tapped the stagnicite windows of the cells she passed.

Everyone she'd spoken to knew what that meant. Stand by.

Phase 1 meant Gloria was sending word to the other floors and ordering them to hold their magic. They'd need a little time for the doses to lapse, and two hours was a safe enough bet. It would also give the strike team enough wiggle room to prepare and make the short trek over from Crescent Vale.

Meanwhile, Nyx had located and stolen the electronic key that would unlock the Recantanyl pumps on the inmates' wrists. Because several doses were stored in the gauntlet, they couldn't rely on them not to work. So as Cora moved from room to room, she pried open the ones she could, making sure to leave them mostly on so the guards wouldn't notice anything was amiss until it was too late. She'd get whoever else she could later.

The minutes dragged, the anxiety humming through her starkly at odds with the unhurried, studious discipline of the researchers. Greer pored over a stack of papers on her desk, then flicked her eyes back to her computer, completely absorbed in whatever it had to say. They all seemed none the wiser.

Cora's last stop was a telekinetic named Archie in the cell next to hers, a graying ex-Marine who'd refused to join ACE when he was outed. As the guard beside her flipped his list over and ran down the names on it, she took the opportunity to tap her nails on Seb's door, alerting him in case Pip hadn't been able to. "He's not on here today."

"I know," she said, doing her best to sound apologetic. "I forgot to ask Greer to add him, but I'll be super quick. He's got a..." she lowered her voice, "manly problem I need to check on."

The guard gave a sympathetic grunt and swiped her in, deciding he'd rather not learn more.

Archie was dozing but shot upward the instant she pushed her cart in. By the time the door had closed, the look on her face told him everything he needed to know. "How long?"

"Ten minutes, give or take. You ready?"

Here was a man who'd worked out every day he was down here, and it showed in the way his chest and arms strained against the fabric of his jumpsuit. He grinned, but nothing about it was happy. "Ready since the day they dragged my ass in here."

She knelt between him and the window, unlocking his gauntlet and handing him a strip of gauze. "Tie this around your wrist when you pull the needle out. Have that list I gave you?"

Archie patted his chest pocket, where she'd written down the names and room numbers of everyone down here whose magic was best suited for an offensive push to incapacitate the guards. There were about forty cells to clear, and she sure as hell wouldn't be able to do it alone.

He saluted her as she left, pretending her cart was stuck on something and wedging it in the door. "Oh crap, I'm so sorry," she said to the guard. "Just give me a second." She knelt, stalling, and stuffed a wadded-up scrap of gauze in the door frame before shutting it behind her. It didn't click. She exhaled, giving the guard an embarrassed grin. "This thing is so hard to steer."

The guard opened his mouth to say something, but the lights overhead flickered briefly. Then the whole lab powered down for a long, breathless moment before the emergency generators whirred on.

Everything stopped.

Cora's eyes met the guard's, and she screamed, "*GO, ARCHIE!*" before shoving her cart into him with all the strength she could muster.

The guard careened backwards as the cart crashed and tipped, pinning him beneath it. She crouched, yanking his key card from its holder, and behind her, Archie burst through the door she'd propped open. The scrape and clang of twisting metal echoed down the hallway as he wrenched cell doors from their hinges, one by one, and sent them flying into guards who'd barely had a moment to realize what was happening, let alone aim their weapons.

Witches emerged from those open cells, most of them haphazardly bandaged from where they'd ripped the gauntlets from their arms. All hell broke loose behind Cora as she swiped the key card on Seb's cell door and threw it wide open.

They locked eyes for a brief, terrifying moment—a promise—and then dashed in different directions.

———⟳———

Even if Pip hadn't warned him, Theo would have known when the whole compound shuddered, plaster trickling down from the ceiling to collect on the shoulder of his jumpsuit. The radio of the nearest guard crackled to life, someone topside screaming for backup, and he joined a group of guards jogging toward the stairwell.

Pip reappeared in the window-slot, holding up the guard's key card victoriously, and swiped it to let Theo out.

Theo *moved*. He grabbed the key from Pip, running from door to door, opening every occupied cell he found. "Your magic is free. Don't ask me how, long story. When it's safe, go up, and find the purple leapstone on the north side of the fence."

"Who are you?" a tan, sixty-something man with thick silver hair asked. He blinked into the bright emergency lights, trying to make sense of the barrage of information and eventually landing on the question physically standing in front of him.

"A friend," Theo said, and at the sound of boots on the concrete, motioned to the small group to stay back. He waited by the mouth of the hallway, listening to the footfalls close in, and watching the reflections of the guards in the dark office window across the way.

The silver-haired man stepped into his periphery, and Theo wasn't about to turn down help. "What kind of magic do you have?"

"Conjuring."

Think, think, think. "Can you give me their weapons?"

"I can't always choose where they come from, but I can try."

"Go for it."

The guards were almost on them. The man stared intently at their approach in the window reflection, and magic rose around Theo, tentative at first, like he was feeling it out, then—

Theo staggered backwards, nearly dropping the combat shotgun that appeared in his arms. He heard a curse from around the corner, and the footsteps paused.

Theo adjusted his grip, stepped out of the hallway, and fired once, twice.

Both guards went sprawling as red exploded behind them. It didn't matter that they were wearing ballistic vests, because Theo hadn't been aiming that low, anyway.

"Christ," one intake technician breathed, dropping the folders in their arms and scrambling back into the room they'd just stepped out of. Two more office drones about thirty feet away did the same, screaming and locking the doors nearest them.

There weren't any other guards on this floor—they'd been more worried about the assault above, which tracked with the plan so far. Theo rifled through the dead guards' things and strapped on the chest rig, which was only a little bloody. He found a sidearm, a knife, and extra ammo for the shotgun, then looked up at the silver-haired conjurer, whose face had lost some color. "You ever fire a gun?"

The conjurer shook his head. "I'll take a knife, though," and he did.

They led the group to the stairwell that spiraled up, and Theo used his key card to open the heavy steel door he knew separated the lower floors from the upper offices and barracks. Voices shouted below them. Shots echoed, and boots thundered up. He propped it open by wedging the tip of a knife holster in its hinges. "I suggest you all make a run for it, right fucking now."

Theo didn't have to tell them twice. The group flowed upward, led by the conjurer and an illusionist who'd seemingly found the nerve to blanket them in the suggestion of an empty staircase.

He didn't follow them. Instead, he headed down.

———————

The growl of an animal made Cora swivel. A massive wolf—who *was* that?—licked at Cora's sleeve and nudged past her, leaping on the next guard to fight his way through the lab's main thoroughfare. A spray of blood fanned along the wall, and someone screamed, lighting a fire under Cora's ass to move.

Most of the guards down there were dead or incapacitated, and the lab techs, once they'd realized the remote-triggered gauntlets were gone, had barricaded themselves in offices or cowered behind machines. A few hadn't been lucky enough to make it even that far. Archie and a witch whose name Cora didn't know held sidearms to the heads of two senior techs, watching them drain the pillars that held the shifters in stasis and bring them slowly out of wherever their minds had been.

Greer had been knocked unconscious, clipped by a flying cell door, but Cora still hated leaving her at her back as she ran down the long corridor toward the room that held the forced organ donors. Seb and Nell followed, along with Gloria, who'd run downstairs to help as soon as she was able.

Oh. *Lupita* had been with her. That was the wolf Cora had seen.

She fumbled with the various tubes and cords sticking out of each sleeping witch, barking instructions for the others and showing them how to extubate the ones who needed it, removing IVs and using her magic to awaken them as gently as they had time for. They were confused and scared, and Cora couldn't begin to tell them what all those scars on their bodies meant, but they understood the basic need to *move*, and move now.

They wobbled on atrophied legs, and Seb carried the weakest one piggyback, a young woman who couldn't have been any older than Cora. Nell was quite tall, and so she and Gloria took another young witch between them, lifting from beneath her armpits on either side. Cora grabbed the middle-aged man who was in better shape than the rest, the one who still had his spleen and gall bladder intact, letting him lean into her as he got the hang of walking again. It was slow going. Too slow, Cora thought, but bit back the urge to tell them that.

Back in the atrium, the pillars had drained, and the only people up and about were the ones escorting the hurt or leveling guns—or in Lupita's case, fangs—at the remaining lab techs and researchers to keep them from trying anything. Cora tensed as the stairwell door burst open, but her knees almost gave out when she saw who it was.

Theo was panting hard, his curls and beard dripping with—water? Sweat? Had he run into a hydromancer?—and he was stripped down to a damn tank top beneath a guard's stolen chest rig. He'd tied the sleeves of his jumpsuit at his waist, or what was left of them—one had been torn in half to create a makeshift bandage around his left forearm, which was already stained red over rippling muscle and old scars.

"Get the fuck outta here," Seb laughed, *genuinely* laughed. "I didn't know they were casting for *Last Blood II*."

"Seb?" Stunned into silence for half a heartbeat, Theo's face went through the gamut of confusion, recognition, and relief before settling on a mix of the three. "Jesus, it's really you." And then he locked eyes with Cora, and Seb might has well have been a signpost. "Both of you."

Cora was so overjoyed to see him in once piece that she almost forgot she was holding someone up.

He slung the gun in his hands over one shoulder and ran to her, and the man she'd been carrying leaned back onto a table, realizing he didn't want to get in the middle of this reunion. Cora dashed forward and he swept her up, kissing her quick and fierce. "We've got to go. Now."

"That's what we're *trying* to do," Gloria said, frowning at both of them. But Cora's eyes locked on Nell, who was staring at Theo as if she knew him from somewhere, and then Cora remembered—

But those were her parents coming through the door behind Theo, luckily, so they wouldn't have to address any of that now. "Emilio!" Seb shouted as he and Sonya darted across the room to their daughter, scooping her up and kissing her forehead. "Can you force the elevator to bypass the other floors?"

Emilio had honed his electromancy into technomancy, Cora remembered Seb saying. "Can do!" Emilio said with a quick salute, setting Nell down but keeping hold of her hand. "Come on folks, let's see how many can pile in there."

Cora swapped places with Sonya, who took the arm of the man she'd been helping earlier, so she could stop the bleeding from the wound in Theo's arm. "How much time do you think we have?" she asked him softly, unwrapping his bandage and knitting the deepest part of the gash together. She wanted to heal it completely, but she had to save her magic.

"Not long. Quinn's our eyes in the sky and hasn't reported anything yet, but it's only a matter of time. Pip and Nyx are back topside, so they'll be able to tell us if that changes."

Cora patted the arm and Theo said, "It wasn't that bad, you know. I had it handled."

She rolled her eyes. "Only you would say that about a fucking stab wound."

The first group, Archie's cadre of the strongest folks down there and the unconscious half-shifted witches they carried fireman-style, piled into the elevator. The rest waited in tense silence as Lupita paced in front of them and Theo paced behind her, shotgun raised at the cowering lab techs and doctors in a dare. Their turn to go up was a claustrophobic mess of bloody, sweaty limbs, not to mention Lupita's fur, and the thundering sound of ten heartbeats as the overweight car groaned upward.

The blast of cold desert air that greeted them in the airplane hangar was a welcome relief until they stepped out and understood what was happening.

Flames roared into the night. Guards bellowed. Smoke billowed. Gunfire blasted through an apocalyptic tableau. Dark shapes lay around them, the bodies of guards mingling with gray jumpsuits. In the distance, the horizon rumbled, and a handful of helicopters drew closer.

Seb stared with wide, unfocused eyes, and everything seemed to slow. Cora realized this was the first breeze he'd felt in over a decade.

It was the first time he'd seen the sky, or the stars, or even known what time of day it was just from being able to look up at them. It was the first time he'd felt the night chill, smelled wood smoke, or seen the craggy cliffs and desert weeds—because he'd been unconscious when they brought him here, just like everyone else.

He looked at the dirt that had been tracked over the concrete floor of the hangar, the earth he was so magically connected to just barely out of reach, right as a voice yanked him out of it.

"Get down!" Dustin hissed, waving them back against the side of the hangar where Archie's group was huddled. Viv and Harry were with them, and a man Cora didn't know. "Goddess, what the hell happened to—"

Harry kicked him as they moved between the prop plane and the wall, joining the rest. They were a group of over twenty now, all taking stock of one another.

Theo crouched beneath the plane to get a better look at the tarmac. "That's wide open." He turned to Dustin, Viv, and Harry, since they'd been covering the refugees running across. Two of them had commandeered assault rifles from dead guards, and all were wearing someone else's blood. "How have they been getting across?"

"Had been an illusion, but I got hit with Crash," Dustin said, slurring slightly.

Emilio's eyes narrowed, sweeping the battlefield. "Do you think if we—"

That was as much as Emilio got out before he sank to his knees, and Cora realized the pile of crates behind him was splattered in red.

Nell was screaming. It was a horrific, lost, strangled sound, and Lupita mowed her over with massive paws, pulling her by her sleeve behind a tower of machinery. Strong arms hauled Cora back, and one of Archie's men fell the same way Emilio had, dropping the body of the half-shifted hawk he'd been carrying as he collapsed to the hangar floor.

"Snipers!" someone called out, and Cora had never seen a group of people move faster, had never been more grateful for Theo or Seb in that moment as they both dragged her into cover. She'd barely processed what she was seeing, let alone been able to tell her feet what to do about it.

Nell's cries were soundless now as she rocked forward on her knees, hugging her chest. Her mother held her back, but her glistening, shocked eyes were only for her husband, understanding what it would mean for her if she crawled to him, and looking like she almost wanted it. Cora had to turn away; it was the only chance she had of getting through the rest of this alive. Of getting the rest of these people out alive.

"Neuromancer," she croaked out. "Anyone here?"

The woman crying on Gloria's arm raised a shaking hand.

"Call out to Helena," Cora said. "There's a witch named Helena on the north fence, out there somewhere. Tell her we're taking sniper fire. See if she can find out where they're coming from."

The woman cried harder but nodded and closed her eyes, reaching out. After a too-long moment, she said, "I...I've got her. They know we're here, they're looking." She paused again. "T-they say reinforcements are incoming. As soon as those snipers are out, we need to move. Humvees, from the west."

"Anyone other illusionists here?" Seb asked. He was met with silence. Fuck.

"We're going to have to just run for it," Theo said, raising his voice over the thrum of the advancing helicopters.

"That's suicide," Dustin shot back.

At the same time Nell yelled, "I'm not leaving him!"

Sonya grabbed Nell around the waist and hauled her up, whispering platitudes into her hair, tears streaming down her face. Nell clawed at her, but she held firm, and Nell didn't have the heart or the strength to push her away.

A chorus of agony rose up from somewhere in the night, gut-wrenching wails that were so quickly cut off Cora felt goosebumps shoot up and down her arms. Then the neuromancer said, "Snipers are down."

Cora didn't have time to think too hard about it. The helicopters were seconds away from clearing the edge of the compound, and one nosedived just beyond the barbed-wire fencing, rotors seizing. It slammed to the ground in a fireball, taking its hunters with them. Another rocked sideways, twisting into a third helicopter, and Theo bellowed, "GO! While everyone's focused on them, go!"

With attention turned toward the fireworks display from the three-helo pileup, they ran.

Lupita led their pack, prowling ahead and taking down two dark figures that moved to intercept them. Gloria swept smoke alongside them with aeromancy, partially obscuring them from view. One of Archie's men had given up carrying his shifter and was instead levitating him and another on a bed of hard wind, straining to keep them airborne as they raced forward through the smoke. Cora, Theo, and Nell brought up the rear behind Seb, who was still carrying the tiny witch piggyback.

Along the northern fence, Mindy directed refugees to the crystal. A telekinetic ward shimmered over her and the altas beside her, deflecting bullets. Two more hunks of crystal abutted a recanting field and Alta Maria's shimmering veil of shadows, which Cora could only spot because she was looking for it. Across the compound, a number of gray jumpsuits had stayed to fight—throwing fire, razor-sharp wind, threads of lightning, the very earth itself at whoever, whatever came at them. Birds of prey circled overhead and coyotes whooped, drawn by wild magic and the witches who could commune with them.

A hail of gunfire erupted as the hunters rappelled down from the helicopters hovering over the compound. Six of them had no weapons at all, just head-to-toe body armor.

"They're...witches. They're *witches*," Cora said, horror dawning. Nobody heard her, certainly not Nell, who chose that moment to pivot on her heel, almost slamming into Cora as she did so.

"Nell!" she cried, whipping around and racing to grab her sleeve. By the time she caught up to the streaming mane of black hair, Theo and Sonya had turned, realizing Cora was no longer behind him.

"Dad!" Nell sobbed, shoving Cora away and dashing toward the hangar's mouth. Theo and Sonya were already running back when the air crackled around them. *Between* them.

It wasn't electricity; it was something different. Something arcane. The fabric of reality distorted in front of her.

Every hair on the back of Cora's neck stood on end.

"Both of you, MOVE!" Cora yelled, wild panic in her voice as he stood rooted to the spot, staring. A twenty-foot *thing* was pushing through the veil, like reality was a sheet it was groping behind.

"THEO!"

The monster pierced the veil with a sedan-sized, clawed fist—not so much a fist as an inky black approximation of one. It groped in the air, then ripped the rest of the veil like tissue paper and crawled through.

It was there but also it wasn't, a shadowy mass but also somehow a void. It had no eyes, or even anything that could pass for them; just a gaping mouth beckoning you to it, like an event horizon.

Someone screamed at Cora to run. She wrenched herself from the creature's thrall and scrambled backwards into Nell, snapping the girl out of her own trance. They made a mad dash for the dubious shelter of the hangar, lungs burning, legs aching, hearts thundering double-time.

Across the tarmac, most of their group had made it through the leapstone, but Seb had stayed with Sonya and Theo, passing the girl on his back to Mindy. Fuck, if he didn't go through...if they stayed behind for her and got themselves killed...

She didn't have time to think about it. The monster roared, not with sound, but a lack of it—a pressure that hollowed out her ears, her chest. Maria was wrapping it in a recanting field, trying to weaken its magic, but there was no way it wouldn't sense them if she and Nell tried to get past again. Sonya struck it with a vein of lightning when it took a step towards Cora and Nell, and it reconsidered, whirling on another gray jumpsuit trying to navigate the pitted asphalt.

Nell had stumbled over to where Emilio's body lay next to the bullet-riddled prop plane, trying to lift him over her shoulders as she crouched. She was strong for her size, Cora would give her that, but her knees still buckled as she strained beneath his weight. Cora stepped towards her. "Nell," she said as gently as she could with the tugging at her amygdala telling her to move, move, *move,* "we are going to die here if we don't go now."

"Dad, *Dad*," she just kept repeating, and then Cora was struck by the weight of it all.

The bodies laying around her. The witches fighting and dying out there, because of her. Emilio, the back of his skull blown open, his blood coating the crates, the floor, Nell's hands and knees. Emilio had been afraid. Afraid for the children, like her, who would see it all and never be the same. Because Cora had had this insane idea to save her brother.

Because she'd fucked up with Nell, and let her be taken, and now that girl's father was dead.

As if merely thinking it had given voice to it, someone said by the mouth of the elevator, "You've really outdone yourself here."

Icy dread flooded Cora's chest as she turned to see Greer, blood matting the hair on her left temple, pointing the barrel of a guard's Recantanyl dart gun at them. Half her gaze, though, was fixed on the battle outside the open hangar, witches fighting guards, witches fighting witches, the void creature struggling against Maria's binding, and the ground force of moonlit Humvees that kicked up dust in the valley below them.

And she hadn't felt it at first, but Cora did now: the dart sticking out of her shoulder.

"Please," Cora said, because her brain couldn't string together anything more coherent in the chaos of that moment. She stumbled forward, yanking the dart from her arm, dredging up the magic she had left to try and reach through its black, sticky barrier.

"Not a step further," Greer hissed. "I have put *everything* into this work. I'm sitting on the cusp of breakthroughs that nobody, *nobody* has ever gotten close enough to prove. I will not," she said, walking towards Cora, finger dangerously near the trigger, "lose that progress now, because of you. I will not let some other scientist at some other prison lab in bumfuck nowhere be the first to reveal any of this shit to the world. You are coming back downstairs with me, you little—"

Cora caught movement from the corner of her eye and ducked as Nell leapt forward with an animalistic scream, slamming Greer backwards into the concrete. The doctor hadn't seen her go still and silent by Emilio's body, creep around the side of the plane.

The dart gun skidded across the floor, far out of anyone's reach as Nell channeled all her rage in grief into the frenzied blows she struck, the scrape of her nails down Greer's face. For everything that girl had been through since she'd lost her parents, she'd come to collect, but not as Nell—as a savage beast with claws of pure lightning, eyes that blazed blue, hair that stood on end from the charged air she'd wrapped around her.

Goddess, what kind of shifter was *she*? She'd molded her lightning into the aspect of a panther, some sort of elemental hybrid. As fascinated as Cora was, and as much as she knew Greer deserved it, they couldn't stick around to kill the woman. They had to go, *now*.

She tore Nell off Greer, who wasn't moving anymore anyway, even though her chest rose and fell. Nell scream-roared, still raging, still lashing forward with her lightning, and Cora said, "We don't have time for this!"

"They killed him," Nell sobbed, collapsing back into Cora's arms, half shifted back. "*She* killed him. They all killed him."

Cora allowed herself to tear her eyes away for half a second. She turned to where Seb and Theo and Sonya were crouched a few hundred feet away, Theo laying down covering fire while Seb burst rocks and roots through the asphalt to try tripping and pinning the hunter witches, breaking their concentration—

No, not all of them. Just three, she realized.

The conjurer who had summoned the void-thing was standing behind a recanting field and a telekinetic ward, deflecting any magic and projectiles levied her way. The two witches who had her six were keeping the wards up, fighting off an assault from Seb, Helena, and another electromancer.

The air crackled again, and the void-thing finally shattered Maria's recanting field with another multidimensional roar. It was synesthesia of another kind, tasting the shrillness of it, smelling the darkness of it, a cacophony of wrong.

Cora squeezed her eyes shut and pried, pried, pried at the Recantanyl, her head splitting, her nose bleeding, and with a scream of pain she ripped through. Magic flowed into her, filled her as she drew from the multiple ley lines she knew ran beneath them to converge mere miles away.

Nell pulled away from her and stared, eyes wide, like she'd just woken up and realized what was happening around her. "You broke through it."

"With all the time I had to practice in that place, I'd damn well better be able to," Cora panted, steadying herself on a crate as a wave of vertigo nearly bowled her over. Greer lay unmoving on the concrete, her face resembling something like raw meat. Cora didn't have time to savor the view.

"Nell, I will help you get your dad's body out of here, but you have to listen to me," Cora said, marking the Humvees' approach. They only had a few minutes to get through that leapstone—and it looked like some of the gray jumpsuits who'd stayed to fight were realizing it, too, moving along the back of the north fence. "That creature is tethered to the conjurer's will only as long as that crystal stays intact. You see it?"

Nell followed Cora's eye line to where a blue, boulder-sized hunk of crystal glimmered, half-buried in rubble, by one of the crashed helicopters. She realized what Cora was about to do. "You're insane."

Cora wiped the blood from her nose on her sleeve. "We're all running out of steam, the altas included, and that thing is mad as hell. Who do you think it's gonna be maddest at when it gets free? My money's on the witch who ripped it from its happy little lair in the spirit realm."

Nell blew a strand of hair from her tear-stained face and finished shifting back, less than thrilled but grappling with the reality of their situation. "What do you need?"

"Cover me while I leyweave. I need to jump into Seb's head for a second. When the monster goes for her, we grab your dad and run. With any luck, it'll distract the folks in those first Humvees long enough for us to make it to the leapstone." It would be close, but Cora was strong, and Emilio had become wafer-thin in his time underground.

Deadlifts, don't fail me now.

"Okay." Nell took a deep, shuddering breath and glanced back at Emilio's body, grief lashing through her eyes again. Fresh tears fell and her mouth wobbled even as she bit down on it.

"For your dad," Cora said gently, grabbing Nell's hand.

"For my dad."

CHAPTER TWENTY-SIX

Theo pumped the last round of his sidearm into a desert coyote. It stumbled forward, sluggish and bloody, collapsing among the rest of its pack. They'd been sent courtesy of the hunter wildermage hiding behind a downed helo, which is also how he'd gotten the deep claw gashes raking down the side of his torso, leaking enough blood to make him woozy.

"I'm out." He hadn't missed the rumbling of the Humvees just down the hill, and said to Seb and Sonya, "We need to get them, and we need to do it *now*."

Seb had shifted the earth enough to raise a chunk of asphalt and rock in front of them as cover, and he was crouched beside Theo, sweating with the effort of trying to break the conjurer's concentration. On his other side, Sonya's hand crackled weakly with lightning. "I can hear Cor," he said, withdrawing and blinking suddenly. "I can—she's leyweaving—"

Theo swallowed his retort and let Seb listen to whatever she'd jumped in his head to say. "New plan," Seb panted. "We're gonna cut the monster loose."

"Oh, fuck me," Theo mumbled.

"She can't be serious," Sonya said breathlessly.

"You got something better? Cuz I sure as hell don't. Stay back, ready?"

Theo tossed aside his useless gun and backed away a step as Seb got on all fours, hands sinking into the dirt. The ground shifted and scattered, more liquid than sand, and the three of them stumbled back a few more

316

steps. Seb gritted his teeth, a noise rumbling in his chest that made its way out as a bellow of pain and determination. They felt the force of the quake echo across the battlefield, the metal siding of the hangar beginning to rattle and clang, and then—*there.*

The earth split open, a chasm yawning and stretching toward...not the conjurer, but something else—and from Cora's position, another fracture shot forward at the same time, meeting Seb's. They joined and exploded toward something glimmering and blue, a rock or boulder, and the blue stone split with a *CRACK* that rang like a lone gunshot through the air.

Something shifted. It was the same kind of magic Theo had first felt with Pip, primordial and bone-deep, mixed with the smell of ozone. The monster stopped, just for a heartbeat, and by the look of terror on the conjurer's face, Theo knew it had worked.

The hunter-witches backed away, slowly, understanding they were no longer predator, but prey. The monster filled the sky with a hollow sound not of this world and launched itself after the conjurer's trio.

"GO, CORA!" Theo bellowed, not sure if his voice could even reach her from this far, but she and Nell were running, running as fast as they could with Emilio's body dragging between them.

The monster swiped a massive fist at the conjurer, swatting her aside like she was a rag doll, then opening its mouth and drawing everything nearby in—witch, hunter, the bodies of guards, the mangled steel corpses of helicopters.

Jesus fucking Christ, what had they unleashed?

Cora and Nell were halfway across, and Theo and Seb sprinted for them. The monster whipped around, deciding it wasn't done with them yet, and took a step in their direction, but one last zap of lightning from Sonya gave them the split second they needed to gain enough ground, stay just out of its reach long enough to...

Mindy was still at the leapstone, screaming at them to go through, and Theo realized she was the last one there. The last one who believed in them enough to stay, to imagine they'd survive. They were twenty yards away.

Ten yards. The Humvees crunched through rocks and dirt, doors opened and shut, a fresh wave of gunfire erupted behind them. Light antitank weaponry sent missiles screaming toward the monster.

Five yards. Mindy and Sonya rushed forward to grab Emilio from Cora and Nell, and they vanished.

The magical tether reached from the leapstone. Nell and Sonya dove through. Then Seb. Cora wrapped it around Theo, then they were yanked off their feet, tumbling upward and forward into silent nothing.

⸻ ∽ ⸻

The immeasurable, unknowable cosmic vacuum spat Cora unceremoniously into the dirt.

She inhaled, gasping, like she'd surfaced from too long underwater. Theo stumbled forward beside her, hands on his knees, and Nell, Mindy, Sonya, and Seb had all been tossed a few feet away. They each sat up slowly, groaning, reeling from the abruptness of coming back to their physical selves.

She'd never traveled by leapstone before. Stories described people forever lost in states of limbo, stuck between worlds, unable to disentangle themselves from one or the other. It was enough to deter most witches from ever trying it.

But they'd made it, she realized, looking at seven of them.

Then she saw Emilio's body and remembered.

Six of them.

Someone she didn't know shoved a bottle of water at her. "Are you hurt?"

"Not my blood," she mumbled. Catatonic, she looked at the water bottle in her hand. It sweated in her palm, and she anchored to the coolness of it. The surrounding sounds blended into a dull roar: people barking orders; people calling out for one another; moans of pain; happy crying; anguished crying; the wind whistling through the rocks; that primordial thrum of magic along her bones.

Someone else gasped, noticing Emilio's body, and Cora looked up.

A small crowd stood around them. Ghislaine, Helena, Archie. A tan, silver-haired man in a gray jumpsuit that was rushing to help Mindy up. Harry and Dustin and Viv. Gloria, who'd handed them the water, tears streaming down her face. Lupita, human again, wrapped in a blanket with a heavy bandage around her head. Behind them, Maria lay on a cot in a healer's tent, along with the half-shifted witches they'd carried out, some of them fully shifted now. So many people milling around that she didn't recognize or only knew the faces of.

On the edge of camp by the rocky outcropping, a row of unmoving forms on the ground spoke of their failures. Loved ones crouched around the lost, shoulders shaking in grief, leaning on one another for support.

Emilio would join them.

Seb rose to his feet, but stumbled, and Cora realized he'd far overextended his magic for that final push. A healer had dashed over to hold him up, and he tried to wave her off and go back to Cora, but she wasn't having it. Theo, instead, helped Cora up. He pulled her closer and slid his free arm across her shoulders, a comforting weight. She relaxed into him, into the intimacy of the gesture, let him care for her in that stolen moment, even as Nell crawled to Emilio's body and collapsed on top of it, sobbing.

If she hadn't already been so shattered, it would have shattered her. If she's had any tears left, she would have cried. Instead, she turned away as Sonya's arms snaked around Nell's body, giving them the privacy to grieve together.

Ezra. Someone would have to tell him. Where...?

There. Beside one of the medical tents, his face was turned toward the moon, breaking into joy and relief as an owl crested the top of the surrounding rocks. It screeched and tucked its wings close, nosediving into his arms. Quinn transformed as she crashed into him and he swung her around, laughing in relief and wrapping her naked body in the blanket that had kept vigil beside him all night.

But from here, Cora could see Quinn's shoulders shaking, and she knew Quinn would bear the burden of telling him Emilio's fate.

Mindy was rushing over to Theo and Cora now, the man who'd helped her up close behind. Mindy's eyes filled, a mix of grief and pride and exhaustion, all threatening to spill over. "Oh, my love. I'm so glad you're okay." Mindy crushed Cora to her chest, and it broke through the daze Cora had slipped into.

She wrapped her arms around Mindy and pressed her face into her shoulder, smelling the faint hint of perfume still lingering under all the dust and dried sweat. That perfume brought her back to the Santa Monica house, put a cup of tea in her hand and sat her down with a fresh-baked cookie, and told her everything was going to be okay.

Mindy pulled away and gripped Cora's shoulders, her lips pressed tight together. Then her eyes locked on Theo.

She saved him the trouble of wondering what to do by pulling him against her, too. She sobbed this time, and a bewildered Theo glanced at Cora before hugging her back. At five feet tall, Mindy only reached the middle of his chest, so her face was buried against his ripped, blood-spattered, sweat-soaked tank top and chest rig. She didn't seem to care.

The silver-haired man lurking just behind them, waiting for the moment to play out, had a mustache to rival Tom Selleck's and dimples highlighting a wide, generous mouth. Even in his gray jumpsuit, he held himself with the dignity of a man in a smoking jacket. "Cor, baby, this is Oscar," Mindy said, pulling away from Theo.

Cora blinked. Oscar. He *had* been in solitary. Nobody she'd spoken to had been able to tell her for sure whether he was still alive. "I looked for you, I...some people said you were..."

"I owe my life to this man here," Oscar said, nodding at Theo. "Didn't lose one of us folks up in solitary."

Theo looked uncomfortable. "Certainly couldn't have taken those guys down without you."

"No question it was effective, if...unorthodox."

Cora glanced from one to the other, figuring they weren't going to elaborate further, and decided to let them keep their little secret.

The following hours passed in a flurry of activity. Most families had been reunited; most injuries had been tended to. Quinn and another shifter scouted the base again, with reports that it was crawling with FBI and ACE. The void monster had done quite a bit more damage before they'd gotten things under control, leaving at least half of that ground force in smoldering ruin, the landscape dotted with craters from anti-tank weaponry.

The cover of night had concealed them, but it was fading now, bringing with it a stain of red along the horizon—the only sunlight that found its way through the smoke-choked air. Cora wondered how they'd explain those fires away to the neighboring towns. Covering up what had happened there would be a nightmare for everyone involved.

But maybe ACE wouldn't cover it up. Maybe they'd use it as ammo to crack down even harder. Only time would tell. For now, they were safe in the Vale, concealed from sight, sound, and pretty much everything else. Refugees would bunk here for as long as they could endure the heightened magic, and when there were fewer hunters swarming the area, they'd be able to start bussing them out to Whitefall.

Because most didn't have homes to return to. The government had seen to that, seizing whatever property and possessions the witches left behind when they were brought in. Those whose families outside the prison had avoided capture might join them and start a new life in Whitefall when they were able to. Others might adopt new names, new identities, and join an allied coven in Flagstaff. Ghislaine had already negotiated the details with an altus there, offering them Harry's invaluable anti-Crash recipe in return.

Some, stubbornly, would go back, but home was home. And that risk was theirs to take.

Cora had seen Ezra and Quinn arguing. ACE might not know exactly how he was tied up in everything that had happened, but he'd never know a moment's peace if he went back. With what Ricky had sent to Fletcher, all the fancy lawyers in the world couldn't keep him safe. And if they didn't lock him up, he'd still draw too much heat to be involved in the Runners again. At least in Whitefall, he'd have Quinn, Sonya, and Nell.

Cora imagined Quinn was trying to convince him of all this and more, but he wasn't having it. Immediately, he turned and went off on *her,* because she'd presumably told him if he was staying, *she* was staying.

And Theo? He was probably near the top of the FBI's Most Wanted list. Cora, Oscar, and Sebastian's names were in the system, their fingerprints. Mindy could have stayed back, but she'd made it clear wherever they went, she went, and that was that. She'd grant use of her home to the Runners in the meantime, until they could figure out something more permanent.

By the time breakfast was served in the meal tent, seventeen graves sat in two rows along one edge of the rocky crescent. They couldn't go back to retrieve the bodies of the witches who died on the base, so after their final head count, they inscribed their names on that large, flat stone altar in the middle of the dais.

Two thirds. Only two thirds of the prisoners had made it out.

Cora lingered at that gravesite long after the mourners left. Theo stood with her, letting her lean backward into his chest, his chin atop her head. They'd waited their turn for the camp showers earlier, wordlessly washing the blood and sweat and dirt off each other, and now they both wore overlarge, donated hoodies and smelled like two-in-one soap. Still, she breathed him in, and he buried his face in her frizzy, desert-air-dried hair, both looking at all that freshly-tilled earth and feeling very much like every moment together was a miracle.

He hadn't been afraid to give everything up for her, to fight for her, to turn his back on the life he'd built for himself. He'd forced her to be honest with herself. To let happiness dethrone grief. To find the courage to live, not just exist.

He'd sacrificed everything to make her family whole. And he'd made it clear, when she told him about her plans to help the Runners from within Whitefall, to do whatever she could for refugees coming to the city from within, that he'd help her make sure other families could stay whole, too.

Whether he'd intended it or not, he'd signed himself up for a life on the run. A life where he might never feel safe again, no matter where they wound up. And she just prayed he wouldn't come to resent her for that.

"I have something of yours," he finally said, pulling something from his pocket and reaching around to press it into her hand. It was warm, metallic, circular.

She stiffened, pulling away from him and turning to face him. Her NA coin. "How did you get this?"

"Ricky took it off you, when he arrested you." Theo's eyes flashed, that wound still fresh. "He told me what happened."

Cora expected to feel shame, expected to want to say something in her own defense, but the urge didn't come. Maybe it was all those graves at her back. Worrying about what he thought of her was laughable. "Then you know I can't carry it anymore."

"I'm not judging what you do or don't do with it. I just thought you should have it back."

She waited for the questions, or worse, the 'I'm here if you need to talk about it.' People who said that never understood what it took out of someone to talk about it, or just wanted to satisfy their own curiosity without seeming like a dick. But that didn't come, either. Theo just raised that scarred eyebrow and put his hands into the pocket of his hoodie.

"Thank you, but I don't want it," she said, shaking her head. She didn't deserve it, and even if she had, she wasn't sure she wanted to carry those years with her, anyway. Maybe a fresh start was a blessing in disguise. She'd figure the rest out later. "Ricky wasn't there, was he? At the base last night?"

Theo looked back at the coin, turning it over in his hands and pocketing it. "No. He's probably shitting himself now, though. I hope they all are." He read the concern on her face and said, "I'm not going to look for him, if that's what you're worried about."

"I'm more worried about him looking for you, honestly."

"He'll have enough on his plate to keep him busy for a good while. All of Metro ACE Command will."

She hoped he was right. She swallowed her next question as Seb wandered up behind Theo, Pip and Nyx on either shoulder, a grin slicing across his freckled face. Theo turned at the sound of dirt crunching beneath shoes and was swept up into rough hug, Seb laughing as he slammed his hand on Theo's back. "Ryland, you sly dog, you."

Pip and Nyx bounced away to avoid being crushed as Theo hugged Seb back, patting his shoulder with equal ferocity. They pulled away and then Seb punched Theo squarely in the diaphragm, knocking the wind out of him and sending him to his knees.

"Seb, what the fuck!" Cora yelled, but both men were laughing—Theo's was more of a wheeze or a choke, but still.

"I...deserve that..." Theo gasped, rising onto one knee and catching his breath. After a long moment he asked, "We good?"

Seb, still laughing, grabbed Theo's hand and helped him upright. She'd missed his laugh so much. It was different now; he used to laugh with his entire body, shaking from the force of it. Now he laughed like he was waiting for someone to brandish a rifle at him.

They'd work on that.

"Yeah, we're good." Seb looked at him, sobering a bit. "And thank you. For everything you did in there."

"I won't pretend it was selfless," Theo said, looking at Cora with an intensity that made her squirm. There was a lot she couldn't decipher in there—maybe a lot he didn't quite understand or want to unpack yet, either. "I still have a lot to answer for, on my own conscience, but maybe I'll be able to lay my head down a little easier at night."

Seb nodded, a quick jerk of the chin. He knew a thing or two about survival, in his own way, but drew the line at giving voice to his own trauma just to try and make Theo feel better. "All the same." He crossed his arms, watched a jackrabbit dart through the brush, and then looked up at Cora. "Time to learn to live in the world, I guess. Seen the old house at all?"

A knot tightened in Cora's chest as she thought about the day they'd spent in the garden. "It's different. The trees are bigger. They put a stupid basketball hoop in the driveway."

"How dare they." Sebastian grinned and sat on a boulder nearby, looking out at the rest of camp. "Mom never liked that house, anyway."

"What? Of course she liked the house. We all liked the house. It was The House."

"We couldn't afford the upkeep, remember? Mom went into so much debt so we could stay at that school. But the roof was always leaking. The layout was like someone had designed it blind. The termites swarmed every summer, no matter how many times we fumigated. The bougainvillea—"

"Don't you dare tell me something was wrong with the bougainvillea. That's my bougainvillea."

"You really spent all this time pining after that house?" he asked.

"No." She scuffed her boot in the dirt. "Yes. Okay, maybe The House sucked. I don't know. But it was ours."

"You know what's still yours, though?"

"What?"

Sebastian elbowed her. "Me, dumbass. And Mindy." He looked over her shoulder at where Theo stood, watching them both with a small smile. "And fine, him, I guess." Pip, not to be forgotten, bounced and flowed up Cora's arm, and Seb sighed. "Yeah, fuck it. This one, too."

Cora finally allowed herself a grin, in spite of everything weighing heavy on her heart as she looked out across the survivors gathered in Crescent Vale. He was right.

And whatever else was true, that was reason enough to do more than just survive after all they'd endured and lost.

"We're definitely lost," Cora grumbled, trying to recalibrate the compass on her phone. The little blue arrow on her GPS was far, far off the road. "I knew it was that last turn-off—"

"She said it wasn't a chain. It couldn't have been that Super 8. I've said this three times now." Seb had begged to drive, but also had yet to find the time to learn, which settled that argument fairly quickly. It didn't, however, stop him from being the most infuriating backseat driver Cora had ever roadtripped with.

"I am going to brake check you again if you don't shut up."

From the rearview, Cora could see Theo leaning his head back against the headrest, pinching the bridge of his several-times-broken nose. He'd shaved the beard a while back to make him less identifiable, but it was springing back with a vengeance, and only served to make him look more haggard in this midway-grown state. "Both of you, just...please."

"Oh! This! This is what Mindy told us to look for, right?" Cora pointed at a run-down motel with a massive, gnarled tree out front, shaped like a fist flipping someone the bird. She jerked Lucy's wheel and braked hard, ignoring Seb and Theo's protests as they veered into the near-deserted motel parking lot.

"I," Theo ground out, "am driving next time." He was out of the car before anyone could respond.

Cora blinked into the chilly January afternoon sun as she and Seb followed Theo into the motel lobby. It was as nondescript as any other roadside stopover, and that was likely the point. It smelled like old A/C, cheap coffee, and soap.

Eau de motor lodge.

Behind the wood-paneled desk, a bored woman with honey-brown hair and glasses didn't even look up from the magazine she was reading. "Reservation?"

"Amspoker. We had a double with a roll-away cot," Seb said. It was the password Mindy had given them.

The woman looked up, sharp eyes raking over them in appraisal, then remaining on Theo. "We wondered when we'd finally be seeing you. Not every day you let the fox into the henhouse."

Theo and Cora stiffened.

"There's not a witch in Whitefall who doesn't know what you did," she continued, winking. "Most of them are even grateful."

"Which are you?" Seb asked, parrying her smile with a winning one of his own.

"Luckily, I'm not paid to have opinions." She tapped long nails on the surface of the reception desk. "I'm just the bridge troll. Here's your key." A smooth, azure pebble slid across the desk, with a symbol Cora didn't recognize carved into it. "Who's driving?"

Cora raised the hand she'd enclosed the rock in.

"I'm gonna tune it to you and you alone. Hold it out."

She did as she was asked and felt magic rise around them, threading around her palm. Just as quickly, it winked out.

"Thread it, and it'll do the rest." The witch looked Theo up and down again, wary. "Welcome to Whitefall."

Back in Lucy, they puttered along the gravel drive wrapping around the motel and through the misty thicket of redwoods, toward the ocean cliffs. Gravel gave way to dirt until the blue stone flared bright in front of a shallow, rocky cave. Cora pulled in with just enough room on either side of the car for them to get out.

Cora read the growing tension in Theo's shoulders as they circled behind the car to the cave mouth and nodded at Seb to give them a moment alone.

Theo looked down at her, face blank with what she knew was considerable effort, and she reached up to put a hand on his cheek. He spoke before she could.

"We knew it might be like this. I'm fine."

She pulled him down to her, pressing her lips against his, pouring everything she couldn't say into that brief moment of contact. "I know. I just wanted to tell you that I'm with you. Every step." She looked down at Lucy's assortment of dings and scrapes. "Every...vaguely phallic dent along the way."

He grinned, despite himself, and she smiled back. "We made it this far. It would be a real shame if some self-proclaimed bridge troll got the better of you when the fucking Creature of the Void didn't."

"Fair," he said, eyes twinkling a little.

She stepped back and turned, holding out the blue stone, and found the shimmering thread spooling outward from it. Following that thread brought her to a small divot in a boulder, and she fitted the stone inside. With a faint click, the glow dimmed.

Theo and Seb finished unloading their bags from the trunk, then each placed a hand on the boulder beside her. She heard Seb inhale by her right ear. "Ready?" she asked.

"I fucking hate leapstones," was all Seb managed before they were yanked upward, inward, outward, through the cosmic vacuum, into everything and nothing, suffocating, suffocating...

Then there was soft grass beneath them, the sound of rushing water, the same redwood spires reaching up into the mist.

The leapstone had spit them out on what appeared to be the other side of the cave she'd pulled Lucy into. The car was gone, though, as Mindy had warned. She wouldn't need it there, anyway, and better to let the Runners make use of it...though they'd probably get more out of it by selling it for scrap.

She'd plucked the Lakers bobblehead from the dashboard, though, and now it burst into Pip as he sensed the wild flow of magic around them. It was everywhere, threading through her, spilling out of her. That primordial hum again, like she'd felt at Crescent Vale, but more muted—controlled.

This forest felt old, so old, and quietly sentient, like it was deciding whether to approve of their being there.

To their right sat a tiny stone cabin in front of a rushing stream, smoke curling from its chimney. The front door burst open, and Mindy's voice carried out from within. "They're here! Oscar! Come out. They're *here!*" Dashing toward them now, barefoot in the misty chill, her gray curls streaming behind them, she kept yelling, "You're here. You're here!"

Nyx and Oscar were hot on her heels, and when Mindy reached them and swept everyone up in crushing hugs, Cora squeaked, "We saw you two days ago—"

"Yes, but that was *there*, and this is *here!*" Mindy planted kisses on Seb and Theo's cheeks, and Oscar opted for handshakes while Nyx and Pip bounced around furiously.

"Where is...here, exactly?" Cora asked, looking through the gloom between the massive trees, where the stream faded from view. "Whose house is this?"

"Mine," said an unfamiliar female voice, and Cora turned to where its owner leaned against the doorway of the cabin. She was Mindy's age, though the woman hadn't let her honey-brown hair go gray as Cora's aunt had, with round glasses perched on an upturned nose. The spitting image of the motel's receptionist—or rather, the receptionist was the spitting image of her. Mother and daughter, probably.

She tugged a hand-crocheted shawl tighter around her shoulders. "I'm Camilla, warden of the East Gatehouse."

"We stayed here last night so we'd be around when you came through," Mindy said to Cora. "Anyone with family making the crossing can wait for them here. Come inside, out of the cold and the damp. We'll get you some tea and get all the paperwork taken care of."

"How far are we from the city?" Theo asked, peering into the mist.

Creatures darted in and out of it, ones Cora had never seen before, sprite-like but some with tails and claws, some with batwing ears, some dark like Nyx's nebula and some bright like Pip's sunburst. Flowers she didn't know the name of clustered and spiraled upward, bearing strange purple fruit. Vibrant winged insects hovered, butterflies as big as her head, bioluminescent dragonflies. This world was close enough to theirs that it felt familiar, but wholly *not* theirs at all—maybe the constant threading of magic changed the way things grew.

Mindy glanced at Oscar, then turned back to them. "You want to see?"

"I'll take your bags in," Oscar said, nodding toward the stream. "Go with Mindy and have a look."

As they followed her, still barefoot, over a worn path that wove into the trees, Seb stopped.

He removed his shoes, too, and Cora watched his feet make contact with the damp earth, saw the breath he took in, the way the breeze played with the rusty locks of hair he'd finally trimmed short. Every step forward was a revelation for him as he felt grass beneath his feet for only the third or fourth time since they'd escaped.

Her cheeks were wet. She knew he was reaching down, down into that earth, sending his magic through the root networks of these ancient trees, pouring himself into every blade of grass, every strange flowering plant.

She kicked her shoes off to meet him there, barely feeling the cold, and took his hand.

They stopped when the river dropped off into nothing, realizing they toed the edge of a cliff. The mist was thinning there, just enough for them to see what lay beyond it.

A seed of hope that flourished, in spite of everything.

ACKNOWLEDGEMENTS

This book weighs about a pound, give or take (if you're reading it in paperback). That always surprises me when I pick it up, considering the number of people it took to carry across the finish line. Maybe it's because this is my first book, or maybe authors never really shake that feeling, but either way, I have so many people to thank for bringing this story to life.

First and foremost, my husband Anthony: Thank you for being a sounding board, an often-needed reality check, a cheerleader, a muse. There are pieces of you sprinkled in both Cora and Theo, and their characters are so much richer for it. I'm incredibly lucky to have you as a creative partner and a life partner, and none of this would be possible without your patience and support (especially when I need to disappear into my writing cave for days at a time).

To my family: Thank you for always encouraging my love of reading and writing, even if I never did let you guys read anything I wrote. Except when I asked Lauren to alpha read the first draft of this book, and then promptly told her to burn it. (Thank you for doing that, too. I'm relieved it barely saw the light of day.)

To Julie Gwinn, my agent, and Galen Surlak-Ramsey, my editor: Thank you for taking a chance on a debut author and for being the first people to see the potential in Cora and Theo's story. And many thanks to the rest of the team at Tiny Fox Press, including Natalie Day and Maya Sherlick, as well as the amazing cover designers at Damonza.

A massive thank you to my beta readers, who persevered valiantly through the earliest versions of this manuscript despite the plot holes, cliches, and info-dumps: Jordan Jones, Ayesha Abdul Ghaffar, Victoria Solomon,

Marta Antonella, and M. B. Saul. I'm also incredibly grateful to authors Janet Walden-West and Anne M. Raven for their feedback during Pitch Wars (and after).

I'm so lucky to have the support of Backspace and an amazing team of coworkers who hype me up constantly; extra-special thanks to author Callie C. Miller for her infinite wisdom and Cat Cheresh who spent many an afternoon with me trying to find the coziest coffee shop in LA to write at.

Last but not least, to all my friends and family who came along with me on this journey: Thanks for believing I could make it here.

ABOUT THE AUTHOR

Sarah K. West began her career as a copy-writer in the ad industry, which is how she wound up on the Los Angeles Westside. She lives with her husband and a sassy chihuahua/spaniel mix named Seymour and spends a good chunk of her time ignoring the beautiful weather to play video games.

Visit her website at:
www.sarahkwest.com

ABOUT THE PUBLISHER

Tiny Fox Press LLC

www.tinyfoxpress.com

Milton Keynes UK
Ingram Content Group UK Ltd.
UKHW040638041023
429927UK00001B/80